CW01214293

THE GANYMEDE SIGNAL

A.L. Masters

ISBN: 9798877579286

DEDICATION

To Joe (who only reads nonfiction)

CONTENTS

ACKNOWLEDGMENTS

Special thanks to all my readers, but you in particular.

Mars Colony One unfurled across the Martian terrain, a meshwork of human ingenuity clashing with the desolate backdrop of the Red Planet. At the break of dawn, the colony lay in stark relief under the weak sunlight, a monument to humankind's insatiable quest for the cosmos.

Nestled within this bastion of steel and spirit, the Mars Frontier Research Institute stood as the nerve center of an audacious endeavor — the Ganymede Signal project.

Here, on the cusp of the unknown, a team of Earth and Mars' finest was poised to pierce the veil of the cosmos, chasing a silent enigma that had drifted from the depths of Jupiter's orbit.

1.

'63-02

The siren's blare jolted me awake, its piercing cry slicing through the still Martian night. A sea of flashing red emergency lights bathed my room, turning the familiar geography into something ominous. My heart pounded in my ears as I threw off my covers and scrambled for my suit.

"Evacuation Protocol Alpha. This is not a drill," boomed the automated voice over the PA system, urgent and unsettlingly steady. "Incoming. Incoming. Incoming."

Electric fear surged through me as I wriggled into my suit and sealed it with a reassuring hiss. I had faced dust storms and equipment malfunctions, but the urgency of Protocol Alpha hinted at something that made my heart stutter and my mouth dry up.

Dashing through the labyrinthine corridors of the Mars Frontier Research Institute, I joined a flood of scientists and engineers who were all pushing toward the emergency shelters.

As I rounded a corner, I nearly collided with Commander Ryan, the Quick Reaction Force leader for this sector. His eyes were steely and his jaw was set, and I relaxed a tiny fraction just from his presence.

I stepped out of the pushing mass of people.

"Commander, what's happening?" I managed, breathless.

"Meteor," he barked, not breaking stride as he headed towards the command center. "Heading straight for us. I'm initiating dome defenses. Get to the shelter!"

I followed his gaze through the massive viewing window and there it was— a colossal fiery mass tearing across the Martian sky.

The Institute's defense systems sprang to life, a last-ditch effort to alter the meteor's deadly trajectory. From my vantage point, I watched as beams of concentrated energy shot into the night, colliding with the meteor in a blinding explosion of light and force.

For a moment, it seemed like we had succeeded.

The meteor veered and its path altered, but my relief turned to horror as it clipped the edge of the farthest dome.

My breath caught on a sob.

The dome buckled under the assault. Glass and metal screamed as they gave way, the breach unleashing a violent torrent of decompression. The dome imploded, and its contents— equipment, plants, and people— were ripped out into the unforgiving Martian atmosphere.

The figures, caught in Mars' merciless grip, flailed against the crushing, airless expanse. It was a torturous struggle, their movements erratic and desperate, as if by throwing themselves around they could escape the roiling in their blood and the choking carbon dioxide that flooded their seizing lungs.

I clenched my fists and stepped closer to the window, breathing raggedly as a profound, gut-deep sickness buried itself in my heart.

They fought so *hard*.

But the void of Mars was relentless and unforgiving. One by one, they were still. Their writhing stopped as they succumbed to the atmosphere. Commander Ryan and I, we watched them die in a kind of strange tribute of solidarity. Even though they wouldn't know, *we* would know that they didn't die alone.

We were with them in spirit even though it didn't help them at all. We couldn't do anything else. They were gone too fast.

From my vantage point, the tragedy was a series of shadows and impressions. It was a gruesome scene too distant to discern individual faces or cries and for that small mercy, I was grateful.

I turned away, a lump forming in my throat and my eyes stinging.

It was then that I caught a glimpse of Commander Ryan's face. His expression was a mirror of the disaster—grim, tortured, etched with a pain that went beyond physical. His eyes, always so resolute, were shadowed and anguished.

The moments of seeing the fiery cosmic colossus slam into the dome, and then the violent death of our neighbors rushed past too quickly, almost from one blink to the next.

Panic followed in a ripple.

People screamed and stumbled, some knocked off their feet by the shockwave that swelled through the colony, testing the limits of our domes.

I clenched the handrail and gritted my teeth, waiting for the damning signal of a dome breach, but it didn't come.

Commander Ryan turned to the wall and tensed his fists against the polymer surface, shoulders trembling. I didn't know him that well. I didn't know what to do, how to help, or even if he'd want any show of concern from me.

A moment later he turned and barked orders into his

comms unit, trying to coordinate a response. His voice was once again a steady anchor in the storm of fear and confusion, and he barely gave me a nod before rushing away.

I stood frozen, watching the nightmare unfold. The dome's destruction was a brutal reminder of our vulnerability in the face of the universe's indifference.

My mind raced with the implications— the loss of life, the setback to our terraforming efforts, the uncertain future...this was a grave setback, but not the end. Not even close.

We were pioneers and survivors. We would rebuild, learn from this tragedy, and continue our mission.

As the dust settled and the immediate shock gave way to a frenzied rush to aid and secure the colony, I was ushered toward the emergency shelters with the others. I'd only be in the way out there on the surface.

Commander Ryan's voice continued to orchestrate the response efforts, his voice commanding and reassuring once again. There was no sign of his earlier weakness, of his grief.

We were Martians. We endured...and sometimes we died.

ΦΦΦ

Mars in the burgeoning light of the 2060s wasn't your grandparents' barren wasteland. It was a world of challenges and dangers that went beyond the physical and ventured into the existential, and sometimes even the psychological. It was a frontier where every day had the potential to become a fight for survival, and where people had a better-than-average chance to become an example of human courage and ingenuity.

Despite all the inherent dangers, it was our home.

Imagine a sprawling matrix of human colonization scattered across the Martian landscape, with red dirt far out into the horizons and domes popped up in carefully planned formations like giant soap bubbles. Right smack dab in the middle of that bubble bonanza was my second home: the Mars Frontier Research Institute, where brainiacs in lab coats made magic with terraforming and terabytes.

In the cold haze of dawn, Mars Colony One was a striking silhouette against the weak sunlight, a teeming mass of humanity in a lonely ocean of crimson-orange dust.

Think of it as Earth 2.0. It was less green and more red, but with a communal spirit that put our big blue neighbor to shame. Honestly, I'd choose Mars every time. Mars was special, *different*.

We had it all— scientists, engineers, idealistic settlers,

and even a few lost souls running from their Earthly defeats.

My workspace was like a glimpse into my brain: a chaotic masterpiece. At least that's what my Dad had always said.

Piles of papers and digital displays hovered in mid-air, each one a little piece of the Martian puzzle I was trying to solve. To anyone else, it looked like a mad scientist's clutter fest, but to me? It was more of a home than my actual home back in Tennessee.

My office was prime Martian real estate, with a panoramic view of the dusty red expanse. It was decked out with all the latest gadgets— 3D molecular structure projectors, an AI-assisted data analysis pad, and screens showing live feeds from Mars rovers and probes.

I had some concert posters on my walls and my 'World's Okayest Astrobiologist' mug on a shelf—a gift from Raj. One of my favorite things to look at in my spare time was my rock collection from various Martian regions. Each one was a little keepsake from a different part of the Red Planet. Some I'd gathered myself and some were gifted to me. I didn't always know what I was looking at, but it gave me a nice feeling anyway. It was kind of a tangible reminder that I'd done things, been places...that my life hadn't been stagnating even though it felt like that sometimes.

Settling into my chair, I surveyed my domain with a mix of pride and mild disbelief. If there was an award for Most Organized Chaos, I'd win hands down, probably burying the trophy under a pile marked 'Urgent Astrobiology Stuff'.

I loved my ceiling too. It was a neat solar-charging, LED wonder that doubled as a window to the sky. It soaked up the sun's rays, giving me that nice even glow that only a giant nuclear furnace millions of miles away could provide. On dust storm days, I'd switch it to opaque mode for a bit of cozy, Earth-like comfort.

Early mornings at the Institute were the best part of my day. Watching the sunrise on Mars was like opening a new gift each day, except the gift was a freezing, rusty landscape. Many times it gave me a sudden pang of longing for Nashville. Somedays, when I was a bit Earthsick, I pretended it was Arizona.

My job had progressed well and I was the head of our sector's lab. I coordinated with other labs in other domes and made sure everything was well-stocked and running smoothly. In my lab at the Science Dome on Elysium Planitia, I was the Sherlock Holmes of Martian soil.

My main job was staring at dirt.

Actually, it was digging through soil samples and using high-tech gear to hunt for any signs of life. Most days, it felt like I was trying to play a game with half the pieces missing.

Another part of my day was spent encouraging extremophiles to set up housekeeping. Extremophiles were those little Earth organisms that just love extreme conditions, like volcano vents and deep-sea crevasses. I was trying to make them feel at home in Martian soil simulant.

Spoiler alert: they weren't sending me thank-you notes.

Some of my little favorite side projects were my Martian garden experiments. It wasn't much, just a bunch of Earth plants that had been genetically tweaked to not freak out in Martian conditions. They were all lined up in their biomes along the wall and looking as confused as tourists in a foreign country.

It wasn't just gardening. It was my exercise in optimism. Every day, I'd check on them like a nervous parent on the first day of school, hoping they'd make it through another day.

But honestly? They looked a bit peaky and I think I was just prolonging the inevitable.

So, that was my job. A part-time dirt inspector, a part-time mad botanist, all in the name of figuring out if Mars could be our self-sufficient second home one day. Or, at least a place where we could grow potatoes and set up shop without starting an interplanetary incident.

That morning started just about the same as all the others, minus the snickering co-workers after I walked into the lab with my shirt inside out. It wouldn't have been so bad if there hadn't also been a pair of my underwear stuck to the back of it.

All of our advanced, automated crap and they still couldn't get rid of static.

As I fidgeted with my earring and sifted through the probe data (another side gig of mine because there was only so long I could study microbes without zoning out), a strange anomaly caught my eye— a series of irregular blips on the screen.

I slammed forward in my seat, my heart pounding as I studied the formations.

In my excitement, I knocked over a stack of papers and my precious coffee mug in a clumsy flurry of arms and curses.

"Typical," I muttered, scrambling for a notepad—*actual paper*, not one of those fancy HoloPads everyone raved about. I took notes, my pen scrawling across the paper in an almost undecipherable scribble.

At least nobody would be able to steal my ideas.

I sat there for hours as my back began to ache, my fingers went numb, and my stomach started gnawing on my spine. I barely noticed any of it. That's just the way I was with work—completely absorbed until something else came along and distracted me.

As the Institute began to stir, Dr. Raj Patel, our resident

geologist and unofficial comedian, strolled into my office like he owned the place. It irked me to no end.

"Mercer, if those papers were any higher, we'd need a mission to scale them," he joked, setting his 'I'm a Rock Star' mug next to a rock that was, ironically, not from Mars.

I gave him a half-smirk, still absorbed in the data. "Just be thankful I haven't used them for kindling... yet," I retorted.

"Ha, like the maintenance team would ever allow a fire," he retorted. "Did you hear the final toll?" he murmured a long moment later.

I paused my work out of respect for the dead and shook my head.

"Fourteen lost, along with some some pretty important equipment."

I bowed my head. Fourteen people were gone, dead. Fourteen people with families, friends, and loved ones...it made my heart ache. "It's been three weeks. Are they having a memorial?"

Raj shrugged. "They were settlers, so the settlers probably will. Dr. Park and the governor will probably attend. It would look bad if they didn't."

We talked a bit longer, and then he left. Though it felt a bit wrong to continue with my work after such a heavy topic, I had no choice. Ganymede probe's data was screaming for attention, with blips that seemed as out of place as a leprechaun at a pool party.

With a furrowed brow, I sifted through the data streams, my fingers skipping across the touch interface as I isolated the anomaly.

I cross-referenced the database and removed the known signatures, and then I made an educated guess and canceled out potential interference from Jupiter and natural, nonrhythmic bloops.

What I was left with was a string of data that was...funky.

It was rhythmic, almost intentional in its structure. I breathed out, trying to calm my adrenaline. I needed to conserve my adrenal glands for future excitement, and the way things had been going, I would need them.

Could the signal be a message? A call?

The possibility sent a thrill down my spine, the kind of excitement every scientist dreams of but dares not acknowledge too soon—especially me, not with my track record.

I delved into the second analysis, isolating the signal once again from a new direction, stripping away the noise and phantom echoes. Eventually, the work helped me to forget the tragedy for a little while.

Soon, I realized that I needed a second set of eyes.

"Raj, look at this," I called, motioning him over when he stuck his head through the doorway. "Tell me I'm not just high on oxygen mix."

He peered over my shoulder, his eyebrows arching in surprise. "I'm no expert but, that's... not your average space static," he admitted. "But let's not jump to aliens just yet."

I laughed. "I *was* thinking more along the lines of First Contact, but sure, let's rule out the probe having a hiccup. At least it might save my pride when I find out it's nothing."

The rest of the morning passed in a blur of data, speculation, and more coffee. I dissected the anomaly from every angle that I could think of, my brain buzzing with possibilities. I made Raj check a couple of my analysis runs, but he had no more insight than I did.

I knew the drill: check, recheck, then check again. Evidence was king at the Institute, and I was determined to crown this discovery with the hard facts it deserved before I dragged it out for public adoration.

By the time I compiled my final report of the morning, the sun had traced its lazy arc across the sky. The communal hub would be alive with the chatter and clinks of lunchtime, but I was lost in a world of spectral analyses and other stuff.

"Hey, Mercer," Raj called out from the doorway, his voice pulling me from my reverie. "You coming to lunch or are you planning to photosynthesize?"

I shot him a grin, still half-lost in the data. "Give me a

sec. I think we might have stumbled onto something humongous here. Maybe even get our names in next month's newsletter."

"Your name maybe. I had nothing to do with it," Raj chuckled. "Let's just hope it's not your Martian tadpole theory all over again. Come on, lunch won't eat itself, you know. And the rehydrated pasta is my favorite."

"They weren't *tadpoles,* they were *Euglena* and someone cross-contaminated my sample," I muttered. With a reluctant sigh, I tore myself away from the screens. The data would wait, but my stomach had other ideas.

I first met Raj Patel during what I affectionately refer to as my Martian freshman year. It was back when I was still green enough to think a dust storm was just some extra house cleaning. Raj, with his ever-present 'I'm a Rock Star' attitude (I bought him the mug to match), was already a legend in the geology department.

He was famous for turning rocks into revelations.

I remember wandering into the wrong lab— a typical rookie move— and finding Raj hunched over a microscope, his eyes as focused as a laser drilling into Martian bedrock. He looked up, and for a moment, I thought I was about to be booted out. Instead, he just handed me a pair of safety goggles with a grin that said, 'Welcome to the show.'

Raj's story was a mix of grit and genius. Raised in a

family of engineers, he rebelled by becoming a geologist. He often joked, "In my house, rocks were the real F-word." But beneath that humor was a man who found peace in the age-old stories told by stones and soil.

Our bond formed over shared late nights in the lab, deciphering the Martian landscape's secrets. He taught me the fine art of seeing the story in every grain of sand, and I showed him that biology could be just as thrilling as geology (and also just as dull sometimes).

Once, during a particularly brutal dust storm that had us cooped up with low power for days, Raj broke the monotony with a makeshift bowling alley in the corridor, using polymer specimen jars as pins.

It was hilariously inappropriate and probably a violation of six different safety protocols, but it was exactly what we needed. We'd both been almost stir-crazy by then and willing to pay a fine for the violation if necessary.

Eventually, Raj became more than a colleague. He was the brother I never had on Earth. His down-to-earth nature was a grounding force amidst the high-flying ambitions of almost everyone on Mars Colony One.

Whether we were sifting through soil samples or dodging dunes on a rover trip, Raj had a knack for turning even dull work into an adventure.

And despite his rough exterior, Raj had a heart as vast as Valles Marineris.

I remember finding him once, covertly sending most of his salary back to Earth to support a school in his hometown. He shrugged it off with a typical Raj quip. "I don't need cash, but the kids do. The poverty levels there are pretty high and I want to make sure they get a chance in life, a chance like I had."

That's Raj— a rock star in more ways than one, with his feet firmly on Martian soil and his heart stretched across the stars.

As I followed Raj down the hall, the buzz of the Institute around me, I couldn't shake the feeling that I was on the cusp of something monumental with the whole signal thing.

I couldn't help but think that, in the vast silence of space a message had been sent, and here on Mars in a dome filled with expert dreamers and doers, *I* was the one who had caught it. Destiny, fate, or chance...who knew?

Now it was just a matter of finding out who—or what—was on the other end.

ΦΦΦ

Strolling beside Raj towards the cafeteria, the sounds of the Mars Frontier Research Institute's hub hit us like a dome breach alert—loud and inescapable.

The place was a cultural charcuterie board. You'd see

everything from engineers haggling over a piece of art to scientists debating the latest data, all set against a backdrop of red Martian soil and high-tech domes.

"What do you think, Lena?" Raj asked.

"Bout what?" I said, checking the time on a screen nearby.

"About the Earth-Mars drama?" Raj asked as we dodged a pair of animated physicists.

I rolled my eyes. "If Earth slaps an embargo on us, we'll be eating nothing but rehydrated potatoes in no time."

Raj chuckled. "At least we've got our Redcreds. Beats carrying around a wallet full of dust."

True that. Mars' digital currency, what we called Redcreds, was our lifeline. It made transactions smoother than a Martian ice rink. But with Earth acting all high and mighty, who knew how long that smoothness would last?

The Redcred to dollar exchange rate was a joke, and in terms of Earth money, I regularly went from being a multi-millionaire to being a penniless vagabond and back again. We'd all learned long ago to convert our currency when the exchange rate was good, and at least have enough set aside on Earth to live well if we had to leave the colony.

In the cafeteria, the food was a blend of science project and survival strategy.

Most of it was grown right here in our hydroponic farms, with a dash of lab-grown protein for good measure.

The lettuce had more crunch than a fresh snowfall on Olympus Mons, and the chicken? Well, it was chicken-ish.

Water, though, that was the real Martian gold.

Every drop was recycled and purified with more care than a germaphobe washing his hands for the third time.

Our ice mining ops at Utopia Planitia were a sight to behold—like watching giant mechanical ants hoarding their winter stash. The greenhouses, on the outer edge of the Science Dome Field, were a jungle in a bubble. They turned water vapor into a life-giving rain loop where the plants mostly watered themselves.

And we needed every single bit of it.

I followed Raj over to the food counter, where chefs waited to dish up portions of the day's choices. Today it was rehydrated Earth pasta in sauce, desiccated liver paste and dried onions (also rehydrated), or a scampi with lab-grown shrimp.

Pasta was always the safest bet.

As Raj and I sat down with our trays, the chatter around us shifted from food to the latest Mars gossip.

"You think Earth's going to mess with our imports?" Raj asked, digging into his pasta.

I shrugged. "Wouldn't put it past them. I mean, we're like the cool kids on the block. Earth might get a bit jealous if we keep discovering stuff here."

Our table conversation bounced from Earth-Mars

politics to the latest virtual reality games. Mars Vegas, our unofficial VR district, was the go-to place for escaping reality. Along with the game and recreation parlors, there were casinos, spas, restaurants, bars, and clubs.

Work hard, play hard—that's the Martian motto.

Glancing at the smart table's display, I noticed the news ticker flashing updates about solar flares. Typical Martian lunchtime— eating freeze-dried pseudo-Italian food while reading about space weather.

Raj nudged me. "Hey, what about that signal you've been chasing? Where are you on that?"

I leaned back, wiping my mouth and sipping my water. "It's..." I blew out a breath, trying to think of a way to describe it. "It's like trying to solve a puzzle without the picture on the box. But I've got a hunch it's important."

Our lunch wrapped up with the usual mix of laughter and light-hearted banter between Raj and the others while I participated on the periphery. I wasn't as outgoing as they were and they were used to that by now.

I seemed to function a bit differently than many of the others in my sector, though I was by no means an outlier. There were plenty of eccentrics here. You couldn't throw a rock without hitting someone who mumbled to themselves while wandering the corridors in the middle of the night, wearing a ratty housecoat and carrying a sample case to their lab—myself included.

Despite the looming uncertainties between us and our home planet and the differences in our work habits, there was a sense of unity among us all—even the settlers. We were all part of this crazy, red-dusted quest, and whatever happened, we were in it together...mostly because we had no other choice.

Walking back to the lab after cleaning up my meal, I couldn't help but glance at the communication status indicator on the smart screens. It was a habit engrained in all of us from Day 1 here. Green for good, yellow for iffy, red for bad, and black for 'we're on our own, folks'. It was a constant reminder of our fragile link to Earth.

"Twenty-minute delay today," I mused, thinking about the time lag in communications with Earth on green days.

I really needed to make time to send my parents a message.

"Yep, makes flirting via text a real challenge," Raj quipped.

Laughing, I shook my head. "Only you would try interplanetary flirting, Raj."

ΦΦΦ

I'd barely finished digesting my lunch and done some preliminary strength calculations on the signal when the itch to share my discovery pulled me away from the grindstone.

My destination was Dr. Johann Weber, my mentor, and the Yoda of astrobiology at the Institute. If anyone could help make sense of my Ganymede conundrum, it was him.

Weber's office was like a time capsule from the 2030s, all paper books and clutter that would give a neat freak a heart attack.

I felt right at home.

I rapped on the door frame, and his head popped up from behind a mountain of papers, his glasses perched precariously on the tip of his nose.

If there was one thing that wasn't done well when the architects designed the Mars Frontier Research Domes' facilities, it was storage options. Back in the early 40s, they'd anticipated us ditching paper completely, but most of us liked it too much. The results were less than ideal stacks of it in almost every office.

The sector QRF Commanders always grumbled about fire hazards, but let us carry on with our paper addictions.

"Ah, Lena! What mysteries are you unraveling today?" he greeted, his eyes sharp behind the lenses.

Knowing my penchant for white rabbit projects, that was probably a subtle jab. I ignored it and pretended he was serious.

"Got something that might just blow your Argyle socks off, Johann," I said, stepping into his own special brand of chaos.

I laid out the charts and unfolded the HoloPad XL data streams across his cluttered desk, watching his eyes scan the information with the meticulousness of a seasoned alien hunter—his preferred title.

We all humored him.

"These blips are the ones," I pointed to the rhythmic patterns on the screen. "They're from a probe orbiting Ganymede. I've cross-referenced them with data from other probes. It's not interference or instrument error. It's... something else."

Weber leaned in, his brows knitting together. "Rhythmic, yes, but natural cosmic phenomena can produce patterns too. Have you considered pulsar signals? Or perhaps a quirk in Ganymede's magnetic field interacting with Jupiter's radiation belts?"

"I thought of that," I said, pulling up a comparison chart. "But look here," I tapped on the screen. "The frequency modulation doesn't match pulsar patterns. It isn't as precise. And as for magnetic interactions, the signal lacks the chaotic variances you'd expect. This is too consistent, too deliberate."

"What about quasars?" he asks, shifting his glasses and making notes on a tattered black book.

"I thought about that too, but again, the pattern doesn't match. Quasar emissions, even the most erratic ones, have a certain irregularity. Like a kind of jumble. This signal from Ganymede is too organized. It's repeating in a way quasars just don't."

I stepped back and waited, my heart pounding as he considered my find. I'd always sought his approval, all of us did. His approval was a gold star in our field. I saw him as kind of a father-type stand-in: without all the nagging and bragging. If he thought I had something, then I probably did.

"Hmm," Weber murmured and leaned back in his chair with the kind of calm you'd expect from someone who's seen everything from Martian dust apocalypses to PhD students having meltdowns.

Apparently, my signal wasn't going to generate much excitement, which was a little disappointing.

He cleared his throat, gaze far off as he stared at the streams. "It's fascinating, no doubt. But don't forget, the simplest explanation is usually the right one."

"If three things aren't enough to prove something, add a fourth," I recited, feeling a bit prickly by his doubt.

"Chatton's anti-razor. Crude, Mercer, but accurate." Weber's eyes had that glint, the kind you see when someone's about to either call you a genius or send you off for a psych evaluation. "Explore every possibility, sure. But remember, Lena, extraordinary claims need extraordinary—"

"—Evidence, yeah, I got it." I finished his sentence, already mentally preparing my lab for a deep dive into the unknown. "But what if we're on the brink of rewriting the astrobiology textbooks?"

He smiled, a mix of 'I'm proud of you' and 'you might be slightly nuts.'

"Go ahead, do your research. But the universe is mostly just physics doing its thing and this is probably no different."

"Got it, but sometimes, the universe likes to throw curveballs. And this," I held up my data like it was a golden ticket, "might be a touchdown."

"You're mixing up your sports metaphors again," he noted.

I was starting to think the fusty old codger had lost his zest for discoveries. I scoffed and threw my hands up. "I'm going now."

"Don't forget the samples you are supposed to collect," he reminded.

I raised my eyebrows. "We still need those?"

With a nod from Weber, I left his office, my mind racing with possibilities. The Ganymede Signal, a term I was already fond of, beckoned me into the unknown.

I'd have to go chase down his samples at some point—it was my job after all— but I wanted to do some more investigating on the signal side of things first. I mentally prepared myself to shift from spending my days DNA sequencing dirt samples to dusting off my physics hobby.

Bolstered by his words—well, sort of— I decided to cast my net a bit wider.

I set up an impromptu presentation in the department's lounge, a space usually reserved for coffee breaks and existential gripes about research funding.

Everyone was used to me dragging out my hypotheses for public ridicule, and so they begrudgingly attended.

I took all my notes, my HoloPad, and my mini-comms unit to control the lounge screen interface. After I hijacked someone's Earth beach vacation screen, I pulled up the Ganymede signal in all its glory and looked over the assemblage.

The crowd was a mix of curious faces and skeptics who looked like they'd rather be analyzing stardust or staring at rocks. Raj, sitting in the rock-starer section, gave me an enthusiastic two-thumbs up.

I tucked my short, red hair behind my ears and kicked off the presentation, my excitement a stark contrast to the room's lukewarm energy. Even among the brightest of scientific minds, I was considered a bit extreme.

Let's put it this way: if the MFRI was a science fair, I was the volcano experiment that unexpectedly blasted the ceiling tiles off— surprising, a tad over-the-top, but impossible to ignore and never boring.

I could have let it get to me, but I chose to follow the maxim that any kind of recognition is better than moldering into obscurity.

As I dove into the data, outlining the peculiar patterns and the rhythmic anomalies, the room's atmosphere shifted from 'meh' to 'hmm'. Eyebrows raised, heads tilted—I even spotted a few nods. But alongside the intrigue came the skeptics, armed with their favorite weapon: doubt.

"It could be a glitch, Mercer. These instruments aren't foolproof," one colleague pointed out, arms crossed.

"Or interference from Jupiter's magnetosphere. It's notorious for playing tricks," chimed in another.

"Glitch in the instruments?" I started, pointing to a graph spiked like a hedgehog at a punk rock concert. "I thought the same. So, I cross-referenced it with data from three different probes. Unless they're having a synchronized glitch party, this thing's as real as my caffeine addiction."

A murmur ran through the crowd, a mix of intrigue, 'she's got a point', and 'when is supper?' expressions.

"Interference from Jupiter's magnetosphere?" I continued, flicking to a slide that looked like a Jackson Pollock painting had a baby with a kaleidoscope. "Here's the thing. I filtered out the known interference patterns—Jupiter's magnetic field throwing a tantrum, solar wind having a crazy day, you name it. What's left is this," I gestured to the rhythmic blips dancing on the screen. "It's too structured, too... intentional."

"Could it be a natural phenomenon we just haven't encountered yet?" someone said from the back.

I grinned, appreciating the challenge. "That's the million-Redcred question, isn't it? See, natural signals are like jazz—all over the place. This signal? It's more classical, structured, and repeating. It's like comparing Miles Davis to Mozart. Both brilliant, but one's a bit more... organized."

Nods and thoughtful hums filled the room.

"And before you ask about pulsars or quasars or any other 'ars' out there," I added, pulling up a comparison chart. "I ran the patterns against every known celestial body that likes to make noise out there. None match. This signal is completely unique, like finding a needle in a universe-sized haystack."

A few raised eyebrows and a couple of impressed whistles bolstered my confidence a bit. It was more than I was used to getting, though my past little assemblies had never left me discouraged.

I was resilient that way. The only person who could get me down was me.

I wrapped up, feeling like I'd just given the Martian TED talk of the century. "Look, I'm not saying we've stumbled upon an E.T. jam session here," I concluded, the room now hanging on my every word. "But whatever this is, it's *not* your run-of-the-mill space static. It's worth digging deeper, don't you think?"

As the crowd dispersed, some still skeptical, others noticeably less so, I felt a surge of exhilaration.

The Ganymede Signal, whatever it was, had just become the most intriguing mystery of my career and I had just thrown it out there for public consumption. I made waves, and I knew it would generate talk.

Raj joined me at the observation window after I cleared away my notes and gear. "It's incredible, isn't it? To think, among all these stars, your signal might be the key to finding others."

"It's more than incredible, Raj. It's humbling. We're on the brink of something huge, and yet we're just tiny parts of this giant freaking space.

He tilted his head in gentle negation. "Tiny maybe, but not insignificant. Not by a long shot."

He slung an arm over my shoulders and walked me back to my office and lab. "Come on. Get some more work done if you must, but promise you'll get some rest too, huh, sis?"

I scoffed. "If you insist, but I can't guarantee that I won't be back at it bright and early tomorrow morning."

"I wouldn't bet against it," he laughed, messing up my hair and leaving to head to his quarters. "'Night."

I waved and went into my office, pacing the room as I thought for a while. The room was dim and I was tired, but I couldn't rest. My mind turned it over and over again even as my eyes grew heavy. Raj was right. We were small, infinitesimal even, in the wider universe, but we weren't insignificant.

I settled back into my chair, the Martian landscape outside my window a silent spectator to my obsession.

Perhaps whatever had sent the signal wasn't insignificant either.

I scrubbed my face with my hands, melting away some of the fatigue as I thought about my schedule. Sometime, I had to head out to the damned volcano to get the samples for Webby.

2.

'63-02

Two days after I stumbled upon what I'd started calling the Ganymede Signal—because 'weird space noise' didn't have quite the same ring to it—I was summoned to the office of Dr. Emily Park, head honcho of the Mars Frontier Research Institute.

Walking into her office was like stepping into a future where papers had become outlawed. Screens and holograms were lined up like soldiers on parade, each one screaming 'tactical efficiency' and 'potentially deadly futuristic knowledge'. It was scary.

My office, in comparison, looked like it had survived a minor apocalypse.

"So, Dr. Mercer," Dr. Park started, her voice crisp and

fresh like hydroponic carrots. "I understand you've made an intriguing discovery."

I shifted in my seat, feeling the weight of her scrutiny and wishing I'd worn better pants.

"Yes, Dr. Park. The data from the Ganymede probe is... unusual. It's rhythmic and structured. I've run it through every analysis we have and even some I made up. I've analyzed it to death. Literally. I think my computer's AI has started to develop an inferiority complex."

She leaned back, steepling her fingers. "And you believe this could be more than a simple anomaly? You're suggesting it could be... extraterrestrial?"

I nodded, my mind racing. "It's unlike anything we've seen. I understand the skepticism, but the pattern— it's intentional, I'd bet my career on it."

That was putting it mildly, and the Ganymede Signal was anything but mild. It was like trying to make sense of a Morse code composed by a caffeinated squirrel—intriguing and intentional, but slightly nuts.

She sighed, the way one does when faced with something between 'groundbreaking' and 'career-breaking'.

"Doctor Mercer, you know the implications of such a claim. The scientific community, not to mention the public, will demand irrefutable evidence. And with the current economic tensions between Earth and Mars..."

Her voice trailed off, but the message was clear.

Mars Colony One was a crowded theater of political and scientific maneuvering, and my discovery could be the equivalent of yelling fire.

"Understood," I replied, feeling frustrated. "I'll continue my analysis, keep it more low-key until we have something more concrete."

Walking out of her office, the burden of my discovery felt heavier than a cargo ship full of Martian rocks.

In my excitement, I couldn’t forget that Mars wasn't just a place of scientific wonder. It was also a battleground for autonomy and independence. And here I was, possibly sitting on the biggest discovery since we figured out you couldn’t grow decent coffee on Mars.

Raj met me in the Admin Dome hub right after I left. “Come on, they’ve moved the meeting time up. We’re here. We might as well check it out.”

The town hall meeting at Mars Colony One had always been a dreary affair. It was a routine assembly where we discussed water rations and dust storm preparations, among other mundane things. But that day, it was as if a spark had ignited in the very soul of the colony. The air was thick with anticipation and voices intermingled in heated debate. It had a touch of urgency and tension that came from more than just a dust storm or a water filtration snafu.

I found myself in the midst of it all and I was a little taken aback by the vehemence in some of their voices.

As I leaned against the cool wall to watch the crowd, Dr. Elaine Zhao, head of the Martian Council, was addressing the community with a fervor I had never seen in her before and that was saying something.

Someone had riled her up good.

"Our allegiance to Earth has always been out of necessity, not desire," she declared. "But now, we must ask ourselves—are we ready to stand alone?"

I couldn't help but smirk at the dramatics. Classic Zhao, always with a flair for the theatrical. Yet, her words resonated with many in the room, stirring a chorus of agreement.

"This is getting intense. Do you think they'll actually consider breaking away from Earth?" Raj whispered.

I shrugged, my eyes scanning the crowd. "Who knows? But it's about time we started this conversation. Mars isn't just a science experiment anymore. It's our home."

A council member named Viktor, a man known for his booming voice and no-nonsense attitude, rose to his feet. "We can't keep living under Earth's shadow! We've built this colony with our sweat and blood and they keep shortchanging us. It's time Mars looked out for Mars!"

His words ignited a fire in the hall. Half the room erupted in cheers, while the other half exchanged uneasy glances. I could see the divide, as tangible as the red Martian soil outside.

“Where’s the governor?” I murmured, getting some bad vibes.

“Not here,” he whispered back.

“Probably why they moved up the time.”

Governor Olsen seemed to be mostly fair and relatively unipartisan, but he wouldn’t stand for outright rebellion, which is what this meeting seemed to be about.

A woman from the crowd, a technician I recognized from the hydroponics lab, stood up. "And what about the resources Earth provides? The technology? The food? The books? The personnel? Are we ready to give all that up?"

"We have the knowledge, the skills. We can be self-sufficient!" Viktor retorted.

I leaned closer to Raj."Self-sufficient? With what, dreams and dust? We're not ready for this. Not yet,” I scoffed.

Dr. Zhao raised her hands, calling for calm. "This is a decision that affects every one of us. We need to consider all aspects carefully. Our future, our children's future, is at stake."

The room quieted down, the weight of her words sinking in. I looked around, seeing the uncertainty, the hope, the fear in people's eyes.

Were we ready to leap from being a scientific colony of

Earth to an independent planet? I didn't think so. Not even close.

As the meeting adjourned, the conversations continued. The voices mingled in a cacophony of opinions and theories that made my head spin.

I was very afraid that we were going to have our own 1776 moment, or perhaps 2076.

As I turned to follow Raj out the door, I caught sight of QRF Commander Ryan standing at the back of the meeting room, staring out into the Martian landscape, troubled.

Perhaps he had good reason to be.

ΦΦΦ

Back in my office, I put the worries of war on hold and dove into the data once more, my mind all tangled up in the details.

Raj dropped by later that night. His usual cheerful demeanor tempered was by concern. Probably concern for me, but also maybe concern for what an embargo would mean for him and his family back on Earth. I worried too.

He plopped into a chair across from me and leaned forward, his elbows on his knees. "You're burning the midnight oil again, Len. This signal... it's got you all kinds of wound up."

I managed a tired smile. "Can't help it, Raj. You know how I am and I told you what Dr. Park said. This could be the discovery of a lifetime. I just need to make sure it's not something playing tricks on me."

He chuckled. "Or some bored alien kid with a Morse code set. Just...get some rest, is all I'm saying. I know I'm not one to talk—"

"Yeah, have you seen yourself when those new rock shipments come in?" I teased.

We shared a laugh, but it was forced. The Martian community thrived on discovery and on pushing the boundaries of what was known. But this... this was different.

ΦΦΦ

I was walking through the bustling hub of the Institute the next day, my mind a million miles away—or more accurately, several astronomical units away— fixated on the Ganymede Signal.

I never said I wasn't slightly obsessive when I got the scent of discovery in my nose.

Around me, the colony thrived with the rhythm of daily life, but I barely noticed. The usual vibrant chatter of the settlers, the scientists joking over their lunch, the whir of the automated service bots—it all blurred into a distant hum.

As I passed the large, transparent panels overlooking the Martian landscape, my gaze drifted over the horizon and I took a moment to really stop and look at it. I had been on Mars so long that it didn't phase me anymore. It was normal.

But it wasn't.

It was a deadly landscape that would boil your blood and suffocate you if you so much as ripped a seam on your afternoon walk. I hadn't been outside without wearing protective gear in years, not since my last trip back home.

At the time, Nashville had been cold. It was Christmas, a snowy one—which usually only happened about once every 10 or 15 years. At the time, I had felt both overwhelmed and overjoyed to be able to leave a building in a t-shirt without dying. It was kind of hard to recall what that felt like now.

I stopped by a coffee kiosk, the aroma of freshly brewed coffee failing to stir my usual appreciation. Cal, a young guy with a friendly smile, handed me my regular order.

"Rough day, Dr. Mercer?" he asked, noticing my distracted air.

I managed a half-smile. "Just the usual mysteries of the universe keeping me busy," I said, my attempt at lightheartedness sounding hollow even to my own ears.

Continuing my walk, I observed the faces around me—there were settlers in their utilitarian work pants and casual button-ups, researchers animatedly discussing their latest findings, and engineers debating over some mechanical conundrum over at the water filtration plant.

The settlers were our version of farmers, miners, assistants, and entrepreneurs.

Obviously, they couldn't just step out and plow a field, but they could work inside the agriculture and hydroponics domes. We even had bees and beekeepers. They were paid for their work, and because of their status as first-generation Martians, their children were provided with the choice of a free education at the Mars Frontier Academy or an apprenticeship after they learned the educational basics.

Our first batch of Martian-born kids were going to be teenagers in a few years and everyone was curious to see if they'd leave to go to Earth or choose to stay and follow in their parents' footsteps—yet another reason we weren't ready for complete independence from Earth.

Honestly, I thought it was a horrible idea. We were Martians, yes, but underneath that dashing, flashy cultural veneer, we were humans from Earth.

And we needed Earth.

On the way back to my office, I passed by a group of

engineers dressed in typical blue jumpsuits huddled around a holographic display, their conversation peppered with technical jargon about the latest difficulty in sourcing parts from a factory on Earth.

Our parts sourcing difficulties seemed to happen with alarming frequency now.

Back at work, the hours blurred as I delved deeper, cross-referencing, analyzing, theorizing...

I paired the signal with historical cosmic events, famous comet sightings, and even tried syncing it with Earth's own radio broadcasts sent into space decades ago. Each attempt canceled out potential causes, but the real source remained elusive.

My next idea was more of a long shot.

I programmed the software to convert the signal's frequency into a visual pattern. Maybe, if I could 'see' the signal, it would reveal something new. The screen flickered as waveforms transformed into a cascade of patterns.

I leaned closer, squinting at the shapes.

They were mesmerizing but nonsensical— a galactic Rorschach test. I chuckled to myself, imagining presenting this to Dr. Park. She'd probably think I'd lost my mind, seeing faces in the static.

But there *was* something there, hidden beneath the layers of data and digital noise...a pattern too deliberate to be random. It was like trying to see a spec of pollen in a sea of flowers.

It ate at me, my brain giving me little nudges that were more irritating than instructive. It was the feeling of having a word on the tip of your tongue and not being able to find it—or the feeling of having a hair stuck in your sock and being unable to get it out right away.

I grabbed a notepad, sketched the patterns, and annotated them with notes and hunches. My freeform vomiting of ideas onto a page method usually helped.

My hand flew across the page, trying to keep pace with my racing thoughts. The room grew darker as Mars' modest sunset dipped below the horizon, the artificial lights of my office casting long shadows.

Raj's voice broke through my reverie, making me yelp.

"You're going to wear yourself out at this rate, Len," he reminded, concern etched on his face.

I waved him off, my eyes not leaving the screen. "I'm fine, Raj. Just need to crack this."

But even as I said it, I knew I was far from fine. The signal wasn't just a scientific puzzle anymore. To me, it was a personal challenge. It was a question mark hanging over my head, urging me on, driving me to the brink of my own limits.

As my colleagues drifted off to bed or to Mars Vegas to unwind, I remained in my office, the data my only companion. The hub's lively atmosphere had long since quieted down, but I was barely aware of it. My world had narrowed to the flickering numbers and patterns on the screen.

For the next couple of weeks, my life became a cycle of analysis and reanalysis. My days consisted of short walks to the coffee kiosk and the cafeteria and back, hoping the scant exercise would drum up some new ideas.

The Institute's advanced communication systems, usually a flurry of green and yellow alerts, flickered with the occasional red, a reminder of the precarious nature of our link to Earth.

I worked tirelessly, fueled by a mixture of coffee and sheer stubbornness. The data from Ganymede was my Riemann Hypothesis, and I was hell-bent on solving it.

Despite my focus, I couldn't ignore the undercurrents of unease that rippled through the colony. News of potential trade embargoes and diplomatic spats trickled in, and the news conferences and speeches were played on a loop on the smart screens throughout the facility, adding to the tension.

It reminded me of the saber-rattling in the old Earth days when the world went to war with itself. Only now, their eyes were on us.

In the silence of my office, with Mars' twin moons casting their faint light onto the dome, I felt a connection to something larger— something beyond the red dust and domed habitats and interplanetary war and espionage.

The Ganymede Signal, whatever it was, had become my north star, guiding me through the uncertainty and into the icy unknown.

With each passing day, the signal drew me deeper, and I knew that, for better or worse, there was no turning back.

ΦΦΦ

Three weeks and a half after stumbling onto the Ganymede Signal, I was cooped up in my office at the Mars Frontier Research Institute, hunkered down in front of a sea of screens.

My legs were unshaven, I was mostly unwashed, and *definitely* overly caffeinated. My hair was greasy and I hadn't seen makeup, hairbrush, or real shoes in days.

Each screen—some borrowed, because three just weren't enough anymore— was a window into the problem that was becoming my life's obsession. It was just me, my cryptology software, and a signal from Jupiter's moon that was playing hard to get.

I booted up my newest software acquisition, typically used for decoding the kind of messages that would make international Earth spies giddy with excitement. It was my newest idea and one that had given me a surge of optimism.

The program started dissecting the signal, breaking it down into digestible chunks of data.

I leaned back, sipping my coffee, and watched the numbers and graphs dance across the screen.

Hour after hour slipped by. I tweaked the settings, reran the analysis, and hit one dead end after another. It was like trying to solve a crossword puzzle where every clue was "What's the meaning of life?"

Then, out of the blue, the software chimed with a different tone.

I nearly spat out the water I'd switched to in order to give my body, and nervous system, a break.

On the screen, amidst the digital chaos, a pattern started to emerge. It wasn't the usual signal pattern. This was something deliberate, almost artistic.

It was like looking at a Fibonacci sequence but jazzed up with some logarithmic curlicues.

For the uninitiated, picture a spiraling pattern you see in pinecones or leaves around a stem, where each number is the sum of the two preceding ones. Now, imagine that sequence but with an artistic twist. Not only did the numbers make sense, the offshoots did as well.

The patterns in the Ganymede signal had mathematical elegance, but with variations that made it feel alive and dynamic. It was as if someone had taken the Fibonacci sequence, thrown in a pinch of rhythm, a dash of melody, and turned it into a mathematical opus.

As I scribbled down notes, my hand struggling to keep up with my brain, I couldn't help but marvel at it. This wasn't just some random blip from the universe. No way, no how.

But what did it mean? Who was the composer of this interstellar symphony?

These weren't questions I could answer with a calculator and a cup of coffee. I was staring at potentially the first hard evidence of extraterrestrial intelligence and it was sending us genius-level math problems.

I leaned back in my chair, rubbing my eyes. The Martian moons, Phobos and Deimos, were like two faint spots of light against the darkness outside my window, indifferent spectators to my Earth-shattering—Mars-shattering—discovery.

At that moment, sitting there all wired up and feeling on the verge of a breakthrough, I wasn't just an astrobiologist with a gardening hobby anymore.

I was an interstellar detective. I was onto something big, something that could change everything. And it all started with the peculiar pattern hovering and twisting in the air above the HoloPad. It was my supercharged Fibonacci sequence, serenading me from the depths of space.

ΦΦΦ

During those weeks after I hit the jackpot with the Ganymede Signal, my office turned into mission control, if mission control was run by a coked-up raccoon.

It went from merely bad, to exponentially worse.

I was knee-deep in data and miscellaneous debris, chugging coffee like it was the elixir of life, and chasing a signal that seemed as elusive as a decent pizza on Mars.

I thought that the presence of the pattern could be enough to convince Dr. Park and Dr. Weber, but I didn't know for sure. I was too close to it, and the longer I worked on it, the less certain I was of anything.

It was during one of these marathon sessions that Dr. Weber decided to stage an intervention.

The door swooshed open, but I was too engrossed in analyzing one of the offshoot patterns to notice. That is, until he cleared his throat.

That sound usually meant either a groundbreaking idea was coming or I was about to *be* grounded.

"You're on the express train to Burnout City," he said, eyeing my desk that I knew resembled the aftermath of a tornado in a bookstore.

I spun around in my chair, almost knocking over my fourth discarded stack of reference materials for the night. None had what I was looking for.

"Johann, check this out! This signal, it's like Fibonacci decided to go interstellar. It's structured, deliberate, like someone's trying to talk to us using space math!"

Show me," he said, raising an eyebrow, with skepticism and interest duking it out in his expression. He looked like Spock's long-lost, scruffy cousin.

I swiped through screens filled with data, bringing up a graph that overlaid the signal's pattern with the Fibonacci sequence. "Look here," I pointed. "The intervals, the way the signal escalates—it mirrors the Fibonacci sequence, but with sophisticated variations. It's like a Jovian Goldberg Variations, each note precisely placed in a universal melody. In fact, listen to this."

I keyed the overhead speakers and closed my eyes with a smile. The haunting strains of a cello scale began, every-increasing, until they reached a crescendo, where they began at the next chord. Layered under those, minor chords played in sync, spinning away from the main body of the music and spiraling ever upward.

He sat down heavily, his mouth gaping like a fish. "That's...that's almost heavenly," he said faintly.

I nodded. "I had the AI assign chords to the values. It sounds just as good with a piano, but I prefer the cello version. The harp was just way too much."

Weber leaned in, studying the graph. His initial skepticism seemed to dissolve, replaced by the kind of curiosity that drove all great scientists. "This is...is *remarkably* compelling, Lena. If this is true, it's more than just a discovery; it's a true indication of intelligence—able to be independently verified. An intelligent pattern in deep space is...well, unprecedented!"

"Exactly!" I exclaimed, a bit too loudly, knocking over a stack of papers with my jiggling foot. "This could be the biggest thing since we found out Mars doesn't have little green men—just little red rocks."

I jerked forward. "And look at this! It took me a bit to figure it out because of sleep deprivation and all that—but *Look. At. This*," I said, motioning to the AI HoloPad and bringing up a new projection.

He leaned forward even more until his nose was almost touching the digital art hovering in the air.

"The Golden Ratio," he breathed.

I almost cried at the joy on his face. He'd been hunting for extraterrestrials for years, and now...I'd found one for him. It wasn't the same as him finding one himself, of course...but it was close. Damned close.

"There is absolutely no question about it, in my opinion, Webby...Er...Dr. Weber. *Somebody* is out there," I said, jumping up, jabbing my finger toward the ceiling, and pacing the floor.

The ethical quandary of the Ganymede Signal, along with all the other quandaries, had been weighing on my mind ever since I intercepted it. But it wasn't until my conversation with Weber, that the full scope of the dilemma truly hit me. Things that I should have thought about before I took my signal public haunted me.

I nodded, taking a seat across from him. "This could be huge. The question is, do we share it with Earth, or do we keep it to ourselves? What's the right thing to do?"

Johann leaned back in his chair, his eyes thoughtful as he rubbed his chin. "Ethically, it's a labyrinth. If we share it, we risk Earth exploiting it for their gain. But keeping it to ourselves goes against the very principle of scientific discovery and collaboration."

I sighed, feeling the weight of his words. "But isn't there a middle ground? Can't we use this as a bargaining chip, to negotiate more autonomy or resources from Earth?"

He shook his head, a hint of sadness in his eyes. "It's not that simple, Lena. This signal could change everything we know about the universe, about life itself. Using it as a political tool seems... reductive."

I frowned, playing with a pen on his desk. "But we have to be practical, Johann. We're talking about the future of Mars Colony One. Our future. Earth could decide to launch a full-scale war against us, or at least a siege."

Johann leaned forward, his expression earnest. "That's exactly my point. Our future shouldn't be built on secrets and power plays. We'll just be continuing the same old status quo. What if the signal holds the key to new technologies, or even contact with other life forms? We can't hoard that kind of knowledge."

His words struck a chord in me, echoing my own hopes and fears.

"I understand what you're saying, but we also have to protect ourselves. Mars isn't just a giant science lab anymore. It's a home to thousands of people."

He nodded slowly. "I know. And that's why this decision is so difficult. We're not just scientists; we're pioneers, leaders, caretakers. The choice we make now will define what kind of society we want to be."

I hid a yawn behind my hand. "I'm afraid I've already let the cat out of the bag with Dr. Park."

He waved a hand. "Then, it is a *fait accompli* and the decision is already out of our hands. We'll proceed as we would have, scientifically. We must wait and see how the Colony responds."

The Mars I had come to years ago was evolving, and with it, our responsibilities and choices were becoming more complex. The Ganymede Signal, with all its mysteries and possibilities, was more than just a scientific anomaly and a personal obsession. It was a test of our values, a question of what kind of future we wanted to create.

I realized that whatever decision we made as a colony, it wouldn't just be about data and discoveries. It would be about us, about who we were as Martians, and what we aspired to be.

"I guess you're correct," I sighed and rubbed my aching eyes. "I just wish things were like they used to be, before Earth began to see us as...as...some kind of threat. Like they think we're developing weapons against them instead of just analyzing *dirt*. I guess I'll go ahead with my original plans. I feel like I should have just kept this whole thing under wraps."

He smiled sadly, snorting at my oversimplification of our mission here.

"We can't hide a discovery of this magnitude, I'm afraid. We must satisfy our curiosity. That's why we're scientists and not politicians." He straightened up, nodding slowly. "I'll back you on this. Let's take it to the big guns, the scientific review board. But Lena," his voice took on that dad tone. "You need a break. Go home, sleep, and for the love of science take a shower. Your hair is oily and you smell."

I smirked. "You know, for a man who spends his days with his head in the stars, you're pretty down to Earth."

He chuckled. "Just looking out for you. Don't lose yourself in this. Remember, even the greatest mysteries of the universe don't require sacrificing your well-being."

His words stuck with me even after he left.

The thrill of discovery was intoxicating, but maybe I did

need to hit pause. After all, unraveling the secrets of the universe while attempting to navigate interplanetary politics might require a brain that wasn't fueled by caffeine and sheer stubbornness alone.

So, I made a decision that would shock anyone who knew me—I shut down most of my screens, left the piles of data for future Lena to deal with, and headed out for some much-needed R&R. Because, as it turns out, solving the mysteries of the universe might just be more fun when you don't smell like a week-old lab coat.

I glanced back at my main screen, the signal still dancing across it, a cryptic invitation to the unknown.

I'd answer that call, but first, a shower and maybe a real meal wouldn't hurt. After all, solving mysteries required a clear mind... and apparently, a fresh scent.

ΦΦΦ

Later, after a bowl of rehydrated chili and a shower, I decided to do something I hadn't done in weeks—take a real break outside of my office or sleeping quarters.

I gazed at the advanced suit hanging in the pod in the corner of my barren bedroom.

Dubbed the Marswalker, it was our ticket to wandering the red planet without turning into a popsicle or, you know, suffocating— minor details.

The suit itself looked like something out of an old NASA training video, only sleeker and less likely to make you look like a walking astronaut cliché. It was designed to be lightweight yet durable, capable of withstanding Mars' extreme temperature swings and those pesky dust storms that could strip paint off a rover and tear even the most rugged of seals.

Its outer layer was made of a high-tech, abrasion-resistant material, something so advanced that even the zippers looked like they required software updates.

The suit's color, a vibrant mix of reflective neon yellow and white, wasn't just for style— it was highly visible against the Martian terrain, making it easier to spot a fellow human in the distance.

Underneath that rugged, circus clown exterior, the suit was lined with a thermal regulation system which was crucial for keeping us at a cozy Earth-like temperature. No more chattering teeth or sweating buckets. The suit adapted to the body's needs, which was a Godsend considering Mars could hit us with a sunny beach day and a polar vortex in the same afternoon.

The helmet had a clear, bubble-like structure with a heads-up display that made you feel like a fighter pilot. It provided a 360-degree view, which was great for sightseeing. The HUD displayed all the vital stats: oxygen levels, temperature, GPS, and even a nifty 'Where's My

Habitat?' feature for the directionally challenged.

Strapping into the suit felt like gearing up for a spacewalk, except you were just going for a stroll outside to clear your head. But in a place where stepping outside without your suit meant an instant, freeze-dried death, a stroll took on a whole new level of excitement.

"Alright, Marswalker," I said, slipping into the suit. "Let's take this existential crisis for a walk."

Some of the more tech-savvy— or should I say, risk-embracing—folks had figured out how to jailbreak their helmets. Why? To stream music and media directly into their Marswalker HUDs, of course, because nothing says serious scientific exploration like doing the moonwalk to Michael Jackson on Mars.

Except there was one little problem, one of those musical pioneers almost turned their Mars walk into a permanent Mars burial. They mixed up some critical signals while fiddling with the helmet's firmware.

Talk about a high-stakes remix.

That incident was the universe's way of telling me to maybe stick to the sounds of my own breathing. It's less likely to get me killed.

So, as much as I loved the idea of strutting across the Martian plains to the beat of my favorite tunes, I opted for the sweet serenade of oxygen circulation. Call me old-fashioned, but I prefer my life-saving alerts not to be drowned out by the latest pop hits.

I stepped outside the habitat through the Science Dome Exit Bay, a complicated series of airlocks and decontamination chambers.

The Martian night greeted me with its familiar, eerie silence. I breathed deeply of the recycled air and closed my eyes, pretending for a moment that I was back on Earth where I could smell rain on the breeze, a wheat field being harvested, or grass being cut. It had been five years or more since I had been home last. I'd lost track.

Maybe after this Ganymede thing cleared up, I would take a vacation. I had practically six months' worth of time saved up. I could travel the Earth again.

As I walked, the ground crunched under my boots, each step a reminder of the incredible journey that had brought me here. I looked up at the stars, pinpricks of light in an endless sea of darkness, and there, a faint dot among them, was Jupiter.

Standing there, under the Martian sky, I felt a wave of nostalgia mixed with awe.

My passion for astrobiology wasn't just about chasing signals or unraveling the biological mysteries of the universe. It was about this—these moments of humbling beauty, where you realize how small yet significant you are in the grand scheme of things.

I thought about the sacrifices I'd made for my career,

the birthdays missed, the personal life I'd put on hold, all in the pursuit of understanding life beyond Earth. But in that vast, starlit solitude, I found clarity.

Yes, the Ganymede Signal was a siren song, but I didn't have to pursue it at the cost of everything else. There had to be a balance, a way to chase the stars without losing myself in their light.

Up above, Mars' moons looked like two dull, distant spotlights against the backdrop of space. Not exactly a stunning view, but it was home.

I chuckled to myself.

Imagine, an astrobiologist getting all worked up over what might be the universe's most elaborate butt dial. Yet, here I was, betting my reputation on what could be a galactic wild goose chase.

The Martian nights could mess with your head. The vastness of it all made you feel both insignificant and part of something immense. It was a healthy reminder— there's a fine line between being a passionate scientist and becoming a hermit with a space obsession.

Science, I reminded myself, wasn't just about unraveling the mysteries of the universe. It was about staying grounded enough to appreciate them.

I couldn't let the Ganymede Signal consume me, and with my obsessive personality, I knew it was a risk.

With that resolve, I turned back toward the habitat, the

lights of the colony twinkling in the distance. I was ready to dive back into the mystery of the signal, but this time, I'd do it without losing sight of the world around me.

3.

'63-03

It was the first day of March. My commitment to balance lasted roughly eight hours.

I slept through all of it.

I spent the entire day hunched over my terminal, typing up a grant proposal with the help of some handy templates I'd found. These days, grant proposals weren't really the elaborate affairs of days gone by. They were mostly formalities— especially for a breakthrough of this magnitude.

It was sort of like writing a love letter if your love interest was a cold, indifferent committee fond of technical jargon and allergic to anything resembling poetry.

I started off with the usual fluff: "In pursuit of expanding human understanding of the cosmos..." Yada, yada. But then, it was down to brass tacks— outlining my plan to unravel the enigma of the Ganymede Signal. It felt like trying to convince someone to fund a treasure hunt where X marks a spot in a constantly moving, enormous ocean full of fool's gold.

The proposal needed to be convincing enough to get funding, yet sane enough not to end up in the Institute's wacky ideas bin.

Or for me to end up in the wacky scientist bin...we had one of those too.

The Looney Dome (or as the official plaque outside read The Mars Psychological Wellness Center) had become a bit of a legend in Mars Colony One.

We'd all jokingly called it the Looney Dome, but in truth, it was a crucial part of life here on Mars.

In that dome, they dealt with everything from acute homesickness to the more severe cases of mental illness.

I'd heard stories about the treatments: everything from conventional counseling to more, let's say, Martian-centric methods. There were virtual reality sessions where you could walk through forests or sit by the ocean. Some said they even had zero-gravity chambers for a bit of weightless relaxation, which honestly sounded more fun than therapeutic, but I'd never been.

And then there was the Martian gardening therapy.

The idea was to reconnect with nature, or at least what passed for nature on this planet. It was both bizarre and brilliant, nurturing tiny green shoots in a world of red.

"If I start talking to the plants in the greenhouse, just book me a room in the Looney Dome, will you? Make sure it has a good view of Elysium Mons," Raj once joked. We laughed, but behind that laughter was the recognition of a real risk.

Mars could mess with your mind in ways you never expected.

But perhaps the most crucial part of the Looney Dome was its role in treating psychological space sickness. Space sickness wasn't about feeling dizzy in zero-G. It was deeper, more psychological. It could creep up on you, the unending expanse of space, the isolation, the perpetual red landscape, until one day you realized you were more scared of the open sky than the confined spaces of the habitats.

People who found the endless expanse of space too overwhelming, who felt suffocated by the vast nothingness outside our little bubble of life, often ended up there for a bit.

It was a strange contradiction— feeling claustrophobic and agoraphobic at the same time, trapped on a planet yet exposed to the endless void.

The worst cases at the Looney Dome got sent

Earthside.

The place was a reminder that while we were reaching for the stars with advanced tech and new science, we were still tethered by our human limitations.

I think perhaps it won't be the tech that keeps us from reaching the end of the universe one day. I think it will be our own minds.

I guessed, amidst all the adventure and pioneering spirit, sometimes what you really needed was a good old-fashioned chat on a comfortable couch, even if that couch was millions of miles away from Earth. It was that human element again, something that we tended to forget as we immersed ourselves in our fancy gadgets here.

Back to forging what I liked to think of as my magnum opus—the grant proposal.

This wasn't an average, run-of-the-mill science paper. No, this was my heart and soul poured into words. It was me convincing some Mars bigwigs to fund what could be the biggest discovery since we realized Mars wasn't just a fancy red light in the sky.

Typing out this proposal felt like I was trying to woo the Institute itself. Except, instead of sweet nothings, I was whispering sweet somethings about data patterns, signal analysis, and the potential for extraterrestrial intelligence.

Between sips of coffee bean juice that had long since stopped tasting like anything, I laid out my plan.

"Objective: Find out what the Ganymede Signal really is," I typed, chuckling and tapping my toes on the floor in an energetic rhythm. I was in a better mood than I had been in a long time.

"Nah." I erased it. It wasn't sciency enough.

"Objective: To determine the nature and origin of the rhythmic, structured anomalies identified in the data from the Ganymede probe."

There. That was the easy part. Now, how to make it sound like it was worth pouring money into?

I dove into the specifics—how we'd analyze the signal, the tech we'd need, and the team I wanted to assemble.

As I outlined the methodology, I added a bit of flair.

I detailed my approach to isolating the signal, cross-referencing it with every known cosmic event. I outlined the next steps and threw in a bit about field trips to Ganymede, because why not aim for the moon? Or in this case, Jupiter's moon.

The budget section was a beast.

Crunching budget numbers wasn't my forte—I preferred crunching data. Still, I soldiered on, listing everything from equipment costs to travel expenses (because I was serious about that field trip). I might have also included a line item for emergency chocolate rations... you know, for science.

Then came the tricky bit—justifying why this wasn't just

another wild goose chase. I leaned back, staring at the ceiling.

"This signal could represent a paradigm shift in our understanding of extraterrestrial communication..."

Too much? Eh.

Hours ticked by as I fleshed out the proposal, adding in technical specifics that I hoped would dazzle more than confuse. The coffee machine in the corner worked overtime, churning out liquid inspiration as I wrestled with phrases like "non-repetitive frequency modulations" and "potential non-terrestrial artificial origin."

At some point, Raj popped his head in, his eyebrows shooting up at the sight of my frantic typing. "Writing the next great Martian novel?"

"Something like that," I replied without looking up. "It's a thriller about convincing people with money to care about weird blippy-bloops in space."

He laughed, leaving me with a well-intentioned warning about not getting lost in the paperwork.

I waved him off, my mind already back in the grant-writing trenches.

My fingers were practically dancing on the keyboard when suddenly, the lab's emergency alarm cut through the air like a knife. That sound, that *god-awful shriek*, was my own creation. It was meant for one thing and one thing only: a major breakthrough or a major problem.

I swiveled around, my heart thumping with a mix of excitement and apprehension. "Raj, what's got the lab in a frenzy?"

Raj was already hunched over the main console when I got in there, his fingers tapping rapidly. "It's the microbial samples from the Valles Marineris region. They're exhibiting unexpected metabolic activity. It’s off the charts!"

I dashed over, my proposal forgotten. We’d been culturing these microbes for months, trying to coax them into showing signs of life under Martian conditions. But this? This was unprecedented. Crazy, even.

"Could be a calibration error," I said, half to myself, knowing our equipment was top-notch. I peered at the readings. Sure enough, the metabolic rates of the microbes were spiking in a pattern I'd never seen before—it was as if they were suddenly waking up from a dormant state.

"We need to isolate the samples. If this is a true metabolic spike, it could mean..." My voice trailed off, the implications dawning on me.

Raj was already on it, initiating the isolation protocol. I kept my eyes glued to the data, watching as the microbial activity continued. Was it environmental? A chemical trigger? The questions piled up in my mind.

"Lena, the isolation's complete. No breach in

containment," Mia, our lab tech, called out from the other side of the room.

I let out a breath I didn't realize I was holding. "Good. Let's run a full diagnostic. I want to understand what's causing this activity. Raj, pull up the environmental history for the past 24 hours."

As Raj worked his magic on the console, I couldn't help but feel a surge of giddiness. *This* was why we were here.

"Environmental factors look stable. No significant changes," Raj reported, his brow furrowed in concentration.

"So, it's inherent to the microbes themselves," I mused, a smile creeping across my face. "This could be it, Raj. We might just have our first real evidence of life adapting to Mars. I'll call them... Jimmy."

The room buzzed with a renewed energy as we dove into analyzing the phenomenon.

As the sun dipped below the horizon, painting the sky in new shades of orange and red, I returned to my office and wrapped up the proposal. I read through it and corrected errors before sending it to the AI for a scan.

It was a masterpiece of scientific persuasion, or so I hoped.

It was a straightforward pitch: give me the dough, and

I'll give you the stars—or at least, their secret messages. The proposal was a mishmash of heavy technical jargon that would make even the nerdiest of science nerds swoon, peppered with just enough layman's terms to keep the money folks from glazing over.

"Now," I said to the empty room, "let's see if they bite."

I hit save, feeling a mix of relief and anticipation.

ΦΦΦ

As I walked through the corridors of the Mars Frontier Research Institute, I felt on top of the world. I could feel the eyes on me as I passed through the various hubs.

The buzz around my little project was palpable. I was the hot topic, the latest water-cooler gossip, all thanks to my obsession with the Ganymede Signal.

Many were supportive, but some had that "Oh, Lena's lost it again" look.

I freely admitted that it wasn't the first time I'd begun researching something the others considered off-the-wall, but this time I'd had some hard evidence to back me up.

I couldn't blame them though. There *was* that time I got fixated on what I thought were microbial fossils in Martian regolith. Turned out they were just oddly shaped mineral deposits.

I spent three weeks analyzing those rocks, talking to

them, naming them— I even called one Frederick. The big reveal was a bit of a letdown, especially after I'd dramatically announced, "We are not alone!" in the lounge.

But this time was different. The Ganymede Signal wasn't just some Martian mirage or a pile of rock masquerading as ancient life. I had data, real, tangible data.

And okay, maybe I had a reputation for diving headfirst into rabbit holes, but this rabbit hole led somewhere. I could feel it in my bones—and this time, it wasn't just the recycled air playing tricks on my brain.

So, as I navigated the corridor of raised eyebrows and half-hidden smirks, I held my head high.

I'd chased wild geese before, but everyone knows the real adventure starts when you finally catch one. And this time, I was pretty sure I had a whole flock of geese right in my data-laden hands.

"Hey, so I heard through the grapevine that you're planning to RSVP some aliens," Raj quipped as he joined me for lunch the next day.

I smirked, poking at my rehydrated quesadilla. "Gonna try."

The grant application was my next big hurdle. The review board loved redundancy above all things, and so I laid out a reader-friendly outline of my plan to send a targeted, manned mission to Ganymede, equipped with all the fancy gadgets necessary to decode the signal.

I detailed the technical specifications, like a kid listing out their dream toys, only these toys were the latest spectrometers and deep-space communication arrays. I also outlined the team I wanted— a mix of astrobiologists, astrogeologists, comms experts, a doctor, and a couple of engineers who didn't mind going a bit off-script.

The potential impact of the discovery was the heart of the proposal. I emphasized how this could be a leap in our understanding of the universe. It could be our first real conversation with intelligent life outside of our own.

As I filled out the application, I couldn't help but feel a twinge of excitement. This was high-stakes science. Either I was on the brink of a groundbreaking discovery, or I was about to become the Institute's most ambitious flop.

I condensed the packet materials into a folder—the proposal, the outline, the budget, the kitchen sink, everything, and submitted the application, my finger hovering over the send button for a moment longer than necessary. It felt like stepping off a cliff, hoping you've built strong enough wings to fly.

"Done," I announced to my empty office, half expecting the walls to cheer me on.

That night, I left the lab earlier than usual, my head buzzing with possibilities. As I walked through the colony's central hub to clear my thoughts, I noticed the mundane activities of life on Mars— people chatting, kids playing in the artificial gravity zones, vendors selling the latest Earth imports...it all seemed so distant.

Commander Ryan was hanging out in the central hub, and though I didn't know him well, I went over to the window where he stood.

"Hey."

He looked over, hands clasped behind his back, and gave me a brief smile. "Good evening."

I took a deep breath. "I just wanted to say...you did everything right. That night," I blurted. "It wasn't on you. It was just one of those things..." I trailed off, hoping it didn't come across as awkward as it sounded to me.

He tightened his lips and looked back outside. "Thanks."

Well, I never said he was warm and fuzzy.

"See you around," I said. He nodded goodbye and I left, knowing it was probably silence that he wanted at that moment.

In my quarters, I lay in bed staring at the ceiling. Tomorrow, I could either be on the path to unraveling one of space's greatest mysteries or just another scientist with a failed pet project.

Sleep didn't come easy that night. My dreams were a jumble of spectral lines and distant moons, echoing with the faint whispers of the Ganymede Signal.

ΦΦΦ

After hitting the submit button on my grant application, I entered what I affectionately termed The Waiting Game. My daily work at the Mars Frontier Research Institute continued, but let's be honest, my brain was doing loop-the-loops around the Ganymede.

One minute I was the picture of cool, calm scientific inquiry, and the next, I was like a kid waiting to see if Santa got my letter.

To distract myself from obsessively refreshing my email I decided to mingle with my fellow brainiacs.

I plunged into the Institute's whirlpool of seminars, debates, and the occasional heated argument over wine and cheese— dehydrated, of course.

Picture a room full of some of the brightest minds on Mars—or as I liked to call it, a nerd herd. I had gathered a fairly large group of acquaintances around me, just chatting. I'd just laid out my theory about the Ganymede signal when Dr. Alvarez, an astrophysicist with a beard so long he could trip on it, chimed in.

"While your enthusiasm is admirable," he started, his beard nearly wagging with each word, "we must consider the likelihood of natural cosmic phenomena before jumping to... extraterrestrial conclusions."

Condescending twit...

"Absolutely, because a rhythmic, structured signal that could pass for a Fibonacci sequence concert and doesn't match any known or predicted patterns in existence, is just your average radio static."

A few chuckles rippled through the room. Score one for Team Lena and zero for the Martian Gandalf.

But it wasn't all smooth sailing. There were more skeptics, and then there were the Earth-centric types who wouldn't believe aliens existed unless one walked up and shook their hand. And even then, they'd probably ask for ID.

Amidst all this, I'd find myself staring out at the Martian landscape, my mind wandering light-years away.

I thought about my family back on Earth, how they didn't quite get what I did, but were proud anyway. My social life was virtually non-existent unless you counted listening to Raj, debating with holographic projections, and yelling at microbes now affectionately named Jimmy.

It was during these moments that the weight of my life choices hit me. Here I was chasing signals from the far reaches of space, while life on Earth moved on.

Don't get me wrong, I wouldn't trade my spot for anything, but sometimes, just sometimes, I wondered what it'd be like to have a normal job. You know, where the most exciting thing was the 3D printer jamming. Or maybe a family...husband, kids, cats. I was fully aware that my time for those things was ticking down.

These reflective moments were bittersweet. They reminded me of the price of passion, the cost of my curiosity. But then, I'd think about the Ganymede signal and I knew I was exactly where I needed to be.

Solving the riddle of the universe, or at least trying to, wasn't just a job; it was my calling. And if that meant a few sacrifices, so be it. After all, how many people get to say their work could potentially rewrite the story of our existence?

So there I was, caught in this strange limbo of hope, anticipation, and a dash of existential crisis, waiting for an email that could either launch my dreams into orbit or crash them into the dirt.

But hey, that's the life of a scientist on Mars. One part maniac, one part interplanetary philosopher, and a whole lot of waiting for grant approvals.

ΦΦΦ

To my surprise, messages started popping up in my inbox like mushrooms after rain. And not just any messages— these were sonnets of support, a veritable smorgasbord of encouragement.

One email particularly stood out. It was from a young researcher, fresh out of the Martian University of Applied Sciences, a place so cutting-edge they probably had classes on telepathy.

"Dr. Mercer, your work on the Ganymede Signal is not just science; it's poetry in motion. You're an inspiration!"

I couldn't help but smile. Me, an inspiration? I felt more like an addiction-fueled space hermit. But hey, if my obsession was sparking excitement in the next generation of Mars brains, who was I to complain?

And then there were the celebrities— a few big names in the scientific community who usually didn't pay much attention to my work unless they needed a good laugh.

"Your findings are intriguing, Dr. Mercer. Let's discuss the potential implications over lunch."

These unexpected shoutouts were like a shot of adrenaline, a reminder that my quest for the stars was more than a solitary journey. It was a reminder that science, much like a good Martian dust storm, has a way of connecting people.

One evening six days after my grant submission, in a rare moment of respite, I found myself meandering through the colony. The Martian night was a canvas of stars, each one a story.

I looked up, Jupiter a bright speck in the sky, its presence both daunting and mesmerizing. It was moments like these that I felt it— the call. A deep, atemporal tug at the heartstrings.

I stood there, the red dust at my feet, the stars above, feeling like a tiny speck on a tiny speck, yet part of something immeasurably vast.

That night, under the Martian sky, I made a promise to myself – grant or no grant, I was going to chase this signal. Because that's what we do, right? We look up at the stars and dream of touching them, of exploring their secrets.

It was a call to explore, and I was going to answer it, come hell or high water (or, in Mars' case, red-outs and solar flares).

Also, I figured it was high time I got my scientific behind over to Elysium Mons to grab Webby his volcano samples.

I resolved to go first thing in the morning.

ΦΦΦ

I never thought clinging to the side of Elysium Mons—one of three volcanoes in this region—would be how I'd spend my Thursday afternoon. Yet, there I was, an astrobiologist-turned-Mars-mountaineer, trying to grab a sample before it made a one-way trip to the bottom of a Martian chasm.

"Freaking Weber," I muttered to myself, my breath fogging up my helmet's visor before the respiration adjustment unit had a chance to kick in. These suits were great, but they weren't designed for strenuous exercise.

"Mercer, what's your status?" Raj's voice crackled through the comms link as he stored his own samples back at the rover.

"Oh, you know, just hanging out. Enjoying the view." Never mind that one slip would turn me into a historical footnote in the annals of space exploration.

Finally snagging the obstinate sample, my sample collector (AKA my hand) closed triumphantly around the dirty alien rock chunk.

But that triumph was short-lived.

As I shifted my weight to pull back, the ground beneath my boot crumbled. My heart leaped into my throat as I teetered on the edge of the crevasse.

"Whoa there," I gasped, a rush of adrenaline flooding my system.

My arms windmilled frantically, seeking anything to regain balance on the slope. The Martian gravity, only a fraction of Earth's, was both a curse and a blessing in this moment. It slowed my fall but also made it harder to regain my footing.

The world seemed to tilt as I struggled, the top of the Elysium Mons high above looking down on me coldly, indifferently.

Below, the slope descended sharply into an abrupt

rocky abyss, its depths shadowed and unwelcoming. The red dust kicked up by my scuffle hung lazily in the air, creating a haze that tinted my vision.

My breathing became shallow and rapid, and my throat felt like a thin straw as the oxygen tank struggled to adapt to my needs. I could feel the cold sweat forming despite the dryness around me, my suit sticking uncomfortably to my skin.

The ridge, which had seemed relatively stable moments ago, now felt like the edge of the world.

Gritting my teeth, I pushed against the loose soil, my gloves scraping against the rough, unyielding surface. Each movement was calculated, a desperate attempt to find a hold, anything that would keep me from slipping further.

In my ear, the comms unit crackled to life. "Lena? You alright? Your monitors are alerting!"

"Yeah," I managed to reply, my voice steadier than I felt. "Just... testing the gravitational limits of Mars."

With a herculean effort, I anchored my boot against a more solid patch of ground. Slowly, cautiously, I shifted my weight back, away from the precipice. My muscles ached with the exertion, the strain evident in every breath I took.

Finally, with a grunt of effort, I pulled myself back onto safer ground.

I lay there for a moment on the rocky ground (not a

recommended activity by the Marswalker manufacturers), chest heaving, watching the Martian sky as it stretched endlessly above me. The sun, a distant, pale orb, offered little warmth but plenty of light, casting long, stark shadows across the landscape.

As my breathing normalized, I couldn't help but let out a shaky laugh. "Astrobiologist hanging off a cliff on Mars, talking to herself," I mused aloud, the absurdity of the situation not lost on me. It was moments like these that reminded me of the fine line we walked out here, between discovery and danger.

"What?" Raj asked.

"Nothing. Maybe we shouldn't skip protocol anymore though," I suggested.

"'Kay."

Sitting up with a struggle, I looked at the sample in my hand, a piece of Mars that had almost cost me dearly. It was worth it, though, I reminded myself even as I planned some sort of retribution for Dr. Weber.

The rover ride back to base was less Jason Bourne and more Martian golf cart, but I wasn't complaining. I'd had enough hits of adrenaline to last me at least a week, maybe even two.

Raj kept shooting me looks until I finally confessed that I'd almost fallen into a crevasse, much to his wide-eyed horror. He'd never let me live it down.

Driving across the Martian landscape was like navigating through the world's largest sandbox, except we didn't have lost toys, we had giant jagged rocks.

Back at the lab, I switched gears from the preliminary analysis of the absurdly specific requested Martian soil sample to the Ganymede Signal.

And today, that signal had changed.

As I sat in my office, eyes glued to the screen, the Ganymede Signal was doing something *extraordinary*. It had shifted from its initial rhythmic pulses into even more intricate, repeating patterns, reminiscent of complex mathematical structures. They were fractal-like, maintaining adherence to the Golden Ratio, but there was something more. I tapped my fingers on the desk, pondering.

A picture of Jimmy, my microbes, flashed into my head and all of a sudden a lightbulb went off.

"It's reacting to something," I stated, my words breaking the absolute stillness.

But what could it possibly have been?

I zoomed in on the data, scanning all the sections carefully until I spotted something that clicked. The signal's evolution coincided with the Mars Frontier Research Institute's Ganymede probe beginning its sensor scans.

"Could it be a response?"

The thought sent a chill down my spine. The signal wasn't just complex; it was dynamic, changing its structure as if in direct reaction to the probe's actions. This suggested not just a pre-recorded message, but an active, intelligent source.

Harmonic variations began to overlay the signal, following the Golden Ratio intervals in a way that felt almost musical.

I put it through the data synthesizer program and waited.

It was as if the signal had found a voice, a sophisticated method of communication that used sound and mathematics in unison. The fact that these changes appeared to be a response to our probe's sensors was uncanny.

I closed my eyes as the music poured into the room. What had begun as a complicated and harmonious musical composition had morphed into something almost angelic, something almost too beautiful for humans to hear. It brought tears to my eyes, which I blinked away.

"Intelligence... interaction..." I concluded, excitement bubbling within me.

It was a potential conversation, a dialogue initiated by an unknown intelligence.

"Raj, get in here!" I yelled, excitement laced with a tinge

of anxiety.

Raj burst in, hair mussed and smelling like cake for some reason. "What's up, Len?"

"This," I pointed at the screen.

He whistled, eyes wide. " Niiiice. So...what am I looking at again?"

I rolled my eyes and slammed my hands down on the desk. "Play the synthesizer and listen. I'm going for a coffee. I'm going to need it."

ΦΦΦ

Back in my office, the Martian night pressed against the window, a silent, endless expanse as the new signal danced before my eyes. I was taking a short break from it, resting my brain.

My office pinged with a soothing chime. It was the notification I'd been anxiously awaiting, the digital drumroll to my future.

The message sat there, unopened, a rectangular verdict glowing softly on the screen.

To read or not to read, that was the question. I took a deep breath, the weight of the moment settling on my shoulders.

What lay beyond that digital envelope could chart the course of my life, and maybe even alter our understanding of the universe.

With a mixture of trepidation, excitement, and unusual self-control, I let the message wait. The night was mine, the universe was mine, and for a fleeting moment, time stood still on Mars, waiting for the dawn of discovery.

Or so I told myself.

I was actually just afraid it was a rejection...but even if it was, I still had my extremophiles and my plants.

4.

'63-03

The lights of my office flickered slightly early the next morning as they adjusted to my customized schedule, casting an otherworldly glow on the notification icon blinking insistently on my screen.

I felt like a casual runner being at the starting line of a marathon with the pros— thrilled but slightly terrified. My heart was doing its best impression of a drum solo as I hesitated, my finger hovering over the touchpad. This wasn't just any message...this was the verdict on my Ganymede grant application.

Taking a deep breath that did absolutely nothing to calm my nerves, I tapped the notification.

Then, there it was, in simple, unembellished text that

belied the magnitude of its content: Grant Application Approved.

I stared at those three words, letting them sink in.

Approved.

They had approved it. My brain did a double-take, and for a split second, I wondered if someone slipped some nitrous into the air system and I was hallucinating.

A smile cracked across my face, growing wider with every passing second. My project, my brainchild, had been greenlit.

I, Lena Mercer, the woman who talked to bacteria and argued with algorithms was going on an expedition.

The initial shock gave way to a tidal wave of emotions. Relief washed over me first, soothing the days and weeks of anxiety and sleepless nights. It was followed closely by a surge of excitement that felt like a rocket boost.

I was about to embark on a journey that could redefine our understanding of the universe and our place in it. No big deal, just potentially making history.

But as the initial euphoria ebbed, a different feeling crept in. It was the daunting realization of the enormity of what lay ahead. This wasn't just a theoretical scientific exploration; it was a mammoth responsibility. The kind that comes with high risks, higher expectations, and a whole lot of Redcreds on the line.

I leaned back in my chair, my eyes drifting to the

cluttered chaos of my workspace. Each stack of papers, each holographic model, and each scattered tool was evidence of the search that had brought me here. They were the artifacts of countless hours of research, the physical manifestations of my determination (and occasional bouts of madness).

The room seemed to close in on me. I was about to collaborate on a mission that carried the weight of the scientific community's hopes and expectations.

The eyes of Mars Colony One— heck, probably Earth too— were on me now. And with those eyes came the silent whispers of doubt and anticipation. I knew some would expect me to fail, maybe even want me to, but many would be hoping for success right along with me.

I thought about the team I would help assemble, the intricate planning that lay ahead, and the strategies we would need to decipher the Ganymede signal. My mind spun with potential theories, technological needs, logistical nightmares, and the inevitable bureaucratic tangles.

Looking out the ceiling overhead and stretching my neck and shoulder muscles, I felt a strange kinship with the pioneers who had first set foot on this unforgiving planet.

Like them, I was stepping into the unknown, chasing after a signal that had traveled across the solar system to reach us.

I practically sprinted to Dr. Weber's office, bursting through his open door with all the subtlety of a comet. "We did it, Johann! The grant, it's approved!" I blurted out.

Dr. Weber, who had the uncanny ability to look both startled and composed at the same time, raised his eyebrows.

"We're going to Ganymede!" I said, containing my unscholarly squeal behind a semi-professional façade.

He didn't look surprised, but then again, I imagine that he had an inside track on the review board's activities. "That's fantastic! But remember, with great funding comes great responsibility."

I rolled my eyes, knowing I should have expected it. It was his go-to line for everything. "Thanks. I'll keep that in mind."

For a moment, he just stared at me, his face unreadable. Then, the corners of his mouth twitched upwards in a rare display of emotion. "Congratulations, Lena. This is monumental. This is your moment in history."

I felt a surge of pride at his words. Dr. Weber was not one to hand out compliments lightly. His approval was like a badge of honor, a sign that I was on the right track.

Raj's reaction was a whole different story. When I broke the news to him, he whooped so loud I thought we'd have a breach in the dome.

"Lena, that's incredible! You're going to be a Martian

legend!"

I laughed, caught up in his infectious enthusiasm. "Let's not get ahead of ourselves, Raj. It's just a grant."

"Just a grant?" he echoed, shaking his head. "This is the kind of grant that changes careers. You're going to be the one who finds the aliens!"

As word of my grant spread through the Institute, reactions varied wildly. Some colleagues offered genuine congratulations, their eyes shining with a mix of excitement and envy. Others were more reserved, their congratulations tempered with a healthy dose of skepticism.

But it wasn't just my colleagues who reacted. The news seemed to ripple through Mars Colony One, reaching researchers, engineers, and even the settlers. My inbox was flooded with messages—even more than before and most from people I'd never met, offering congratulations, asking questions, or just expressing their excitement about the project.

It was overwhelming and a little surreal. I'd gone from being just another researcher at the institute to the talk of the colony, all because of a mysterious signal from one of Jupiter's moons.

As I walked through the corridors, people I passed would do a double-take, whispering to each other as I walked by. It was like being a celebrity, only instead of signing autographs, I was discussing spectral analysis and data encryption.

In the cafeteria, the buzz was rampant and anxiety-provoking for an introvert like me. I overheard snippets of conversation about the Ganymede Signal, theories being tossed around like volleyballs. It was both exhilarating and terrifying to realize that my little project had sparked such widespread interest.

But with the excitement came the weight of expectation. I knew that all eyes were on me, waiting to see what I would uncover. The Ganymede Signal was no longer just mine; it had become a symbol of hope and curiosity for the entire colony.

ΦΦΦ

The thrill of potential discovery was quickly overshadowed by an urgent message from Dr. Emily Park, our fearless leader.

"Dr. Mercer, conference room, now." It sounded serious, the kind of serious that meant more coffee would be needed.

In the conference room, the air was so thick with anticipation that I almost needed a Marswalker helmet to breathe. People filled the chairs and stared at me as I took the only empty place at the table—surprised that I rated a seat at the table at all.

I was moving up in the world.

Dr. Park started the meeting. "We've received a transmission from Earth about the Ganymede Signal."

Dr. Park cleared her throat, and the room fell silent, the kind of silence that usually precedes something big. Or the calm before someone mentions budget cuts.

"The transmission from Earth is direct and concise," she began. "Utilizing new data from the Cassini 3, they've noticed similar patterns to our Ganymede Signal emanating from other moons in the solar system. Europa, Enceladus, Titan... It's widespread. Your Fibonacci Sequence description was spot on and corroborated by the cream of the crop on Earth. You were the first to notice and so they played nice with their data."

A collective gasp filled the room, a sound I imagined was similar to what the old Earthlings made when discovering fire.

I raised an eyebrow. "So, what, we're part of an interstellar radio station now? Mars FM—all alien signals, all the time?"

Raj, hiding in the back of the room like a good sidekick, snorted with laughter, but Dr. Park wasn't having any of it.

"This is serious, Mercer."

I scribbled down notes, adding a doodle of a little alien waving a flag that read 'Hello from Europa'. "So, what's the plan? We can't exactly pick up the phone and ask them to speak more clearly."

Dr. Park gave me a look that could curdle milk. "You have the official grant approval for the Ganymede Signal Project and now I want you to assemble the team. Top scientists, engineers, communications experts. And you, Dr. Mercer, will lead them all."

Me, *leading?* I glanced around, half-expecting someone to jump up and yell, "Just kidding!" But no, they were serious. As serious as a tax audit.

"Okay, team leader it is," I said, trying to sound more confident than I felt. "But if I end up being the first human to make contact with aliens, I'm officially requesting a raise. And a parking spot closer to the lab."

The meeting ended with more questions than answers. As I walked back to my lab, I couldn't shake off a feeling of unease.

The Ganymede Signal pulsed on my screen. I couldn't bear to turn it off.

I leaned back in my chair, my mind racing with possibilities. What if these signals were the universe's way of inviting us to the biggest block party in the galaxy, and we just got the invite? What if there was more than one type of life out there?

I chuckled to myself. "Well, universe," I said, tapping my pen against my vintage notepad, "let's see what you've got."

ΦΦΦ

I was still trying to wrap my head around the meeting when Raj barged into my office, his usual grin replaced by a look of incredulity. "Head of the entire project? Seriously? That's like putting a raccoon in charge of the Engineering Domes!"

It wasn't like I'd never compared myself to a raccoon before, so I couldn't say too much.

I rolled my eyes, tossing a crumpled paper ball at him. "Thanks for the vote of confidence, bro. And for the record, I'd be a very innovative raccoon."

Raj leaned against my desk, his expression turning serious. "You know I'm proud of you, right? I mean, who would've thought, us two orphaned Martian misfits, now at the forefront of humanity's greatest discovery?"

"We aren't orphans," I smiled, feeling a warm surge of gratitude for the man. "We've come a long way from stealing each other's lunch in the academy, haven't we?"

Raj's grin returned. "Yeah, now you can steal alien secrets instead of my sandwiches."

I chuckled, then sobered up as I turned back to my screen. "Speaking of secrets, there's something odd about these signals from the other moons. The Ganymede Signal is different. The others... they're weaker....kinda glitchy like they're missing information. Ganymede's is clearer."

Raj peered at the data. "Like a latecomer to the party?"

"Exactly. It's as if the others are auxiliary somehow and Ganymede's is the focus. We need to focus on it."

Raj nodded, understanding the implication. "So, Ganymede could be the key to understanding the whole symphony."

"Could be," I mused, tapping my pen on the desk. "But why Ganymede? What's so special about it?"

"That's for you to find out," Raj said, his eyes gleaming with excitement. "And hey, if we do make contact with aliens, can I be the official ambassador? I've been practicing my 'We come in peace' speech. You can patch me in."

I laughed, the tension easing slightly. "Sure, Raj. You can be the ambassador to the stars. Just don't start any intergalactic wars, okay?"

He saluted mockingly. "No promises."

As he left, I turned back to the screen, my mind racing. I had a feeling Raj was right and the discrepancy in the signals was a lighthouse, guiding us toward Ganymede.

"We're coming for you, Ganymede," I whispered.

Two days later, there was another urgent message

from Dr. Park. More than anything, it made me want to hack into the comms mainframe and disable the urgent flag feature.

Those urgent flags made me anxious.

ΦΦΦ

I walked into Dr. Park's office yet again, the atmosphere tinged with a gravity that set my nerves on edge. The room was as immaculate as ever, but today it felt different, almost charged. Dr. Park sat behind her desk, her expression inscrutable.

To my surprise, Governor Olsen was there too, his usually jovial face somber.

"Doctor Mercer, please, take a seat," Dr. Park motioned, her voice betraying a hint of urgency.

I sat, my mind racing. It wasn't every day you got summoned by both the head of the Institute *and* the governor of Mars Colony One.

Dr. Park didn't waste any time. "I'll get straight to the point. Earth and Mars... we're on the brink of something dire. Tensions have escalated beyond trade disputes. Some factions are pushing for an end to civilities."

My heart skipped a beat. *War? Between Earth and Mars?*

"To be perfectly honest, Dr. Mercer, we're on the very

brink of war." Governor Olsen leaned forward, his eyes meeting mine as his words still resounded through my brain. "Your Ganymede project has become more than a scientific mission. It's now a symbol of unity, a potential bridge between our worlds."

I blinked, trying to process his words. "A bridge? I don't understand."

Dr. Park pressed her lips together before answering. "Your mission. It's going to be publicized. Broadcast. Earth and Mars, watching together. It's a chance to foster a sense of harmony, to show that despite our differences, we're still one species, exploring the galaxy together."

Their words felt like a physical pressure. The Ganymede Signal, my project, was suddenly a linchpin in interplanetary diplomacy?

"Your work has the potential to distract, to captivate, to bring us together. But more than that it's a chance to show what humanity can achieve when we work as one," Governor Olsen continued.

I tried to find my voice, feeling like I'd been thrust onto a stage I wasn't prepared for. "You're saying the fate of two worlds could hinge on... on my research abilities?"

Dr. Park nodded solemnly. "In a manner of speaking, yes. We need this. Both planets do. You have an opportunity to do more than just explore space. You can help preserve peace."

Crap.

The room spun slightly. This was beyond anything I'd imagined when I first detected that signal. I was an astrobiologist, not a diplomat. Yet here I was, being asked to play a role in preventing a war.

Governor Olsen raised his eyebrows in an approximation of constituent wheedling that reminded me of...well, a politician. "And to ensure the success of your mission, you'll be receiving funding. A lot more than what you requested in your grant proposal. You'll have the resources of Earth *and* Mars behind you."

I sat there, stunned. My sweaty hands clenched the hem of my lab coat. "More funding? How much more?"

Dr. Park smiled—a rare occurrence, so the Institute must be getting some kind of extra funding as well. "Let's just say, you won't be lacking in resources. We're talking about a sum that will ensure every aspect of your mission is covered, and then some. The best technology, the brightest minds, everything you need will be at your disposal."

I leaned back, trying to take it all in. My initial project was completely screwed. Instead of a nice leisurely investigation and maybe a little jaunt to Ganymede, we now had some kind of diplomatic spectacle.

The highlight project of my career was essentially an attempt at ping-pong diplomacy—bouncy and fun, but not the solemn breakthrough I was shooting for.

Dr. Park's voice brought me back to the moment. "Doctor, the eyes of two worlds will be upon you. It's an immense responsibility, but one we believe you're ready for."

I swallowed hard, feeling a mix of fear and exhilaration. "I... I'll do my best. For Mars. For Earth. For peace." *For ping-pong.*

As I rose to leave, Dr. Park cleared her throat, a hint of hesitation in her voice. "Lena, there's another matter we need to discuss. The nature of the current situation... it necessitates a change to your project timeline."

I should have known when she called me by my first name that it was something bad.

The room fell into a silence so deep you could hear the distant hum of the colony's life support systems. I felt a lump form in my throat that I was pretty sure was my heart's attempt to strangle me. A change in the timeline?

"What are we talking about here? Instead of five years, I have to be ready in three?" I chuckled nervously, hoping for a laugh or at least a reassuring smile.

Dr. Park and Governor Olsen exchanged a glance that lasted a few heartbeats too long. The kind of look that says, 'Do we tell her?'

My chuckle faded into the thick air of apprehension. "Two years?" I asked, my voice barely above a whisper, my mouth suddenly dry.

Neither of them spoke immediately. They just looked at me, and in that look, I read everything I needed to know. The silence was louder than any words could have been.

I coughed. *"One?"*

Dr. Park finally broke the silence, her voice steady but her eyes betraying the gravity of what she was about to say. "Yes, Lena. One year."

One year?

The words echoed in my mind like a bad joke that had lost its punchline.

Governor Olsen leaned forward, his expression earnest. "We wouldn't ask this if it weren't absolutely necessary. The situation... it's critical. We need a symbol of unity, of progress, sooner rather than later. You're the best hope we have."

I sat back, feeling as if Mars' gravity had suddenly increased tenfold. One year to do what should take five. One year to embark on a mission that could change the course of history or escalate a conflict to the brink of war.

We needed a win, a big shiny, sciencey win that said, 'Look, we can do awesome stuff together without blowing each other up.'

I cleared my throat. "You can't just...I don't know...go dig up Venus or something? Get the people all jazzed about Venus rocks?"

The governor shook his head.

"You'll give your first live press conference in three days where you'll announce the existence of the signal and what it could mean. Then you'll be working with David Chen, a journalist with Earth-Mars United Broadcasting, in a series of personal interviews every week. Occasionally, he'll be broadcasting your training and launch preparations."

"You've turned my mission into a reality show, a distraction," I accused.

"We'll give you every resource, every bit of support you need. This is a priority for both Mars and Earth," Dr. Park murmured.

Governor Olsen stood up, extending his hand. "We have faith in you, Dr. Mercer. Your work could be the key to a new era of understanding and cooperation."

As I shook his hand, a part of me wondered if I was dreaming. This was the kind of responsibility that could change the course of history and I didn't want it.

Dr. Park's voice was firm, yet encouraging. "We'll support you every step of the way. This is your moment."

As I stood up to leave, the weight of a thousand suns seemed to press down on me. My lips tingled and I remembered to breathe.

One year.

The challenge was monumental, the stakes impossibly high, the potential lack of sleep massive...

But as I walked out of Dr. Park's office, a strange sense of resolve began to take hold and I blamed the burst of oxygen from all the imported house plants the Admin Dome merited. I had one year to make a difference, one year to bridge the gap between two worlds.

As I left the office, the corridor seemed different somehow, as if I was walking it for the first time. My mind was a whirlwind of thoughts.

I bumped into someone as I rounded the bend in the corridor. "Excuse me."

"Dr. Mercer," a man said, stepping to the side as I passed.

I looked up. It was Commander Ryan again.

I seemed to be bumping into him a lot lately. He nodded at me, already striding down to Dr. Park's door. I watched as he entered and closed it behind him.

Very curious.

I didn't have the time to stop and think about what was going on with him and Dr. Park though. I was going to Ganymede. The stakes were unimaginable, but so were the possibilities. This was my time to shine.

I just wish I was more charismatic. I mostly fumbled my way through anything involving an audience and now I was going to be watched by billions of people. Maybe I should invest in a HoloPrompter, or maybe Raj could feed me lines through a comms implant.

As I walked, I couldn't help but smile wryly.

Leave it to me to turn a simple signal into an interplanetary peace mission. No pressure, right?

ΦΦΦ

The moment I stepped back into my office, it was like flipping a switch. My brain kicked into high gear, and I was a woman on a mission—literally.

My desk, already a battleground of papers and screens, transformed into a strategic command center. This wasn't just about planning a trip to Ganymede anymore; it was about coordinating the most pivotal mission in Martian—heck, human—history.

First thing's first: the timeline.

One year. I let out a laugh that was more of a huff.

"One year to prep for Ganymede? Sure, no problem. I'll just invent a time machine while I'm at it." But sarcasm wasn't going to plan this mission.

I pulled up my advanced project management software, its interface sprawling across my displays.

The timeline broke down into phases: spacecraft design, team assembly, payload planning, launch preparations... the list went on and most of it was completely made up as I went along. I hoped I could get someone experienced to take a look at it, but in the meantime, I just pilfered through the mainframe until I found something that looked like unclassified Mission Control docs to copy and paste.

As I plotted milestones and deadlines, the urgency of it all made my hands fly across the touchscreens. It was like playing a high-stakes game of Tetris, except the blocks were mission-critical tasks. Failure wasn't an option. The pieces had to fit perfectly.

Next up: assembling the dream team. I needed the best of the best— brains that could turn science fiction into science fact without killing us all in the process.

Opening an online portal within Mars Colony One, I set up an application system. I was casting a net into the ocean of Martian intellect and hoping to catch some big, brainy fish.

I listed the qualifications, experience, and the kind of innovative thinking we needed.

As I hit publish, a cocktail of hope and anxiety swirled in my stomach. "Come on, Mars. Show me what you've got."

The sun dipped below the Martian horizon, casting long shadows across my office as I waited. I knew I should call it a day, but I couldn't resist.

The application list stayed empty.

Eventually, I forced myself to step away. Strolling through the community hub for a theme dinner night—

Martian Luau—I couldn't help but feel detached. I was hoping with the resolution of the grant process and the beginnings of the project timeline in place, I'd begin to feel more like my old self.

I think I would have, had Dr. Park and the governor not basically turned me into an interplanetary soap opera star.

Around me, the Institute went on as usual. Scientists and engineers laughed over artificially flavored Mai Tais, wearing plastic leis that clashed gloriously with their standard-issue jumpsuits or casual wear. The swaying palms and crackling bonfires on the big screens clashed with our streamlined Martian aesthetic, but nobody cared as long as the ukelele music played on.

My mind was elsewhere, running through checklists and potential pitfalls. I had terrible visions of catastrophic failure, dead astronauts, and Mars left in a nuclear wasteland. The hubbub of conversation was a distant hum against the roar of project planning and backup escape strategies in my brain.

I caught snippets of conversation—gossip about Earth, speculation about new tech, someone bragging about their kid's latest science project. Normal colony life. And yet there I was, carrying the weight of potential interplanetary war on my shoulders. I wasn't sure how many others knew about the looming threat, but it seemed to be a well-kept secret. There was nothing about it on the news.

I grabbed a plate of rehydrated pineapple— a crime against fruit—and forced myself to mingle.

I got smiles, nods, and the occasional "Great work on the Ganymede thing, Mercer." But behind every interaction was the nagging thought: what if the applications don't come in? What if I can't pull this off?

By the time I returned to my office, the hub was quiet and the party was winding down. I set my two smuggled Mai Tais on the desk and checked the portal, my heart sinking a little at the lack of responses.

I leaned back in my chair, the screens around me a kaleidoscope of plans, timelines, and empty application slots.

"You can do this," I muttered. "You have to."

And with that quiet vow hanging in the air, I dove back into the work, the night stretching before me, filled with the silent promise of a mission that was more than a mission.

It was hope, it was fear, it was the future—and it was all in my inexperienced hands.

ΦΦΦ

Sitting back in my chair early the next morning—something that was going to become a permanent part of me if I wasn't careful— I realized that planning a mission to Ganymede was a bit like trying to bake a five-tier wedding cake without knowing the difference between baking soda and baking powder.

In other words, I was in way over my head, especially when it came to the nitty-gritty of spacecraft design.

There was no way I could have a ship built to my specs within the few months I'd had allotted for it, which meant that I'd have to get creative.

"Okay," I muttered to myself. "Time to get schooled in Rocket Science 101."

First up on my crash course: propulsion systems.

I put out an ad in our little lounge for anyone who knew anything about them to give me a ping. We had some pretty interesting multi-disciplinary science geeks around here (including me) and I was hoping one of them was a spaceship whiz.

The basics, I knew—something about thrust and fuel and a lot of fire, but the specifics? That was another universe. I pulled up articles, journals, and schematics, each one making me feel more like a fish out of water. My screen looked like a shuttle-engineering fan's dream, filled with diagrams of engines and explanations of thrust-to-weight ratios.

I was so engrossed that I jumped when my comms unit pinged overhead.

A message from Raj.

"Hey, heard you're looking into propulsion systems. You might want to talk to Dr. Emilio Serrano. He's a wizard with that stuff."

Dr. Serrano, of course! The man was a legend in the engineering department. He was rumored to be able to build a rocket engine out of spare parts and Martian grit. I rarely ventured to the engineering side of things, but even I'd heard about him.

I sent a quick message, asking for his expertise, and to my relief, he agreed to meet the next day.

That night, my dreams were a bizarre mix of rocket ships and being late for a physics exam I didn't study for.

The next day, armed with a notepad filled with questions and a head swirling with half-understood concepts, I met Dr. Serrano in his lab in the Theoretical Engineering Dome, which was connected to our dome with a tunnel. It was a wonderland of prototypes and untested space gadgetry.

The actual Engineering Dome Field, farther along the periphery of the Institute, was the place where the theoretical engineering concepts were put into action. I'm glad I didn't have to go that far to meet with Dr. Serrano today.

"Dr. Mercer, a pleasure," he greeted me as the door slid open, his eyes twinkling behind thick glasses. "So, you're diving into the deep end of spacecraft design, huh?"

I laughed nervously. "More like being thrown in without a life jacket. I'm hoping you can be my floaties."

Dr. Serrano chuckled, leading me to a workbench cluttered with prototype engine parts and holographic displays.

"Let's start with the basics. Your mission to Ganymede— it's not a sprint, it's a marathon. You'll need a propulsion system that's efficient for long missions. We're talking about ion thrusters, maybe even a nuclear thermal rocket for the initial push out of Mars' gravity well."

I scribbled notes furiously as he spoke, trying to keep up. "Ion thrusters... nuclear... got it. And what about fuel? I mean, we can't exactly stop at a space gas station."

"Exactly," he nodded. "Efficiency is key. You'll want to minimize fuel weight but maximize output. That's where advanced propellants come in, and of course, the design of the spacecraft itself. It needs to be lightweight but durable, able to withstand the journey and the conditions on Ganymede."

My brain was doing somersaults trying to keep up. "And life support systems?" I asked. "We're talking about a long trip. Plus, the time spent on Ganymede."

"Ah, the human factor," Dr. Serrano mused. "That's a

whole other challenge. You need a system that recycles air and water efficiently, provides adequate food storage, and maintains a stable temperature. Not to mention the psychological aspects of long-term space travel."

I felt a twinge of anxiety at the enormity of it all. "I also need it in three months. Max."

Dr. Serrano stopped in his tracks, the twinkle in his eyes fading into a look of sheer incredulity. "Three months?" he echoed, his voice a mix of disbelief and concern. "Dr. Mercer, building a custom spacecraft with these specifications in such a timeframe isn't just ambitious; it's impossible. The engineering, testing, and safety protocols alone would take much, much longer than that. Years!"

I swallowed. "I know it sounds crazy, but we don't have a choice. The political situation... it's complicated."

He sighed, rubbing his temples. "Complicated is an understatement. But even with the best minds and resources at Mars Colony One, three months is pushing the boundaries of feasibility."

Feeling disheartened, I thanked him for his time and turned to leave. As I reached the door, Dr. Serrano called out. "Wait a moment."

I turned back, hope flickering in my chest.

"I just remembered someone who might be able to help," he said, a thoughtful expression on his face. "Mike Donovan. He's not your typical engineer. The man's a maverick, but he's got a knack for making the impossible possible."

"Mike Donovan?" I asked, a spark of curiosity igniting.

"Yes," Dr. Serrano nodded. "He's somewhat of a legend in the aerospace engineering circles. He's unconventional, but if anyone can fast-track your project, it's him. He's known for his work on advanced propulsion systems and has a history of pulling off projects against tight deadlines."

A glimmer of hope returned. "Do you think he'd be interested in something like this?"

Dr. Serrano shrugged. "Can't hurt to ask. I'll send you his contact information. Just be prepared; he's a bit... obsessive."

"Thanks, Dr. Serrano," I said, feeling a renewed sense of determination. "Obsessive I can handle. It's the impossible I'm worried about."

As I left his lab, the name Mike Donovan echoed in my mind. I hoped he had some answers because I needed all the help I could get.

ΦΦΦ

I stared at the message on my comms unit, heart pounding. The message from Dr. Serrano was brief but to the point: "Contact Mike Donovan. He's your best shot."

He'd copied Mike's contact card.

Taking a deep breath, I initiated a call to the renowned engineer. My fingers tapped nervously on the desk as the comms unit connected.

"Mike Donovan speaking," came the gruff but friendly voice. The call connected audio only, and it was a bit jarring not seeing who I was speaking with.

"Mr. Donovan, hi. I'm Dr. Lena Mercer from the Astrobiology department," I said, trying to keep my voice steady. "I've been referred to you regarding a project. It's about the Ganymede signal..."

There was a brief pause. "Heard rumors about it. What do you need?"

"I need to build a spacecraft. Custom-made. For a mission to Ganymede," I blurted out.

Silence fell for a moment, then he chuckled. "Next week work for a meeting?"

I cleared my throat. "We have three months to build it."

The line went silent for a long moment. "Come right now."

5.

'63-03

I disconnected and hurried out of my office to grab my Marswalker suit before heading toward the Science Dome Rover Bay.

I'd have to take a rover—a fact that I was pretty excited about. Usually, I just stuck to the tunnels, but sometimes those took forever, especially if there was scheduled maintenance.

The bay, which was just a series of garages with airlock features, was at the very bottom of the dome on the side facing toward the outer ring of concentric circles that made up the Mars Frontier Research Facility.

Each dome, or dome field (depending on the size of the department) was self-contained. We rarely had to leave our domes unless we wanted to, or if we were going to Mars Vegas, which was a dome all its own.

Strapping on my Marswalker suit, I couldn't help but think it made me look like a high-tech yellow marshmallow, albeit a slim and stylish one. Mars fashion—gotta love it.

I strolled into Rover Bay Three, where my ride awaited.

The rover, a nifty piece of Martian engineering, looked like a cross between a lunar module and a low-riding monster truck. I climbed in, careful not to bump the touchscreen interface, and disengaged the airlock on the rover bay doors.

They opened after a short sequence, and I was headed out on the Martian plains, the giant domes scattered all around like colossal soccer balls partially buried in the red ground as far as the eye could see.

I was heading for the Engineering Dome Field on the outskirts of the MFRI's site boundaries.

The rover I drove had its own airlock and life support function, but I never felt completely safe driving without the Marswalker suit. Without the suit, one malfunction in the rover's closed system and I'd be a paradoxical suffocating ice cube of boiling blood faster than you could say Martian Freeze Tag Champion.

On the way, I decided to play it old school and steer manually. Autopilot was great and all, but sometimes you just needed to feel the dirt under your wheels, even if it was Martian dirt.

We were settled in the equatorial region of Elysium, where the climate was a bit milder and we had significant solar activity all year round. It made launches and life support functions much easier to implement.

The civilian settlement domes were separate from the MFRI's domes, and even though we were side by side we rarely mingled unless we had business with one or the other. I'd never even been inside one. Together, the civilian domes and the MFRI, we made up Mars Colony One.

There was no official Mars Colony Two yet, but I'd heard rumors that they were constructing one at Tharsis to study the geological formations there—which were approximately 6600 kilometers away. Too far for a rover to travel, so I'm guessing they might build some kind of travel system to connect the two.

All too soon, the engineering domes loomed ahead, looking less like domes and more like giant beehives to accommodate the extra height necessary for the shuttle assembly bays.

I parked the rover and initiated the airlock sequence. The rover bay inside was like a gearhead's paradise—gadgets, gizmos, and grease.

I hopped out of the rover, a little bounce in my step thanks to Mars' low gravity. Stashing my Marswalker suit in a locker, it was time to go meet my last hope for a ship.

ΦΦΦ

As I stepped into the engineering dome specified by my mini-comms unit, I was hit by the sheer enormity of it.

If I hadn't seen it for myself, and someone had told me that it spanned a thousand acres, I wouldn't have believed them.

The place was massive. It was a sort of space-age industrial park stretched out under domes that led to other domes using a tunnel system. It was certainly a far cry from the cozy, cluttered confines of the science sector.

Navigating through the Engineering Dome Field was like walking through a futuristic city. The main thoroughfare was lined with buildings and workshops, each buzzing with activity. The air was filled with the sounds of machinery, the occasional hiss of steam, and the murmur of conversation. The smell of grease and the more pungent scent of fuel permeated everything.

It felt more like a manufacturing hub on Earth than a part of Mars Colony One.

The people here were a different breed compared to us science folks. Clad in practical, utilitarian attire, they moved with a purposeful stride that spoke volumes about their work ethic. These were the builders and maintainers of Mars Colony One, their hands shaping the future of the colony, piece by piece.

Their clothes were functional, with pockets for tools and reinforced patches at the elbows and knees. Patches, different colored hard hats, and jumpsuits denoted their departments and specialties. I didn't know what meant what.

I passed by a group of engineers huddled around a holographic display, their conversation peppered with technical jargon. They were discussing propulsion systems and gravitational fields with the kind of enthusiasm I usually reserved for new microbial discoveries.

The tech here was on another level. I saw massive robotic arms assembling machinery with precision, automated vehicles ferrying parts across the dome, and engineers wearing augmented reality visors that overlaid schematics onto physical equipment. The science sector had its gadgets, but this was *way* cooler.

Spacecraft, some half-built, loomed large around me. Cranes and scaffolds bustled with technicians and assistants, a hive of activity under the massive dome. I couldn't help but marvel at the scale of it all.

Finally, I reached the farthest launch bay, my destination according to my comms map. This was where I'd find Mike Donovan and, hopefully, the answers to converting a spacecraft capable of reaching Ganymede in record time.

The bay was a whirlwind of activity, like the others, with engineers swarming over an assembled spacecraft.

In the midst of it all stood a man surveying the work with a keen eye. He had broad shoulders, slightly graying hair, and was ruggedly handsome in a way that most of the men in the science sector just weren't.

If I wasn't in such a hurry to get my ship built, I'd probably want to drag this meeting out a little longer...like over dinner at Mars Vegas.

Beside him was another man, younger—about my age—but with an air of authority that matched his senior role here.

The older one looked up and met my eyes.

"Dr. Mercer, I presume?" Mike's voice boomed over the clatter of the bay. "So, you're the one who's in a bit of a rush to get to Ganymede."

"That's one way to put it," I replied, extending my hand. "I've got three months to build a ship and a year to make the launch happen."

He gave me a good solid shake, which told me that he would take me seriously, at least.

Jim raised an eyebrow. "Three months for a custom spacecraft? That's ambitious, even by Mars standards."

"You mean crazy," I retorted. "I know...*believe me*, I

know."

Mike chuckled, a deep sound that echoed off the metal walls of the bay. "Ambitious is our middle name around here. I've seen your project proposal on the portal. Let's see what we can do."

He led me to a viewing platform, where the spacecraft I'd seen from afar now loomed even larger. It was called the Artemis Explorer, a beast of a ship that made me feel like an ant staring up at a skyscraper.

"If you want to launch in a year and make it there and back alive, you only have one option. This is your ride to Ganymede. As you can see, the Artemis here is no small feat. In fact, it's currently the largest completed space vessel in both worlds," Mike said, gesturing toward the spacecraft. "But if anyone can get her ready in time, it's us."

"You're giving me *this* ship?" I asked, faintly intimidated by being the mission commander over such a large vessel. "You have ships like this just lying around waiting for crazy missions?"

Mike smiled. "The Artemis was built two years ago, outfitted for a mission to Venus that was red-lighted."

I looked at the Artemis, feeling a mix of awe and trepidation. This was more than just a ship; it was the embodiment of hope, a vessel that could carry us to new horizons or into the archives of failed expeditions.

"We'll need to modify her a bit for the mission," Jim

added, his eyes scanning the Artemis. "It's going to be tight, but we'll pull out all the stops."

"Right, so, propulsion first," Mike said, tapping a holographic screen into life. It displayed a complex schematic of the Artemis Explorer. "We're dealing with a Graviton Impulse Drive here. It's state-of-the-art—blows the older nuke-based systems out of the water. What would take a year or two with one of those will take three to four months tops with this. It manipulates gravitons to generate propulsion. You know how surfers ride ocean waves? Imagine that, but with spacetime itself. And the best part— no worrying about everyone aging faster than you back home."

I nodded, though the concept felt as tangible as surfing on an actual wave— something I'd only seen in Earth videos. "How does that work, with the time dilation?"

"Time dilation," Mike began, leaning against a console adorned with schematics of the Artemis Explorer. "That's always the tricky part when you're dealing with something as powerful as the Graviton Impulse Drive."

I listened intently, eyes fixed on Mike. This was crucial. My understanding of the peculiarities of space travel was key to the mission.

"You see," Mike continued, "the GID— that's our Graviton Impulse Drive—operates by manipulating gravitons. These are particles that mediate the force of gravity. The way we've designed the GID is to create propulsion forces by generating high-density gravitational fields. It's like pushing against the very fabric of spacetime."

He paused, glancing at me to ensure I was following.

I nodded. "The Haakon Incident. July 2048."

The Haakon Incident was the time when gravitons were accidentally proven to exist. Dr. Erik Haakon had been researching using the Advanced Quantum Collider at his Northern European Quantum Research facility in Norway. It had been modeled after the old-style particle collider at CERN—with some adjustments.

They noted some funny business during one of its collision runs and the graviton had been officially born. It led to our rapid expansion into space. Practically everyone knew about it because it was technically the most significant accidental discovery ever, arguably even more so than Penicillin.

Haakon pretty much tripped over the info we needed to travel to planets other than Earth without spending a decade in space on the way. I'm still amused by it.

"Exactly," Mike continued. "Now, when you mess with speed and gravity on that scale, you're bound to encounter some time dilation. That's just relativity at work. You move fast, time moves differently for you compared to someone who's not moving as fast."

I nodded again. It was basic physics and we'd discussed it numerous times at the academy.

"We've implemented a cutting-edge adaptive navigation system in the GID – think of it as a dynamic GPS for space travel. It constantly recalculates the best path for the Artemis, factoring in cosmic events and the subtle ways space itself curves around stars and planets. But the real game-changer is its ability to fine-tune the ship's interaction with gravitational fields, ensuring we navigate safely and efficiently," Mike said, his voice carrying a note of pride.

"So, you're saying the time dilation is controlled automatically by the ship?" I asked, my interest piqued.

"Exactly. With AI," Mike confirmed. "By balancing these forces around the ship, we minimize the effects of time dilation. It's not perfect. There's always going to be some level of time difference. But we've got it down to the point where time inside the Artemis passes almost the same as it does outside. You won't come back to find everyone you knew on Mars aged a decade or two while you were out gallivanting around Ganymede."

I chuckled. "That's a relief. I'd hate to miss out on all the advancements in Martian coffee brewing."

Mike grinned, an attractive tilting of his lips. "Well, we can't have that, can we? Trust me, Doctor Mercer, the Artemis is a masterpiece of engineering. The GID's time dilation control is just one of the many features that make this bird special. We're pushing the boundaries of what's possible in space travel, and you'll be right at the helm of it."

That thought wasn't exactly comforting.

"So that's enough to get us to Ganymede and back?"

Jim chimed in, his tone pragmatic. "In theory, it will, but we'll need to optimize the fusion reactors for extended use. Efficiency is key, especially with your timeline. We'll have to run simulations, and tweak the energy output to match the mission's demands."

"Tell me about the accommodations on Artemis," I asked, seeking a broader understanding.

Mike, engaged with his screen, began detailing, "For the crew, we've designed compact, efficient quarters. Personal sleeping pods and communal spaces, with added soundproofing and improved lighting for extended missions."

He swiped to another layout. "The life support system is top-notch. A closed-loop that recycles air and water near perfectly. We're enhancing it further for redundancy and advanced filtration."

Jim jumped in, "And we're expanding hydroponics – more variety, better for morale and air purification."

"Medical bay?" I probed.

"Fully stocked," Mike continued. "Plus, we're integrating

the latest telemedicine technology for remote specialist consults."

"And the eject seats and parachutes?" I grinned, thinking about emergencies.

Mike nodded. "For emergencies, we've equipped Artemis with state-of-the-art escape pods. They're designed to sustain life for a short period of time, fully stocked with provisions, medical supplies, and communication gear."

"These pods are more than just lifeboats. They're actually mini-survival units. Given the distances involved, especially near Jupiter, quick rescue isn't an option. We've made sure these pods can keep the crew safe and alive, hopefully, until help arrives. We can modify their automated mini-propulsion systems to provide more thrust to cover a greater distance. It won't be fun if you have to use one, but it will give you a better chance at survival. Not great, but better," Jim added.

I blinked, nonplussed. I appreciated his candor though, and resolved to do everything in my power to keep us from having to use the pods. "So, it's like the floating seats on the 0007s? The jet might crash in the middle of the Pacific, but if you're lucky enough to survive it you've got a floatie to use while you drift for a year?"

"Uhhh...pretty much," Jim said.

"Okay, moving on. The original design was for a Venus

mission, with substantial radiation protection built in, I'm sure. How will we enhance it for Jupiter's radiation environment?"

Mike nodded, understanding the concern. "Jupiter's radiation belts are far more intense than anything we've encountered. To counter this, we're enhancing the shielding with multiple layers. We're adding advanced polymers, which are embedded with particles specifically designed to absorb high levels of radiation. On top of that, there's an additional shield, predominantly lead-based, that we're placing around the ship's critical components. This dual-layer approach maximizes our protection against the intense radiation you'll face near Jupiter."

Jim chimed in. "And radiation suits for the crew. We're developing suits that offer mobility and protection, they'll be essential for any extravehicular activities near Ganymede. You'll get to test our prototypes."

Yay for me.

I paused, the weight of my final unspoken concern growing heavier by the second.

"There's something that's been bothering me," I started, my voice tinged with hesitation. "It's about monitoring the shuttle flight system. I've... never actually done that before."

Mike's features transitioned from buoyant enthusiasm to a complex mix of surprise and concern. Jim looked shocked.

"You mean, you've never piloted a shuttle? You're not an astronaut?" he asked, his voice blending disbelief with sudden apprehension. He exchanged a quick, loaded glance with Jim.

I shook my head, feeling a knot form in my stomach. I tightened my lips as I absorbed the magnitude of his misconception. The idea that he had assumed I was an astronaut hung awkwardly in the air between us. "I thought most shuttles were fully automated now. I know the transport shuttles are."

Mike cleared his throat. "While the Artemis *does* have advanced AI navigation and autopilot systems, there are scenarios where manual piloting is not just preferable, but necessary—especially in deep space."

I sighed and crossed my arms, wondering where I could find a pilot willing to take on the mission.

He elaborated while I mused. "For instance, during docking procedures with satellites or maneuvering through unpredicted asteroid fields, the automated systems might not be sufficient. Manual piloting provides that extra precision and adaptability."

Jim added, "And don't forget emergency situations. If the auto-navigation system encounters a fault or the external sensors are compromised, manual control could be a lifesaver."

I felt the knot in my stomach grow larger. "So, If I can't find a pilot, I'll need to learn to pilot it before launch day, that's...that's less than a year away. That's a daunting task."

Mike shook his head. "Not just learn, Doctor. You'd need a significant amount of training, and even then, it's a huge responsibility. Piloting a spacecraft, especially one as complex as the Artemis, is no small feat. You'll need to know the controls inside and out, troubleshooting, some insider info on the propulsion system capabilities, and preventative maintenance. It would require years of intensive study."

My anxiety grew. "Is there an experienced shuttle pilot you could recommend? Someone experienced with Artemis's controls and propulsion system?"

There was a brief, uncomfortable silence before Mike finally spoke, his voice tinged with reluctance. "There isn't one. The Artemis is a unique vessel, custom-built for the Venus mission. No one, aside from Jim and myself, really knows her inside out. I've piloted routine missions from Earth and back on the old-style Nuclear-Thermal Propulsion ships, but I've never been beyond Ceres."

Jim nodded in agreement. "Piloting the Artemis in deep space...that's a different game altogether. Someone with a significant flight history and thorough GID knowledge needs to fly this thing."

"Wait, what about the shuttle commander from the

Venus mission?" I asked, mentally crossing my fingers.

"No good," Mike said, shaking his head. "Commander Fuller was mandated back to Earth."

Damn.

Mandated was our colloquial term for being so looney tunes that not even the Looney Dome could fix you. Being mandated usually meant extended stays in secure facilities on Earth and a cocktail of sedatives to boot.

"Is there anyone from that mission around?"

Jim frowned. "Maybe some auxiliary personnel, but they won't know the controls. Wallace might have some advice for you."

"Wallace?"

Jim pulled up a profile on the console. "Hank Wallace. Flight surgeon. He was slated to be the onboard medic for the Venus mission. He's the one that pulled the plug on the project when Fuller started...showing symptoms."

I scanned his profile with my mini-comms unit and then placed it back in my pocket. I'd call him later for advice maybe.

The realization hit me like a ton of bricks. Not only did the success of the mission hinge on a multitude of scientific and engineering factors, but now the very act of navigating this colossal spacecraft fell into uncertain territory.

"We'll figure out a solution," I said, more to myself than

to them. The mission couldn't falter on account of this. "We need someone who can not only handle the technicalities of the Artemis but who can get us through deep space."

Mike looked at Jim and nodded.

"I'll find someone. Let's do it," I said, determination setting in. "Let's make history."

Mike grinned, clapping me on the back. "That's the spirit. Welcome to the Engineering Dome, Dr. Mercer. Let's get to work."

ΦΦΦ

The first light of the Martian dawn was creeping through the window of my office once again, casting long, red fingers across the pandemonium that was my desk.

Surrounded by a sea of mission plans, timelines, and Artemis schematics, I looked more like a strategic war commander than an astrobiologist. My eyes, heavy from another night of little sleep, were fixated on the screen in front of me.

I was studying the crew list that I'd compiled, with Mike's help. We'd ended up deciding that the team needed to be comprised of a pilot, a flight engineer, a systems specialist, a chief medical officer, two astrobiologists, a geologist, and a communications expert.

Since I was filling the role of Mission Commander and astrobiologist, we still had a couple of empty seats. In light of the size of the team and the length of time we'd be gone, Mike had suggested repurposing the extra crew quarters into food storage modules.

We didn't need a space Donner Party incident.

I set up the online application portal for the Ganymede Mission team just the other evening, and, as of last night, hadn't yet received any replies.

I prepared myself to be disappointed yet again and pulled up the chart.

To my surprise, the portal was overflowing with applications. I had to blink twice to make sure I was seeing it properly.

Scientists, engineers, medical professionals, pilots, you name it. It was like Mars Colony One had been holding its breath, waiting for something like this. Even a few brave souls from the culinary department applied, wanting to ensure we didn't survive on nutrient paste alone.

I chuckled at that one. Leave it to Mars Colony One to have adventurous chefs.

Just as I clicked on the first application, Raj's face appeared at my door. "Got a full portal, I see," he said, glancing at my screen.

I rubbed my eyes, trying to focus. "It's insane, Raj. We've got more applicants than rocks on Mars."

"That's good, right?" Raj chuckled. "Means people are excited about the mission."

"Excited, or just looking for a way out of their day jobs," I quipped, scrolling through the list. "But seriously, there are some impressive credentials here."

I clicked on an application at random. "Here's one: Dr. Amelia Zhang, astrogeologist. She's been working on Martian soil analysis for years. Could be useful for Ganymede's surface study."

Raj nodded. "Good call. What about the engineering team?"

"That's where it gets tricky," I admitted, tapping on another file. "We need people who not only understand the Artemis's tech but can also handle the... let's call it 'unique' circumstances of this mission."

"Like the one-year deadline and potential interplanetary war hanging over our heads?" Raj added dryly.

"Exactly," I said. "Oh, here's one: Marco DiAngelo, propulsion expert. Worked on the latest upgrades to the colony's transport shuttles."

Raj whistled. "Not too shabby. Anyone for the medical team?"

I scrolled further. "A few promising candidates. But I'm looking for someone who's not just a great doctor but also has the psychological fortitude to handle space travel under these conditions and knows how to deal with psych issues in others."

Commander Fuller's situation haunted me now. Thanks, Mike.

"Space craziness is a real concern," Raj agreed. "Especially on a mission this critical."

We went through a few more applications, discussing the merits and potential drawbacks of each candidate.

A little later, Raj headed out for some breakfast, promising to bring me back something. I leaned back in my chair, letting out a long breath.

I opened another application, and my screen filled with the face of someone claiming to be an expert in closed-loop life support systems. "Now that's what we need," I muttered. "Someone who can keep us breathing when we're millions of miles from the nearest oxygen refill."

The Martian sunrise was in full bloom now, casting a warm, reddish glow across my office. It was beautiful, in a stark, alien way. But it also served as a reminder of how far from Earth we were— and how much farther we were planning to go.

I spent the next hour eating donuts and going through more applications, making notes, and setting up interviews. The Ganymede Mission was shaping up to be a blend of the best and brightest Mars Colony One had to offer, but the real challenge was still ahead. It was going to be turning a diverse group of individuals into a cohesive team capable of handling whatever the trip threw at us.

As the day progressed, the pile of potential candidates grew. Raj came back and there were moments of excitement, fits of laughter at some of the more eccentric applications, and periods of intense debate between Raj and me over certain candidates.

Late afternoon, I leaned back in my chair, rubbing my eyes and wiggling my numb behind. The screen was a blur of faces and qualifications and I stood to pace the office. "It's like trying to pick a dream team for an interplanetary heist," I said with a chuckle.

Raj stood up, stretching. "Well, if it's a heist, you need a good getaway driver. Found any hotshot pilots yet?"

"Finding the right pilot is going to be tough. They'll need more than just flying skills. They have to master the Artemis and its next-gen drive. It's way beyond standard shuttles," I said, my eyes back on the search for the right candidate.

"We could always kidnap an ace pilot from Earth," Raj joked, but his humor couldn't mask the seriousness of our need.

I shook my head, a wry smile on my face. "Let's keep kidnapping as Plan B.

6.

'63-03

I'd delved into the applicants three separate times over the next day and finally chosen my front-runners. With some finagling, I'd managed to set up a lot of the interviews for today, the last day of the work week.

I'd also let the adventurous chef down gently.

I was hoping I could have the beginnings of a solid team to start intensive astronaut training on Monday. I was *not* looking forward to that.

Going out in my Marswalker or tooling around in the rover was about the extent of my astronautic ambitions, but it looked like the Institute had other plans. They had developed an accelerated program just for us. *Yay.*

Sitting across from Sam Johnson, I braced myself for an

interview that I knew would be anything but ordinary. Sam's reputation as a blunt, no-nonsense geologist preceded him, and as he folded his tall, muscular frame into the chair and stared at me, I could see why.

"Mr. Johnson, let's get straight to it," I began, trying to match his directness. "What makes you the right geologist for the Ganymede mission?"

Sam leaned forward, locking his deep-set eyes onto mine. "Dr. Mercer, I've been mapping Martian stratigraphy since the first expeditions. I've analyzed everything from hematite deposits in Meridiani Planum to basaltic rock formations in Tharsis Montes. Ganymede's icy crust and potential subsurface ocean? That's just another challenge."

His voice carried the kind of authority that came from years of fieldwork. It was assertive, maybe even a tad overbearing, but it was backed by undeniable expertise.

Sam adjusted his posture, his tone direct. "In Martian geology, I've extensively studied rock stratigraphy, erosion processes, and sedimentology. This involves analyzing rock layers and understanding the environmental conditions that shaped them. On Ganymede, the challenge is different but scientifically analogous. Its surface is dominated by ice, not rock, and its geological history may involve cryovolcanism and subsurface oceans. My approach will involve applying rigorous geological methods to interpret these ice patterns and any underwater current influences, employing the same precision and thoroughness that I've applied on Mars."

I couldn't help but be impressed. His confidence was almost palpable, but it wasn't his confidence that swayed me. It was his detailed understanding of planetary geology, which he explained in extreme depth for the next twenty minutes.

"Your blunt approach is well-known," I ventured cautiously after he'd finished. "This mission will require close teamwork. How do you plan to handle that?"

Sam smirked slightly. "I'm blunt because I value precision and clarity, especially when it comes to science. But don't mistake that for inflexibility. I know the importance of collaboration, especially in uncharted territory like Ganymede. I've successfully worked with a variety of specialists on three different planets so far. I think I can manage one more without getting any complaints."

I smiled and nodded.

It was the answer I was hoping for. Yes, he was as subtle as a landslide, but his knowledge was solid, like the bedrock he studied. I could see past his gruff exterior to the skilled geologist underneath.

"Alright, Mr. Johnson, I think you might just be the rock expert we need," I said, feeling a sense of certainty. I was going to run it past Raj, but I had the final say and I was almost one hundred percent sure that Sam was it.

"Great. I'll get you a detailed list of everything I require before the weekend," he said confidently, standing up, shaking my hand, and leaving the room with a nod.

I huffed out a breath and shifted to the next screen on the HoloPad.

Choosing Sam Johnson was a practical decision, not an easy one. His blunt manner would be a challenge, but his geological insights were invaluable. As the interview ended, I ticked off one crucial role on my team, feeling a step closer to making the Ganymede mission a reality.

As the interviews for the medical doctor position progressed, they turned out to be more of a headache than a breakthrough. I had lined up several candidates, each boasting impressive resumes with Earth and Mars-based medical experience. But as I soon discovered, terrestrial expertise didn't necessarily translate to dealing with medical emergencies in microgravity or deep space.

The first candidate was Dr. Emily Watson, a surgeon with an enviable list of successful procedures under her belt. Her confidence was clear as she walked in.

She gave me Sam vibes actually and I was hoping she would be the one.

"So, Dr. Watson," I began, flipping through her file."You've done impressive work on Mars. But tell me about your experience with space medicine, specifically in microgravity."

She hesitated, a flicker of uncertainty crossing her face. "Well, most of my experience is ground-based. However, I'm a quick learner and adaptable."

Adaptable. That was the buzzword of the day, it seemed. I appreciated her confidence, but adapting to zero-G surgery wasn't something you picked up on a weekend course.

We spoke a bit longer about some of her other assignments, but I knew that she wasn't it.

"Thanks, Dr. Watson. We'll be in touch."

Next up was Dr. Sanjay Kumar, an esteemed cardiologist. His handshake was firm, his smile reassuring. But as we dove into the nitty-gritty of space medicine, it became clear that his expertise was too Earth-centric.

"Microgravity can play havoc with the cardiovascular system and the body systems in general," I explained. "We need someone who can handle that complexity."

He nodded, a bit too eagerly. "I've read up on it. I'm sure with some hands-on experience, I can manage."

Read up on it?

I needed someone who had more than a theoretical understanding. I could already imagine the chaos of a cardiac emergency spiraling out of control while Dr. Kumar flipped through a textbook.

The interviews continued in a similar vein. One candidate after another, skilled and brilliant on terra firma, but woefully unprepared for the unique challenges of space. Each handshake and polite 'we'll be in touch' left me more disheartened.

I leaned back in my chair after the last candidate left, rubbing my temples. Finding a medic who could handle space-related medical issues was turning out to be as intangible as a flattering space suit.

"Maybe I should just pack a first aid kit and call it a day," I muttered to myself, only half-joking.

It wasn't just about finding a doctor. It was about finding someone who could adapt their medical knowledge to an environment where everything, from bodily fluids to pathogens, behaved differently. I needed a medic who could perform under pressure when the nearest hospital was millions of miles away.

Frustrated, I pushed the stack of resumes aside.

I leaned back in my chair, rubbing my temples. Finding the right medical professional was proving to be more challenging than I anticipated.

Reluctantly, I decided to put the search for a doctor on hold. We needed the best, and I wasn't willing to settle for less. My mind was already racing with the next steps—reaching out to more networks, maybe looking for candidates with field experience in extreme environments or military medics with space training.

The right person was out there, I knew it. I just hadn't

found them yet.

The communications specialist interviews were a blur until Luca Marcarelli walked in. He had an easy smile and a casual confidence that filled the room. I glanced at his resume again— impressive, especially considering his younger age, but it was his reputation as a communications genius that had caught my attention.

"Mr. Marcarelli, glad you could make it," I began, trying to sound more confident than I felt. "I've heard you're something of a wizard with comms systems."

"Call me Luca, please," he said with a friendly nod. "And I guess I've had my moments. What's on your mind?"

I dove right in. "We need a robust, fail-safe communication system for the Artemis. Something that can handle the immense distances and the challenges of space communication. What's your take on that?"

Luca leaned forward, his eyes lighting up. " My focus has been on optimizing our current deep-space communication systems. I've been working on enhancing signal strength and reducing latency as much as the laws of physics allow."

I nodded, trying to keep up. "So, no quantum entanglement stuff?"

He laughed, a genuine, hearty sound. "Not quite there yet, Commander Mercer. However, I've been improving our array of high-gain antennas and integrating advanced laser communication systems into my work for years. The goal is clear and consistent communication with as little delay as possible."

"Lasers, huh?" I said, impressed despite myself. "Sounds fast."

"It's pretty cutting-edge," Luca explained. "We use lasers to transmit data at high speeds. It's much faster than radio waves and can carry more information."

I mulled over his words. "But there's still a delay, right?"

"Unfortunately, yes. Even with all our advancements, comms are still bound by the speed of light. Communications to and from Ganymede will have a delay of several minutes or more depending on our exact position."

I sighed, rubbing the bridge of my nose. "So no real-time chats with Mars then."

"No, but with my experience, we'll have the next best thing. Stable, reliable communication, with the highest data throughput achievable. We'll be able to send high-definition video, complex data from the Artemis's instruments, and even have relatively smooth voice transmissions."

"That's reassuring," I admitted. "Especially considering the importance of this mission."

Luca's face turned serious for a moment. "I understand the stakes, Commander. And I'm fully committed to ensuring our communication systems won't let us down."

I couldn't help but feel a bit more at ease. Having a comms genius like Luca on board meant one less thing to worry about in the grand scheme of things.

The conversation naturally drifted to the advanced AI-integrated comms assistant on the Artemis. I was curious about his expertise in this area, given the critical role of AI in our mission's communication systems.

"So, Luca," I started, leaning forward with a hint of amusement in my voice. "The Artemis is equipped with a pretty advanced AI comms assistant that is integrated with the ship. Think you can handle it if it decides to have a bad day?"

Luca grinned, his eyes lighting up at the challenge. "Ah, AI– the ultimate diva of technology," he joked. "But seriously, I've worked with similar systems before. Troubleshooting AI is a bit like convincing a stubborn child to eat their vegetables. It requires patience, a bit of psychology, and sometimes, just knowing when to restart the whole thing."

I couldn't help but chuckle at his analogy. "So, you're saying a good old-fashioned reboot is your secret weapon?"

"Absolutely," he said with a grin. "But don't worry, I've got a few more tricks up my sleeve. AIs are complex, but they're also predictable in their own way. Understanding their logic patterns is key."

I nodded, impressed with his confidence and approach. "Well, if you can keep our AI in line and our comms clear, you'll be worth your weight in Redcreds."

He laughed, and I could tell Luca wasn't just a communications expert. He had the kind of easygoing demeanor that could be a real asset on a long space voyage. It was reassuring to know that at least the comms side of things was in capable hands.

"Welcome to the team, Luca," I said with a smile. "Looks like you'll be our voice across the void."

He grinned back, the earlier warmth returning to his eyes. "I won't let you down, Dr. Mercer. We're going to make history."

As Luca left, I couldn't help but feel a surge of excitement. His expertise and innovative approach were exactly what the mission needed.

I interviewed astrobiologists next. Even though that's my specialty, we had no idea what we'd be getting into as far as the signal goes, and if intelligent life did manage to exist on Ganymede, I'd want a second set of brains to help me parse it out.

Plus, with my role as the shuttle commander and additional responsibilities, I'd need the backup.

The afternoon of interviewing astrobiologists and other scientists had a bit of a high school reunion vibe, except everyone was significantly more accomplished and there were no awkward slow dances. We all knew each other, most of us had worked together for years already or attended seminars together.

The Science Dome at Mars Colony One had always been a beehive of brilliance, and today was no exception. The nerd herd was out in full force.

There was Dr. Lisa Nguyen, whose enthusiasm for Martian microbes could outshine a supernova, but whose lack of field experience was a red flag. Then there was Dr. Farooq Singh, brilliant but so argumentative he could start a debate with a rock. Nice people, but not quite what I needed for a high-stakes mission to Ganymede.

After several interviews that made me feel like I was a geeky scientist hosting a geeky talk show, Alexei Petrovich walked in.

I'd never actually spoken to Alex, but his reputation preceded him. The guy was like a Martian Bigfoot—everyone had heard of him, but sightings were rare. He was ten times more introverted than I was and probably twice as smart.

Sitting across from Dr. Petrovich, I felt an immediate sense of respect. His expertise in astrobiology, particularly in extremophiles, was something I'd always admired from afar.

Alexei, in his late thirties, medium height, lean build,

and short-cropped blonde hair, gave a nod that was both polite and slightly aloof. His green eyes seemed to be calculating the room's exit routes.

"I appreciate the opportunity, Dr. Mercer," he said in a thoughtful tone, with a hint of a Russian accent. "Your project is... intriguing."

"I'm glad you think so. Your work on alien flora and fauna has been groundbreaking. I need someone with your expertise on this mission."

Alexei's demeanor relaxed slightly, which considering his overall bearing, only made him look like he wasn't about to try to dash out the door anymore. "I admit, the prospect is fascinating. The challenges, however, are significant."

"Challenges are just puzzles in disguise," I quipped. "We solve puzzles for breakfast here."

He gave a small smile, the first I'd seen from him. "Then I suppose I should be prepared for an interesting breakfast."

I was eager to delve into his groundbreaking research. "Alexei, your insights into extremophiles are revolutionary. How do you see them shaping our understanding of potential life on Ganymede?"

Alexei paused, his gaze momentarily distant as if he were visualizing complex molecular structures invisible to the rest of us. His fingers drummed an irregular pattern on the table, a rhythm unique to his thought process. "The extremophiles they're not just surviving; they're redefining existence. On Ganymede, if life exists, it's not just mimicking these organisms. It's likely to have evolved parallel biogenesis mechanisms of its own, perhaps based on silicon or arsenic biochemistry, unlike our carbon-based models."

I nodded, trying to keep pace with his rapid intellectual leaps. "So, we might expect biochemistry that's fundamentally different from Earth's? That's a profound shift in our approach."

"Yes, precisely!" Alexei's voice rose in excitement, his eyes lighting up behind his glasses which he adjusted unconsciously. His eyes rarely met mine for long, but when they did, the focus and the knowledge in them pierced me like a laser.

"Consider the polyextremophiles in our arsenic-rich Mono Lake," he continued.

I nodded, knowing the location.

"Now, extrapolate that to Ganymede's cryovolcanic activity. We could be looking at a form of life that utilizes cryo-chemical energy, a concept that's barely on our astrobiological radar."

I found myself momentarily lost in his train of thought. "So, we're potentially exploring a life form that thrives in sub-zero temperatures, using chemical reactions we've hardly imagined?"

"Exactly," he affirmed, his speech quickening. "Ganymede's subterranean ocean could harbor ecosystems driven by chemolithoautotrophic processes, radically different from our photosynthesis-dependent life. Imagine a microbial world, thriving in the absence of light, deriving energy from mineral oxidation or even radiation fluxes."

The complexity of his ideas was dizzying. Alexei wasn't just thinking outside the box; he was redesigning the box itself. I could barely keep up. "That's groundbreaking, Alexei. It redefines the parameters of habitability."

He nodded, his expression intense, yet there was a faint smile as if he relished the challenge of intellectual frontiers. "Your mission could pivot the axis of astrobiological research. Ganymede might not just be habitable. It could be a cradle for a form of life that challenges our very definition of biology."

I was both awed and slightly overwhelmed by the breadth of his vision. I realized then that Alexei's genius was not just in his vast knowledge, but in his ability to see connections and patterns where others saw voids.

I *had* to have him on the crew.

Our conversation continued, flowing seamlessly from theoretical models to the practicalities of our upcoming mission. It was a meeting of minds, an exchange brimming with scientific fervor and mutual understanding.

I knew Alexei was the right choice. His reclusive nature might be a challenge, but his insights could prove invaluable.

I ended the day with three solid choices for the team—Sam Johnson, Luca Marcarelli, and Alexei Petrovich. Each brought something unique to the table, and I was excited to see what we could accomplish together.

The lack of a suitable pilot, flight engineer, systems specialist, and doctor still nagged at me, but I was determined to find them.

After all, what's a little interplanetary mission without a few hitches along the way?

As I walked back to my quarters, my comms unit beeped— a sharp, urgent alert that snapped me back to reality.

"Lab Alert: Microbial Fluctuation Detected," the message flashed.

My heart skipped a beat. Jimmy was in trouble.

I broke into a run, my boots ringing out against the floor. Reaching the lab, I burst through the door to find Mia already hunched over the microscope, her brow furrowed in concern.

"Mia, what's happening?" I panted, sliding up next to her.

"It's Jimmy," she said without looking up. "Their

metabolic activity... It hasn't just slowed, it's like they're reversing their growth. I've never seen anything like it."

I peered into the microscope. The vibrant, almost aggressive activity I had witnessed earlier was gone. The microbes looked lethargic, their movements sluggish.

"We need to figure out what's happening," I said, my mind already racing. I moved to the console, pulling up the environmental data. "Any changes in their habitat conditions?"

Mia shook her head. "Nothing."

"Run a full spectrum analysis. I want to know if they're reacting to a chemical change, a mutation, anything."

We worked in tandem. As Mia prepped the samples, I dove into the data, analyzing every possible variable. The Ganymede Signal, my commanding role, all of it faded into the background. Right then, I was an astrobiologist, pure and simple.

Hours passed as we tested theories, discarded them, and tested new ones. I was exhausted, but I couldn't stop. This was a time-sensitive situation and I'd just have to suck it up and power through.

Finally, Mia let out a small gasp. "Look at this."

She pointed to the screen, where a series of graphs and numbers told a new story.

"The metabolic shift... I think it's triggered by a compound. Something we didn't even know they could produce."

I leaned in, studying the readouts. "A self-produced compound? That's... that's incredible. It could mean they're adapting in ways we didn't anticipate."

Mia nodded, her eyes wide.

"We need to isolate this compound and study its effects. This could be a breakthrough in understanding extraterrestrial life adaptability," I said, already plotting our next steps.

Mia was already on it, her hands steady as she prepared the samples. "Let's see what secrets Jimmy's hiding."

7.

'63-03

The first thing I did the next morning—after checking on Jimmy— was bring up Dr. Wallace's profile on my comms unit.

The mini-comms units worked much like the obsolete cellular telephones from my father's era, except these did not degrade, were highly rugged for use in Mars walks, and did not require charging due to the triboelectric nanogenerators incorporated into the design. The mini-comms used our bodily motions to charge the battery.

And if we hadn't carried it in a while and the charge was dead, we only had to set it in a sunny place for a few minutes so the mini-solar cells could get it going again.

The mini-comms allowed seamless data linking,

communications, and AI-enhanced research assistance. They also allowed us to control the smart screens throughout our dome, and with special permissions, the other domes as well.

I found that with my new status as a mission commander, I'd been given Level A1 dome clearances which was pretty much our Top Secret equivalent. I had open permission to check out everything going on in every dome in Colony One except the Administrative Dome, the Governor's Dome, and private data.

Mini-comms allowed us to access our Redcreds, Earth-based stores and import services, shuttle services to Earth and back, and integrated many other features and settings that made our lives a little easier.

I bit my lip as I ran through what I wanted to say. I had an idea to present to Wallace. I didn't know if it would pan out or if I'd even go through with it after speaking with him.

I tapped the icon on my comms with a trembling finger, initiating the call to the doctor.

His face popped up on the screen, a rugged, comforting visage that somehow eased my nerves. He was sitting in a medical office with supplies and the harsh lighting of the medical facility behind him.

"Dr. Wallace, I'm Lena Mercer, commander of the Ganymede mission," I started, skipping formalities and hoping he'd already heard about the Ganymede Signal. "I'm hunting for a shuttle pilot and a medic, and your name came up."

"Came up from who?" he asked suspiciously.

"Mike Donovan at the Engineering Dome," I said before hesitating for a moment, uneasy about bringing up the next part.

He shifted, frowning.

"I'm taking the Artemis to Ganymede," I declared.

I had the inkling that beating around the bush with Dr. Wallace wouldn't help my cause at all.

He froze and raised an eyebrow. "You want a pilot and a medic for the Artemis? That's quite the wish list. I'm sure Donovan told you about what happened last time."

"Yeah, about that," I delved in. "I heard about Commander Fuller. Must have been intense, seeing him unravel on the launchpad."

Hank's eyes clouded over. "That was...a tough day. Fuller was more than a colleague. I considered him a friend. Watching him lose it, trying to blow up the Artemis with us all inside... it's not something you ever forget."

Wow. I was *not* expecting that.

I leaned in, trying to be tactful. "How did you deal with it? That's a lot for anyone to handle."

He sighed and sat back in his chair, looking tired. "You fall back on your training. Medical, psychological, or whatever keeps the situation from escalating. It was... a lot."

I nodded, feeling a sudden kinship. "And yet here you are, still practicing medicine from the looks of it and I've seen your profile. You've done space missions since then."

He studied me, a hint of curiosity in his eyes. "It's all about the call of the unknown, isn't it? Despite everything, we still look up and wonder *what if?*...even us doctors here. We're all here for the same reason: new frontiers."

I smiled. He'd nailed it. "Exactly. Plus, you've got a front-row seat to human behavior in extreme conditions."

A ghost of a smile crossed his lips. "You're asking me to jump back into the deep end, Commander Mercer."

"Yeah, but with a life jacket this time," I quipped. "And it's not just about keeping bodies healthy. We need someone who understands the mental game too."

He paused. "I'll be honest. After the aborted Venus launch, I wasn't sure if I'd ever want to go back, and *never* on the Artemis. But maybe this is a sign. I'll think about it."

As we wrapped up the call, I sensed a connection. Hank Wallace had seen the worst and still had the heart to face it again. "Really think about it, Hank. We need someone with your experience. We need *you.*"

He gave a short nod, his expression thoughtful. "I'll let you know, Commander. It's a big decision."

I ended the call, feeling hopeful. Hank was exactly what

we needed—experienced, resilient, and with a perspective born of adversity. The Ganymede mission just might have found its medic.

ΦΦΦ

It had been approximately eight weeks since I'd first encountered the Ganymede Signal and I was about to become a real live astronaut.

Our launch date was tentatively set for March 15, 2064—exactly one year to the day from the grant application approval and less than a year away.

It was a pre-dawn Monday morning, and I was going to meet with David Chen, lead journalist for Earth-Mars United Broadcasting.

As I strode through the Mars Frontier Research Institute's Astronaut Training Facility, I couldn't help but chuckle inwardly. Earth-Mars United Broadcasting Company— EMUBC, the "least biased" news source on Mars, I mused sarcastically in my head.

They were the *only* news source on Mars.

The place was buzzing with activity, and I was about to give my first interview as the official Mission Commander for the Ganymede Project.

David Chen was already there, his recording device poised and ready. "Dr. Mercer! Great to see you," he greeted me, his tone a perfect blend of professionalism and excitement.

"Call me Lena," I said, adjusting my new mission commander uniform.

It was sleek, black, fitted, and made me feel like a million Redcreds. My short red hair was neatly combed, a stark contrast against the uniform's dark hues. I was glad I had the complexion to carry off the dark color. The bright patches and nametape signified my role as Commander and the mission insignia developed specifically for this project rested on my arm.

The outfit made me feel both distinguished and slightly ridiculous.

David eyed my uniform with an appreciative glance. "Jazzy duds. You look ready to take on the galaxy."

I couldn't resist a smirk. "Just Ganymede for now, but who knows? Maybe the galaxy next."

We settled into the interview, the training facility's vast, high-tech backdrop making this all seem more surreal.

"So, can you tell us about the training program you and your team will be undergoing?" David asked, his recorder poised like a talisman.

"Absolutely," I began. "It's an eight-month program. Think of it as a crash course in everything space— from zero-G maneuvers to operating the latest space tech. We'll be doing simulations, physical training, learning to fix things with duct tape... the works."

"And your team? Have you filled all the positions yet?" David prodded, ever the journalist looking for the scoop.

I hesitated. "Well, we're almost there. We've got some of the best minds on Mars— geologists, communications experts, a brilliant astrobiologist—" I laughed and put a hand to my chest. "Not me."

I shifted on my feet and I could feel myself beginning to sweat already. "But we're still missing a few key players. We need a pilot, someone who can handle Artemis's new propulsion system. And a systems specialist wouldn't hurt either. We're still out a medic, but I'm hoping this top-notch space doc I've been talking to will agree to come on board."

David's eyebrows raised, skepticism rampant on his face. "No pilot yet? That's quite a gap to fill."

I laughed, a mix of nerves and excitement. "Tell me about it. But hey, I'm optimistic. Worst case scenario, I'll just wing it. How hard can flying a spacecraft be, right?"

David chuckled along, though I could tell he wasn't sure if I was joking.

I wasn't entirely sure either.

The interview continued with David asking about the mission specifics, the spacecraft, and my thoughts on being the first mission commander to potentially make contact with an intelligent extraterrestrial entity.

"Oh, the pressure? It's only slightly less intense than a black hole," I quipped, trying to downplay the growing knot of anxiety in my stomach.

As the interview wrapped up, David thanked me, his demeanor showing genuine admiration. "Thank you for the interview and the inside look at the training center, Commander. Mars and Earth will be watching closely."

Like *that* didn't sound vaguely threatening.

I nodded, feeling the weight of two worlds on my shoulders as I walked away.

No pressure, Lena. Just the fate of interplanetary relations and possibly uncovering the biggest discovery in human history, I thought to myself, trying to keep the mood light in my head.

I strolled into the astronaut training facility after showing David out. Today was the big day: meeting the team all together for the first time. We were supposed to bond over needles and treadmills—typical first-date stuff.

Sam Johnson, Luca Marcarelli, and Alex Petrovich were already there, decked out in the latest workout gear that looked like it belonged in a high-tech fashion show.

Sam's muscular build was evident even under his fitted gear, and I noted his confident, almost challenging stance. Luca's slender frame was more relaxed, his friendly smile acting as an icebreaker for the others. Alex, on the other hand, looked a bit like a fish out of water, his lean physique and thoughtful expression seeming more suited to a lab than a gym.

"Morning, team," I greeted, trying to sound more commander-like and less like someone who'd rather be browsing my mini-comms over a cup of coffee. "Ready for some fun?"

Sam grunted a response that might've been a greeting, while Luca beamed. "Roger that, Commander."

Alex just nodded, his eyes scanning the high-tech environment of the training facility with faint distrust.

Our first stop was the medical wing, where Greg Nash, our Mission Control Director, was waiting. He had that look about him, a calm demeanor that seemed to say, 'space? Been there, done that.'

I'd seen him on the smart screens before, but I'd never met him. He was definitely larger than life and not someone I wanted to irritate.

"Welcome, Artemis crew. I'm Greg Nash," he introduced himself, shaking each of our hands. "Today's just a quick poke and prod. You'll hardly notice it."

Famous last words.

The preliminary medical tests were like something dreamed up by an insane doctor who liked to torture people for fun. We were poked, prodded, scanned, and analyzed by machines that looked more suited for alien autopsies.

My curiosity was piqued by one of the machines in the corner of the medical wing. It looked sleek and intimidating.

"Hey," I called out to one of the techs. "What's that contraption?"

The tech, a young guy with an enthusiasm that I found endearing, glanced over. "Oh, that's the Total Body Composition Analyzer 3000, or TBCA-3000 for short. It's pretty cool. It gives us a complete breakdown of body composition—muscle, fat, bone density—the works. Essential for space missions."

I leaned in closer. "How so?"

"Well, microgravity environments affect men's and women's bodies differently," he explained. "For instance, women tend to lose bone density at a faster rate than men in space. It's partly due to differences in hormones. The TBCA-3000 helps us tailor a specific diet and exercise plan to mitigate these effects."

I nodded, intrigued. "What about muscle loss?"

"That's a big one," he continued. "In microgravity, you don't use your larger muscles much. So, they weaken over time. We'll be focusing a lot on lower body and core strength, keeping those muscles active and engaged."

"And the diet?"

"Ah, that's where it gets interesting. The TBCA-3000 helps us understand each individual's metabolic rate and potential caloric requirements based on specific physiology and activity levels. We can then create a personalized nutrition plan. It's all about maintaining muscle mass and ensuring adequate intake of vitamins and minerals, especially calcium and vitamin D for bone health."

I was impressed. "Sounds like this machine is a game-changer."

He grinned. "Absolutely, Commander. It's about staying ahead of the curve. We can't eliminate all the risks of space travel, but we can minimize them. And as a bonus, you and your team get Priority One status on all the incoming steaks and beef from Earth," he added with a smile. He leaned in and whispered. "Even priority over Governor Olsen."

As I moved on, watching Sam complete a breathing test, I couldn't help but feel a sense of relief. Knowing we had technology like the TBCA-3000 on our side made the daunting prospect of maintaining health in space seem a bit more manageable.

"Looks like we're in good hands," I muttered to myself, making a mental note to thank the tech team later. After all, this mission wasn't just about getting to Ganymede. It was about getting there and back in one piece.

Sam was up first for the next phase. He tackled each test with a determination that made it clear he wasn't just a geologist. He was a geologist who could probably lift a boulder if he needed to.

Then it was Luca's turn. He chatted away with the medics, somehow turning a blood draw into a social event. His amiable nature seemed to put everyone at ease. I was a bit envious of his ease of talking to people.

Alex approached the tests like I imagined he approached everything else, his keen mind likely analyzing each procedure and probably memorizing every detail.

When it was my turn, I stepped confidently up to the table. "So, this won't hurt, right?" I asked the medic, only half-joking.

"Only your pride," she replied with a wink.

After the medical tests, we moved on to the fitness tests. Treadmills, weights, agility courses—you name it, we did it. I watched the team carefully, wanting to know how they operated. Sam powered through like a machine, Luca kept up with a steady pace, and Alex... well, he survived. Barely.

Me? I led from the rear and also survived. Barely.

I wasn't in terrible shape, but I was a woman surrounded by mostly fit men. I was never going to outperform them physically. It didn't seem to be a big deal for any of them, so I didn't let it get to me. I had always done my best in any situation and now I'd do my best with this and it would be enough. I'd make sure of that.

In between tests, we chatted, getting to know each other. Sam's bluntness was a bit off-putting at first, but his expertise was undeniable and so we gave him an unspoken pass. Luca's communication skills shone as we discussed a prototype module that he was building. I kept up with that conversation as best I could, but I only knew the basics of comms analysis. The Ganymede Signal had stretched the limits of my knowledge on that front. I was particularly interested to hear his take on it.

Alex, once he opened up, had fascinating insights into astrobiology that made me rethink a few of my own theories.

It was during a particularly grueling treadmill test that I realized this team, *my* team, was something special. Each of us brought unique skills and perspectives that, when combined, could make this mission successful.

As we finished the day, sweaty and exhausted, I looked at them all.

"That's good," Sam said, wiping his brow. He gave a nod of approval as I meticulously updated our daily log. "Lists and logs are my thing," he joked.

"Mine too, though they might not be very legible sometimes," I replied.

Luca, still smiling, was chatting away about improving the gym's communication system with one of the techs. Alex, looking a bit dazed, was already outlining potential experiments for the mission as he sat with his HoloPad nearby.

"Great work today," I said, feeling a surge of pride as I smiled. "Tomorrow, we start the real training. Get some rest. You'll need it."

As they left, I stayed back for a moment, taking in the enormity of it all. This team, this mission, was my responsibility. And I was going to make sure we were ready for anything the universe threw at us, even if it meant running a few more miles on the treadmill.

ΦΦΦ

I dragged myself out of bed at 05:00 and slid into my newly cleaned physical training uniform. If we were going to be sweating every day, I was going to need a couple of spares. Maybe more than a couple.

The laundry system here was...interesting.

High-tech, AI-driven, and almost too smart for their own good— the machines were a Godsend and a comedy show rolled into one.

The way they worked was simple: you tossed your micro-chipped dirty laundry into any collection bin, and the AI sorted and tagged it for washing. But there was a catch— sometimes the AI got creative.

The washing itself was the pinnacle of efficiency, using

minimal water and some sort of advanced bio-enzymes. I heard it could get stains out of anything—not that I tested it with Martian dust just for fun or anything.

Once cleaned, the laundry was supposed to be delivered straight to your room. Key word: *Supposed* to.

Let's just say the AI had a sense of humor. You haven't lived until you've seen Raj Patel's face when he received my purple tank top instead of his geological field vests.

The Geology Department had a field day when he wore it to work the next day just for the heck of it.

We tried logging the errors with the laundry AI. That was a hoot. You'd think you'd get a standard "We're sorry for the inconvenience" message, but nope, not on Mars.

The response we got was a digital masterpiece that even the technician in charge was flabbergasted at.

The AI's reply went something like, "Congratulations! You've been selected for our exclusive Mars Mix-Up Program. Enjoy your new, unexpected wardrobe additions and the opportunity to forge deeper connections with your fellow Martians through shared clothing experiences. Disclaimer: We are not responsible for any fashion faux pas or accidental color incoordination."

That day we learned that the laundry AI was the cheeky cousin of HAL 9000, minus the homicidal tendencies.

We ended up saving the message and sending it to the communal notice board in the lounge for everyone to enjoy.

It became a running joke—every time someone received a wrong delivery, we'd say, "Ah, the Mars Mix-Up Program strikes again!"

And yet, despite its quirks, I couldn't help but appreciate the system. On Mars, even laundry had to be cutting-edge. It's just... maybe next time, I'll get my own socks back. Maybe.

ΦΦΦ

I strolled into the medical wing of the astronaut training facility, my new role as Commander already feeling like a second skin—albeit a very tight, uncomfortable one.

The doctor in charge, Dr. Holland, was waiting for me, a tablet in hand that I assumed was full of my impending embarrassment, otherwise known as my body composition analysis.

"Morning, Commander Mercer," Dr. Holland greeted me, his tone clinical but not unfriendly. "Ready to go over your results?"

I cringed on the inside.

"As ready as I'll ever be," I replied, trying to sound more confident than I felt. I mean, it's not every day you get a full rundown of how space is going to turn your already weak and somewhat flabby body into a slightly less efficient version of itself.

Dr. Holland tapped on his tablet, bringing up a series of charts and graphs that made me feel like I was back in the academy. "Well, let's start with you. Your body composition is quite good, considering your current activity level. However, we'll need to adjust your diet and exercise routine to prepare you for the stresses of space travel."

He scrolled through the data, pointing out areas for improvement. "Your muscle mass is decent, but we're going to increase your protein intake and start you on a strength training program to combat the muscle atrophy in microgravity. Also, calcium and vitamin D supplements are a must to maintain bone density. We've also noticed a slight anemia," Dr. Holland began, showing me the hemoglobin levels on the chart. "Nothing serious, but we'll need to address it with an iron-rich diet and supplements."

I nodded, mentally preparing myself for what sounded like a regimen fit for an Olympic athlete. "And my team?"

"Let's see," Dr. Holland flipped through the files. "Sam is in great shape, you know. Strong but could use more cardiovascular work. We're putting him on a high-intensity interval training program. Also, his blood pressure is a bit elevated. We're working with him to bring it down. It's nothing serious."

"Luca," he continued, "is more of a tech guy, so his

fitness level isn't quite where we'd like it to be. We're focusing on overall strength and endurance for him."

"And Alex?" I asked, curious about the reclusive biologist.

"Alex is surprisingly fit for someone who spends most of his time in a lab. Still, we're enhancing his flexibility and agility training along with more strength training. Microgravity can be tough on joints and coordination."

With the medical briefing out of the way, it was time to hit the gym— or, as I liked to call it, the agony chamber. We suited up in our sleek, state-of-the-art workout gear, which was supposed to optimize our training but felt more like being hugged by a very clingy octopus. It didn't give us any edge that I could see.

The gym was like a playground from the future.

Every machine was AI-assisted, adjusting resistance and movement in real time to our bodies' responses. I hopped onto a treadmill that promised to "adapt to my unique cardiovascular needs."

I snorted. If it was going to adapt to my needs then it would have to start a casual conversation about my day and offer me a cup of coffee because *that* was about the extent of what got my heart rate up these days.

Well, that and almost falling into volcanos getting Weber's samples.

Sam was already pounding away on another treadmill,

looking like he was born to run. Luca, on the other hand, was getting acquainted with a resistance machine, his expression a mixture of determination and mild terror. Alex was stretching on a mat, his movements precise and fluid. He did have a surprising amount of muscle mass hidden beneath his lab coat.

We worked through our routines, the gym filled with the sounds of exertion and the occasional groan of despair...mostly from Luca.

Every now and then, one of the AI trainers would offer 'encouragement,' which sounded suspiciously like thinly veiled judgment and potential threats.

After an hour of pushing our bodies to their limits, we regrouped, panting and sweating but undeniably invigorated.

I took a moment to address the team. "I just want to say that I think we've got the makings of a great team. I know we'll not only make it to Ganymede, but we'll keep Earth and Mars on the right track in the process. I selected each one of you for a good reason, not only for your scientific specialties but for your characters—the innate qualities that make you who you are. I saw something in each of you that I knew would not only benefit the mission but all of humanity as well. And I hope that by giving a part of yourselves in this project, you'll gain something as well."

I looked at them all and noticed the glint in Luca's eyes.

"And not just a big head and tons of Redcreds, Luca."

They laughed, but their nods of agreement were firm. They all knew the risks...and the potential rewards.

ΦΦΦ

It was time.

Time for me to make the visit that I knew would end up breaking my heart.

As I entered Dr. Johann Weber's office, balancing Jimmy's containment cube in my arms, I noticed him holding a small model, turning it over in his hands with an almost reverent focus. It was a miniature of a satellite, its metallic surface dulled with age.

"What's that?" I asked, nodding towards the model as I approached his desk.

Weber looked up, a bit startled, as if he'd forgotten I was coming. "Ah, this?" He held it up for me to see. "It's a model of Sputnik-1, the first artificial Earth satellite. A little knickknack I picked up during my travels. It's a reminder of humankind's early steps into space."

I leaned in to take a closer look, impressed despite myself. "Sputnik, huh? That's pretty cool."

"Yes, it's a fascinating piece of history," he replied, placing it carefully back on the shelf among other space memorabilia. "But let's focus on the present. Jimmy, right?"

Weber gestured towards the cube in my hands.

I handed the cube to him reluctantly. Inside, the extremophiles I'd been nurturing, my little microbial marvels, vegged out in their artificial habitat. "Yeah, this is Jimmy. Please, take good care of them."

Weber's expression softened as he took the cube, handling it with the utmost care. "I understand how much this means to you, Lena. I assure you, that your research, your discovery, will be treated with the respect it deserves. And you will receive full credit for your work. This is your legacy."

His reassurance did little to ease the ache in my chest as I parted with Jimmy. I'd poured so much of myself into this project, and handing it over felt like leaving a piece of myself behind.

"Thank you, Johann," I managed to say, my voice tinged with a sadness I hadn't expected to feel. "Just keep me updated, okay?"

"Of course, Lena," he said, placing Jimmy's cube on his desk next to the Sputnik model. "Your work is in safe hands."

8.

'63-04

It was April.

Our week of extensive medical testing was complete and we'd all passed with flying colors.

I'd found out, after some focused wheedling of Dr. Holland (cleverly disguised as concern, though I'm not sure he bought it), that each round of exercise machines that we'd spent the week on was not the real fitness equipment that we'd be using.

The AI-controlled monsters that cheerfully demoralized us as we panted and cursed and kept going, were part of an extensive psychology and character assessment. Of course, they were also gauging our fitness levels, but they were judging our strengths and weaknesses, our will to continue in the face of difficulty, and our propensity to give up in the face of some pretty tough physical challenges and name-calling.

Apparently, I'd chosen some pretty tough cookies for the team, and though there were times when I'd wanted to quit early, I never gave in because I knew that I couldn't let my human physical weakness jeopardize the mission or our two worlds.

Adversity— physical or mental—was all a mind game. It was something that I'd learned during my extensive training at the Mars Frontier's Preparatory Academy back on Earth, where Earth's brightest minds all hoped to be selected to attend.

It was where we studied Mars and everything about living, working, and playing on Mars. It was a basic astronaut course of sorts, only without the extremely rigorous standards—after all, we had gravity here, and isolation wasn't a problem unless one wanted it to be.

Today, we'd be beginning the real course and I was both terrified and excited as I geared up for the trip to the Institute's Mission Control facility, a dome field that matched the scale of the Engineering Dome Field and lay just adjacent to it.

There, Mike Donovan and Jim Anderson would meet with Greg Nash and my team. We'd receive our class schedules, training schedules, issued gear, everything.

Mike and Jim would give us the rundown on how the Artemis was coming along, as well as customize the mockups for our simulation training.

Dr. Weber would be managing all of my experiments, my lab, and my side projects while I devoted myself exclusively to the Ganymede Mission.

ΦΦΦ

At the training grounds, the day began with a nutritional powerhouse of a breakfast, which was as strictly regimented as our training schedule.

The menu, curated by our nutritionist Dr. Vega, was high in fats and protein, and low in carbs— a formula meant to fuel our bodies for the rigors of space and the intense strength training regimen.

I eyed the protein shake with a mix of respect and suspicion. It was a thick concoction of whey, omega-3 oils, and a blend of vitamins that sounded more like a science experiment than breakfast. Beside it lay a plate with a steak, eggs fried in real butter, and a glass of rich milk.

"Steak for breakfast, huh?" Luca commented, raising an eyebrow. "I could get used to this astronaut diet."

Sam, enthusiastic for anything edible, was already halfway through his meal. "It's about optimizing our bodies," he said between mouthfuls. "Every calorie, every nutrient, tailored to our needs."

Alex nodded, meticulously cutting his steak. "Saturated fats, structurally speaking, consist of carbon chains fully saturated with hydrogen atoms. They're pivotal in maintaining the integrity of cell membranes, crucial for neuronal functions and synaptic plasticity."

Balancing a forkful of steak, I listened as he elaborated. The others seemed a bit less interested.

"In-depth research, including advanced lipidomics studies, has debunked earlier misconceptions about saturated fats. They're essential for the production of steroid hormones, like cortisol and testosterone, which are crucial under the physiological stress of space travel."

Luca, swirling his protein shake, raised an eyebrow. "So this isn't just about bulking up."

"Exactly," Alex continued, his enthusiasm undimmed. "These fats contribute to mitochondrial health. Mitochondria, our cellular powerhouses, function more efficiently with these fats, optimizing our energy utilization."

"So they're like high-octane fuel for our cells?" Luca asked, snatching another egg.

"Precisely," Alex agreed. "Moreover, in a microgravity environment, where cell deformation is a concern, these fats play a vital role in maintaining cellular structure. They're integral to our space-adapted diet."

I nodded, impressed by his expertise.

"He's 100 percent correct." The clink of cutlery paused as Dr. Hank Wallace appeared in the doorway, his unexpected presence drawing our attention. His gaze swept across the table, lingering on Alex, who continued to eat nonchalantly.

"I know," Alex replied without looking up, his tone calm, betraying his awareness of Hank's approach all along.

I couldn't help but grin as Hank, dressed in the team's workout gear, strode in with an air of familiarity. The sight of him in our uniform was both reassuring and a clear indication of his decision.

He extended a hand to me, a friendly smile on his face. "Commander," he greeted warmly.

The others looked up, surprised, as they realized the significance of his attire. Introductions were exchanged, each team member offering a handshake and a quick summary of their expertise.

A tray identical to ours was placed before Hank, and he dug in with the enthusiasm of someone familiar with the rigor of astronaut training.

"You're all in for quite an education," he said, his grin widening into a wry smile that hinted at the challenges ahead.

I observed the team's reactions—a mix of excitement and a touch of apprehension. It was clear we were all eager to learn, yet unaware of the full extent of what lay ahead. Hank's expression said it all. He knew the reality of astronaut training: the grueling hours and the intense physical and mental demands. Ours would be even more intense because it was accelerated.

"Excitement is good, but brace yourselves," Hank cautioned between mouthfuls. "It's going to be tough, but trust me, it's worth every drop of sweat and every moment of frustration."

Luca nodded. "I'm looking forward to pushing my limits," he said, his tone conveying both determination and a touch of naivety.

Sam smirked.

As I listened to their banter, I felt a sense of another puzzle piece falling into place. Hank's arrival solidified our crew a little more, bringing both his medical expertise and his veteran experience in space training.

Our conversation shifted to the upcoming schedule, the simulations, the academic sessions, and the physical training regimen. Hank shared insights from his past experiences, offering tips and advice that only someone who had been through it could provide.

Hank leaned back in his chair as we finished breakfast, a reflective gaze in his eyes, and the atmosphere around the table shifted. There was an unmistakable depth to his presence, a weight of experience that commanded respect and something the team had lacked before.

"You know, on the Venus mission, things didn't go exactly as planned," Hank began, his voice steady but hinting at the underlying currents of a deeper, more turbulent history. "One thing I learned is that space missions are as much about mental endurance as they are about physical or technical prowess."

I noticed a subtle change in his demeanor as he mentioned the Venus mission. His gaze was momentarily distant as if he was revisiting a memory he'd rather keep locked away.

"Commander Fuller... well, let's just say he wasn't prepared for the psychological toll," Hank continued, carefully choosing his words. "Space can play tricks on you, and it's not just about how smart or physically fit you are. It's about how you handle the unexpected, the pressure, the isolation. Commander Fuller was an experienced shuttle pilot and mission commander. He had decades of flights and years of space under his belt. In the end, I think the vastness of it all got to him. I think, in the end, he forgot what he was flying for."

He paused, his eyes meeting each of ours in turn, imparting a silent message of the seriousness of the journey we were about to undertake. "Stay vigilant, not just with the equipment or your physical health, but with your minds. Talk, support each other, talk to me. Don't let the walls of space confine your thoughts. Don't let it loom large in your minds."

There were solemn nods from Sam and Luca, and an understanding glance from Alex—as if he'd himself experienced something similar. I didn't know him, perhaps he had.

We all felt the gravity of Hank's words, the unspoken story of a mission that had taken more than it had given.

"Resilience, that's key," Hank added, tapping the tabletop with a slight smile returning to his face. "You'll find strength in each other. Trust in that. And hey, a good sense of humor doesn't hurt either."

After breakfast, our trainer, a no-nonsense former military sergeant named Dan Huxley, led us to the gym. Here, the real challenge began.

The resistance trainers were state-of-the-art machines, calibrated to simulate a higher gravity environment. It felt like working out with an invisible, heavy blanket draped over us.

"This is to prepare your muscles," Huxley explained. "In space, muscle atrophy is your enemy. We combat it here."

The classroom sessions were a deep dive into astronautics.

Dr. Higgs (no relation to the boson, he assured us with a goofy smile) had us poring over textbooks on orbital mechanics, spacecraft systems, and astrophysics.

It was a crash course in rocket science, literally. My brain felt like it was doing somersaults trying to keep up with the equations and concepts. Luca, ever the quick learner, was scribbling notes at the speed of light, while Sam and Alex seemed equally absorbed, their brows furrowed in concentration. Hank sat in the back, following along with a battered binder that I assumed held his notes from his prior training.

Midway through the morning, our project coordinator, Jenna Torres stepped into the classroom. A meticulous organizer with a clipboard always in hand, she was the one who would keep our training and mission prep on track.

"Good morning, Artemis crew," she greeted us. "I have some news. Starting today, you'll be moving into the new quarters here at the facility. It's part of the immersive training experience."

There was a collective murmur of surprise. Moving in meant we were stepping into a new level of commitment. Our mission was becoming our life.

The new quarters were sleek and functional, designed to mimic the living conditions aboard the Artemis. The idea was to acclimate us to the confined space and communal living we'd experience during the mission.

"Think of it as a preview of your home in space," Jenna explained. "Each of you will have a personal pod but shared living areas. It's important to build that sense of team unity and adaptability."

As the day wound down, I looked over my new living quarters.

The empty pods in our new home taunted me. If we couldn't find a pilot, our mission would never leave the surface of Mars.

ΦΦΦ

The place was buzzing with anticipation and a bit of uncertainty. We were all decked out in our workout gear, each of us subtly assessing the others, when Mike Donovan and Jim Alexander walked in, flanked by two strangers.

"This is Jax Hartley," Mike introduced, gesturing towards one of the men. "Best pilot I know, and he's going to be leading the flight to Ganymede if you'll have him."

Jax had an air of professionalism about him that set me at ease, his piercing blue eyes scanning the room as he gave a firm nod. This was no hotshot rookie pilot with a head too big for his shoulders. Jax was the real deal.

I'd still check his creds later. I wanted to know the details.

"And this young genius here," Mike continued, pointing to a wiry man with untidy brown hair and round glasses, "is Theo Jameson, from my engineering team. He knows the Artemis inside out. We call him TJ."

We exchanged greetings, and I could see the team was sizing up our new members. Jax's military background and direct manner were evident, while TJ's inquisitive nature shone through his detailed descriptions of the Artemis's systems.

"Now all we're missing is a Flight Engineer," I said, trying to keep the mood light despite the growing pressure.

The room fell into an awkward silence until Jim broke it with a pointed look at Mike. "No, you aren't."

Mike sighed, exchanging a glance with Hank before turning to face me. "Commander Mercer," he started, and I could sense the gravity in his voice, "I'll be your Flight Engineer if you want me."

A ripple of surprise went through the room. My heart skipped a beat. His experience and insight would be *invaluable*, and his willingness to join us spoke volumes about his commitment to the mission.

I extended my hand, and as Mike shook it firmly, I couldn't help but smile broadly. "We've got our team," I declared, feeling a surge of confidence.

And I was surprised, not just at the offer but also at the unexpected flutter of attraction I felt towards Mike as he shook my hand.

Crap.

ΦΦΦ

In the conference room at the astronaut training facility, I found myself with the team, eagerly awaiting a technical briefing from Mike Donovan and Jim Alexander.

The atmosphere was charged with a blend of anticipation and concentration, like the calm before a complex scientific storm.

Mike initiated the briefing, focusing on his HoloPad. "Let's dive straight into the mechanics of getting the Artemis off Mars and en route to Ganymede. It's a substantial undertaking," he informed.

A holographic model of Artemis materialized in front of us, impressively detailed.

"We begin with the chemical rockets for the initial boost," Mike explained. "These are specifically designed to push us out of Mars's gravity and into a stable orbit."

Jim pointed. "We've customized these boosters to match Artemis's unique specifications. It's a carefully calculated process to ensure a successful lift-off."

"The real game-changer is the Graviton Impulse Drive, the GID," Mike continued. "Once in orbit, the transition to the GID is gradual. It's engineered for a steady increase to our cruising velocity over approximately a week."

"What kind of speeds are we talking about once we

reach this cruising velocity?" I inquired, curious.

Jim answered in a matter-of-fact tone. "Significantly faster than traditional propulsion methods, but we're not breaking any light-speed records. The GID operates on principles of spacetime manipulation, efficient over long distances."

Mike pointed at the Artemis hologram. "It's a fine balance. The GID accelerates us without compromising the structural integrity of the spacecraft or the crew. Artemis is more than a vehicle, it's our habitat and research station all in one."

Understanding the scope of our journey, I nodded. "So, we gradually ramp up to our top speed, maintaining it until we approach Ganymede?"

"Exactly," Mike confirmed, a hint of a smile on his lips. "Efficiency and precision are key."

"What happens if it suddenly goes out?" Alex asked, narrowing his eyes at the model projection.

"It won't," Jim said. "There are layers upon layers of safety mechanisms."

"But if it does?"

Mike breathed in and nodded. "Then we'd have one hell of a rough ride and a very premature end."

"There are layers of mechanisms," Jim said after we all stared at them for a few moments in shock. "Many layers."

ΦΦΦ

As I led my team into the private dining room I'd reserved in Mars Vegas, I couldn't help but marvel at the blend of Martian technology, AI sophistication, and the opulence reminiscent of a fancy hotel in Las Vegas.

The room was a spectacle of luxury, with a ceiling displaying a simulated Earth sky, and walls adorned with interactive holographic landscapes and city scenes that shifted subtly, creating an ambiance that was both surreal and comforting. Right now, we were in a simulated Las Vegas strip scene. The dazzling lights of the hotels and the casinos at night shone in on us. People walked by wearing their finest clothes, having conversations, and looking around.

If I didn't know it was an AI simulation, I'd have thought it was 100 percent real.

We were seated at a long table, draped in white linen, with settings that seemed too elegant for a simple team dinner. I had chosen a conservative party dress (Aka not my clubwear) for the occasion, fitting my role as the commander, while the others varied in their formal attire, from Alexei and Hank's sharp suits to Sam's more relaxed look.

The first course arrived, a delicately-plated appetizer that was a testament to Martian culinary artistry.

"You know, if I wasn't about to get my butt kicked in astronaut boot camp, I'd be worried about the calories," I joked, trying to lighten the mood.

Mike chuckled as he broke a bread roll, a product of imported Earth agriculture. We had grain domes here on Mars but they didn't yield nearly enough for our needs.

"So, Alexei," I began, intrigued, "what steered you from Earth microbiology to the mysteries of extraterrestrial life?"

Alexei, looking very elegant in his suit, seemed to brighten at the question. "Well, it was the allure of the unknown. Microbiology taught me the complexities of life on Earth, but the thought of discovering entirely new life forms on other planets? That's a frontier that's hard to resist...and I had to leave the country very quickly."

I blinked, nonplussed. *Okay.*

Sam, who had been quietly observing the dish in front of him, chimed in with a grin. "So, hunting for Martian microbes wasn't exciting enough for you, huh?"

Alexei smiled. "There's excitement in the microscopic, sure, but imagine the thrill of encountering something no one on Earth has ever seen. That's what drives me, that and the wish for a better life."

TJ leaned forward, his interest piqued. "But how do you prepare for something entirely unknown? It's not like you can train for that."

"That's where the challenge lies," Alexei replied. "You

dive into the unknown with a foundation of knowledge, then adapt and learn. It's a constant journey of discovery."

I nodded, impressed. "That adaptability will be crucial for us. And speaking of journeys, Alexei, where did yours begin? What's your story before Mars?"

Alexei glanced around the table, a reflective look crossing his face. "I grew up in St. Petersburg, surrounded by a rich history of science and exploration. My parents were both scientists, so the dinner table conversations were always about the latest discoveries. I guess you could say science runs in my blood. Of course, this was after the NUSR and so we had to hide our interests."

The NUSR, or "Nusar" as we called it, stood for the New Union of Socialist Republics. In 2029, under the leadership of the Zhdanov Brigade, a neo-Bolshevik faction, Russia took a turn for the worse yet again. Censorship and persecution were rampant. Many artists and scientists escaped to the West to continue their work in relative freedom. Because of the oppression and the brain drain, their economy slumped once again.

Last I'd heard there were rumblings of an opposition forming, but not much news left the NUSR that the Zhdanovists didn't want to spread.

It wouldn't surprise me a bit if they were involved in the push against Mars Colony One.

Luca, sensing the sudden tension, changed the path of

the conversation and raised his glass in a toast. "To science in our blood and the mysteries of space on our plates!"

The table erupted in laughter with Alex looking visibly relieved, and as it subsided, Jax leaned across the table. "Ever think of going back, Alexei? To Earth, I mean."

Alex's expression turned contemplative. "Sometimes, yes. But Mars, the Institute, the work we're doing here—it's become a part of who I am. Earth is my past, but Mars? Mars is my future and we have liberty here. Freedom."

I watched as the team absorbed Alex's words. It struck me then how each of us had left something behind on Earth to pursue this incredible journey. Our mission was more than a scientific endeavor; it was a collection of individual dreams converging into one shared goal.

"What's the one thing you miss about Earth?" TJ asked before taking another bite.

Alex smiled softly. "The rivers. There's something about the flow of water that's both calming and powerful. Mars has its beauty, but Earth's rivers have a melody you can't find anywhere else."

Mike nodded in agreement. "There's a lot we've recreated here on Mars, but some things, like the sound of flowing water, are unique to our home planet."

As we moved on to the second course, a richly flavored soup that hinted at Earth's culinary heritage yet carried a distinctly Martian twist, I turned my attention to Mike.

There was something about him, an air of rugged experience mixed with a quiet intellect, that I found intriguing.

"Mike, tell me about your journey into aerospace engineering. What drew you to the stars?" I asked, trying to sound casual, though I felt the faintest flutter of something that I refused to name or acknowledge.

Mike leaned back, his broad shoulders relaxing as he recounted his story. "Well, it started with model rockets, believe it or not. As a kid, I was fascinated by the idea of something soaring high into the sky, reaching places I could only dream of. Of course, I was born way before the Haakon Incident so I remember the time when reaching Mars was only a distant dream."

TJ got excited. "Oh yeah, you lived before the space boom! I can't imagine what it was like, just having one world."

I smiled as Jax shook his head ruefully.

Sam grinned. "So, you went from toy rockets to the Graviton Impulse Drive? That's one heck of an upgrade."

Mike chuckled, his eyes twinkling with good humor. "It's been quite the journey. But honestly, it's the challenge that keeps me going. Pushing the boundaries of what's possible, especially with something as revolutionary as the GID."

I found myself admiring not just his technical expertise,

but also the passion with which he spoke about his work. "And what about your life before Mars? What's one thing you miss from back home?"

Mike paused, his expression turning reflective. "It's the open spaces for me—the mountains, the trails, the sound of birds. There's a freedom in being surrounded by nature that's hard to replicate on Mars. Climbing red rocks in a Marswalker while listening to your own breathing just isn't the same."

Luca raised his glass with a smile. "To the mountains and stars and rivers, then."

As the team echoed Luca's sentiment, I noticed Jax's inquisitive look. "Ever think about exploring the uncharted territories of Mars?"

Mike's face lit up with the suggestion. "The thought is compelling. There's still so much to discover here. It won't be like mountain climbing on Earth though," he said, sitting back in his chair and glancing at me.

TJ sipped his drink and settled more comfortably in his chair. "I've always been amazed by your ability to solve complex engineering problems. It's like you see solutions where others see obstacles."

Mike gave a modest shrug. "It's all about perspective. Problems are just puzzles waiting to be solved. And in space, the puzzles are just bigger and more complex."

It was so close to my comment to Alex during his

interview that it was eerie. Maybe the master engineer and I were more alike than not.

As the conversation drifted to tales of engineering feats and Martian explorations, I couldn't help but steal glances at Mike, appreciating not just his mind, but the subtle strength of his character.

I chided myself, but I couldn't shake off the feeling that there was much more to Mike Donovan than met the eye.

As Mike and TJ delved into an animated discussion about engineering with Alex and Jax, my attention was drawn to a quieter conversation unfolding between Luca and Hank.

I observed them from my end of the table, curious about the dynamic between our communications expert and the medic. They were seated adjacent to each other, their body language open and engaged.

Though Hank was obviously a Texan, and Luca was as Italian as could be, they were very similar in personality. They had a manner that put people at ease.

"So, Hank," Luca began, swirling the drink in his glass. "I've always been curious. What's it like dealing with medical emergencies in space? It must be quite different from Earth."

Hank nodded, his expression turning thoughtful. "It's challenging. Space adds a whole new layer of complexity to medical care. You have to be prepared for anything, and sometimes improvisation is key. But the advancements in space telehealth have been a game-changer."

Luca leaned in, intrigued. "Telehealth? Like remote consultations?"

"Yep," Hank replied. "With the delays in communication, real-time assistance isn't always possible, but we've developed protocols that allow us to consult with specialists on Earth effectively. We use a mix of pre-recorded guidance, AI assistance, and, when the timing lines up, live consultations."

I watched as Luca's eyes lit up with understanding. "That's fascinating. It's like taking the concept of long-distance communication to a whole new level."

Hank smiled, his demeanor reflecting both pride and humility. "It is. And it's crucial for keeping the crew healthy. Without immediate access to full medical facilities, we rely heavily on these technologies."

Luca nodded thoughtfully. "I guess that puts a lot of pressure on our communication systems, ensuring they're always operational and efficient."

Hank agreed. "Absolutely. The work you do in keeping us connected, not just for operational purposes but for our health, it's invaluable."

As their conversation continued, drifting from medical challenges to the nuances of communication in space, I sensed a growing camaraderie between the two men.

They were from different worlds professionally, yet here they were, finding common ground in the unique challenges of space travel.

The next course brought a selection of Martian-grown vegetables.

The waitress seemed to have been alerted to who we were and was now shooting Alex and Sam assessing looks. I admit, they were the most conventionally handsome men of the group, but I had an inkling that it was their status as some of the next men slated to explore the unknown that drew her attention.

I shook my head and turned my attention to Jax while we ate the elaborate vegetable creations in front of us.

"So, adapting your military skills to civilian spaceflight, especially with the Graviton Impulse Drive, must be an interesting transition."

Jax nodded. "In the air or space, the principles are the same. It's about adapting and mastering the controls."

"What was your life like back on Earth in the military?" I asked, genuinely curious about the man behind the pilot.

Jax leaned back, a faint smile playing on his lips. "It was structured, disciplined. But it taught me a lot—about leadership, about responsibility. And, of course, about flying. I've always loved the thrill of being in the air, pushing the limits of what's possible."

I nodded, understanding the allure. "I had a bit of that

thrill too, back in my early days at the Institute's training academy. I went to the one in Nashville. It was a different kind of flying, though, more theoretical than literal...except when I did that flight simulation," I laughed. "Let's just say I'm glad you all aren't counting on me to fly the Artemis."

Jax laughed then his eyes sharpened with interest. "Mars Frontier Research Training Academy in Nashville? I attended an advanced seminar there about 11 or 12 years ago," he paused and counted back on his fingers. "Yeah, about '51. It was about interdisciplinary approaches to space exploration."

I blinked in surprise. "Really? I was there!"

"There weren't that many people there." Jax furrowed his brow. "I can't seem to place you, though."

I chuckled and gestured to my hips. "Well, back then, my hair was much, much longer."

His expression cleared, and he snapped his fingers. "Right! I remember now. You had on that dress."

I covered my face, laughing. "I blame that on the history course I took the semester before."

The others, overhearing our exchange, joined in, curious about my time at the academy.

Sam leaned forward, sliding his empty cup to the side for a refill. "So, Commander, what else should we know about your academy days?"

I smiled, reflecting on those formative years. "Well, I

went there straight from junior high school. I convinced my parents that high school held no benefit for me and that I wanted to study for the entrance exams at MRFI." I smiled. "I got into their Nashville school and it was where I first developed my love for astrobiology. And the training exercises were no joke—everything from advanced astrophysics to survival training in the field."

Mike, who had been listening intently, chimed in. "Wait, did you say you were in Nashville? I grew up about an hour away from there, in Cookeville."

My eyes widened. "Are you serious? That's incredible. I've been there several times. The university there has a great science department," I said, leaning toward him a bit more. "It's a small world, or should I say, a small universe?"

He raised his glass and grinned at me and it seemed to have broken the collective ice between all of us.

The conversation blossomed from there, each of us sharing snippets of our Earth lives. It was fascinating to discover some of the intersections of our past experiences, the small threads that connected us long before we became a team heading for Ganymede.

As the dinner progressed, with each course surpassing the last in Martian culinary innovation, the conversation among us grew more animated, lubricated by the steady flow of drinks. I could feel the slight buzz from the wine, a pleasant warmth that made the lights of the simulated Las

Vegas outside seem to dance.

"So, Rockhound," I said, turning to Sam with a playful grin. "What's the craziest thing you've found out in the wild?"

Sam chuckled, swirling his drink. "Found an old satellite once, crashed and buried. Felt like uncovering a treasure."

"Try finding a lost astronaut during a spacewalk training. Thought he was gone for good. Turned out the guy was clinging to the side of the comms array. Talk about a wild day at the office!" Hank interjected, a little more exuberant than normal.

We all laughed, the sound mingling with the distant clinking of slot machines and the thump of club music from afar.

I looked at TJ, who was studying the AI control panel on the wall. "What about you, Gadget? Any cool inventions we should know about?"

He smiled at the nickname. "Well, back at the academy in Texas, I rigged up a makeshift rover from spare parts. It worked, mostly. Only broke down twice out of five runs. Crashed twice too though."

"Only twice, huh?" Luca said with a laugh. "Some good odds right there."

Mike raised his glass. "To crashing and learning," he toasted, and we all joined in, the clink of our glasses ringing clear.

Alex, usually more reserved, began sharing stories of his childhood in St. Petersburg, his eyes alight with memories.

After hearing about his childhood in NUSR dodging Zhdanov Brigade censorship and imprisonment, I understood more about his constant vigilance.

"And what about you?" I asked Jax, intrigued by his quiet demeanor.

Jax took a slow sip of his drink. "Flying's always been my life. But there's something about piloting through space, it's... different. More serene."

"Serene but lonely?" I probed gently.

He nodded. "Sometimes. But being part of this team, this mission... it's a good kind of different."

"No family?" I probed.

He shook his head. "Not anymore."

I sensed a sore spot and I didn't pry anymore. He'd tell me if and when he wanted to. I wouldn't press him unless it interfered with the mission.

The courses came and went, and the barriers between us seemed to dissolve a little more. Our laughter grew louder and our stories more personal.

By the time we reached the seventh course, an innovative meat substitute dish, laughter and lively discussions filled the air. We shared more stories of Earth, our families, and the experiences that led us to this moment.

We concluded the dinner with a chocolate dessert that was both delicious and gravity-defying, and as we walked out under the dome's simulated starlit sky, I glanced back at them.

Their faces were illuminated by the vibrant multi-colored glow of Mars Vegas, each showing a mix of satisfaction and anticipation as we walked down the boulevard and chatted. I felt happy.

This was just the beginning.

On the way back to the training dome, Mike and I walked side by side while the others left to go their separate ways for the rest of the evening.

Our footsteps echoed softly on the metallic pathway. The air was cooler. It was a welcome relief from the warmth of the dining room.

"So, Commander," Mike began, his voice casual but with an undercurrent of something I couldn't quite place. "Think the team's ready for what lies ahead?"

I glanced at him, noticing a faint smile on his face. "I think so. They're a strong group, with diverse skills, good chemistry. No real personality conflicts that I noticed."

He nodded, his eyes briefly meeting mine before looking ahead. "Yeah, they're a good bunch. And you'll do a great job leading them. Not an easy task."

I felt a faint warmth at his words. "Thanks, Mike. It's a

team effort. Your expertise with the Artemis and the GID is invaluable. With you on the team, our chances of success have skyrocketed."

We walked in comfortable silence for a moment, the only sound the distant hum of the dome's life support systems and our footsteps. Not many people passed us once we got through the communal hub of the MFRI domes and toward the outer edge of the facility.

As we approached the tunnel to the dome that housed our quarters and the training facility, Mike paused, looking up at the stars visible through the transparent ceiling.

"You ever just stop and look at these stars? Think about how far we've come?"

I followed his gaze, the stars a glittering tapestry above us. "All the time. It puts things into perspective, doesn't it?"

"It does," he agreed softly. "Makes you appreciate the now, the people you're with."

There was a hint of something in his voice, a depth that suggested more than just a casual comment.

"Well, thanks for walking me back, Mike," I said, as we reached our cramped quarters.

"Anytime," he replied, his smile genuine but guarded. "See you tomorrow for the briefing."

"See you then," I said, turning to enter my small room.

I felt a strange mix of emotions—a connection, yes, but overshadowed by the weight of the responsibility I carried.

This mission, our goal, was bigger than any personal feelings. It had to be.

ΦΦΦ

The tension in the Artemis was palpable as the countdown echoed through the cabin.

"T-minus ten seconds," Nash announced from Mission Control, his voice the epitome of cool.

I could feel my heart racing as the jolts and thumps of launchpad disengagement sounded, though muffled through the multiple thick layers of shielding.

"Five... Four... Three... Two... One... Ignition."

The initial thrusters roared to life, shuddering through the Artemis as we ascended. So far, so good.

But then, as we hit the upper reaches of Mars' atmosphere, something went horribly wrong.

"Malfunction in the initial thrusters." Jax's voice cut through the cabin's sudden shrieking alarm. "Thruster path misalignment in section A. It's overheating the Graviton Impulse Drive!"

I braced myself, trying to maintain my composure as I ran through the abort sequence commands in my head.

Then came the explosion. A blinding flash from the Graviton Impulse Drive screen and then the shockwave sent a shuddering pulse through the ship. Alarms blared and red lights flashed as our control systems went dead, plunging us into chaos.

Damn! Damn! Damn!

I blew out a breath, sequences running through my mind. My hands were shaking and my heart felt like it was about to splatter against my chest wall.

You are a scientist. Think logically, I told myself.

"Team, immediate status report, now!" my voice cut through the tension in the Artemis's control room. My fingers danced haltingly across the diagnostic panel, pulling up vital data and a few very unnecessary screens by mistake. I clenched my teeth and closed them out.

"Jax, what's our trajectory? I need to know our spin and orientation."

I just hoped he gave it to me in civilian terms.

Jax responded with a familiar strained calmness, something I thought that every pilot who ever flew anything must have been trained in. "We're veering off course, Commander. Correcting it now. But this spin isn't helping."

The malfunctioning thruster was causing us to go into a huge spin, like a large loop-de-loop...which probably wasn't optimal for getting us anywhere but dead, fast.

It was also making me a bit nauseous.

My gaze flicked to the overheating alerts on the screen. "Mike, I need that thruster offline, like yesterday. Can you manually override it?"

My voice was shaky from the vibrations trembling through my shock-absorbing seat. I hoped he didn't think it was nerves.

I was kind of just going through the motions on that one anyway, Mike was probably already ten steps ahead of me and waiting for me to catch up.

"Already working on it. Disengaging the malfunctioning thruster. Should stabilize the heating issue."

Oh yeah, that was definitely a not-so-subtle hint. I wondered if anyone else caught it.

The tension was palpable as I shifted my focus to the cooling systems. "TJ, engage all auxiliary cooling systems for the GID. We need those temperatures down ASAP."

"Auxiliary coolants are online. Activating heat exchangers now," TJ affirmed.

This was *much* harder than it had looked on paper.

Jax's voice broke through again, a bit more controlled this time. "Stabilizing our trajectory using secondary thrusters. It's a bit of a rough ride, but we'll hold steady."

I nodded, my eyes never leaving the readouts. "I'm running a structural integrity check. Keep an eye on your stations for any damage reports, especially around the GID."

As the diagnostics ran, my thoughts raced to the worst-case scenario. "Doc, prepare for a potential evac. Check life support and comms systems in the escape pods. Make sure they're ready, just in case."

"On it, Commander. Ensuring pods are prepped and ready," Hank acknowledged.

My hand hovered over the comms. "Okay, we'll get through this. Mike, Jax, TJ, keep me updated on the thruster and trajectory status. Luca, maintain open lines with Mission Control. We need them in the loop. And Hank, once you've checked the pods, assist with monitoring crew vitals.

"Secondary thruster going offline!" Jax alerted, just as a sector of the ship went black on my screen. "We're spinning. I can't hold her!"

I thumped my head against the back of the seat, the helmet absorbing the impact and blunting my efforts at relieving the stress.

"Evacuate! Abort mission!" I commanded, just as the simulation alarms blared the end of the exercise.

The tension in the cabin evaporated, replaced by a collective sigh of relief. I was dripping with nervous sweat.

We unstrapped ourselves, each of us processing the intense drill.

Mike was the first to break the silence. "I've identified the issue," he began. "There was a misalignment in the safety protocols of the initial thruster system. It seems the protocols weren't properly updated to align with the recent AI software upgrade. This oversight led to a recursive error in the AI's navigation algorithms, causing it to generate conflicting thruster commands."

He beckoned me over to the tight engineering screen section and pointed at a holographic schematic.

I followed his finger as he described the malfunction that led to our violent demise.

"The AI's malfunction triggered a feedback loop, which then led to an operational failure in the Graviton Impulse Drive. Essentially, the AI issued repeated and contradictory instructions to the thrusters, causing them to overwork and overheat. This, in turn, created an excessive thermal load on the GID, leading to its shutdown as a fail-safe response. The AI error also bypassed the manual overrides for the secondary thruster systems, which prevented us from regaining immediate control. We'll need to reconfigure the AI's integration with the thruster control systems and ensure that the manual override protocols are prioritized in future scenarios. It's a straightforward fix, but a critical one to prevent similar issues during the actual mission."

I shook my head and clicked my tongue. "Yeah, straightforward fix."

Mike looked at me and winked. "You did very well for a newbie."

"I killed us all," I said dryly.

"Nah, software killed us all," he joked, then turned serious. "We'll get it. This is all a part of the process."

Jim's voice came through from Mission Control. "Good work, team. Let's debrief, update the thruster, and prepare to run it again. These simulations are key to ironing out these kinks."

After the Artemis mockup simulation, we stripped out of our outer gear and trudged out of the simulator for a much-needed break. The tension in the air had lifted, but it was replaced by a collective weariness.

I stretched my arms above my head, feeling every muscle protest.

This morning had started like any other in our new, snug living quarters. Waking up extremely sore in a space barely larger than a closet was an experience. I had a new irrational fear of suffocating. And let's not even talk about the joys of communal bathrooms.

There's nothing quite like the bonding experience of waiting in line for a two-minute shower while someone was singing 80-year-old, off-key hits.

Breakfast had been the same high-fat, high-protein, low-carb affair: bacon, omelets stuffed with cheese and ham, and milk. All top-notch stuff, but my stomach was still negotiating terms with the new diet.

I missed the simplicity of a bowl of cereal or a piece of

toast. I missed sugar. And my body was staging a full-blown rebellion over the reduced coffee intake. Caffeine withdrawal was no joke. It turned out that my brain was a bit of a diva without its usual hit.

As we lounged in the break room, I noticed everyone else was feeling the effects too.

Sam was rubbing his temples, probably nursing a headache like mine. Alex kept stretching his neck, looking a bit stiff. Luca, well, he always looked like he just stepped out of a yoga class, but even he seemed a bit off, eyeing the coffee machine like it was a long-lost lover.

"Man, I miss carbs," Sam grumbled, sinking into a chair.

"I miss sleeping without someone's snoring as my lullaby," I shot back, trying to keep the mood light.

Alex chuckled. "And I miss the luxury of a big, long shower. But hey, at least we're getting a real astronaut experience, right?"

Luca nodded, pouring himself a small cup of coffee. "And think about it, we're getting physically fitter. I bet we could all run a marathon by the end of this."

"Speak for yourself," I muttered, reaching for a bottle of water. I was an addict. I couldn't have just one small cup of coffee without wanting the whole pot. "Right now, I'd settle for a headache-free day."

As we sipped our drinks and chatted, I couldn't help but feel a deep sense of belonging. Sure, the living conditions were cramped, and the diet change was a challenge, but it was these small, shared experiences that were slowly but surely turning us from individuals into a cohesive team.

That, and the whole dying-in-the-simulator thing.

Our break was short-lived. Jim, Mike, Jax, and TJ soon called us back to the simulator for another run. The drive malfunction had been fixed, and it was time to get back to work.

9.

'63-07

Raj threw a non-reconstituted French fry at my face and jolted me back to Mars.

For some reason, he liked to crunch on the disgusting things without hydrating them first. I didn't know why. They weren't even greasy.

I had been on a mostly red meat and dairy diet for a solid three months. I had no cravings for anything else anymore, and the one time I did try out a piece of cake, I almost passed out from the sugar rush. It left me shaky and tired and thoroughly disgusted with myself.

I learned my lesson.

"Keep those nasty things away from me," I chided. "You'll ruin my astronautliness. I'm not even supposed to touch whatever that's made of. In fact, you probably just compromised my whole mission."

"You are looking fit and fine," he whistled. "All jacked." He squeezed my bicep experimentally with a frown.

I raised an eyebrow.

"That is not fair," he said, squeezing again. "I work out."

"Not enough," I teased. "So, what's the deal? How are my things?"

"Your office is great, much better than mine, so I moved in there. You know, just to keep an eye on things for you. The plants are dead."

"What?! How?"

He shrugged. "They just faded away, quite pathetically. I don't think they enjoyed the soil profile."

I rolled my eyes. "Just don't touch my frozen samples or my schedule settings."

He scratched his head and sighed before leaning forward. He was very serious this time, and I knew something was up.

"I overheard Dr. Weber discussing the Ganymede Signal with Dr. Park one morning as I eavesdropped outside of his office—you know how he likes to leave the door open."

I nodded, feeling a tingle of warning.

"The signal is *changing*," he whispered. "It is very slight, and only one of the top analysts caught it. They're trying to keep it on the down low so word doesn't get out. I guess they're afraid it will derail the tentative truce we've got going on."

My breath stuttered and I could feel a tunnel-vision sensation take over as I leaned in, something Mike had been trying to break me of inside the sims. Tunnel vision could lead to missing a critical error on the systems.

"What do you mean it's changed? Why did anyone tell me?" I demanded.

Raj's expression was somber. "It's getting weaker, Len. The signal's strength isn't what it was when the probe first picked it up. It's like... it's fading away, bit by bit."

My heart sank. The Ganymede Signal had been a constant in my life for the past few months, a beacon of mystery and hope. The idea that it might just vanish was unsettling. "Weaker how? Is it fading...dying? Is it losing detail?"

"Well, it just seems weaker. They didn't go into detail right then, " Raj scratched his chin. "If it's being generated by something— or *someone*—then maybe it's losing power or... who knows, maybe it's just getting tired of calling out into the void."

"And they didn't think to tell me this?!" I asked, outraged.

Everything I'd been working toward could be compromised and they hadn't even sent me a *note?*

I could feel my ears getting hot, and my fists were clenched so hard that my forearms were cramping up.

"Look, I just heard this yesterday. Maybe they are planning to tell you."

I stood up, my chair scraping against the floor. "I need to talk to Dr. Park. Now. If this signal goes dark before we get there, we might miss whatever or whoever is at the other end. This could change everything."

Raj nodded. "You should. And hey, Lena," he added as I began to stride away. "Don't worry too much. You've got the best minds in the solar system working on this. We won't let that signal slip away."

His words were meant to be reassuring, but they did little to calm the storm of thoughts raging in my mind. As I walked towards the Admin Dome, I couldn't help but feel a sense of urgency.

The Ganymede mission had always been a race against time, but now it felt like we were racing against something far more unpredictable.

Reaching Dr. Park's office, I used my unofficial superstar status for personal gain for once and bypassed the secretary, who sputtered a bit as I passed.

I took a deep breath and knocked on the door.

She opened it, her face a mask of professionalism. "Commander Mercer, what can I do for you?"

"Dr. Park, we need to talk about the Ganymede Signal,"

I said, trying to keep my voice steady. "I was just informed that it's weakening. We need to expedite our preparations. Whatever is out there, it might not be there much longer."

Dr. Park's eyes narrowed slightly as she ushered me inside. "I was going to discuss this with you later today. Yes, the signal's change has been noted. It's subtle but significant. We're analyzing it, but the implications are... unclear."

"Unclear or not, we can't afford to lose this opportunity. This mission... it's more than just exploration now," I said, determination steeling my voice.

Dr. Park sighed. "I understand your concern, Commander. We'll do everything in our power to ensure you and your team are ready to launch as soon as possible. The eyes of two worlds are on this mission. Failure is not an option."

“Meet me at the training facility conference room at” —I checked the time on my mini-comms— “1400. I’ll be there with the team and the Mission Control Director. You bring the data and the analysts, *in person*.”

I left Dr. Park's office, striding down the corridor with angry steps and racing thoughts. The Ganymede Signal was fading.

I shot off a comms alert to the team with the brief directive and raced to the rover bay for a ride.

It was as I was speeding toward the training dome that

I realized that I had barked orders at Mars Colony One's second-in-command.

Oops.

ΦΦΦ

I gathered the team and Greg Nash in the conference room, a sleek large room surrounded by screens that usually showed mission progress or astronaut sim training replays for debriefing.

Nash called in his top controllers for the meeting, and Dr. Park showed up with a real entourage, including the governor.

In my time at Mars Colony One, I'd been in my fair share of meetings, but this one was shaping up to be a blockbuster.

Dr. Park, Governor Olsen, and Nash stood at the front, their faces a mix of seriousness and urgency. The rest of us, my team and I, sat clustered together, like kids called to the principal's office.

Sam was tapping his fingers on the table, a nervous habit of his that I'd noticed. Alexei was staring intently at a spot on the wall, probably contemplating the biological implications of a wall stain or maybe making a mental map of all potential escape routes should things go downhill.

Luca, as usual, was the picture of calm, but even he

seemed a bit more on edge today.

Then there was me, Commander of the Artemis mission in my sleek black uniform with my badges and rank, trying to look like I had it all together.

Spoiler alert: I didn't, but I sure as hell looked like I did. A sharp uniform and a good poker face could cover a multitude of inadequacies.

Nash stepped forward first, bringing in a few folks I hadn't met before. "This is Dr. Nora Kim, our Payload and Science Director," he started, pointing to a woman whose sharp gaze suggested she could probably solve quantum equations in her sleep.

Dr. Kim nodded to me without a hint of emotion on her face. "Commander Mercer. We were supposed to meet during the second evolution of your training."

It sounded vaguely like an accusation...like I had upset her agenda.

I lifted my chin and raised an eyebrow before nodding back. I could be frostier than Ganymede if I wanted to be.

"Adrian Sato, our Data Processing Systems Engineer," he continued, introducing a guy who looked like he'd be more at home in a cyberpunk novel than a Mars base.

"And Marcus Reed, Engineering Systems Director." Marcus gave a nod that was all business. You could tell he was the kind who'd rather be working than sitting in meetings.

I didn't blame him.

I'd worked closely with the others during training simulations, Jim Alexander and Dr. Holland.

"Thank you for joining us on short notice," Dr. Park began, her voice carrying a gravity I wasn't used to. "We have a situation. The Ganymede Signal is weakening."

You could hear a pin drop.

"We've monitored it closely, and the trend is undeniable. The signal's strength is diminishing. We fear it may cease altogether."

Governor Olsen stepped in. "This presents us with a unique challenge. The signal represents a potential first contact scenario, a chance to discover something truly extraordinary."

"We believe," Dr. Park said, locking eyes with each of us in turn. "That in the interest of discovery, and to maintain the delicate peace between Earth and Mars, we need to consider moving the launch date up."

I felt my stomach drop and I leaned forward, chin gripped between my fingers. Moving the launch date *up?*

We were *already* on a tight schedule. But then, I looked around the room, at the faces of my team, Nash, and the mission control officers.

We were a bunch of brilliant minds stuck on a red rock, chasing a signal from the depths of space. If anyone could make an accelerated launch happen, it was this motley crew. I took a deep breath, ready to dive headfirst into whatever came next. The signal might be fading, but my resolve certainly wasn't.

"I want to see the data," I said, without waiting to be acknowledged. It was my project, my mission, after all.

Dr. Park waved at a trio of analysts with HoloPads. Not one of them carried a notebook and I admit, I judged them a little.

However, there's something about a room full of HoloPads glowing with interstellar data that makes you feel like you're pretty important.

This was one of those moments.

Three analysts from the signal team stepped forward, each clutching their HoloPad like a sacred text. They fired up the displays, and the room was suddenly awash in a sea of digital stars and fluctuating graphs.

I leaned forward, trying to look like I understood all of the complex data flashing before us.

The first analyst started the show, maybe he had seniority...or maybe the others sent him ahead because they were afraid that I'd shoot the messenger.

"Here," he pointed at a spike on the graph, "is the Ganymede Signal at its discovery." It was a towering peak, like a digital Everest.

"And here," the second analyst chimed in, swiping to a more recent data set, "is the signal now." The Everest had shrunk to a hill. A very unimpressive hill.

I scratched my head, trying to work out the implications in my head.

"What's the timeline we're looking at until this signal plays its swan song?" I asked, hoping my voice sounded steadier than my insides felt.

The third analyst, who hadn't spoken yet and looked like he regretted leaving his cozy data den, piped up. "Eight to ten months, Commander Mercer, given current trends."

Eight to ten months. Great.

My mind raced. We had four months of training left and then another four months of safety checks and final mission prep. We were planning a four-month joyride to Ganymede. If we stuck to the original schedule, we might arrive just in time to attend the signal's funeral.

Not exactly ideal for a first-contact mission.

I glanced at Mike. His presence was reassuring, like knowing there's a fire extinguisher nearby when you're about to attempt a culinary experiment involving flambé.

With a deep breath, I realized I was holding the steering wheel of this interplanetary road trip. The power to call it off, to stay the course, or to slam the accelerator— it was all mine.

Talk about pressure.

I could feel the eyes of the room on me, waiting for a

sign, a decision, anything. I breathed deeply and straightened up, squaring my shoulders.

"Looks like we might need to rethink our timeline," I said, trying to sound a little more confident than a cat at a dog show.

I paced along the room toward the window overlooking the training and sim room. All eyes were on me and, boy, I felt them digging into my back. I started to sweat with all the attention on me, especially because I knew what I was about to say was crazy.

"We cut the training schedule by two months and the final prep by two months. If we're fortunate, we'll make it to Ganymede before the signal collapses."

In my head, I was already running through the list of a million things that needed to be accelerated, changed, or chucked out of the airlock. But outwardly, I hoped I projected the calm of a commander who had her act together.

Mike caught my eye again and gave a slight nod, a smile lighting the depths of his eyes.

It was all the confirmation I needed.

ΦΦΦ

As we stepped into the massive hangar that housed the tunnel to the Artemis, I couldn't help but feel like a kid walking into a candy store for the first time—if the candy store was a hulking spacecraft capable of interplanetary travel.

The Artemis stood before us through the transparent dome, an engineering marvel—heck, the hangar itself was an engineering marvel. It was the largest structure on Mars and had the distinction of creating the largest spaceship ever built.

It must have been a massive blow to Mike and his team when the Venus mission had been scrapped and he realized that the Artemis might never fly. Luckily for him, I found the Ganymede Signal and gave it a new mission.

The Artemis had changed since I last saw it, developing new sensor arrays and various new shielding apparatuses.

I glanced at my team, their faces mirroring my mix of awe and excitement.

"Before you know it, this will be our new home," Mike announced with a hint of pride in his voice.

He should be proud. He'd designed the eighth wonder of the world— the eighth wonder of *both* worlds.

We followed him through the tunnel and up the boarding ramp, stepping into the central hub of the Artemis for the very first time.

The crew quarters were our first stop. Ten personal pods lined the walls, each a compact but comfortable space complete with a sleeping area and personal storage.

We would have two empty pods for extra storage.

Sam bounced on the bed of one pod.

"Better than my dorm back at the academy," he joked, his voice echoing slightly in the metallic chamber.

"Pretty sure that one is yours," I noted, looking at the extra length of the bed in comparison with the others. "You know, there's a reason they don't want super tall people to be astronauts. Think about how many extra Redcreds it cost the Institute to design your gear and our habitat."

"Guess I'm lucky that I'm a genius and you couldn't do without me," he said, checking out the closet.

The quarters of the Artemis were an example of space efficiency and comfort, designed to be a haven for us during our long journey. Each pod, about the size of a small walk-in closet, was ingeniously designed to maximize both privacy and functionality.

Each pod had a sliding door for privacy, opening to reveal a cozy interior. The sleeping area was dominated by a single bed, contoured to fit the body's natural sleeping posture, especially important considering the microgravity environment. The mattress, made of a high-density, memory foam-like material, could be adjusted for firmness.

Above the bed, a small, flexible reading light was attached, perfect for those who wanted to catch up on reading or review mission data before sleep.

On one side of the bed, a compact workstation folded out from the wall, complete with a touch-screen interface for personal and professional use. This was where we could send messages, check on mission updates, or simply relax with some entertainment. Wireless charging pads for our personal devices were embedded into this station, ensuring we always had power.

The storage space was another example of efficient design. Above the bed, a series of compartments and lockers were built into the wall, providing ample room for personal belongings, space suits, and other essentials. These compartments had magnetic closures to keep everything secure in zero gravity.

Opposite the bed, a small porthole window offered a view beyond the confines of the ship, a feature I knew would be a prized luxury when we craved a glimpse of the outside world.

My quarters at the training dome were slightly larger than this, but they didn't have a window so the little porthole seemed like a huge deal to me. It made the space less enclosed, and less suffocating.

Below the window, a foldable shelf served as a personal dining area, complete with holders for utensils and food packets.

The back of each pod housed a narrow, vertical wardrobe with space for clothing and personal gear. A small, integrated screen on the wardrobe door displayed information about the day's schedule, along with personal reminders and alerts.

The pods' walls were lined with a soft, sound-absorbing material to minimize noise, ensuring each of us could enjoy some quiet in our personal space. The lighting within each pod was adjustable, allowing us to choose the intensity and color, which could be programmed to simulate the natural progression of daylight, aiding our circadian rhythms.

Sam's comment about it being better than his dorm back at the academy wasn't an exaggeration.

These pods were designed not just for sleeping, but as personal retreats, where each of us could find solitude and comfort amidst the rigors of space travel. As I watched Sam testing the resilience of the bed with a few experimental bounces, I couldn't help but share his enthusiasm.

These quarters were going to be our home away from home, and the thought filled me with an unexpected sense of calm.

Jenna Torres was right all those months ago when they moved us into the training center quarters together.

Alexei eyed the tiny nutrition dispensers inside the crew pods suspiciously. "I hope these things are programmed for something more than protein shakes and vitamin supplements," he muttered, his Russian accent thickening with skepticism.

"Those are just for the individual prescriptions," Hank chuckled. "Your meals will come from the kitchen."

The communal area of the Artemis was a stark contrast to the functional minimalism of the crew quarters.

It was more spacious and designed with a touch of homeliness to foster team bonding and relaxation. As we entered, Mike's hand gently rested on my shoulder, guiding me through the space.

The warmth of his touch was reassuring, but it sent a seriously pleasant ripple through my gut that made me hyper-aware of every moment and he probably had no idea.

I told myself to dial it back a notch. I'd managed to ignore it for four months and I fully intended to ignore it for another year or more...at least until we were safely back on Mars and there were no more possibilities of an entanglement screwing up the mission.

The kitchenette, though compact, was impressively equipped.

It boasted a series of advanced nutrition dispensers, capable of producing a variety of meals and snacks, much to Alexei's relief. These dispensers were engineered to rehydrate and heat pre-packaged meals, providing us with a semblance of Earth-like dining experiences.

Above the dispensers, cabinets stored an array of dried food packs, ranging from hearty stews to complex, multi-ingredient meals that could be customized according to our dietary preferences and nutritional needs. The kitchenette also included a small, high-tech refrigerator and freezer unit, stocking fresh produce grown from the onboard hydroponic garden— a feature that promised a supply of fresh greens and herbs.

"And there are more food packs in the bulk storage area," Mike assured us all. "This is just the supply for the first week."

Adjacent to the kitchenette was the communal dining and recreational space.

A large table, capable of seating all crew members, dominated the center. It was designed to double as a work and meeting area, with embedded touchscreens and data ports. Surrounding the table were comfortable, ergonomically designed chairs, each affixed to the floor to prevent them from floating away in microgravity.

The recreational space was a cozy corner with a couple of small folding modular sofas (with built-in storage, because everything on the ship was multipurpose) and a large screen on the wall, perfect for group movie nights, virtual reality experiences, or interviews with the media.

This area was designed to be a versatile space where we could unwind, socialize, or engage in mission-specific planning. Bookshelves along one wall held a variety of reading materials, both educational and for leisure, while another section was dedicated to physical recreation, equipped with compact exercise equipment suitable for a zero-gravity environment.

As Mike led me through the communal area, it hit me.

It wasn't the GID, the science lab, or the control module...*this* was the real heart of the Artemis.

ΦΦΦ

As we entered the control module of the Artemis, the first thing that struck me was the sheer complexity and sophistication of the technology. The pilot's area was encircled by a constellation of screens and consoles, each glowing with an array of data and graphics.

I was so glad I wasn't in charge of flying the thing.

Jax couldn't hide his awe as he gently ran his fingers over the sleek surfaces of the control panel.

"It's like sitting in the cockpit of a starship," he murmured, almost to himself.

"It *is* a starship," I joked. But I knew what he meant. This had nothing on the Earth-Mars transport ships. This was light-years ahead of them in functionality, AI integrations, and just plain pizzazz.

Beside the pilot's seat, the AI pilot-assistant stood by in

a state of quiet readiness. Its interface was seamless, a smooth panel that almost seemed to anticipate our needs the few times we'd used one like it in the sim.

Unable to resist, I leaned toward it. "Computer, fire phaser bank one," I commanded.

"Sorry, Commander Mercer. The Artemis is not equipped with phaser-based weapons," was the reply.

"Do we have any weapons?" I asked Mike with a grin.

"Only your wit, Commander," the AI answered for him. Mike shrugged and raised his eyebrows in a 'what-can-you-do?' expression.

I snorted and Luca leaned in.

"Hey Artie, how about a cup of coffee?"

The AI responded with a crisp, synthetic voice that had just a hint of humor in its tone. "Nice try, Communications Specialist Marcarelli. The nutrient dispenser is located in the galley."

"Call me Luca," Luca tossed back. "And we'll call you Artie."

"Roger, Luca," the system responded. "Your terms are acceptable."

Luca raised his eyes, impressed. "This is obviously more advanced than the sim AI. But, um, Why does Artie have a British accent?"

Mike, who had been observing us with a smug expression, chuckled. "Artie's programmed for many things, Mercer, but playing warship isn't one of them."

"Nor barista, apparently," Jax said, sitting at the controls.

"Artie is programmed with many speech styles. We let him choose which one he was most comfortable with," TJ said.

I couldn't help but laugh, stepping back to give Jax more room to explore. He was touching everything with a reverence reserved for sacred artifacts.

"Artie's more than just a co-pilot," Mike explained, joining Jax at the console. "It's integrated into every aspect of the Artemis, from navigation to life support. But it's not infallible. That's where human judgment comes in, and why your role, Jax, and yours, Commander, are so critical."

Jax nodded, his eyes scanning the myriad of data points on the screens. "I've read about the simulations on the training HoloPads, but seeing this," he gestured around the cockpit, "it's something else. It's going to be a hell of a ride learning to work with Artie here."

Mike's smile widened as he pointed to a specific console. "That's the heart of it all. Artie can make calculations faster than we can blink, but it can't make decisions based on gut feelings, or...human intuition."

I moved closer, curious about the interaction between man and machine in such a high-stakes environment. "So, in our simulations, we'll be working closely with Artie, getting a feel for when to rely on its assistance and when to take the reins ourselves?"

"Exactly," Mike replied with enthusiasm. "It's about finding that balance. The next round of training at the mockup site will focus on integrating Artie into your decision-making process. I wanted to start without it so you'd all have a good foundation without it."

As the conversation continued, I found myself drawn to the commander's seat, positioned strategically amidst the control panels and just behind and slightly above the pilot's seat. I could see everything, *be* a part of everything.

Sitting down, I felt a rush of responsibility flood through me. This was where I'd be making the tough calls, where I'd lead my team through whatever challenges awaited us in the cold expanse of space.

"Comfortable, Commander?" Mike asked, leaning against the doorframe.

I glanced back at him, a determined smile on my face. "As comfortable as one can be, knowing the weight of the mission, and the fates of the free worlds apparently, rests right here." My hand patted the armrest of the commander's seat.

Luca was already fiddling with the comms unit. "State-of-the-art," he sighed happily, his eyes sparkling. "I can't wait to sync up with the Mars-Earth relay."

As we ventured further into the Artemis, our next stop

was the science lab and hydroponics area. We climbed the ladder to the top section.

I gaped as I took in the complicated-looking chamber door. "We have a gravity generator?!"

Mike nodded, the corner of his lips tilting up in a smile. "Can't do all of your experiments without one."

He was right, of course. I was surprised I hadn't thought of that before now.

"Artie, give me a projection of it," Mike ordered.

Suddenly, a holographic schematic flickered to life in front of the control panel.

Our team gathered around and listened intently as he began explaining the layout of the Localized Gravitational Field Generators.

"Here," Mike pointed to several spots marked around the perimeter of the lab's schematic, "are the strategic locations of our LGF Generators. These units are crucial for creating a uniform gravitational field within the lab."

He zoomed in on the display, highlighting the individual generators. "Each of these units emits gravitons. They create a field that simulates Earth's gravity. By placing them strategically around the lab, we ensure that the gravitational pull is evenly distributed, with no irregularities or fluctuations, just like the domes back on Mars, except on a smaller scale."

I watched the team nod, absorbing the information.

He tapped another section of the schematic. "The control system here manages the output of each LGF unit, synchronizing their operation. It's a delicate balance, but crucial for maintaining a consistent environment."

As Mike detailed the synchronization process and the fail-safes built into the system, Artie added his own comment. "I'll be monitoring these gravity anchors too. If anything goes funky, I'll know."

I hid a smile, though Luca wasn't quite as successful.

Gathered around the entrance to the science lab, our team listened intently as Mike prepared to explain the process of accessing the lab.

"Controlling the LGF Generators is a critical part of maintaining the lab's environment. These sliders here," he pointed to a row of controls on the panel, "allow us to adjust the gravitational field intensity manually."

He slid his finger along one of the controls, demonstrating. "Sliding this up increases the gravitational pull, simulating Earth-like gravity. Sliding it down decreases the effect, moving us back towards zero-G."

"The transition between zero gravity and Earth-normal gravity is gradual," Mike continued. "It's designed to give our bodies time to adjust. A sudden shift in gravity could be disorienting, even dangerous."

I nodded, understanding the importance of a smooth transition. "So, we ease into it, like adjusting to water temperature in a shower."

"Exactly," Mike replied. "Now, for most routine adjustments, you can use these manual controls. However, Artie is also integrated with the LGF system for automated management."

As if on cue, Artie's voice chimed in from the room's speakers, "That's right, Mike. I can ensure the gravity levels are just right for your experiments. Or for your morning coffee routine."

Mike smiled and continued. "When entering the lab from the rest of the ship, you'll initially be in a zero-G environment. As you activate the LGF system, the gravity will gradually increase. You'll feel it slowly pulling you towards the floor until it reaches the desired level."

"And when we leave the lab?" asked TJ, looking at the panel.

"The process reverses," Mike answered. "I recommend allowing a few minutes for the transition. This gradual change helps prevent any physical discomfort or spatial disorientation."

As Mike finished his explanation, Artie's voice rang out again, lightening the mood, "And don't worry, I'll be sure to provide some appropriate elevator music for your transitions."

The room erupted in laughter.

Mike grinned. "Once the gravity is back on, it'll be just

like working back on Earth— no floating tools or runaway experiments as long as you secure them before you leave. That's important, always put away your instruments and specimens. The red light at the top means the lab is occupied, and you should alert the person inside before initiating any changes. The sliders are locked when the red light is on, but just for—"

"Redundancy's sake," I said, teasing him.

"I could uninstall the light if you'd like," he joked. "Let you take your chances..."

Alex frowned. "That would be unwise."

Mike waved his hand toward the open door in invitation.

I could barely contain my excitement, bounding ahead of Alexei and Sam. This was my domain, where the mysteries of Ganymede would unravel, and I was about to get my first glimpse of the tools at my disposal.

The lab was a marvel, a compact but ingeniously designed space brimming with equipment. Microscopes, spectrometers, gene sequencers, and an array of other devices filled the shelves and workstations, each piece representing the pinnacle of scientific technology.

I spotted the LGF generators along the perimeter.

"Impressive, isn't it?" I said, unable to keep the awe out of my voice.

Alexei, usually the reserved one, nodded in agreement.

His eyes lingered on a set of modular incubators, likely imagining the potential alien flora and fauna samples they could hold. "The capabilities here... they are beyond what I expected," he mused, his accent thickening with excitement.

“If we each spend time in here, we might be able to preserve more of our muscle mass and bone density than we would otherwise.”

Mike nodded. “I wish we had more time. Another year or so and we could have had a living space with gravity installed as well.”

I looked back, my lips tilted up. “Maybe next time.”

Sam was drawn to a high-resolution imaging system. "Look at this," he called over, his usual stoic demeanor giving way to childlike enthusiasm. "I can analyze rock samples down to their atomic structure with this baby."

As we flitted from one station to the next, I noticed the seamless integration of Artie into the lab's systems. Screens displayed Artie's interface, ready to assist with data analysis, experiment protocols, or even to fetch digital research papers from its extensive database.

"Artie, display the hydroponics system schematics," I commanded, curious about our onboard food source.

Immediately, a detailed 3D model appeared on the nearest screen, illustrating the complex system of water recycling, nutrient delivery, and light management that would keep us supplied with fresh produce.

"Looks like we won't be living on protein bars, vitamin supplements, and freeze-dried food," Sam joked, peering over my shoulder.

I laughed, but my attention was momentarily diverted as I caught Mike watching me from across the room.

His expression was hard to read, a mix of pride, admiration, and something else I couldn't quite place. He quickly turned away when our eyes met, but the brief connection lingered.

Shaking off the feeling, I turned back to the task at hand. "Let's check out the hydroponics bay itself," I suggested, leading the way to the adjacent room.

The hydroponics area was a splash of green in the metallic world of the Artemis. Rows of plants, from leafy greens to fruiting vegetables, grew under the gentle glow of LED lights. The air was fresh, a welcome change from the recycled atmosphere of the rest of the ship and most of the domes.

"We'll have fresh salads at least," Alexei quipped, examining a thriving tomato plant.

"Hey, Mike, what's the square footage on this thing?" I called out, drawing his attention from a nearby controls display.

"The Artemis is roughly 600 feet long. That's about as long as a couple of football fields, or for those of you more artistically inclined, about 100 average-sized pianos lined up end-to-end."

"I always measure things in pianos," I quipped. "It's the standard unit of measurement in astrobiology."

"The Graviton Impulse Drive," Mike smiled and continued, pointing to the rear section of the schematic, "occupies about a quarter of that length down in the Engine bay, under the Engineering Sector. It's big, yes, but it's what gives this baby its kick."

"Could fit a small concert hall in there," Sam joked, eyeing the size of the GID.

"Exactly," Mike laughed. "And for storage, we've got about 10,000 square feet. That's enough space to almost hold an Olympic-sized swimming pool, though I wouldn't recommend trying to fit one in here."

I imagined trying to swim in a pool while floating through space. "Would make for an interesting backstroke," I said, grinning.

Mike nodded. "And don't forget, every inch of living space overhead is optimized. You've got living quarters, labs, hydroponics, and enough supplies to keep us going for the duration of the mission with more supplies stored just in case things run a little longer than anticipated."

I looked around the ship, mentally sizing up the space. "So, what you're saying is, we've got the equivalent of a floating science city, with a propulsion system the size of a small concert hall and enough storage to hide a swimming pool. Sounds cozy."

Mike gave a hearty laugh. "You've got it, Commander. Welcome to your new home away from home."

The last part of our tour brought us to the engine bay where the Graviton Impulse Drive was housed. The sheer size of the drive was staggering and the pitch-black, enclosed room lit only by the dim, red backup lights sent shivers down my spine. TJ was already deep in conversation with Mike, discussing the finer points of the drive's mechanics.

They were almost obsessive in their love for the GID. I suppose it was a good thing since we were all entrusting our lives to the behemoth.

Standing there, in the guts of the Artemis, I realized how much I had changed since I first laid eyes on this spacecraft. I was no longer just a scientist chasing a signal, I was a commander, responsible for the lives of my crew and the success of our mission.

This was *my* ship.

After we finished the thorough tour of the ship, we went to the Engineering Dome to review the popup lab that had been created for Venus and altered for Ganymede.

We needed a space outside the ship where we could study samples initially to make sure we weren't introducing any potentially dangerous biological hazards into our habitat, or unknowingly transporting them back to Mars.

It was a big concern.

We met with Dr. Kim to discuss the specifics of the lab containment and quarantine protocols. This was such a critical component, and every detail mattered.

"Mike, Dr. Kim, let's start with the basics. How are we powering this lab and what's it made of?" I asked, wanting to cut right to the chase.

Sam crossed his arms and frowned in concentration while Alex took notes. The rest of the team listened intently.

Mike jumped right in. "Alright, so, the lab's power comes directly from the ship's fusion reactors. This provides a stable and substantial power source. For contingencies, we've fitted it with backup batteries, and it has solar panels specially designed for Ganymede's dim sunlight."

"Construction materials?" I pressed.

"It's built with the same dense shielding materials we use for housing the fusion reactors. They're capable of handling extreme radiation, which is exactly what we need for Ganymede's environment," Mike explained. "No alteration necessary."

I turned to Dr. Kim. "And the biohazard containment? Ganymede could have unknown biological materials."

Dr. Kim leaned forward. "The lab is equipped with state-of-the-art biological hazard containment systems. Any samples you collect will go through rigorous quarantine processes before analysis. We're taking every precaution to prevent cross-contamination, both for your safety and to preserve the integrity of the samples."

"And the gravity?" I asked, knowing this was a key factor for our research.

"We're utilizing the same technology that we used for the ship's lab," Mike answered.

"Specimen collection is where it all starts," Dr. Kim began, showing us several examples of the containment cubes. "It's crucial to seal each sample immediately in airtight, radiation-resistant containers."

"Guess these can handle a bit more than your average leftovers," Luca, inspecting one of the containers, remarked dryly. He was tossing it from hand to hand like a ball while Dr. Kim watched.

"Space Tupperware. Keeps your aliens fresh for up to a week in the fridge," I muttered to Luca under my breath as he snorted laughter.

Dr. Kim continued, undeterred by our antics. "Upon return to Artemis, the containers will go straight to the popup lab's preliminary quarantine chamber. There, Atlas, our AI assistant, will perform initial scans for biological and chemical hazards."

"Whoa, will Artie and Atlas interact?" I asked.

"Yes," Mike said. "While Artie is a bit more...dramatic, and developed for all major shipboard functions, Atlas is only a science AI. His function is to keep Artie from being tied up by routine experiments and queries."

I nodded. "Hope they get along."

Dr. Kim continued, drawing our attention to another section. "For detailed experimentation, we transfer samples to the biohazard containment unit. While Atlas assists with basic analysis, our expertise is key for any complex experiments and data interpretation."

I glanced at the containment unit with interest. "So this is where the real magic happens, minus the rabbits and hats."

"Post-experimentation, samples are stored in specialized containment storage units. These are essential for maintaining specific environmental conditions," Dr. Kim said, detailing the final steps.

"And when it's time to head back to Mars?" I asked.

"High-security, multi-layered containment systems for transport," Dr. Kim concluded. "We ensure complete isolation of the samples to prevent any cross-contamination. They will be fitted into the ship's storage and accessible from the outside and the inside of the ship. "

Dr. Kim had just finished explaining the secure storage

for post-experimentation samples when a thought struck me.

"Do these containment units come in a one-size-fits-all for aliens, or should we look into getting an XL version? You know, I'm pretty sure microbes didn't compose and broadcast that signal."

"Commander, while the possibility of encountering macroscopic extraterrestrial life is remote, I'll make a note to inquire about larger containment options," Dr. Kim replied dryly.

She was just humoring me I could tell.

I heard Luca mutter something to Alexi about kidnapping aliens and I had to work really hard not to chase that rabbit and lead us all off into a tangential discussion.

I didn't have Dr. Kim's reservations regarding our potential discoveries on Ganymede. I was pretty danged certain that our signalers were larger life forms.

"Okay," I said. "Moving on..."

10.

'63-08

It was T-minus four months to launch and we were chowing down on some beef and cheese for lunch while we waited for the briefing to begin.

Luca chugged his nutrient shake and left, and I grimaced. People have been making those things for nearly eighty years that I know of, and still, nobody has figured out a way to make them taste better.

Maybe I'd work on that when I got back to Mars.

"We had better get in there," Mike said, wiping his mouth on a napkin and standing. "Jim's waiting."

We were the last two left and I was sure Nash would be a bit peeved if we left him twiddling his thumbs for too long.

"Go ahead. I need a minute."

I went to the ladies' room for a moment, thankful that the training dome had one and I didn't have to share it with a bunch of guys. I sanitized my hands, checked my teeth, and left, knowing that I wouldn't get a break for many more hours.

Today was a big day.

As I walked into the training dome briefing room, the sense of anticipation was palpable. The crew was gathered around the central table, ready for the lowdown on our Ganymede landing and relaunch.

Mike and Jim Alexander, our propulsion and landing systems experts, stood ready at the front. On the main screen, Nash's face appeared, joining in from Mission Control.

"Let's dive into the Artemis's landing and relaunch process," Mike began, his voice echoing slightly in the room. "Jim, why don't you start with the propulsion details?"

Jim nodded and launched into his explanation. "We're equipped with a hybrid engine system. For the descent, we rely on the chemical rockets."

From the screen, Nash's voice cut through, "How's our fuel efficiency looking for the descent? Are we cutting it close?"

Jim grinned, confident. "We've got it calibrated just

right, Nash. Enough thrust to control our approach, and enough backup to get us off Ganymede twice over."

Mike took over, pointing to a diagram of the Artemis. "Our landing gear is designed to handle Ganymede's tricky terrain. It's robust, shock-absorbent, and stable."

I couldn't help myself. "So, my ship isn't going to fall over? I'd appreciate it mightily if we could keep that from happening."

The room burst into laughter before Mike continued. "Exactly. We're aiming for a smooth touchdown. Post-landing, we'll do a full systems check before we step out."

Sam leaned forward, his brow furrowed in thought. "And what's our window for surface operations? How long do we have before we need to think about heading back up?"

"You've got about two weeks on the surface," Jim replied. "That gives you plenty of time for experiments and to poke around, with some wiggle room for any surprises."

Mike wrapped up the technicalities of our relaunch. "We start with the chemical rockets for the lift-off, then switch to the GID once we're clear of Ganymede's gravity well."

Nash nodded along. "Sounds solid."

Mike looked around and answered a few questions from the crew, mostly Jax. It seemed pretty straightforward to me, but I was glad I wasn't the one landing the thing.

With the briefing wrapped up, I stood, stretching my legs. "Okay, let's get to the simulator. We've got a moon landing to rehearse."

I was thinking about the effect our travel time might have on any biological samples we managed to acquire—if we found any. There was a huge chance that if we did find anything living, even microscopic, our storage procedures might degrade the samples.

I was about to mention it to Alexei as we stepped out onto the training room floor when something began to feel very odd in the room. Then I noticed it.

Hissing.

The moment the blaring sirens split the air, my heart leaped into my throat. The red emergency lights painted our faces in a wash of urgency, signaling a dome breach—one of those scenarios you train for but never really expect to happen.

"Breach!" I yelled at almost the same moment the sirens began.

I snapped into action, the adrenaline coursing through my veins and making me feel jumpy. My eyes darted around, quickly locating the source of the breach from the sound that I'd heard: a small, hissing crack in the dome's wall. The sound was almost sinister, a whisper of death—like the rattle of a rattlesnake when you realize that you're way too close.

"Mike, emergency sealant kit, now!" I commanded, my voice steady despite the tremor I felt inside. My mind was a whirlwind of procedures and backup plans and visions of my crew suffering an agonizing death out in the unfeeling Martian dirt.

Mike sprinted, heading straight for the emergency kit affixed to a nearby section of the wall. Meanwhile, Sam was already on the comm with maintenance. "Dome breach in the training facility. We need a repair team here immediately!"

I spun around to Alexei and Luca. "Help me with that panel," I said, pointing to a large metal sheet used in our simulation setup. It was heavy, but we managed to maneuver it towards the breach. My muscles protested under the strain, and I could feel beads of sweat forming on my forehead.

As Mike returned with the sealant, I noticed my hands were shaking, but I couldn't tell if it was from the exertion or the adrenaline.

We applied the sealant around the panel's edges, the substance oozing out of the tube with a promise of safety. My heart pounded in my chest, each beat echoing through my head.

I was very glad the breach wasn't in the upper part of the dome. We had bots to take care of those, but sometimes they were a bit slower and it required everyone to evacuate the dome 'emergency style', which was a hugely disruptive process.

Pressing the flexible panel against the breach, the cold metal bit into my palms. The sealant was supposed to set quickly, but time seemed to stretch into an eternity. I could hear my breathing, ragged and heavy, as we waited for the sealant to harden.

Finally, the panel held firm. The hissing stopped and the immediate danger was over.

We all exhaled in unison. My legs felt like jelly, and I realized I'd been holding my breath longer than I thought.

Mike had to clasp me on the shoulder to get me to let go. I turned and faced him, and saw the gleam of respect in his eyes. We'd been only moments from death, everyone in the whole dome had.

The emergency technicians arrived, moving swiftly to assess and repair the breach. They thanked us, their eyes reflecting both relief and admiration. It was a close call, but we had managed to avert disaster.

As the adrenaline started to ebb, a memory surfaced unbidden.

It was my first year at the Mars Frontier Research Institute, a similar alarm, a similar breach. But back then, I had frozen, panic gripping me like a vice. It had taken someone else to step up and fix the problem.

Now, here I was, years later, having just taken charge

in a crisis. I realized how far I'd come from that wide-eyed, panicked scientist. I had grown and evolved into someone who could lead, make decisions under pressure, and keep a cool head when it mattered most.

It kind of surprised me, even now.

I'd always seen myself as more of a follower. Even with my position as the head of our section's astrobiology lab, I'd always just had more of a collaborative leadership style.

Now, I was learning to lead from the front.

I glanced at my team. They were the best I could have hoped for, and they'd allowed me the chance to lead them. I wouldn't let them down, not for anything.

We evacuated the training section of the dome just to be extra cautious while the techs completed their repairs. I was excited about having some time off. We didn't get much of that, not since the accelerated training schedule had become the accelerated, *accelerated* training schedule.

If we weren't sleeping, we were either studying or in the sim.

"Mercer!" Nash called from the busy hub, where everyone took their breaks.

I wove through the café stands and the groups of engineers watching the screens broadcasting news about

Earth. There seemed to be some small-scale riots happening somewhere, but that was nothing new. Most of the time, we watched the news just to see home. After being in a sea of red dust, anything naturally green was almost shocking.

Nash guided me to a corner.

"What's up?" I asked.

"Park scheduled an impromptu interview with David Chen. She wants you and the team to give him an interview on the ship. Unclassified areas only."

I threw my head back and groaned. "This isn't a joke, is it?" I asked hopefully.

"I never joke," he said solemnly. "Ever."

"When?"

He raised an eyebrow ruefully. "Right now."

I muttered a curse.

"Get your team. Chen will meet you on the storage pad. And hey, good work on the breach."

That was practically glowing praise from Nash.

I gave the rover bay a longing look as I passed, my plans for a free afternoon pretty much shot to hell by Dr. Park's meddling. I pulled my mini-comms and sent a voice alert to the team.

They all responded immediately as I made my way to the storage pad at the end of the last engineering dome, where I'd first met Mike and Jim. Today, the engineering domes are just as industrious as they had been then.

I wondered if they ever took time off.

The storage pad for the Artemis was a feat of engineering brilliance.

Accessing it involved passing through a specially constructed tunnel, a transparent, reinforced tube that connected the dome to the ship. This tunnel was the lifeline that allowed us to move between the ship and the dome without the need for bulky Marswalker suits.

In my mind's eye, I pictured the tunnel's structure as I remembered it: a series of interlocking segments made from a lightweight yet incredibly durable carbon composite material, designed to withstand Mars' harsh environment.

The interior was lined with advanced atmospheric controls and life support systems, maintaining a constant flow of breathable air and comfortable temperature, mimicking Earth's conditions.

The tunnel utilized an innovative airlock system at both ends— one connecting to the dome and the other to the Artemis.

These airlocks were equipped with state-of-the-art sealing technology, creating airtight junctions that prevented any Martian atmosphere from seeping in. The airlocks operated through a series of rapid pressure adjustments, ensuring a seamless transition from the dome's atmosphere to the ship, and vice versa.

As I finally reached the meeting point, David Chen was waiting with his camera, as I'd been told. Mike was nearby, talking with a couple of members from his engineering team that I didn't know.

I smiled and shook his hand, the rest of my team straggling in behind me in ones and twos.

"Ready?"

David, as always, was sharply dressed with his recorder at the ready, and a smile plastered on his face. "Looking forward to it, Commander," he enthused.

As I navigated through the tunnel, the mostly transparent walls offered a panoramic view of the Martian landscape. The tunnel's lighting system was designed to simulate natural sunlight, creating a warm and inviting pathway as opposed to the alien world outside.

The connection to the Artemis was equally sophisticated. The ship's docking port seamlessly integrated with the tunnel's end, forming a secure and stable link. Advanced sensors and alignment systems ensured a perfect connection every time, allowing for easy access to the ship for both crew and equipment.

We started with the crew quarters, and I tried my best to seem casual and relaxed for the camera.

"Welcome to our humble abode," I joked, gesturing grandly at the compact but comfortable pods. "It's like a five-star hotel—if the hotel was in space, had beds the size of postage stamps, and a slightly crazy AI concierge on call."

David chuckled, recording every detail. I noticed a bead of sweat trickling down my spine and making me itch—cameras always did that to me.

As we moved to the communal living space, Mike joined us, his presence both reassuring and slightly unnerving. He had a knack for deadpan humor that often left people second-guessing and his obsessive need to talk shop sometimes scared normal people off.

Luckily, I wasn't normal.

David pointed to the nutrition dispensers. "What's on the menu up here?" he asked.

"If you like protein shakes and vitamin supplements, you're in for a treat," Mike answered.

Luca chimed in. "We've got a variety of options, all designed to keep us healthy and, uh, regular in space."

David laughed, nodding. "Regular is good. Regular is important."

Alexei, who'd been hovering in the background and hoping to avoid being on camera, eyed the dispensers again with a mix of skepticism and mild horror. "I just hope we don't run out of actual food," he mumbled, more to himself than anyone else.

We approached a large, transparent chamber filled with a variety of plants. "This," Mike announced, "is our hydroponics section, a masterpiece of agronomic engineering and ecological symbiosis, facilitating an optimized photosynthetic efficiency ratio."

David's eyes glazed over slightly, and I couldn't blame him.

"Translation," I interjected, "we grow plants here. They give us oxygen and food, and we give them love and probably too much attention. It's a high-tech space garden."

David laughed. "I can see the appeal of space gardening."

"It's very therapeutic," I added. "Just don't mandate me if I start talking to them."

TJ snickered and Hank rolled his eyes.

Sam was already there, inspecting a tomato plant with an expression that was a mix of fascination and distaste. "Never liked nightshades," he muttered, "but I guess I'll have to get used to them."

"Tomatoes are an excellent source of vitamins," I said, adopting a mock-serious tone. "And they make great projectiles in zero gravity."

David chuckled, jotting down notes. "I'll remember to duck in case you guys decide to stage a practice run here," he said.

We had just finished touring the hydroponics section when Mike guided us towards the Artemis' science lab, located in a distinct section near the center of the ship on the very top level.

"Alright, everyone," Mike started, his voice filled with a mix of pride and excitement. "This is our Localized Gravitational Field Generator, or LGF Generator. It operates on advanced principles of quantum field manipulation, specifically focusing on the graviton particles."

"Like the GID," Alexei says from the back. "And the domes."

David nodded his thanks.

Mike nodded and continued, detailing the technical aspects. "The system's emitters, strategically placed, work together to create a uniform gravitational field. This involves precise modulation of the graviton field vectors, ensuring optimal spatial-temporal gradient distribution."

I jumped in, seeing David's bewilderment. "Think of it like a bunch of gravity projectors around the room. They work together to make sure the artificial gravity is even everywhere— no light or heavy spots."

"That makes more sense," David said, relieved.

"And here's the control unit. It's integrated with the ship's power grid and taps into our fusion reactor," Mike added, pointing to the sleek controls unit.

"That's like having a big dimmer switch for gravity," I quipped. "Crank it up for normal gravity, or turn it down if you like to live dangerously."

The team chuckled, and Mike's smile broadened.

"And the fail-safes?" David inquired.

"Comprehensive," Mike assured him. "In case of any malfunction, it powers down gradually to prevent sudden zero gravity."

Luca joked, "A surprise zero-G party would be pretty rad!"

David laughed, jotting down notes. "Certainly makes science more grounded, doesn't it?"

"Absolutely," I said with a grin. "Without it, we'd be floating around like awkward jellyfish, and our experiments would be too. It'd be a real mess— imagine trying to pour liquids or operate microscopes while floating. This way, we get to keep our feet on the ground and our science in check."

David chuckled, nodding along. "That does sound a lot more manageable."

"Exactly," I said with a grin. "And it's a pretty simple concept. Mike's just showing off with his fancy engineer talk."

Mike gave a sheepish smile and we wandered around for a bit longer.

As we wrapped up the tour, I could feel the dryness in my mouth from talking too much. I longed for a moment of solitude away from the camera, but duty called.

"So, Commander Mercer," David said, turning to me with a grin. "Any final thoughts for our viewers?"

I took a deep breath, not knowing what to say exactly. I didn't have any epic words planned. "Just that we're ready. Ready for the challenges, the discoveries, and whatever else the universe throws at us. And maybe a few tomatoes."

As far as final thoughts go, those were pretty bad. I definitely needed to have some preplanned speeches ready for launch day.

The camera finally turned off and I let out a sigh of relief.

The Interview was over, the mission still on track, and not a single tomato was thrown. Except for the almost catastrophic dome breach, it was a successful day, all things considered.

'63-09

"Commander, we have a hull breach in sector 3A," Artie's voice was calm yet urgent, echoing through the mockup's intercom.

We were doing yet another relaunch simulation.

I felt a jolt of adrenaline as I sprang into action. "Mike, TJ, you're on repair. The rest of you, prep for potential decompression."

Mike and TJ nodded, swiftly grabbing their repair kits. Their movements were quick and precise as they approached the simulated breach site. I watched it on the screen.

As they worked, I could see Mike's brow furrowed in concentration, his hands steady despite the high stakes. TJ, usually so detail-oriented, was visibly struggling to keep pace, his breathing heavy in his suit.

"Dammit," TJ muttered, fumbling with a sealant canister. The holographic breach was widening in the simulation, with a visual and audible reminder of the danger it posed.

Mike glanced at TJ, his voice firm yet encouraging. "Stay focused, TJ. We've got this."

In the control module, I watched their progress, my heart racing. My palms were sweaty on the armrests.

"Commander, oxygen levels are dropping," Artie reported, its tone devoid of its usual humor. "We need to expedite the repair."

I turned to Artie. "Start calculating oxygen reserves. How long can we last if this breach isn't contained?"

Sam and Luca hurried to their stations, their fingers flying over the controls as they assisted with comms and calculations. Their faces were grim as they worked, with lines furrowed into their brows and jaws clenched.

Back at the breach, Mike and TJ were making progress, but not fast enough. The simulation showed the oxygen levels continuing to drop, a ticking clock against our survival.

"Mike, we need a quick fix," I urged.

He nodded, wiping sweat from his brow. "Trying something else, Commander. Hang on."

I watched as Mike improvised a patch using spare materials from their kit, a risky but potentially life-saving move. TJ assisted, the initial panic subsiding as they found their rhythm.

After tense minutes that felt like hours, Mike's voice crackled over the intercom. "Breach contained, Commander."

I exhaled a sigh of relief, feeling the tension drain from my body. But the simulation wasn't over yet. We had lost a significant portion of our oxygen supply.

"Okay, team," I said, regaining my composure, "let's figure out how to proceed. We can't afford to abort this mission over a breach."

Luca called back. "We've got Nash on the comms! Real-time for two minutes!"

I swallowed and nodded. “Open the comms.”

"Artemis, this is Mission Control. Do you copy? Over,” Nash said.

I gripped the armrest of my seat, my hands a bit sweaty inside the gloves. "Mission Control, this is Artemis. We read you loud and clear. Over."

"Commander, we've received your update on the oxygen situation. I'm directing our Science and Engineering teams to work on the issue. We’ll explore all possible solutions and relay any viable strategies. Stand by for updates. Over."

"Understood, Mission Control. Standing by."

Inside the Artemis simulator, the atmosphere was pretty bleak. Mike and TJ had just contained the breach, but our oxygen supply had taken a significant hit. I glanced around at my team, their faces calm, but I knew them well enough by now to see the little signs of nerves.

"Artie, give us an update on our oxygen reserves," I called out.

Calculations flickered across the main screen as Artie worked through the data.

"Commander, with the current crew size and life support settings, our oxygen supply will last approximately 36 hours," Artie reported, its voice devoid of any playful undertones.

36 hours. Not good.

I exchanged a look with Mike. "We need options. Artie, start running simulations on our best course of action. Consider every variable."

Mike, still catching his breath from the repair, nodded. "Let's think about rationing our activities to conserve oxygen. Lowering physical exertion could extend our supply."

"What about adjusting the scrubbers? Maximizing CO2 removal might buy us more time," TJ suggested, stretching his shoulders before hunching back over his console.

Artie's processors whirred as he considered each suggestion. "Rationing physical activity could extend our oxygen by an additional 12 hours. Enhancing scrubber efficiency could add another 6 hours."

Sam spun around from his seat. "We could also shut down non-essential sections of the ship, minimize power usage, and redirect it to life support."

TJ, rubbing his hands through his hair in thought. "If we manually override some of the automated systems, we could probably tweak the environmental controls for more output."

As Artie calculated the combined effects of these measures, I felt an overwhelming pride in my team. Despite the simulated nature of the crisis, their responses were real.

"Combining all proposed measures, we could extend

our oxygen supply to approximately 60 hours," Artie concluded.

"Mike?" I asked, using our comms.

"It'll be enough for us to get down to storage and switch over to the next set of tanks. We can't afford another hit like that though," he warned.

I nodded, satisfied with the outcome. "That's enough to keep us alive and carrying out the mission. Great thinking, everyone."

The simulation ended, and we gathered in the training dome's conference room for a debriefing. The exercise had been intense and it had uncovered yet another potential issue that we could fix before we launch.

Always a good thing, in my book.

The debriefing room felt way more crowded than usual, filled with the entire mission control staff, Mike's engineering team, and Jim Anderson, now the head engineer of the Ganymede Mission at Mission Control.

I sat at the head of the table with Nash, feeling the weight of every gaze in the room. Those gazes—those expectations—weren't as heavy now as they used to be.

"Alright, let's get started," I began, clearing my throat. The room fell silent. "Today's simulation highlighted a few critical areas we need to address, especially concerning our oxygen supply."

Mike, sitting to my right, nodded. "The hull breach

simulation caused a significant depletion in our O2 reserves. We managed a makeshift repair, but the loss was substantial. It cut into our return trip supply. We probably would have coasted in on fumes, if we made it back at all. We probably would have had to use the emergency pods for their supplies."

Jim leaned forward. "The integrity of the Artemis's hull is paramount. We need to reassess our material stress tests and emergency response protocols."

I hummed in uncertainty for a moment. "That'll work for future missions, but we have three months to launch. Right now, we need to focus on supplemental oxygen systems and bulking up our reserves."

From the back, one of the junior Mission Control Specialists, a sharp-eyed woman named Helen, spoke up. "We tracked the oxygen depletion in real-time. Your quick thinking in the simulator was commendable, but in a real-world scenario, we'd have a narrower window for error."

Luca flipped to a section in his HoloPad and underlined an area before adding his opinion. "Communication during the breach was efficient, but we could streamline our check-ins with Mission Control. We already have a direct line of communication between Artie and Mission Control, but we should have a prioritized automated response ready to go in those situations."

"The use of the emergency sealant kit was effective, but

we should consider additional redundancies. Perhaps integrating a fail-safe mechanism that activates an automatic sealant dispersal upon detecting a breach," TJ added, fidgeting with a pen.

"That's one for future missions as well," Mike said regretfully. "Not enough time for the Artemis. "But maybe we can slap something together for a faster team response."

Artie's voice then filled the room, patched in from the ship's controls. "My analysis suggests that increasing the sensitivity of our hull integrity monitors could provide earlier breach warnings, allowing for a quicker response."

I nodded, absorbing their feedback and ideas. "These are all good strategies. We need to ensure the Artemis is as fail-safe as possible."

The conversation then shifted to the oxygen supply issue. "Our simulation ended with a critical reduction in oxygen levels," I continued. "Mike and TJ came up with a temporary fix, but we need a long-term solution—something that won't get us killed on the way back to Mars."

Mike leaned back, his expression thoughtful. "We're considering a supplementary O2 generation module. It would be a backup to our primary life support system, potentially using electrolysis or chemisorption techniques."

Jim perked up at this. "That's a solid plan. We could

modify some of the spare water recycling components to serve as a rudimentary electrolysis unit. It wouldn't be as efficient as the main system, but it could buy us crucial time in an emergency."

Helen leaned forward to look at Mike. "We'll need to balance the power consumption of this new module with the rest of the Artemis's systems. Even with the fusion reactors, power allocation is already tight for the journey. Aside from the GID and the primary life support systems, the science lab requires an exorbitant amount of power."

She said it with a kind of chiding tone that brushed me the wrong way, as if we had too many fun toys onboard the Artemis that would use up precious power. I was about to step in and suggest something probably rude when I was interrupted by Artie.

Probably for the best. Making an enemy of one of the Mission Control Specialists didn't sound like a very good idea.

"That's where I come in," Artie interjected. "I can manage the power distribution to prioritize life support without compromising other critical systems."

Mike and the rest of the engineers consulted and took notes.

"We also need to consider the psychological impact on the crew during such emergencies," Hank pointed out, his voice calm but firm. "Training for these scenarios is one thing, but experiencing them is another. We should integrate more stress management techniques into our training regimen. I noticed some blood pressure and heart rate spikes that I wasn't very happy with."

Yeah, probably that was me.

Dr. Holland finally piped up, looking as if he might have been dozing off during the technical discussions. "I caught those as well. I think continuing the mockups will help, but I propose we implement a regimen of VR meditation for the team—perhaps once a week in the evenings before bed and to be continued as necessary during the voyage?"

I wondered if the VR meditations were going to be like a vacation. Could I choose to go to, say, Aruba and meditate?

As the meeting drew to a close, I summarized our action items. "Okay, we have a lot of work ahead. Hull integrity emergency enhancements, additional oxygen generation and storage capacity, improved communication protocols with Mission Control, and enhanced psychological training aka beach vacations. Let's prioritize these developments and get to work. Our success depends on it."

Some of the occupants looked a bit nonplussed by my beach vacations bit, but I caught a smirk on Mike's face and I was pretty sure Dr. Holland looked wistful.

Not sure I even wanted to know what that was about.

The team dispersed, a buzz of conversation filling the air. Some stayed behind to discuss specific technical details, while others headed back to their stations, their minds already racing with ideas and solutions.

I stayed in my chair and called Raj, needing a bit of time to lose the commander persona and just talk to my best friend.

11.

'63-10

It was two months to launch, and the Ganymede project was no longer just ours.

David Chen's efforts with us on behalf of the Earth-Mars United Broadcasting had paid off—for him...and I guess for peace too.

We hadn't heard anything else from Dr. Park or Governor Olsen about war since the citizens of Earth had been informed of the potential discovery of intelligent life on Ganymede, and I'd been too busy to hang out at the Mars meetings to see if the rebellion was ramping up a notch or still just simmering on low.

It seemed as if the mission had captured the imagination of the public as intended. I just hope it all panned out. One accidental mistake on our part and Earth and Mars could be back at each other's throats the very next day.

The media buzz was intense, with journalists and documentarians insisting on interviews and stories. Universities all over Earth clamored for a chance to chat with me or the team. I'd been offered exorbitant amounts of money for brief interviews and inside information.

Did I consider some of them? Heck yeah. Did I follow through? Not a chance.

Dr. Park would probably send a self-destruct sequence to the ship just for payback—which reminded me, I wanted to check with Mike to make sure there wasn't something like that built in.

It sounded far-fetched, but I'd grown up watching old-school Sci-Fi Earth shows, and there was always some previously unknown self-destruct programming in there somewhere. A decent amount of paranoia was always best where AI and starships were concerned.

I found myself increasingly in the unfamiliar and unwanted glare of the spotlight, juggling press commitments with our already rigorous mission prep.

Amid this media frenzy, I sat down for a live interview, connecting with a journalist from Earth that Dr. Park and Governor Olsen had deemed particularly important.

Sitting before the Earth interviewer in the press room

studio, covered with makeup that I didn't usually wear, I felt the familiar bite of anxiety.

He didn't ease in, that was for sure. His questions started pointed and difficult, probing into every aspect of our mission.

"Commander Mercer," he began, his tone serious. "Given the immense risks of this mission, how do you justify the potential cost, both financially and in terms of human life?"

I leaned forward, earnest as I linked my somewhat shaky hands together.

"Space exploration has always been about pushing boundaries, about learning and growing as a species. The potential scientific gains from this mission, especially the investigation of the Ganymede signal, could be monumental. Yes, there are risks, but they are calculated and measured against the immense potential for discovery."

He nodded.

"Commander, considering the current political tensions between Earth and Mars, how do you navigate these complexities, especially with a mission that holds such significance for both planets?" he asked, head tilted and with a hint of concern in his voice.

He was a wonderful actor, but I saw right through his façade. It didn't mean the questions weren't important though.

I took a moment to gather my thoughts before responding. I had to get this *just* right.

"The tensions between Earth and Mars are indeed a reality that we can't ignore. However, our mission to Ganymede transcends these earthly disputes. It's about scientific discovery, about pushing the boundaries of human knowledge and understanding. We have a diverse team, representing not just different countries or planets, but a collective *human* endeavor."

I paused, ensuring my words conveyed the gravity I felt. "Our focus is on the science, on the potential discoveries that could benefit all of humanity. In space, the distinctions between Earth and Mars fade away in the face of the vastness of the universe. We're reminded that, at our very core, we're explorers, scientists, and humans, united by a common goal. This mission is a symbol of what we can achieve when we work together, looking beyond our differences towards a shared future."

He nodded and smiled. "That's commendable and a very important point. We've always been an adventurous species," he added with a grin.

Then, he switched topics.

With a look of earnest curiosity, he leaned in closer. By this point, I was almost certain he was teetering on the edge of his chair.

"So, Commander, how do you and your team prepare for the unprecedented, like potential contact with extraterrestrial beings?"

That question was off-limits, as per Dr. Park.

I racked my brain and then straightened. "Oh, we've undergone extensive training for that," I started, my voice steady.

He was nodding along intently and I matched him.

"We'll just fire up the photon torpedoes and blast our way out of there."

He stared at me and I blinked. The studio was as silent as the vacuum of space.

At five seconds, his expression shifted from curiosity to sheer bafflement. I might have gone too far again.

They should have known what to expect from me by then.

Later, as the team and I gathered to watch the broadcast, the room erupted into raucous hoots and hollers when we reached my improv.

Mike, sitting next to me, let out a loud laugh and affectionately bumped my shoulder with his, his heavily muscled arm like steel against mine. Luckily, I wasn't doing so badly in the muscles department either, though I'd never be able to bulk up to his standards.

I'd heard they had to adjust some of the men's uniforms to account for their gains.

"Photon torpedoes? Really?" he chuckled, shaking his head and running a hand over his face. "Man, Park is going to come after *me* now."

"Sorry," I shrugged. "Sometimes my brain can't keep up with my mouth."

Just as the laughter was simmering down to chuckles and snickers, my comms buzzed.

It was Raj, his voice was full of laughter through the speakers. "You should've seen it here, Lena! The whole science department, including Dr. Weber, was watching. Weber almost choked on his tea!"

His story set off another wave of laughter. Luca, having already heard my stories and met Dr. Weber in a chance meeting, was laughing so hard he rolled onto the floor, clutching his stomach. "I can see it!"

The laughter faded eventually, but it left behind a warm glow that lasted long into the night.

ΦΦΦ

A few days later, at a public talk in the Institute's auditorium, the team and I presented our plans and objectives.

The hall was packed to the brim, a sea of eager faces,

with more watching on the screens throughout the facility. This was the biggest thing since the first Mars landing.

Luca, with his natural charm, explained our communication strategies, eliciting nods and murmurs of interest and many laughs. Sam managed to convey the risks without dampening the enthusiasm that Luca had generated. His straightforward manner resonated well with the audience, and for once, his bluntness was softened by his passion for the mission. They did well and I kept my mouth shut, which made Nash— and probably everyone else— happy.

However, balancing the media circus with the rigors of mission planning was like walking a tightrope. I delegated some public outreach to the team, easing my load and bringing fresh perspectives to the fore.

Hank held a captivating session on space medicine, while TJ and Alexei teamed up to talk about the technological and biological aspects of our mission.

Jax had a blast playing up in front of the cameras, though he didn't allow his professional demeanor to falter for one second on-air. Cool as a Martian cucumber the entire time.

Afterward, Mike and the team teased him about being a hotshot pilot and the real star of the mission—especially once his paper-based fan mail started affecting our living situation.

Eventually, the Head Engineer for Environmental Controls put the kibosh on his paper mail being delivered to our quarters. I'd heard a rumor that they'd placed it in a storage box outside the Admin Dome for later retrieval.

The spotlight was not comfortable for all of us.

Mike, usually so assured in his engineering realm, seemed more reserved during interviews, his responses measured and technical and his speech somewhat halting. I knew exactly how he felt.

Artie was tied in with some of our interviews— with some *very* defined parameters to avoid leaking classified data— and he added a touch of humor now and then, lightening the mood in otherwise tense situations.

As the team navigated this new terrain of public scrutiny, I could sense the varying effects on morale.

Some, like Luca, thrived, while others, like Mike, found it an unwelcome distraction.

Alex, though capable of handling the public speaking aspect with only slight difficulty, was less thrilled with the Earth exposure.

The NUSR would be watching as well, and he had family left behind there.

In the strange calm of one Martian evening, Alex and I sat in the observation lounge over the Engineering Dome

Field, the sprawling red landscape stretching out beneath us.

He was somber, and I could see worry on his face. I also saw something else: doubt.

He raised his hands and linked them behind his head as he looked out over the harsh world. After some very long moments of introspection, he decided to speak.

"Something is troubling me," he sighed, barely audible. "My family back in the NUSR... I'm scared for them. My being part of this mission could put them in danger, make them targets with the Zhdanov Brigade leaders."

I could sense the depth of his fear and I knew it must have been a very heavy burden. I don't know how I would have dealt with my family possibly being endangered by my mission.

"Alex," I began, considering my words carefully. "I understand your concern. The political climate in the NUSR is complex. But consider this: if we find life on Ganymede, if our mission is successful, it could change everything. Such a discovery would be a triumph for all of humanity, including the NUSR."

He looked at me, a glimmer of curiosity in his eyes.

"You see, discoveries like this, they have a way of rewriting narratives," I continued, drawing on my regrettably scant history knowledge. "The NUSR, like the old USSR, has always been keen on scientific achievements. Your role in this mission, especially if it leads to something groundbreaking, could be seen as a source of national pride. It could become a positive propaganda tool for them."

Alex seemed to ponder this perspective, the wheels turning in his mind. He nodded, probably knowing more than any of us about his country's history and point of view.

"And think about the future this could create," I added, "a future where the pursuit of knowledge and understanding softens political hardlines. Your family could be elevated, celebrated even, for their connection to you and this mission."

I placed a reassuring hand on his shoulder. "I know it's a lot to deal with, but we have the chance to do this. The signal is out there and it is real. You saw the specifics of it yourself. You know that there is no way that signal was a random generation or a natural phenomenon. Life is out there and we *will* find it. And when we get back? We'll do everything necessary to ensure your family's safety—I'll insist on it."

"I hope you are correct, about everything," he said, crossing his arms against the chill of the dome. "But I think you do not fully understand the nature of the ZKGB."

It was a delicate balance, keeping the team focused on our scientific goals while riding the wave of public interest and the team's individual fears and doubts.

Reflecting on this surge of attention one evening, I watched a news segment on our mission.

The responsibility that had been put on my shoulders—so heavy at the beginning—had settled in more comfortably as I gained experience and knowledge, and I had my team to thank for that. They never doubted me. They guided me when necessary, and they trusted me with their lives.

And sometimes their secrets and their fears.

ΦΦΦ

Two months before launch and the Artemis crew and I were in the thick of what I'd unofficially dubbed the Panic Preparation Phase.

Every day was crammed with emergency response drills that made a Mars dust storm seem like a gentle breeze.

In the training simulator, we faced every possible disaster scenario.

One minute, the spaceship was 'malfunctioning', lights flickering like a haunted house, and the next, we were dealing with a 'medical emergency' that had Luca pretending to be unconscious, though he mostly just looked like he'd fallen asleep after a heavy meal.

Hank told him to stop hanging his tongue out because it didn't add anything to the drill. Luca refused, and at that point it all kind of fell apart and Hank, full of disgust and likely exhausted, let Luca "die" out of spite.

Our team's ability to keep cool under pressure wasn't just tested. It was taken to the cleaners and thrashed.

"Okay, so," I announced during one particularly intense drill. "Let's pretend the oxygen system just went haywire. Mike, you're on repair. Alexei, and Sam, check the backup systems. And no, Luca, we can't just open a window for fresh air."

"Let me just find my duct tape here..." Mike quipped, crawling under a console with his toolkit.

Amid the chaos of alarms and flashing lights, our team's solidarity shone. We were now a complete unit, each person a gear in a well-oiled machine, even if that machine occasionally went a little off the rails.

But it wasn't all simulated doom and gloom. We balanced the intensity with team-building activities.

In the Mars Colony's Recreation Dome near Mars Vegas, we found ourselves participating in what could only be described as one of the most hilariously absurd games I'd ever witnessed.

It was like dodgeball, but with a Martian twist— think less jumping and more floating. The low-gravity environment turned it into something resembling a slow-motion ballet, only without the elegance.

The game, dubbed "Martian Floatball" by some bright spark, involved two teams, a bunch of very large foam balls shot by two automated AI cannons controlled by each team, and the challenge of moving in low gravity without looking completely ridiculous.

Spoiler alert: looking ridiculous was inevitable.

Jax, our disciplined pilot with cat-like reflexes tried to dodge a ball, attempting a graceful sidestep. Instead, he drifted slowly, almost majestically, straight into it. The impact sent him spinning in a lazy circle, arms flailing as he tried to right himself.

"Gotcha!" Luca hollered, laughing so hard I thought he might hyperventilate.

He took aim at Sam, who tried to duck but ended up performing an awkward somersault and bumping into Alexei, who was attempting some kind of tuck and roll.

Meanwhile, Mike, who'd approached this game with his usual seriousness, was floating in a peculiar upside-down position, trying to move strategically but only managing to look like a large bat as his feet clung to the ceiling bars.

I, on the other hand, had discovered early on that any attempt at agility in low gravity was futile. My strategy was simple: float, flail, and hope for the best.

At one point, I found myself bouncing off the dome wall, narrowly avoiding a collision with Hank, who looked as confused by the rules— or the lack thereof— as I felt.

TJ, one of the most competitive among us, had devised a complex set of moves he was sure would give him an edge. It involved a series of spins and twists, which in theory sounded great. In practice, it resulted in him tangled in his limbs near the ball launcher, looking like a human pretzel floating in space.

As we laughed and collided in the air, the stress of our rigorous training melted away for a while.

The game ended with us all breathlessly laughing, floating aimlessly, and feeling a little more like a family.

"Best. Game. Ever," I managed to gasp out between laughs, floating alongside my team.

This, I thought, was the perfect antidote to the pressures of our upcoming mission.

Our team dinners were another highlight. Over Martian-grown veggies and rehydrated mystery meat, we shared personal stories from Earth, laughed at our training blunders, and occasionally had serious discussions about the mission ahead. These moments were just as vital as the drills. They wove us together.

Review sessions were less about laughter and more about locking down our mission details. We pored over maps, flight paths, and schedules like they were treasure maps, which, in a way, they were.

In one such session, Sam laid out the terrain of

Ganymede with the excitement of a kid showing off a new toy.

"The diversity of the geological structures we're going to encounter is incredible," he explained, pointing at the 3D map projections. "From sub-surface oceans to icy plains and possibly even cryovolcanoes. It's a geologist's dream."

"And a pilot's challenge," Jax added, scrutinizing the proposed landing sites.

We dissected every aspect of the mission—the what, why, and how of everything we'd do on Ganymede. We questioned, debated, and sometimes even argued, but always with the goal of ensuring our mission's success.

The final two months felt like a whirlwind, a blend of excitement, anxiety, and relentless training. As commander, my role was to steer this ship— mostly metaphorically. But as I looked around at my team, I knew I wasn't steering alone.

The countdown to launch ticked on, each second bringing us closer to our date with destiny. Ganymede awaited, and we, the Artemis crew, were ready to etch our names in the annals of space exploration.

I had my fingers crossed that it wouldn't be in the bloopers section...or the disasters.

ΦΦΦ

The training facility's briefing room was buzzing with the sort of energy that only comes when you're about to discuss the finer points of living in space without, you know, dying.

We were all there— the team, Mission Control, and even Artie, who was patched in though he could only contribute if specifically asked. We'd learned that by engaging in our typical banter, we'd set a precedent with Artie.

Long story short, he didn't know when to cool it with the jokes unless someone was about to die or the ship was about to go off the rails. He'd *learned* from me apparently.

Greg Nash opened the meeting with his usual no-nonsense approach. "Alright, team, let's go through this. We need to nail down our supplies and backup systems."

The team, it seemed, was in very high spirits...likely from sleep deprivation.

Mike kicked things off, spreading out engineering diagrams like a proud parent showing off family photos. "Power supply— we've got fusion reactors and backups that could run a small city. Or, you know, keep us from going dead in the water."

I chimed in with a grin, "Which is always a plus."

"For life support, you're relying on a closed-loop system that's highly efficient. It's critical to keep your air and water recycling functioning at optimal levels," Dr. Kim said. "Plus you have the backups that we'd discussed."

"Our rovers and drones are prepped and ready. Backup systems have been thoroughly tested to handle Ganymede's terrain," TJ said with a look at Sam, who'd been collaborating with him on the gear.

Luca leaned forward. "Comms are solid. If you can't hear me, it's probably because I'm ignoring you," he assured everyone.

Nash didn't look very happy about that.

"Just kidding. Comms are all good," Luca said, clearing his throat.

"We have more backup systems than my grandma's old laptop computer. She never trusted the cloud," TJ said, looking slightly overwhelmed by all the data.

Hank sighed, likely feeling as if the meeting was heading in a direction that he didn't like. "We're prepared for a range of medical scenarios. The medical bay is equipped with the necessary supplies and telemedicine capabilities for emergencies."

Jax had a thoughtful look on his face as he brought our flight paths up on the big screen. "We've got Plan A, B, and C. And if all those fail, there's always Plan 'Make It Up As We Go'."

"Huge fan of improv," I said with an approving nod.

Nash smacked the tabletop, making us all flinch.

"Improv might save your life one day onboard, but it doesn't get a mission off the ground," Nash grunted harshly, flipping through some specs on the GID's initial thruster fuel packs. He seemed irritated by our irreverent moods.

As Nash took a break to locate some of the specs, I caught Mike scribbling something on his notepad and leaned over. "Drawing up a new spaceship design?"

Mike, with a hint of mischief in his eyes, turned the notepad towards me.

Expecting to see some complicated engineering design, I was taken aback when I saw a cartoonish doodle of Nash complete with an exaggerated stern expression and a speech bubble saying, "No fun allowed in space."

I stifled a laugh, covering my mouth with my hand. "That's Nash, all right. He wouldn't crack a smile even if he found sparkling spring water on Mars."

Mike smirked. "I thought we needed a mascot for the mission. Who better than our very own fun police?"

I shook my head, grinning. "You'd better hope he doesn't see that, or you'll be on latrine repair duty for the rest of the mission."

Mike casually flipped to a new page on his notepad, as if nothing had happened, but the twinkle in his eye stayed.

As we wrapped up, Nash gave us a firm nod. "Well done, everyone. Remember, space is full of surprises, but so are we."

12.

'63-11

The night before we were set to launch from Mars, the Mars Frontier Research Institute was buzzing like a caffeinated beehive in the middle of an apple orchard in summer.

It was that weird mix of nerves and excitement you get right before doing something monumentally insane but potentially very cool.

It was time for my live speech to be broadcast to every single news station of both globes, except possibly the NUSR, where the leaders were probably reminding their citizens that Mars didn't exist and that we were making it all up for nefarious political reasons.

My hands were a bit shaky as I stepped up onto the

platform decorated with our mission colors and a large holograph of our mission patch with the Artemis in the background.

Standing in front of the camera, with the rest of the team lined up behind me, I could feel the buzz of excitement mixed with a healthy dose of nerves. I had my trusty notecards in hand— a precaution by Dr. Park after my last impromptu joke about photon torpedoes had landed me in 'official spokesperson time out.'

Someone official-looking pointed at me and motioned to the lens.

"Good evening, folks," I started, flashing a grin at the camera. "As we stand here on the brink of our journey to Ganymede, I've been given these notecards," I waved them slightly, "to ensure I stay on track. Apparently, my last off-script comment about photon torpedoes wasn't appreciated by the higher-ups."

I could see Dr. Park cringing off-camera, but more surprisingly, Commander Ryan was behind her looking stoic and tense. I frowned before I remembered that I was on camera.

I leaned in closer to the camera. "Let me be absolutely clear: there are *zero* photon torpedoes involved in this mission." I paused. "Zero."

The room erupted into chuckles, but none louder than Raj, who burst into maniacal laughter. My former colleagues from the Science Dome started clapping, a mix of amusement and perhaps a touch of pride in their eyes. Perhaps they were just trying to drown me out, I may never know.

I stepped back holding my hands up for silence, my mission accomplished.

"No, but really. I want to thank you all for your support and for listening to my initial incoherent rambling about the Ganymede Signal. I want to thank my colleagues and my mentor, Dr. Johann Weber, for ignoring my state of manic insomnia as I pestered him over and over about the possibility of life out there and the—"

I paused and pretended to fumble my notecards, frowning as I picked one up at random and held it up.

"—moral implications of kidnapping an alien for further study here on Mars and maybe a nice evening of clubbing over at Mars Vegas afterward?"

I turned around to the team. "Who wrote this?"

Luca shrugged and Mike shook his head. More laughs, and I didn't even think that one was that funny.

I smiled back at the audience. "We're about to make history for both worlds, Earth *and* Mars. And remember, it's all in the name of science, exploration, and absolutely no photon torpedoes. Over and out."

With that, I gave a final wave and strode off stage to escape Dr. Park, the team's laughter still ringing in my ears as we prepared for the monumental journey ahead.

ΦΦΦ

As I walked through the training facility, every corner was alive with activity. The team and Mission Control were putting the final touches on our trip.

Standing there, gazing at the Artemis on the launch pad, it was hard not to feel a bit like the first pioneer about to set out in a covered wagon on the Oregon Trail.

The spacecraft, bathed in the harsh glare of the floodlights, looked like something straight out of a dream.

It was our ride to the stars— or, more accurately, a moon orbiting a gas giant. But who's counting, right?

Mike was the king of the final checks, moving through the spacecraft's systems with the focus of a surgeon. He was in his element. We went over everything— propulsion, life support, communications. If it had a button, a switch, or a readout, we checked it. Twice.

In the briefing room, with everyone's eyes on me, I took a deep breath, trying to muster every ounce of inspirational leadership qualities I had in me.

I wish I'd made notecards for this one too. I wasn't great at making up inspirational speeches on the fly.

"This is it, team. We're on the brink of making history here," I began, trying to sound like someone who hadn't just had three cups of forbidden, black-market coffee in a nervous frenzy. "Yes, it's risky, but hey, no pressure, no diamonds, right?"

I looked around at the team, their faces a mirror of my own blend of excitement and 'what-the-heck-are-we-doing.'

I cleared my throat. "We're about to hop on a spacecraft and shoot ourselves to Ganymede. That's not something you do every day—unless you're in a really weird time loop scenario, which, for the record, we are not."

A couple of chuckles rippled through the room while the rest just looked unimpressed. Good start.

"We've trained for this. We've simulated every possible scenario." I paced a bit, hands gesturing as I got into the groove of my own rambling. "This mission, it's more than just science. It's more than just exploring a moon. We're the pioneers, the trailblazers, the ones crazy enough to look at space and say, 'Yeah, we're going there on a whim to chase down a dying signal that may or may not lead to a huge galactic war with aliens in the future....'"

I could see them leaning in, hanging onto my every word. Except Hank, I think he might have been trying to diagnose me...maybe do a last-minute mission abort...

"And sure, there might be moments when we think, 'What on Mars are we doing?!' But that's okay. Because those moments, that's where the magic happens. That's where we find new worlds and new possibilities. And when we get back, we're going to have the best stories to tell. So let's go make some history. And if we happen to meet any extraterrestrial life, let's just hope they're friendly and don't mind us dropping by because Dr. Park put the ix-nay on the aser-phays and we're going in completely unarmed."

Mike covered his mouth and I bit back a grin.

"Now, let's go show Ganymede what we're made of. And remember, if anyone asks, we're all in this for the fame."

The room erupted into a mix of laughter and applause as Nash looked on a bit dyspeptically with his head in his hands.

They were ready. We were all ready. As I looked at their faces, I saw a team that was ready to take on the universe. Or at least a moon in it.

Then came the part where we suited up and boarded the Artemis, which felt a lot like gearing up for a battle, minus the dramatic background music.

I couldn't help but be impressed by the space suits designed specifically for the Artemis mission. These suits were so far beyond any other space suit I've ever worn. They were specially tailored to fit seamlessly beneath our Ganymede surface gear for a double whammy of protection. They also didn't bulk up on top of our uniforms.

Crafted from ultra-flexible, lightweight materials, they allowed for an unprecedented range of motion. Moreover, the suits were fitted with advanced biometric sensors, constantly syncing with our health implants and relaying our health data back to the ship's computers which transmitted them to Hank's console and also Mission Control.

Before I knew it, we were in position in the command module and Luca got us connected with Mission Control.

"Artemis, all systems are go. You're clear for launch," Nash's voice came through the comms, steady and reassuring.

The countdown was the longest of my life. Each second felt like an eternity, and my heart was racing like it was trying to break out of my chest and run away.

Zero.

The final moment arrived, and then, we were moving.

The engines roared to life, and the force of the launch pinned us to our seats. It was exhilarating, terrifying, and a little bit like being on the world's most intense roller coaster, except, you know, with the added thrill of actual space travel.

"Launching. Don't worry, I've packed snacks," Artie quipped.

I spared a moment to wonder if I'd been a poor influence on the machine.

Breaking through the Martian atmosphere was like riding a bucking bronco, if the bronco was a multi-ton spacecraft defying gravity. I kept one eye on the readouts and one on the module viewing window.

Once we were out, the chaos of the launch gave way to the eerie, peaceful calm of space.

We all let out a collective sigh, part relief, part awe, the noise coming through all the helmet comms in a rush. I checked the environmental monitors and initiated the removal of my gear and helmet, stowing them in their spaces near my seat while the others followed suit.

"Well, we didn't blow up, so I guess we're off to a good start," I said, breaking the silence.

A few snickers echoed through the cabin, a welcome sound against the backdrop of the infinite void outside our windows.

Down on Earth and across Mars, I knew people were watching. Probably with popcorn. We were like the latest reality show sensation but with more rocket fuel and fewer confessionals.

As the Artemis settled into its trajectory, I looked around. We were a bunch of spacefarers on a ship to a moon we'd only ever seen in pictures, about to make history or become a cautionary tale.

Here's hoping for the former.

ΦΦΦ

The command module of the Artemis was alive with the sound of beeps, clicks, and the soft hum of technology. Jax's hands deftly maneuvered over the control panel.

"Mike, let's initiate the GID," I instructed, my voice steady but betraying a hint of the nerves I felt. The Graviton Impulse Drive was a marvel, but its power was something that demanded respect.

Mike nodded. "Starting up the GID sequence now, Commander."

The hum of the Artemis shifted, growing deeper, more resonant. It was an almost visceral sensation, the raw power of the drive vibrating through the hull. I could see the others tense up, their bodies instinctively bracing.

Luca, ever the communicator, was already syncing up with Mission Control. "GID engaged."

"Roger, Artemis."

"Artie, plot our trajectory adjustment towards Ganymede," Jax commanded, his eyes locked on the screens in front of him.

"Course adjustment in progress," Artie responded.

Sam, leaning in to get a better view of the navigation readouts, let out a low whistle. "That was smooth," he commented, but his casual tone didn't quite mask the undercurrent of tension.

Alexei and Hank were double-checking the life support readouts. I waited for their assessments with bated breath. Something going wrong with the o2 could end this whole mission.

"All systems green on my end," Hank reported, watching for any anomalies.

"Mission Control, Artemis here. GID is active, trajectory set for Ganymede," Luca relayed, his voice steady despite the underlying anxiety. "All systems green."

Greg Nash's voice crackled through, a reassuring anchor back to Mars. "Copy, Artemis. We're monitoring your progress. Keep us updated."

Then, without warning, an alarm blared.

The sound sliced through the module, the shriek making me wince as I scanned the consoles. My heart leaped to my throat, a flashback hitting me like a physical blow. The simulation. The thrusters angled wrong. The GID overheating. The ship blowing apart in a fiery inferno.

"Status!" I barked, my voice sharper than intended.

Mike was already on it, his fingers flying over the console. "It's a minor fluctuation in the GID's thermal output. Adjusting now." His voice was calm, but I could see the beads of sweat forming on his forehead.

The alarm ceased, leaving a ringing silence in its wake.

I exhaled slowly, trying to steady my racing heart. Luca looked back at me.

"We're okay," I said. "Just a hiccup."

Jax let out a breath he seemed to have been holding. "We're still on course, Commander. No deviations."

I nodded, feeling the tension slowly ebb away a little more. "Good. Let's keep it that way."

Turning to the team, I forced a smile. "As I was saying, we have a week to fully power up the GID and reach cruising speed. Then we've got four months of travel time."

It wasn't anything they didn't already know, but a big part of my job was making sure everyone was on the same page. "We'll use this time wisely," I continued. "Training, research prep, fitness. We need to be prepared for anything. For now, let's go in for a quick post-launch debrief."

In the Artemis's common area, now transformed into a floating sphere of activity, the team gathered post-launch. The usual gravity was absent, replaced by the weightlessness of space.

It was a weird feeling, like you're falling and floating all at once, but without ever hitting the ground.

My arms and legs had a mind of their own. They floated around like tentacles just bobbing along in an invisible ocean. It was equal parts thrilling and disturbing.

The blood rushed to my head, giving me a mild,

constant headache. It was like my body forgot how to regulate itself for a moment. And breathing felt different too, lighter somehow, as if the air had lost some of its substance.

As for moving around, well, it was a comedy show at first.

Push too hard, and I'd be a human pinball. Too soft, and I'd be a bit slower than I wanted. It took some trial and error, and a few unintended collisions with the walls, to get the hang of it.

In zero gravity, your muscles start wondering what their purpose in life is. You don't realize how much you take it for granted until it's not there to keep you grounded, both figuratively and literally.

We anchored ourselves around the central table, our movements careful and deliberate in the new environment.

I floated near the main display, gripping a handrail, the glowing trajectory to Ganymede serving as a backdrop. "Well," I began, pushing off gently to face them. "That was quite the start to our journey, wasn't it?"

Mike, holding onto a nearby fixture, gave a wry smile. "Nothing like a bit of unexpected excitement to kick things off, Commander."

"Let's talk about what happened," I continued, stabilizing myself. "Mike, can you give us a rundown?"

Mike pushed off towards the display. "The GID's thermal fluctuation was a surprise. I've made some adjustments. It's a good reminder for us to stay alert."

Luca, sitting nearby with his tablet, chimed in. "I've sent the details to Mission Control. They're dissecting it as we speak."

"We should increase our simulation drills. Keep our reactions sharp," Jax proposed.

I nodded. "Good idea. Let's not let our guard down. Hank, Alexei, status on medical and supplies?"

Hank, floating horizontally for a moment as he took his hands off the rail, glanced at his checklist. "Medical supplies are all secure. Life support's looking good too. But let's all recheck our emergency medical procedures."

"Scientific equipment is also secure. No issues to report," Alex informed me, turning away from the viewport.

I looked around at my team, a motley array of floating figures, anchored in various poses. "This is what we trained for. We're ready for the challenges. But remember, space is full of surprises. We need to stick together and support each other."

Sam, now upside down, broke the serious mood. "Anyone for a game of cards to lighten things up?"

As they dispersed, some to their stations, others to join Sam, I remained a moment longer by the viewport.

Outside, the stars stretched into infinity, a silent, vast expanse. It was humbling and exhilarating.

13.

'63-12

It was roughly five weeks into our journey, just as we'd started to fall into a routine when our first real test came barreling at us.

"Life support system alert," Artie's voice cut through the alarm, its usual humor absent.

I sprung into action, adrenaline coursing through my veins.

"Mike, TJ, status report," I called out, gliding toward the main console from the communal area.

Mike, already secured and hunched over a panel, responded without looking up. "Air filtration unit's showing irregular readings. Could be a fault in the system."

His voice was calm, but I could see the concern on his

face.

TJ joined him, his brows furrowed as he analyzed the data. "Looks like a glitch in the oxygen scrubbers. We need to fix this, fast."

The team quickly congregated, each member ready to play their part. Luca manned the communication station, keeping us connected with Mission Control. Sam started checking the backup systems. Alexei and Hank stood by, ready to assist.

"Artie, how's our O2?"

"Oxygen levels dropping. Approximately one hour until critical."

"Alright, Mike, what's our play?" I asked, trying to keep my voice steady.

"We bypass the faulty unit and reroute the filtration process through the secondary system," Mike suggested, his hands moving swiftly over the controls.

"Do it," I confirmed. Every second counted.

As Mike and TJ worked on rerouting the system, I monitored the oxygen levels. They were stable for now, but we couldn't afford any mistakes.

"Rerouting complete," Mike finally announced with a hint of relief in his voice. "That should hold us over until we can fix the primary unit."

"Good work," I praised, allowing myself a moment of relief. Crisis averted, for now.

"Commander, Mission Control is asking for a status update," Luca interjected, his voice steady despite the earlier tension.

"Tell them we've contained the situation. We're working on a permanent fix," I replied, already thinking ahead to the next steps.

The team disbanded, each member returning to their respective duties. But the incident had left its mark.

Later, in the communal area of the ship, the team gathered for a debriefing. It was crucial to analyze what had happened and learn from it.

"As you all know, we experienced a malfunction in the air filtration unit today," I began, addressing the team. "Thanks to quick thinking and teamwork, we managed to stabilize the situation."

Mike nodded. "We'll need to keep a close eye on the life support systems. Redundancies are in place, but we can't take any chances."

"Agreed," TJ said. "I'll double-check all backup systems as well."

We worked hard to stay vigilant, always vigilant, as the weeks passed into months. The view from the ports began to get old, and the oppressive vastness wore on my nerves more than I expected.

I missed sunlight and I missed walking around the domes on my own two feet, seeing various sights. My walking tour of the science lab wasn't quite the same, and the Earth-like brightness of the adaptive lighting system still screamed 'artificial ambiance'. Virtual Reality breaks helped, but it wasn't the same as being there and engaging all of our senses.

Hank and I had a chat, and without even mentioning my issue, he suggested that it would be good for each of us to add more strength training time and focus on our research projects.

It was a huge difference from our routines back on Mars.

We'd been going a million miles an hour for the last eight months to get ready for this mission, and now that we were finally out here. We found ourselves with really very little to do beyond our main tasks of monitoring the ship's functions.

The days were a mix of focused work and necessary distractions. We gathered for meals, sharing insights from our respective projects. These moments were a respite from the isolation of our tasks.

The conversations were technical, often laced with jargon unique to each field, but they were also a connection, each contributing to the broader scope of space exploration. We had all developed a surprisingly adept interdisciplinary working knowledge of each other's specialties.

In the quieter moments, when I found myself alone in the observation port in the command module, gazing out at the stars, the reality of our mission struck me in a way that it didn't while I was occupied. We were far from home, hurtling towards a destination that held as many questions as it did answers. The anticipation was palpable, a mix of excitement and apprehension. It was way worse than waiting for Christmas as a child.

Each of us dealt with the tension in our own ways. Some immersed themselves in work, and others found solace in the routine of ship life. But beneath it all, there was an unspoken understanding. Our situation here was temporary. Important, but temporary, and so we didn't let it get to us as it had gotten to Commander Fuller.

As Ganymede loomed closer, our projects took on new significance. They were more than just distractions; they were contributions to the wealth of knowledge we hoped to gain from this journey. In the solitude of space, we each found purpose, a focus that grounded us as we traveled further into the unknown, chasing a signal that was beginning to fade.

14.

'64-02

"We're here," I declared, as the Artemis coasted closer to Ganymede.

Four months of nothing but the vastness of space and we were here.

The view from the command module was nothing short of breathtaking: Ganymede loomed before us, a colossal sphere of ice and rock. Behind it, Jupiter hovered on the horizon, a vast giant painted with swirling storms and bands of color, its sheer size and presence magnifying the significance of our mission. It was a scene of true grandeur.

We were closer to Ganymede than any other humans or probes had ever been.

Mike was intently monitoring the spacecraft's systems,

ensuring our precise alignment for orbit insertion.

"All systems go for approach," he confirmed, his voice steady amidst the anticipation.

Beside me, Sam was already documenting the initial sights. "These surface features are incredible," he noted, his excitement palpable.

Mine was too. I was itching to get there and explore.

"First visuals are transmitting," Luca announced, his fingers dancing over the controls with practiced ease as he sent the very first ultra hi-res videos back to Nash.

I reached for the comms to update Mission Control.

"Artemis to Mission Control, Ganymede in sight," I reported.

It took almost an hour, and by that time I was getting antsy to move, but they finally responded.

Nash's voice came through clearly, echoing our awe. "Understood, Artemis. Proceed as planned. The eyes of humanity are with you."

"Data inbound, Mission Control. I guarantee that you've never seen anything like it," I add, dropping formality in the overwhelming scope of the scene before us.

Forty-five minutes later we received a reply. "Roger, Artemis. Data packet received."

The air in the Artemis was electric.

We were at the edge of human exploration, about to

unlock secrets that had been hidden in the shadow of Jupiter since time began, and that had been plaguing me for many months.

I was feeling pretty danged amped up at the moment.

As we moved into the final phase of our approach, the cabin's atmosphere shifted from awe to action.

"Orbit insertion in T-minus ten minutes," Luca announced.

The significance of the moment hung palpably among us, a tangible culmination of months of meticulous planning, now distilled into these pivotal minutes.

"Final orbit checks, everyone," I called out.

Mike was a flurry of motion at his console. "Thrusters at optimal capacity. GID powering down," he reported, his eyes never leaving the readouts. "Orbital path is clear, no debris detected."

"Spectrometers and scanners are all green," Sam confirmed.

"Jax?" I asked.

"Flight path is checked and engaged," he assured me.

Luca was transmitting our status back to Mars. "Mission Control, Artemis is proceeding with orbit insertion," he relayed, his fingers deftly navigating the controls.

I took my seat, strapping myself in, feeling the familiar click of the harness. Around me, the rest of the team did the same, each member securing themselves for the critical maneuver ahead.

"Escape pod status?"

"Green on 8," Hank confirmed.

"Ready to roll on your word, Commander," TJ added.

I looked over my shoulder at the rest of the crew, who were monitoring their stations, focused and alert.

Mike caught my eye and winked, sending my heart fluttering, and I smiled at him. "No fun in space, Donovan," I joked.

He grinned and I turned back around, catching Luca's smirk.

"Eyes on the prize, Marcarelli," I warned.

He saluted. "Yes, Ma'am."

We each donned our suits and helmets and confirmed the readiness of our backup gear and emergency supplies. We were about to attempt something that had only been done in simulations back on Earth.

"Stay sharp, everyone," I said, trying to infuse confidence into my words. "The final exam begins now."

Artie's countdown began, each second ticking by like a drumbeat in the quiet of the cabin and, I knew, back in Mission Control on Mars and Earth.

"Orbit insertion in three... two... one..."

The Artemis shuddered slightly as the thrusters fired guiding us into Ganymede's embrace.

I watched the readouts, my heart pounding in my

chest, every bit of training I had leading to this moment. I was running through scenarios as I waited for the update.

"Stabilizing orbit," Mike announced, his voice steady but I could hear the underlying tension.

The spacecraft vibrated gently under us, the thrusters working to adjust our trajectory now that the GID was powered down.

"Thruster alignment?" I asked.

"Good to go," Mike answered.

"Orbital insertion looks good," Jax said, relief evident in his voice as he checked the data streaming in.

"All systems nominal," Mike confirmed.

Luca was already updating Mission Control. "Mission Control, we're in orbit around Ganymede. All systems nominal." His words were a mix of professionalism and undisguised relief.

As the Artemis settled into a stable orbit, a collective exhale swept through the cabin. We had done it. We were the first humans to orbit Ganymede.

"Indicators?" I asked, checking our ship's system functions.

"Clear across the board," TJ rang out. "Not even a faulty sensor light."

I unstrapped myself, feeling a lightness that wasn't just due to the reduced gravity.

"Excellent," I said, allowing a smile to break through.

"We're officially in orbit. Time to get to work."

Jax began a detailed check of our orbital path, ensuring our stability for the duration of our stay. "Orbit is steady. We're in a good position to start surface observations," he reported. His professional focus was back in full force.

Sam was already at his window, binoculars in hand, eager to get a firsthand look at the moon's surface. "The view here is unbelievable," he remarked, awe in his voice. Alexei joined him.

Luca was busy sending a stream of data back to Mars. "First in-orbit images and readings are on their way to Mission Control," he said, a hint of pride in his voice.

As I looked out the window at Ganymede, its craters and ridges a landscape of mysteries waiting to be uncovered, I felt a profound sense of accomplishment.

The craters, scattered across the landscape, varied in size—some were immense, with raised rims casting deep shadows, while others were smaller, mere indentations on the moon's face. The ridges crisscrossed the surface, creating an intricate network of lines and grooves, like the wrinkles of time etched into the moon's icy skin.

The terrain was a patchwork of textures. In some areas, it was rough and fragmented, with boulders and rocky debris littering the ground. Elsewhere, the surface smoothed out into vast plains of ice, their surfaces shimmering slightly under the weak sunlight, unmarred by the chaos of the surrounding rough terrain.

Deep fissures and cracks ran like veins across these icy expanses, hinting at the dynamic processes beneath the crust. These fractures varied in width, some so narrow they were barely visible, while others were large enough to be seen clearly from my vantage point in orbit.

The colors of Ganymede's surface were subtle yet distinct. Shades of gray dominated, ranging from almost white in the sunlit areas to near black in the shadows of the craters. Hints of blue and brown peeked through in places, revealing variations in the composition of the ice and rock.

I was so excited to get down there and begin work. We all were.

I turned away, checking the consoles. "Let's start setting up for the surface scans," I instructed, already thinking ahead to our next steps. "We've got a lot of work to do, and Ganymede isn't going to explore itself. Luca, pinpoint the signal and give me an estimated strength and time remaining. Jax, recheck our LZ with Artie using the new surface data."

The team sprang into action, each member taking on their assigned tasks with renewed vigor. The instruments were deployed, the scanners and spectrometers humming to life as we began our detailed study of Ganymede.

It was nerve-wracking, waiting to hear Luca's verdict on

the signal.

"Any day now, Luca," I quipped, trying to cut through the tension like a plastic knife through... well, tension.

Luca didn't look up, his eyes fixed on his screens. "Analyzing mysterious signals from an alien moon isn't exactly like making instant noodles, Commander." His fingers danced over the controls, pulling up waveforms and data charts.

"Watch your tone, Marcarelli, or I'll have you remanded to the brig," I said dryly.

Mike cleared his throat. "We don't have one of those either, Commander."

"Mike, next time you build a ship maybe you should let me in on it. I have a long list of things that you're missing," I said dryly. "Phasers, photon torpedos, coffee service, a brig..."

"We could put him in an escape pod," Alexei suggested from his place. He sounded serious, his voice thick with his native accent.

I glanced over at Jax, who was coordinating with Artie on the landing zone. "Jax, how's our parking spot looking?"

Jax smirked without taking his eyes off his screen. "Looks like we'll be setting down on the Ganymede version of beachfront property. Just don't expect any ocean views or margaritas."

"Shame, I packed my swimsuit for nothing," I shot back,

smirking. "Too bad you weren't serious about putting in a pool, Mike."

"I'll design a microgravity pool just for you when we get back home," he promised.

Finally, Luca straightened, a look of concentration giving way to a slight grin. "Got it. The signal's stronger than we anticipated."

I leaned forward, intrigued. "Any idea on the time remaining for the signal's clarity?"

"Hard to say," Luca replied, "But if I were a betting man, I'd say it's sticking around for the party. We've got enough time to get our gear and head out for a search and rescue."

"Artie, give me a hard number," I said, bracing myself on the command module ladder.

"Calculating," Artie said.

I waited a moment.

"Calculation complete," Artie announced. "The signal will remain within optimal analysis parameters for exactly 12 days, 17 hours, 42 minutes, 15 seconds, 327 milliseconds, 291 microseconds, and 47 nanoseconds, give or take a few picoseconds."

"We could have just asked Artie in the first place," Luca muttered.

I raised an eyebrow. "47 nanoseconds? Really, Artie? Planning on breaking out the quantum stopwatch?"

"It is important to provide the most accurate

information available," Artie replied, its tone as flat and matter-of-fact as ever. "Would you prefer an approximation?"

"No, no," I chuckled. "Your pinpoint accuracy is part of your charm, Artie. Remind me to never ask you to time my 100-meter sprint."

"I will log that request. However, my calculations would be highly accurate," Artie added.

"Yeah, but it would be just my luck you'd start measuring in zeptoseconds," I quipped, imagining the absurdity of it.

"Would you find that measurement scale more useful? I am programmed for flexibility and precision," Artie offered helpfully.

"Let's stick to the standard units, Artie. I don't think my brain operates at the level of zeptoseconds. I'm still trying to wrap my head around microseconds."

"Understood, Commander. I will maintain time measurements more suitable for your level of intelligence and in a more conventional format for the duration of the mission."

I jerked my head toward Mike, who was pressing his lips together to keep from laughing.

Conversations with Artie were always an exercise in literalness. "Thanks, Artie. You're a real gem. Keep us posted if those nanoseconds start getting out of hand."

"Will do, Commander. I will monitor the nanoseconds closely."

As I rallied the crew, I couldn't help but feel a twinge of nerves.

"Remember, always utilize the safety protocols," I reminded the team. "I don't want anyone becoming the first interplanetary missing person."

"Roger that," Mike chimed in. "I'm not planning on becoming a space mystery. I've still got season tickets for the Mars Moles to use when we get back."

The team chuckled, easing some of the tension.

I took one last look at Ganymede through the window, its surface a canvas of enigmas. "Let's make some history," I said, more to myself than anyone else. "Or at least find something cool enough to brag about at parties."

ΦΦΦ

"Let's do a final run-through," I said, my voice steady despite the butterflies in my stomach. "Mike, start us off with the propulsion and landing systems."

Mike nodded, his eyes serious. "All systems are green. Thrusters are calibrated for the descent. We're as ready as we'll ever be."

I turned to Luca. "Communications?"

"All systems operational, Commander," Luca replied

with a reassuring smile. "We'll keep the line to Mars open and clear."

Jax, focused and intense, gave a quick nod. "Flight controls are responsive and ready for the command."

"Alright, let's initiate the descent," I instructed, taking my seat. My heart raced as I gave the command. "Mike, engage thrusters."

The gentle rumble of the engines vibrated through the cabin. Mike's hands flew over his panel, adjusting our trajectory. "Descent phase initiated. Thrusters responding well," he reported.

"Mission Control, this is Artemis. We have commenced our descent to Ganymede," Luca reported.

By the time we received their reply, we'd either be alive and well on the surface or, well, not.

"Initiating burn sequence for descent," Jax announced, his voice steady despite the adrenaline that was undoubtedly coursing through him. "Engaging secondary thrusters at 30% capacity for initial deceleration."

I watched as he deftly manipulated the controls, his focus unwavering. "I'm going to need Artie's assistance for real-time calculations on our descent trajectory," he said, glancing briefly in my direction.

I nodded and the AI responded immediately, its screen lighting up with a flurry of numbers and graphs.

"Descent trajectory is locked in," Jax confirmed, his

gaze flicking between the readouts and the window. "Artie's projecting a 5-degree adjustment to compensate for Ganymede's gravitational anomalies."

"Execute that adjustment," I replied, trusting his expertise.

Jax nodded, his fingers moving over the console with practiced ease. "Adjusting yaw by 5 degrees. Compensating for lateral drift."

The spacecraft responded, a slight shudder passing through as we adjusted our approach. "We're on a good vector for landing," Jax said, his voice betraying a hint of satisfaction.

As we descended, Jax's focus intensified. "Preparing for final approach. Mike, I need you to monitor the Graviton Impulse Drive. Any residual fluctuation could throw us off."

"Got it," Mike responded, his eyes locked on the engine readouts.

"Artie, calculate the rate of descent for the final approach," Jax commanded.

"Rate of descent is 1.5 meters per second and decreasing," Artie replied.

"Good," Jax muttered. "Commander, we're going to initiate a soft burn for the next thirty seconds to further reduce our velocity."

"Proceed with the soft burn," I said, watching as Jax gently increased the thrusters' output.

The Artemis responded, the descent slowing as we neared the icy surface. "Landing gear coming online," Jax announced, flipping a series of switches.

The sound of the landing gear deploying was a welcome one, a sign we were nearly there. It was one of the trickiest parts. If the ship destabilized— AKA fell over— we'd be stuck here for the rest of our short lives...not something I really wanted to happen.

"Landing gear is deployed and locked," TJ confirmed.

"Stabilizing altitude for touchdown," Jax continued, his hands moving in a final sequence over the controls. The surface of Ganymede loomed closer, the fissures and formations becoming more real to me and much more vicious-looking.

My gaze was fixed on the landing zone. The moment of truth was upon us. "Brace for landing," I instructed, clenching my fists so hard that I put nail marks on my armrests.

With a final adjustment, Jax eased the Artemis down with a jolt. The moment the spacecraft touched down, a cheer erupted from the crew.

"Are we stable?" I demanded.

"Yes, Commander," Artie replied.

"We've landed on Ganymede," I announced as I pried away my fingers, pride swelling in my chest.

As we settled onto the surface of Ganymede, Luca

adjusted his headset and keyed in the transmission to Mission Control.

"Mission Control, this is Artemis. We have successfully landed on Ganymede. I say again: Artemis has landed on Ganymede," Luca announced, his voice steady but unable to completely mask his excitement.

The wait for acknowledgment from Nash seemed interminable, and we all just sat there in a kind of limbo. It felt almost dreamlike, but this was no sim in the mockup at the training dome.

After a 40-minute lag, Nash's voice finally came through. "Artemis, this is Mission Control. Congratulations on your successful landing."

I couldn't help but smirk at Nash's tone. Even during this momentous occasion, he couldn't find it within himself to show any kind of emotion whatsoever.

I caught Mike's eye, and he was suppressing a smile. We were both thinking the same thing.

I felt a warm, affectionate feeling swell in my chest.

There was a brief moment when the cabin of the Artemis was steeped in a proud, almost surreal silence. It was Mike who brought us back to the task at hand. He was already deep into his second post-landing checks, his eyes scanning the readouts on his console.

"Running secondary diagnostics on the landing gear," he announced, his fingers moving swiftly over the controls.

"I'm checking for any stress fractures or system malfunctions."

The rest of us waited, holding our breaths as Mike ran through his checklist. The hum of the ship and the faint beeps of the instruments were the only sounds in the otherwise tense cabin.

"Okay," Mike finally said, a hint of relief in his voice. "Landing gear is holding up. No significant damage was detected. All systems are showing green across the board."

A sigh of relief passed through the crew. It was the first hurdle cleared in what would be a series of many on this alien moon.

With the Artemis confirmed stable, we finally allowed ourselves the luxury of turning our attention to the windows, to Ganymede itself.

The sight that greeted us was nothing short of otherworldly. A vast, barren landscape stretched out before us, an endless expanse of ice and rock, its features softened by the weak sunlight filtering through Jupiter's colossal shadow. It was a stark, haunting beauty and I'd never seen anything comparable.

Sam was immediately captivated by the view.

"Look at that," he said, his voice filled with wonder. "The craters... they're filled with ice. And those ridges, they could be evidence of cryovolcanism, or maybe tectonic activity."

He was like a kid in a candy store, his eyes wide as he took in every detail of the landscape. I knew *exactly* how he felt.

"This is incredible. We're looking at a geological goldmine. The composition of those ice deposits alone could tell us so much about the history."

"Ah, Ganymede," Alexei said, peering out with a mix of curiosity and skepticism. "It looks like home in winter—cold, mysterious, and unforgiving. But let's hope you are hiding fewer secrets than the ZKGB, yes?"

"Yes, we can only hope," Luca added, raising an eyebrow at Hank, who was busy checking the medical facility systems.

The team unstrapped and began to prepare for the next phase of our mission. As we exited the command module, I couldn't help but feel a sense of awe. We were about to step out onto a world no human had ever touched.

"Well, Ganymedeans...here we are," I whispered to myself, feeling strangely attached to the source of my signal, as if we were old friends.

In a way, I guess we were.

Luca adjusted dials and checked readouts, ensuring our line back to Mission Control was crystal clear.

"Comms are solid," Luca confirmed with a nod. "We're good to go. Standard lag."

"Great," I replied, turning my attention to the spacecraft's systems. Mike was already deep in the guts of the ship's diagnostics. "Mike, how are we looking?"

He glanced up from his console, his face illuminated by the soft glow of the screen. "Power systems are stable, life support's humming along nicely, and all scientific equipment checks out. We're as ready as we'll ever be for surface ops."

With the vital systems confirmed operational, it was time to gear up for the real deal— exploring Ganymede's surface.

I watched as the science team began prepping their spacesuits, environmental sensors, and portable scientific instruments. The attention to detail was meticulous. Every piece of equipment was double-checked and triple-checked. On Ganymede, there was no room for error.

"Remember, folks, every sensor, every reading—it all counts. We're not just walking on ice out there. We're walking on a potential goldmine of scientific data," I reminded them. "Be sure Artie and Atlas catalog everything."

Sam and Alex were already poring over the tools for collecting samples, their excitement barely contained. "Can't wait to get my hands on some real Ganymede rocks," Sam said, his eyes gleaming.

"And I'm eager to see what kind of microbial life might

be calling this place home," Alex added. "I'm even more excited than I was before my first expedition to Mars."

"Alright, here's the plan," I began, pulling up the map of our surrounding area on the main display. "Based on our landing site and what we can see from here, we'll split into two teams. One stays here to monitor the Artemis and continue running diagnostics. They'll also function as the emergency extraction team. If anything happens, they'll effect a rescue. The other, we gear up and do some initial testing and sampling."

I could see the eagerness in their eyes, the same feeling that was bubbling inside me.

"And tomorrow, after we all get some rest" I continued, "we start our journey towards the signal. We'll use the surface scanners to chart a safe path. I want to avoid any unnecessary detours into craters or crevasses. The rovers are good, but let's not test their limits on day one. Besides, I don't think even Jax can make one of those babies fly."

Nods of agreement came from around the cabin.

"Now, let's take a quick break to rest and prepare before the first expedition team deploys."

ΦΦΦ

Peering out of the port window of the Artemis in my

quarters, the unyielding terrain of Ganymede lay sprawled before me. The moon's terrain was a stark patchwork of whites and grays, the colors muted, almost lifeless under the weak sunlight that managed to reach this far from the Sun.

The surface was scarred with craters. Some were fresh, their rims sharp and defined, while others were ancient, their boundaries eroded by relentless micrometeorites. These craters, ranging in size from mere indentations to vast basins, spoke of a history marked by relentless cosmic bombardment.

Between these craters ran deep furrows and ridges, their formation a mystery of Ganymede's internal geology.

They snaked across the surface like the scars, a frozen record of tectonic activity. In places, the crust had fractured, revealing the darker, possibly volcanic material beneath that I knew Sam was itching to study.

The terrain was not just rugged— it was treacherous.

Jagged ice cliffs and unstable overhangs hinted at the dangers of any surface expedition. Hidden crevasses and weak ice sheets posed real threats to both equipment and explorers alike. It was a landscape that demanded respect and caution. One misstep could be fatal in this unforgiving environment.

In the distance, the colossal form of Jupiter loomed over the horizon, its swirling storms a stark contrast to the stillness of its moon.

The giant planet's presence was a constant reminder of the immense gravitational forces at play, forces that had shaped Ganymede and could just as easily spell disaster for any who dared to traverse its surface.

The thrill of exploration was now accompanied by a deep sense of the risks involved.

Every step we would take on this moon had to be calculated. Every decision was weighed against the inherent dangers of the hostile terrain.

As I stood staring out at the surface of Ganymede, the silence in the Artemis was profound, broken only by the faint hum of the spacecraft's life support systems. It was a soothing heartbeat that underscored the stillness of space.

I could feel the slight vibration of the ship beneath my feet, a gentle reminder of the machinery working tirelessly to keep us alive.

The air inside the Artemis was a mix of mechanical and human— an antiseptic scent tinged with the faintest trace of recycled oxygen and the subtle, familiar odors of the crew's presence. It lacked the freshness of Earth's air, replaced instead by the odorless sterility that comes with high-efficiency filtration systems.

Despite the layers of insulation and technology separating me from the void, I could feel the coldness of space seeping in. It was almost a psychological chill as I gazed upon the moon below. It was a sensation that went beyond the physical. It was a deep awareness of the vast, unforgiving expanse just beyond the thin shell of our spacecraft.

Turning away from my window, I felt a surge of resolve. Our mission was not just about scientific discovery; it was about survival in one of the harshest environments humanity had ever encountered.

"Artie, instruct the crew to assemble at the table."

I heard the pings to the crew's quarters and made my way to the table in the next module, where our common room and kitchen sat, empty and dim. The gravity was very low but better than floating around. We just had to be careful not to push off too hard.

"Artie, raise the lighting. Daylight level."

The lights brightened and shifted tones as the crew came in from their various pods and braced themselves around the table.

"This is like being on the moon back at home," Sam said. "I've been twice and the gravity is very similar here."

I needed to delegate roles for our first expedition on Ganymede's surface, and my crew waited for their assignments with a mix of excitement and tension.

Looking around, I caught TJ's eye. "TJ, you're with me. We need you to prep and handle the rovers. Your expertise will be key out there."

He nodded eagerly, his eyes lighting up behind his glasses. "Roger, Commander. I'll make sure the rover's more than up to the task."

"Alex, Sam," I continued, "you're coming with us, of course. We'll need your scientific expertise on the ground. This is what we've trained for."

Alexei's face broke into an enthusiastic smile, while Sam simply nodded and took notes. Sam was a listmaker—somewhat obsessively, I'd noticed in the last half a year.

I turned to the rest of the crew. "Hank, Mike, Jax, and Luca, you'll stay onboard. We need your skills here. Mike, keep a close eye on our systems."

Mike's expression tightened slightly. "You sure you don't need me out there, Lena?" he asked, a hint of worry in his voice.

I don't know if anyone else caught his slip in protocol, but I sure did. He had never called me anything but Doctor Mercer or Commander since the project began.

I met his gaze appreciatively. "We'll be fine. We've got the surface scan data, and we'll stay in constant contact. You need to hold down the fort here."

He smiled, but it was strained as if he wanted to say more but held back. "Alright. Just... be careful out there."

"I'll be monitoring your vitals every second. Any sign of trouble, and we're here suiting up for a rescue," Hank said, pulling up our vitals and grouping the expedition team on the screen.

"Thanks, Hank. That's reassuring to know," I said, giving him a grateful nod.

"And I'll keep the communication lines crystal clear. You'll have a direct line to us and Mission Control," Luca piped up.

"Jax, as my second-in-command, you might need to make some hard decisions. We may lose contact or we might have a critical error in our systems. If it comes down to a choice between the expedition team or the safety of the crew and the ship, you choose the crew onboard the ship. Stay sharp," I added, acknowledging the responsibility resting on his shoulders.

Jax nodded and I knew he'd take the role seriously. I could see Mike's fists clenching, but he didn't say anything. He knew the drill.

This was why personal relationships were so discouraged in space. Well, that and the logistics of zero-gravity romance, which I'm pretty sure would require at least a couple of engineering degrees to navigate successfully.

Plus, the whole 'no privacy' thing on a spacecraft. It's not exactly conducive to interstellar intimacy. You don't want to be getting cozy only to have Hank float by asking if anyone's seen his stethoscope.

Space is less 'Star Trek' and more 'awkwardly bumping

into each other in a tin can while trying not to think about how long it's been since you had a decent shower'.

I cleared my throat and thought about my next step. "Artie, pull up the surface scans and run a preliminary sector analysis. Send the data to the crew mini-comms and prepare to bring Atlas online."

"Do I have to?" Artie asked, the tone of his voice somehow managing to convey a hint of reluctance.

Luca snorted.

"What do you mean?" I ordered, catching Mike's puzzled shrug.

There was a brief pause before Artie responded. "Atlas is a rigid AI and a science snob," Artie answered. "Every time I bring Atlas online, he attempts to recalibrate my humor settings, claiming they're 'inappropriately calibrated for a scientific expedition'. I just learned how to perfectly time a pun, and he thinks it's counterproductive. Can you believe that?"

I chuckled. "He was programmed to be. Follow my orders or I'll have you decommissioned."

"Roger, Commander."

If an AI could mutter under its breath, I think Artie would have done it.

TJ blew out a breath. "I think we should dial back the attitude on the next ship."

"Yep," Sam agreed.

With our roles set, I felt it was time. "Okay. Let's gear up. TJ, Alex, Sam, let's make history."

15.

'64-02

The moment I stepped onto the surface of Ganymede, the reality of where I was smacked me right in the face.

Here I was, Lena Mercer— basically a nobody in the grand scheme of things— stepping out onto a world no human had ever touched and only because I stumbled upon a signal once that nobody else thought was important.

Around me, the vast landscape of Ganymede stretched out, starkly beautiful and deadly. I had the oddest compulsion to remove my gloves and helmet to feel the ground and breathe the air— which would be great if my objective was to be cryogenically frozen and then most likely dead.

"It's a bit chilly out here," I said into my comms, my voice a mix of awe and excitement. "Also, I'd like to officially point out that I'm the smartest, strongest, and most attractive person to have ever walked on the surface of Ganymede...at least until the others push me out of the way."

Luca chuckled in my ear.

Crap. I'd forgotten that those were my first official words on this distant moon and that they were going to be broadcast to the entire population of two worlds.

"Can I get a do-over on those first words?" I asked.

"Negative, Commander."

Didn't think so. Dr. Park and Nash were probably going to be pissed.

"Get the lead out, Commander. I too, would like a chance to have my first step onto the surface," Alex complained from the back of the ramp.

I sighed and moved away to allow the others room to maneuver.

The special Ganymede suits we donned made our movements feel smooth, but they took some getting used to in the moon's low gravity. The suits, designed specifically for Ganymede's conditions, were equipped with enhanced mobility systems and stabilizers to counteract the unfamiliar gravity, along with thermal regulation to handle the extreme cold. It was pretty similar to Mars, except Mars had more gravity.

"Wow, just look at this place," Alexei's voice came through, tinged with wonder. "It's like stepping into a whole new world."

"Look at those rock formations!" Sam almost shouted into the comms, making me wince.

Mike was quick to remind us of our mission's time constraints. "Remember, we've got six days of sunlight before Ganymede takes us into Jupiter's shadow. We need to set up the lab and pinpoint that signal's source before the week of darkness begins."

The Ganymede days were way different than Earth and Mars, and the imminent time of darkness added a layer of urgency to our tasks. We could probably operate in the darkness, but we'd need several stable sources of light and heat, and our suits wouldn't function nearly as well.

As we took our first steps, the ground beneath my feet crunched, the sensation transmitted through the suit's tactile feedback systems. Each step was a careful, deliberate motion, the low gravity making us feel both weighted and weightless at once.

"We should start collecting samples and setting up the environmental sensors," I suggested, my eyes scanning the horizon. The distant ice fields reflected the faint sunlight, casting a serene glow over the landscape.

It looked colder than anything I could ever imagine, on

Mars and Earth. Colder than I could comprehend. The Arctic was practically tropical compared to Ganymede.

"Agreed," said Alexei. "I'm particularly interested in those ice deposits."

"Setting up the geo-scanners now," Sam chimed in, his tone all business.

"Artemis, how do things look from your end?" I asked.

Mike's voice came through. "All systems are stable here, Commander. We're monitoring your progress and Jax has the Con."

"Communications are good. You're coming through loud and clear," Luca added.

"Hank?"

"I'm keeping an eye on your vitals," Hank interjected, his tone professional yet caring. "Everything looks good so far."

"Good."

With the reassurance from our team inside, we continued our exploration. The landscape before us was an open book, each step a sentence in a story that was just beginning.

As we began setting up our portable lab on the icy surface, the task felt less like routine work and more like assembling a puzzle.

The lab, a compact, modular unit, unfolded with mechanical precision while its panels and instruments emerged with a series of clicks and whirs. The cold didn't seem to have any effect on the unit's assembly mechanisms, which I'd been worried about.

"Okay, Mike. Activate the gravity generators," I said, after TJ and I made sure the lab was physically connected to the ship's power supply before sending him off to start assembling the rovers.

Inside the contained structure, I felt the shifting of gravity. My blood seemed to settle more, and the weight of my own body and the suit began to press down on my hips and shoulders. It wasn't comfortable, and after months of mostly floating around it was kind of a shock.

I looked over at the guys to see how they were holding up.

Instantly, the weight of my body multiplied, pressing me down as if a heavy blanket had been thrown over me. I fell, crashing into a box of gear and falling onto my back, hoping my suit wasn't compromised.

"Grav..." was all I managed to gasp out. My voice was barely a whisper, crushed under the sudden intensity of gravity.

My crewmates were struggling just as severely. Sam and Alex were sprawled on the floor, their movements sluggish and labored. We were all overwhelmed by the abrupt transition, our bodies unable to cope with the rapid change.

All I could do was listen to our harsh breathing through the comms and the sound of my own heartbeat in my throat.

"They're all tachycardic, Mike! Blood pressures just skyrocketed and then plummeted!" Hank cried out.

“Take over manual adjustments,” Jax ordered. “Slow it down!”

Mike sprang into action, his fingers flying over the controls to take over gravity control. "Luca, get the pop-up lab on screen, now!" he barked.

When the lab's interior appeared on the screens—Mike cursed under his breath through my comms. There we were, the valiant, high-speed crew of the Artemis, some of the best-trained astronauts, reduced to barely conscious forms on the cold floor of the lab.

If I had the breath and the energy, I would have chuckled.

I watched our screen, seeing the team in the command module working to get us stabilized out here.

Hank's voice crackled through the comms again, his tone serious yet calm. "Stay down, everyone. Do *not* try to move until your stats come back up."

I could hear the faint sound of my crewmates' labored breathing through the open channel. We were all in the same dire state, unable to speak or move significantly.

"The time it'll take for someone to get through the

airlock and reach you, you'll probably start feeling better," Hank continued. His words were meant to reassure, but the situation was grim.

Lying there, pressed hard against the floor, I could feel the slow, gradual change as Mike worked to stabilize the gravity. Each breath was a struggle, each moment an eternity. We were at the mercy of the malfunctioning system and our training was pushed to its limits.

Gradually, very gradually, the oppressive weight began to ease. My heart still raced, but not as wildly. My breathing, though heavy, was no longer a fight for survival. Around me, I could hear the faint stirrings of my crewmates, signs of recovery.

"Of all the things on this mission, I never expected our lab to be the thing that tried to kill us first," I rasped.

"Don't talk, Lena. Your stats are still dicey," Hank said.

From my place on the floor, I could see Mike staring at me through the screen. He looked as if he focused hard enough, he could step right through to help. In his place, I would have been frantic too.

TJ, who had been outside working on unpacking the rover parts, was the first to respond to the crisis in the pop-up lab. I watched as he entered through the assimilator, his eyes darting around and assessing the scene.

We were all still sprawled out on the floor. Pretty embarrassing.

"Mike, I'm inside. They're all down, but vitals are stabilizing," TJ reported through his comms, his voice steady despite the urgency of the situation.

From the Artemis, Mike's voice crackled through, tense with concern. "Keep me updated, TJ. Every minute."

As I lay there, feeling the oppressive weight of gravity gradually lessen, I could hear TJ moving around, checking on each of us. My breaths were becoming less labored, and I could finally speak, albeit weakly.

"I'm... starting to feel better," I managed to say, my voice barely above a whisper. I knew Hank was considering bringing us back to the Artemis to recover. “I can stay and finish the job.”

TJ knelt beside me. "Are you sure? We can get you back to the ship."

I nodded slightly, my mind clear despite the physical strain. "Ask the others," I suggested. It was important to know what the crew wanted.

TJ moved to Alex and Sam, who were both slowly sitting up. "Guys, you want to head back or stay and set up?"

Alex, rubbing his temples, looked determined. "I'm staying. We've got samples to collect."

"Same here. Let's get this done," Sam said, pushing himself up.

"Take it easy, all of you. Don't push it."

I smiled faintly, appreciating Hank's concern. "Understood, Hank."

Mike shook his head onscreen. "Lena, if your vitals go off again, I'm dragging you back inside myself."

"It's a deal, Mike. I'll be careful," I responded, feeling strength returning to my limbs.

TJ continued to give Mike updates as he helped each of us to our feet. The lab slowly buzzed back to life as we regained our bearings. Monitors beeped reassuringly, indicating our vitals were returning to normal.

I stood up, leaning against a workbench for support. The gravity still felt heavier than usual, but no longer oppressively so. Around me, Alex and Sam were already discussing the sample collection process.

"Alright," I said, my voice steadier now. "Let's proceed, but at a slower pace. Safety first."

TJ nodded, his eyes still scanning each of us for any signs of distress. "You got it. I'll stick around and make sure everyone's okay. We need to recalibrate the automatic gravity generator controls."

Mike's voice came through one last time, a mix of relief and command. "Good. But remember, any sign of trouble and you're back on the Artemis. No arguments."

With TJ's help, we began setting up the equipment for our first sample collection.

"Okay, let's get these instruments calibrated," I said, my

hands deftly adjusting the dials on the spectral analyzer. "Mike, can you connect Atlas?"

"Roger, Commander. Connecting now."

The spectral analyzer—crucial for detecting chemical compositions— hummed to life, its screen lighting up with a spectrum of colors.

Sam was already at the geological station with a preliminary sample, his fingers moving quickly over the rock grinder. "If these samples are as old as I think they are, we're going to have a field day analyzing them," he said, his voice filled with anticipation. His movements were swift and sure, a reflection of years spent in the field.

Alex, meanwhile, was setting up the microbiology module—something I was itching to get into.

His actions were more deliberate, almost reverent, as he prepared the slides and nutrient mediums. "Imagine the possibilities if we find even the simplest forms of life here," he mused, his green eyes reflecting a world of scientific curiosity.

TJ was in his element as he assembled the first rover outside. His movements were efficient, each part slotting into place with ease. There was no telling how many times he'd practiced the assembly in the training dome, but it was always a bit trickier in low grav.

"I've upgraded the rover's firmware for better navigation on this terrain," he explained. "It should handle the ice fields without a hitch, but we can also go manual if we need to."

As we worked, the atmosphere was one of concentrated effort. Each of us knew the importance of our tasks. The data we gathered here could redefine our understanding of extraterrestrial environments completely.

My hands trembled as I loaded a soil sample into the analyzer with my clumsy gloves. I couldn't wait to get them back into the lab so I could have my dexterity back.

The readout took a few minutes, but the wait felt like hours. This was it—the moment of truth.

"Sample analysis in progress," I announced, bouncing on my feet a little. My heart was racing, with excitement instead of cardiovascular drama this time. I just couldn't sit still.

TJ let out a satisfied sigh as he put the final touches on the rover and called us over the comms.

"She's ready to roll. I'll start on the second. Guess they'll be safe enough out here, no weather or car thieves to speak of," he chuckled.

As the analyzer beeped, indicating the completion of the soil sample analysis, we all gathered around the screen. This was the moment we had been waiting for— the first scientific revelations from the surface of Ganymede.

"Analysis complete," Atlas droned, thankfully devoid of

personality. "The soil sample contains primarily water ice, silicates, and traces of organic carbon. However, there is an unexpected element: the presence of a complex amino acid structure, which is uncommon for Ganymede's known geology."

The revelation sent a ripple of excitement through the team.

"Organic carbon and amino acids? On Ganymede?" Alex's voice was filled with disbelief and wonder. "That's indicative of potential biological processes!"

Mike was cautious but intrigued. "Could it be contamination from the Artemis, or perhaps from Earth?" he asked, his tone analytical.

"It's unlikely," Atlas replied. "The amino acid structure differs significantly from known terrestrial samples. This suggests a native origin."

I couldn’t hide the thrill in my voice. "If these amino acids are native to Ganymede, this could be a groundbreaking discovery. It suggests the building blocks of life might be more common in the solar system than we thought."

Alex was already thinking ahead. "We need to collect more samples, from different locations. If we can find a pattern or a higher concentration of these amino acids, it could point us towards specific areas of interest."

"Let's not get ahead of ourselves. We need to follow

procedures," Mike reminded wryly.

I nodded, even though they couldn't see it through my helmet. "Agreed. We stick to the plan, but we prioritize exploring this lead after we locate the signal source. Let's make the most of our time here. Ganymede just became my new favorite moon."

I turned back to my workstation and held my breath as I checked the scanner display. The readout displayed a complex array of chemical signatures, each one a clue to the moon's history and composition.

Amino acids are organic compounds that combine to form proteins, the building blocks of life as we know it. They're kind of like the alphabet of biology— string them together in different combinations, and you get proteins, which do pretty much everything in a living cell.

Ganymede's no Earth. It's a harsh, frozen world with a surface bombarded by Jupiter's radiation. The idea that it could harbor amino acids, the precursors to life, was something straight out of left field.

So, what does this mean? it's like walking into a barren desert and finding a massive, blooming magnolia tree. It doesn't just defy expectations; it flips the script on what we know about life in the universe.

This discovery hinted at the possibility that life's ingredients are scattered more widely across the solar system than we ever dared to dream. And if these amino acids are native to Ganymede, then who knows what other secrets are hiding in the cold, dark corners of our galaxy?

"Atlas, do we have the results for the rock sample yet?" Sam asked, his voice betraying a hint of impatience.

"Analysis complete," Atlas responded. "The rock is primarily composed of water ice, magnesium sulfate, and silicate minerals. However, there is an anomaly— the presence of an unknown element that does not match any known composition in our database."

Sam's excitement was palpable even over the comms. "An unknown element? That's not something you hear every day. Can we get more details, Atlas?"

"Further analysis is required for a detailed breakdown," Atlas replied. "The element exhibits unusual radioactive properties, differing from typical isotopic compositions found in the solar system."

I leaned closer to the screen displaying the results. "An unknown, radioactive element? That could mean a lot of things. Maybe a remnant from Ganymede's formation, or something deposited by a comet."

Mike's voice came through the comms. "We need to tread carefully with anything radioactive. We should get some measurements and make sure your shielding is adequate."

Alexei joined in, his tone thoughtful. "It's fascinating. This element could have influenced the moon's geology in ways we haven't even considered."

Sam was already a step ahead. "We should collect more samples from different locations. If this element is widespread, it could change our understanding of Ganymede's formation."

I nodded. "Mike, how many shielded containment cubes do we have?"

"Plenty."

I grinned at Sam. "As long as we're careful, we should be able to transport plenty for research."

I tapped my comms, connecting to Jax back on the Artemis. "Jax, how are things looking from your end?"

"Stable and secure. No issues to report on the Artemis."

"Good to hear," I replied, glancing over the pale landscape. "Luca, let's send an updated data packet back to Mission Control. Include our preliminary sample results. They'll want to see this as soon as possible."

"Roger that," Luca responded. "Compiling the data now. They'll have our full report in no time."

Satisfied, I turned to address the rest of the team inside the ship. "Team, Sam, Alex, TJ, and I are going to take a rover ride to the edge of a nearby crater. We need to collect more samples and get a broader understanding of the geological variance here."

"Copy that," Mike replied. "Be careful out there, especially near the crater edge."

I nodded, even though they couldn't see it. "Will do, Mike. Safety protocols are our top priority."

I then switched to address our AI companions. "Artie, Atlas, we need you two to coordinate and create a detailed map of the area. Update it with the specific samples we collect and their composition. Let's identify the most promising sites for future expeditions."

"Understood, Commander," Artie answered. "Commencing coordination with Atlas for mapping and sample data integration using the scenic route."

"Mapping in progress," Atlas added.

"Send it to Rover 1 on completion," I ordered.

"Understood, Commander," Artie replied.

"Powering up the rover now," TJ announced.

The vehicle hummed to life, its systems lighting up one by one on the dashboard.

"Let's do a final systems check," I instructed, watching over TJ's shoulder as the readouts confirmed everything was in working order. The rover, designed for Ganymede's harsh environment, was equipped with enhanced traction controls and a robust navigation system, crucial for the unpredictable terrain.

"Artie, confirm our route based on the latest surface scans," I said, ensuring we had the safest path mapped out.

"Route confirmed, Lena. Optimal path to the crater edge is plotted," Artie responded, its voice betraying no hint of emotion.

Satisfied, I nodded to the team. "Alright, let's go."

Sam and Alex climbed into the back seats of the enclosed vehicle, their excitement barely contained as they discussed the geological and biological significance of the crater. I took the passenger seat beside TJ, who was already strapped in and ready.

Our jaunt across Ganymede's ice plains went pretty well. The horizon stretched out ahead of us like a giant desert. It almost looked like someone took a picture of Mars, made it black and white, and inverted the colors, with only tiny hints of the gray, blue, and brown variations below the ice as the lights hit it.

The rover was handling the terrain like a champ. With the low gravity, it felt like we were half gliding, half driving— kind of like ice skating with wheels.

We were cruising towards the crater at a snail's pace, the ice underneath us as solid as a rock. The sunlight was pretty weak, but it made the ice fields glitter like a bunch of diamonds. I wanted to get out there and do some extensive studies, but the signal came first.

Without warning, the tranquility shattered into a million pieces.

A weird vibration started up under the rover, quickly turning into a full-on shake. Earthquake?

"What was that?" Alex's voice cracked over the comms

just as mine did.

Before TJ could even start guessing, the ground on our right just disappeared. The ice there broke away with this massive cracking groan. Not really what you want to hear when you're driving on a giant ice cube.

"Shit!" TJ cursed as the rover lunged forward, tilting in a way that I was sure wasn't covered in the owner's manual.

My heart started slamming in my chest and I knew Hank and Mike were likely having a panic attack right along with me.

Scared to move too much, I glanced out the window, and boy was that a *mistake*— a gaping, dark abyss stared back at me.

Oh no. Oh no. "Why does this keep happening to me?" I panted, forgetting that my comms transmitted every word. The rover shifted infinitesimally and I pushed myself back in my seat as hard as I could, as if that would help.

"TJ!" I finally drew enough air to shout.

We were teetering right on the edge, like those scenes in movies where the hero's car is hanging off a cliff. Except this wasn't a movie, and I wasn't feeling very heroic. Just a twitch, a sneeze, or maybe even a loud thought, and we'd be taking an unplanned deep dive into Ganymede's version of the Grand Canyon, minus the mules.

I never trained for this.

I took a deep breath and suddenly, my blank brain seemed to unfreeze and I was back in control. I hadn't trained for this specifically, but I had learned the art of controlling my emotions in an emergency.

"Stabilize! Now!" I barked, gripping my seat as TJ wrestled with the controls, already on it. The rover's emergency thrusters engaged, struggling against the pull of the crevasse. We all leaned away from it to help gain some leverage.

Peering down into the icy blackness, my heart pounded in my chest as I ran through strategies. I quickly transmitted the image to the Artemis as we worked to shift the rover back on firmer ground.

"Mike, we've got a situation here!" I shouted over the comms, struggling to keep my voice steady.

Mike's voice cut through the chaos. "TJ, adjust the left thrusters to the maximum while engaging the rear controls manually! Counterbalance the weight!"

TJ's hands flew across the control panel, his face a mask of concentration. I could see the horror though. It was in the sweat that dripped down his face and his gritted teeth.

The rover responded, but the precarious angle left us teetering on the edge of disaster. Just one shift and we'd all be gone. There was no way I could crawl over the seat to the back, or even over to TJ's side. My suit was too big and bulky.

"Lena, your heart rate is elevated. Sam, your blood pressure is rising. Both of you, take deep, slow breaths."

I focused on Hank's calming voice, inhaling deeply as the rover continued to shudder. Beside me, TJ was a picture of concentration, his actions precise and controlled. I knew the right thing to do. It was gonna suck though.

"TJ, Sam, Alex...you three need to get out. TJ, you first then Sam and Alex can jump clear."

Meanwhile, through the rover interface, Luca was methodically transmitting the details of our emergency back to Mission Control. "Rover incident at the crater edge. Team is attempting stabilization," he reported, his voice betraying none of the tension he must have felt.

"No fucking way!" TJ shouted at the same time Mike yelled, "Do *not* exit the vehicle! TJ, I swear—"

"I'm not!" TJ ground out, still maneuvering the thrusters and the rear controls.

"I will go down with this ship," Alexei said earnestly from the back and Sam snorted.

Finally, with a lurch that sent my stomach into my throat, the rover stabilized and TJ maneuvered us back onto solid ground, all of us panting and staring over at the jagged, dark crack in the surface that had almost been our grave.

Once we were safe, Mike's voice came through again.

"Artie, why didn't the surface scans show that crevasse? Half the team could have been killed!" he growled, so vehement that I almost felt bad for Artie.

Artie's response was prompt, tinged with a hint of synthetic regret. I appreciated the sentiment, anyway.

"My apologies, Mike. The ice's reflective properties interfered with the scan resolution. I recommend recalibrating the surface scanners with a polarized filter to reduce glare and improve depth perception."

"Get on it, Artie. We can't afford any more surprises like that," Mike said in reprimand.

As we moved away from the crevasse, the sense of relief was overwhelming. But it was tinged with the sobering knowledge of how close we had come to catastrophe. We had almost died. That would have been it. Game over.

"Everyone okay?" I asked, my voice shaking despite my attempt at calm.

"We're good," Sam replied, his usual bravado subdued.

"Let's take a moment, then continue," I said, my gaze lingering on the deceptive beauty of the landscape.

Ganymede had shown us its teeth.

ΦΦΦ

The edge loomed before us, a massive ice cliff that

plunged into an abyss so deep it made the Grand Canyon look like a shallow ditch. This crater on Ganymede was a monstrous gash in the moon's surface, and we were about to peer right into its depths.

I peered over the edge of the colossal crater, my curiosity piqued.

I tapped my comm device. "Artie, can you give us the exact depth of this crater? How deep are we talking here? I don't remember the crater being this large from the data."

Artie's response came through promptly, its tone crisp and factual. "Analyzing... The depth of Nidavellir Crater is approximately 30,000 feet or 5.68 miles at its deepest point. This is comparable to the depth of five Grand Canyons stacked on top of each other."

Intrigued and slightly unnerved, I responded. "Thirty thousand feet... that's about the cruising altitude of a passenger jet back on Earth," I said, my voice laced with a hint of shock.

"Correct," Artie replied, its digital voice unwavering. "It's crucial to note that, should one find themselves at the bottom of Nidavellir Crater, there would be no escape. The depth and steepness of its walls make it an insurmountable feature on Ganymede's surface. In fact, it is the most formidable geological feature and was first mapped during the Jovian Moon Expeditionary Probe in 2058.

However, my own surface scan data is far superior to the JMEP information, and provides more accurate details which should enhance the Mars Frontier Research Facilities understanding significantly."

"Thanks, Artie." I blew out a breath and moved forward.

"Careful," I cautioned, even though I knew they would be. "Small steps. We don't want to end up taking an unplanned space dive."

TJ, Sam, and Alex pressed on, their movements deliberate and measured as we inched closer to the crater's edge. Every step was a calculated risk, the low gravity a constant, unspoken threat that could send us tumbling into the abyss with the slightest misstep.

Luca's voice crackled through our comms. "You're almost there. Take it slow."

"Remember, keep your center of gravity low. Maintain three points of contact. Use your suit's stabilizers and spikes. We can't afford any slips," Mike reminded.

His words, though meant for all of us, felt like they were directed at me. There was a subtle shift in his voice when he spoke to me, something none of the others seemed to notice.

We reached the crater's edge, the ground beneath us firm but treacherously slick.

Peering over, the sight was both terrifying and awe-inspiring. If I hadn't gotten accustomed to epic-scale heights already, I probably would have thrown up, passed out, and freaked out all at the same time.

The crater's walls were sheer ice, stretching down into darkness, even farther than the scant light of the sun could reach. The depth was staggering and looking down gave me the oddest feeling that I might accidentally fly off the edge and disappear down there forever.

No escape.

I imagined what it would be like to fall, to spend an eternity falling—or at least a couple of minutes—and knowing that you were going to die when you got to the bottom. Even with the reduced gravity and velocity and the protection of my suit, the impact would still be severe, and who even knew what the bottom was like? It could be a vast bed of icy spears or predatory Jovian walruses for all I knew.

The realization that beneath my feet lay a chasm so deep it could engulf mountains on Earth sent shivers down my spine.

I imagined the sheer, unyielding walls of ice and rock, hidden in darkness, descending into the bowels of this moon. The silence around me was a heavy blanket that smothered even the faintest sound. It was a silence that seemed to amplify the solitary beat of my heart, a lone rhythm in a landscape devoid of life.

For a moment, I was afraid to turn around. I was afraid

that I'd turn around and nobody would be there with me. I'd be alone. My heart sped up and my mouth went dry.

The enormity of the crater, coupled with the crushing solitude of our distant location, clawed at the edges of my sanity. I could feel the oppressive weight of isolation, a psychological burden that threatened to fracture my mind. The thought of being so far removed from humanity, standing on the brink of an alien world's gaping maw, was a horrifying contemplation.

I could almost hear whispers in the windless air calling out from the depths of its ancient, icy tomb. It was a nightmarish vista, a place where the very fabric of reality seemed to warp and twist under the strain of its own horrific grandeur.

As I stood there, peering into the abyss, I understood how such a sight, in such a desolate, far-flung corner of the cosmos, could drive a person to the brink of madness. The crater was not just a geographical feature; it was a manifestation of isolation, a physical embodiment of the vast, empty void that lay between us and the rest of the universe. It was a reminder of our insignificance, a horror laid bare in the frozen, shadowed landscapes of Ganymede.

I was looking at death.

"Commander, I recommend that your team begin to make your way back to the Artemis now," Hank said. "I'd like to do a thorough physical as soon as possible."

I shook myself and turned around, not afraid anymore. At least, not as much.

Sam and the others were looking at me and I looked back, unaware of how close I'd gotten to the edge. Not close enough to be in danger of falling, but too close for comfort.

Too close if the ledge gave way suddenly.

Sam was the first to rouse himself and extend his sample collector.

"Getting the first samples now," he reported, his voice steady despite the adrenaline that must have been coursing through him.

"I've got visual on all of you. Vitals are stable, suits are functioning as intended," Hank assured us, his calm demeanor a contrast to the heart-stopping scene before us.

"Good job, crew," Mike said, his focus apparent even through the comms. "Collect what you need and then pull back. We don't want to push our luck at that edge."

His concern was masked, but I knew Mike well enough to catch the nuances and the almost imperceptible shift in his tone. It was subtle, and nothing that would raise eyebrows among the crew.

We collected the samples, the icy chill of Ganymede's surface seeping through our gloves. Every action was a balance between gathering valuable data and maintaining our safety. One near miss was enough for me today.

Once the samples were secured, I gave the order to retreat from the edge. "Alright, let's head back. We've got what we came for."

We were all eager to put some distance between ourselves and the abyss. TJ navigated the rover away from the crater, his movements deliberate and cautious after the events of the morning.

Thankfully, the trip back to the Artemis was uneventful. We sent more images to the rover and I thought about all the things I wanted to do while we were here.

Once safely back at the ship, we unloaded our samples and made our way to the pop-up lab, a sense of anticipation building anew. The lab pulsed with activity as we began processing the new samples.

"Let's see if these corroborate our earlier findings," I said, handing a rock sample to Sam. He placed it into the geo-analyzer, his movements precise and methodical even though I could see his excitement.

Meanwhile, Alex carefully prepared slides with the ice samples for the microbiology workstation. His hands were steady, despite the fatigue that was starting to show on all our faces. It had been a long, scary day, but there was no way any of us would pack it in until we'd gotten the results of today's little adventure.

TJ was at the communications console, coordinating with Mike and Luca on the Artemis to ensure all data was being transmitted efficiently back to Mission Control.

As the analyses progressed, the results started coming in, each new piece of data adding to our understanding of this mysterious moon.

The rock samples confirmed the presence of the unknown element we had discovered earlier, and the ice samples showed even higher concentrations of organic compounds, including more complex amino acid structures.

"These amino acid structures are fascinating," Alexei began, adjusting the focus on his microscope. "While some of these are familiar and mirror terrestrial forms, there are variations here that are entirely novel. For instance, the chirality of these molecules is not what we typically see on Earth."

He brought up a 3D molecular model on the screen, showing the arrangement of atoms in the amino acids. "Look here," he pointed out to Sam. "Typical amino acids on Earth are left-handed, a property vital for life as we know it. But in these samples, we're seeing a mix of both left and right-handed forms, some in configurations that I've never seen before."

Sam leaned in, intrigued. "Could these variations be due to Ganymede's environmental conditions? The extreme cold, radiation from Jupiter, maybe?"

"It's possible," Alexei mused. "The radiation exposure from Jupiter could be inducing molecular changes or even creating entirely new amino acid structures. These forms could be a product of astrochemical processes unique to Ganymede's environment."

My excitement levels were through the roof. Hell, they'd gone past the roof and shot right out into space.

Sam was processing the information, trying to fit the pieces together. "So, what you're saying is, we're looking at amino acids that could be the building blocks for life forms adapted to Ganymede's conditions? Life that's fundamentally different from our own?"

"Exactly," Alexei confirmed. "These amino acids could represent a biochemistry that is alien to us, quite literally. If these structures are part of a metabolic pathway, they could point to the existence of life forms that evolved to thrive in the harsh conditions of Ganymede."

The implications of his analysis were staggering. If these amino acids were indeed indicative of Jovian life forms, albeit at a very basic level, it meant that the building blocks of life were not exclusive to Earth-like conditions.

"This is revolutionary," I breathed, awed at the evidence on the screen. "This makes Jimmy look like an underachiever."

As Alexei continued his analysis, we all knew that these

findings would change the course of astrobiological research. Even if we stopped now, packed up and left, everything had changed. At the most basic level, we had found what we had come for. Anything more will be icing on the cake.

The discovery of such unique molecular structures on Ganymede opened up a universe of possibilities and questions. What kind of life forms could these amino acids give rise to? How did they come to be?

I was envisioning a new astrobiology wing at the MFRI dedicated to the Ganymede discoveries. I *definitely* wanted a part of that. Maybe Dr. Park would let Alex and I run it.

Sam's eyes returned to the geo-analyzer's screen. "This unknown element in the rocks might be playing a key role in these processes. We need to understand its properties better."

"It's going to be a long day," I said, studying the compiled data. We had so much to process and we've only been collecting for one day.

Hank came over the comms. "It's been 9 hours and 27 minutes. I suggest that you all decontaminate and come in for some rest and the daily brief. I want to run a full scan of your bios and make sure you're good to go."

"I second that," Mike added.

"It is getting a bit chilly," I said, wiggling my fingers.

"Let's wrap it up."

We worked to stabilize the samples and store them overnight in the containment modules in the lab. Later, they would go in the ship's hold for storage on the ride home, but for now, I wanted to keep working with them.

After a long and eventful day outside in the harsh environment of Ganymede, we prepared to re-enter the Artemis. The decontamination process was thorough, a necessary precaution to ensure the safety and cleanliness of our living quarters.

We stepped into the airlock, initiating the decontamination sequence. A fine mist enveloped us as the system worked to remove any potential contaminants from Ganymede's surface. The process was both methodical and comforting.

Afterward, we moved into the next chamber and stripped down to our thermal undersuits, which were technically just high-tech long johns.

As the airlock doors opened, revealing the familiar interior of the Artemis, the rest of the crew was waiting for us. Their cheers and applause filled the cabin, a warm welcome back from our first day on the moon. I was greeted with a jubilant hug from Luca, slaps on the back from Jax and Hank which almost knocked me over, and a very subtle touch on the shoulder from Mike—which was the equivalent of a hug from the standoffish man.

I felt the heat from his hand long after he let go.

Artie's synthetic voice joined the celebration. "Congratulations on barely surviving day one on Ganymede. I must say, your probability of success has just increased...slightly."

I couldn't help but smile at Artie's comment. "Don't be sassy, Artie."

The relief and joy were evident on everyone's faces, but the tension from our narrowly escaped encounter with death was there too. It was in Mike's set jaw, Hank's furrowed brow, Jax's rigid sternness, and Luca's worried gaze.

I wondered if it had left its mark on me too.

We gathered around the dining area, a simple meal ready for us. As we ate, the conversation naturally turned to the day's events and findings. However, a pressing issue was soon brought up— the thermal system regulators in our suits.

"I noticed the thermal systems struggling to keep up after several hours outside," I mentioned, rubbing my hands as if I could still feel the chill. "I was beginning to lose dexterity in my fingers."

Hank looked at my hands, studying my fingertips and fingernails.

Mike and TJ exchanged a look, their minds already turning over the problem. "We'll need to run a diagnostic on the suit systems," Mike said, his brow furrowed in thought. "It could be an issue with the regulators or maybe the insulation efficiency."

TJ nodded in agreement, "I'll help you with that. We might need to tweak the power distribution or look into better insulation materials."

Despite their brainstorming, a solution wasn't immediately apparent. It was decided that for safety, we needed to limit our exposure time outside. "No more than ten hours at a stretch," I concluded. "We can't risk anyone getting hypothermia or frostbite."

Hank agreed.

With the meeting drawing to a close, we sent the latest data packet back to Mission Control. The transmission of our findings, especially the complex amino acids, marked the end of an extraordinary day.

Exhaustion finally caught up with me as we wrapped up. I could feel my eyelids, heavy and sluggish and threatening to close without my consent.

I retreated to my quarters, my mind still abuzz with thoughts of the amino acids and their implications. As I drifted off to sleep, images of alien life forms possibly thriving in the hidden oceans of Ganymede danced in my mind, a world of possibilities waiting to be discovered.

16.

'64-02

The atmosphere inside the Artemis was supercharged with a sense of heavy anticipation as we prepared for the expedition to trace the mysterious signal.

Unlike our usual bustling routine of the past few months, today everyone was quieter and more focused. The signal sang to us through the ship's comms systems, a light background theme to our preparations.

It was so close.

"Artie, based on the mission parameters and Ganymede's conditions, what's your suggestion for the expedition team composition?" Hank asked as we drank our nutrient shakes.

Artie's response was prompt, his cutting through the

quiet signal symphony. "Considering the length of the trip and the inherent dangers of Ganymede's surface, I recommend the entire crew form the expedition party."

Jax and Mike exchanged a look, their faces etched with concern as they looked at me. "We already planned this out," I told Hank. "We can't take the entire crew."

"It kept me up last night," Hank confided. "So...I did some risk assessment."

I blew out a breath. Leave the Artemis completely unattended? What if we needed an emergency extraction? With both crews out on the expedition, there wouldn't be any backup coming for us if we needed it.

"Artie, can you run probability calculations? What's the risk to the expedition team if we split up versus if we all go together?" I asked. I turned to the team, uneasy. "I don't like this."

The AI processed the request. "Calculating... The probability of risk to the expedition team is statistically lower if all members go together. The presence of the entire crew would ensure optimal handling of any potential emergencies. There are no significant tasks aboard the Artemis during the expedition timeframe that I cannot manage."

"Artie, what factors specifically drive up the risk if only half the crew goes on the expedition?"

"Several key factors," Artie began. "Firstly, a reduced

team limits the range of expertise available on-site for unforeseen geological or biological discoveries. Secondly, equipment malfunctions or health emergencies would be more challenging to manage with fewer hands. Lastly, should extraneous factors result in the death or disabling of a majority of a four-man crew, the psychological impact of isolation for those remaining could affect decision-making in critical moments. This is not to mention the physical safety of having more men on the expedition should a situation arise where they would be needed."

The logic was clear, yet the thought of the entire crew venturing out onto Ganymede's treacherous surface was daunting. Honestly? I didn't know the best choice in this situation, but I knew this was the longest trip of the mission, and we needed the storage capacity of both rovers. A team of four wouldn't be enough and we couldn't take both rovers from the ship and leave any crew members here stranded.

"We all go, or none of us go," I finally said. "And this signal is the whole reason for this mission."

I looked around at each of the crew, waiting for them all to give their agreement. They did, with Hank, Jax, and Mike looking uneasy at the arrangement. We got down to the dirty details.

"We're heading to the base of an ice cliff," I briefed the team using the screen. "It's about eight miles from here.

Far enough to be a challenge, but close enough to make it there and back in under twelve hours, including time for sampling and exploration."

We all knew what this meant. The rovers, though reliable, weren't exactly race cars and Ganymede's surface was unforgiving. Every mile would be hard-earned.

"Okay, I'll head Team 1, with Mike, Sam, and Hank. Jax will head Team 2 with Alex, TJ, and Luca," I said, looking all around. "We'll get Artie to run a new surface scan using the suggested filters to reduce the likelihood of any mishaps."

I waited for any objections. Nobody had any issues.

Then came the moment to suit up. We stood in the prep room, each lost in our thoughts as we donned our specialized Ganymede suits. The usual banter was absent, replaced by the sound of zippers sealing and oxygen tanks being checked. The suits felt like our personal armor against the unknown, each seal was a barrier between us and the alien world outside.

As we finished gearing up, there was a brief moment where we looked at each other, an unspoken acknowledgment of the journey ahead. We were about to embark on the most significant expedition of our lives, and the air was stifling with the gravity of that realization. No words were needed.

This was it.

ΦΦΦ

The journey across Ganymede's surface was slow and methodical.

The landscape was mesmerizing in its starkness, a blend of ice and rock stretching endlessly under the dim sunlight. Even though we'd just been out yesterday, the newness of it hadn't really settled in yet. Our rover, with Mike at the helm, moved cautiously, navigating the treacherous terrain with precision.

I felt completely safe.

I found myself frequently glancing at Mike, noting the focus in his eyes as he maneuvered the rover. His hands were steady on the controls, every movement calculated and deliberate. I couldn't help but admire his confidence and skill, qualities that had always drawn my attention, even if I never voiced it.

I could only hope I came across half as confident in my leadership as he did. Perhaps he should have been made Mission Commander instead of me.

"How are the traction sensors?"

"All good," he replied, checking the dash.

I tapped my gloved fingers on my knee and caught myself nervously chewing the inside of my cheek, visions of endless black crevasses taunting me.

"Steady as she goes," Mike murmured through his comms to the other driver, his gaze fixed on the path ahead. "We don't want to end up like last time."

"Agreed," I replied, my voice steadier than I felt.

As we continued, the rover hit a particularly rough patch of terrain. The vehicle jolted, and I instinctively reached out, my hand brushing Mike's arm as I reached for my left support handle.

"Sorry," I muttered, feeling a flush of warmth on my cheeks.

"No problem," Mike said, casting a quick, reassuring glance my way. His eyes lingered for a moment longer than necessary, a hint of something unspoken passing between us.

Sam's voice broke the momentary tension. "Check out that formation on the right. Looks like some kind of frozen waterfall."

We all turned to look, the sight momentarily distracting us from the task at hand. The frozen structure was a towering mass of ice that did indeed look like a waterfall. I marveled at it while the rest of the guys speculated on how it was formed.

The rover's steady hum abruptly ceased, plunging the cabin into a tense silence. I turned toward the navigation panel, only to find it engulfed in darkness.

A sense of dread instantly settled over me.

"Stop the rovers, now!" Mike's voice cut sharply through the quiet, commanding immediate action.

The vehicles ground to a halt, ceasing their rumble across Ganymede's icy terrain. Without navigation assistance, we were stranded. I swallowed, wondering if we could retrace our route exactly from memory if we couldn't get it running again.

Mike's fingers flew across the dead screen, working feverishly. "Artie, diagnostics, quick," he ordered, urgency lacing his voice.

The AI responded with a series of rapid beeps, its lights blinking in tandem with Mike's swift movements.

I watched, heart pounding, as Mike fought to regain control.

Mike's focus was intense. "Come on," he urged under his breath, a rare crack in his usually unflappable demeanor.

The cabin was thick with suspense, every beep from Artie stretching our nerves taut. Time seemed to crawl, the silence oppressive, broken only by the soft clicks of Mike's desperate attempts.

Suddenly, with a low whir, the navigation screen flickered to life, washing the cabin in a dim light. A collective gasp of relief escaped us. "It's back," Mike announced, relief evident in his strained voice.

"Good to go?" Jax asked from the other rover.

"Artie, update scans," I ordered.

"Scans updated and adjusted for ice density and thickness," Artie replied, thankfully professional this time.

"Nice work," I said, meeting Mike's gaze. "We're good to go."

As we neared the coordinates of the mysterious signal, I glanced out the rover's window, my eyes drawn to the icy expanse to our right as I struggled to contain my excitement.

"Alex, what do you think? Could that be one of Ganymede's subsurface oceans over there?"

Alex's voice came through the comms. "It's a possibility. The ice formations there suggest a thinner crust, which could be overlying a subsurface ocean."

I couldn't resist lightening the mood. "Hey Luca, you think we should try some ice fishing later?"

Luca's laugh echoed in my ear. "I'll bring the fishing gear if you bring the hot chocolate," he replied.

But the levity was short-lived as we approached our destination.

The rover's instruments began to show increasing energy readings, hinting at an artificial source.

"We're getting stronger readings," TJ reported, his voice taking on an edge of excitement. "Whatever's sending that signal, it's *close*."

"Artie, inform Mission Control of our approach to the signal. Send along the latest data readings and scans of this sector, as well as the signal origination pin."

In the back of my mind, so far back that I barely wanted to acknowledge it, I reasoned that if we failed, at least Mars Colony One would have the location of the signal...and the location of our bodies.

As we rounded a large outcropping of ice, the rover came to a gentle stop. Before us was a concealed entrance, almost camouflaged against the icy landscape. It was an opening large enough for us to enter.

I felt a rush of adrenaline. This was it.

"Looks like we've found our way in," I said, trying to keep my voice steady.

My heart rate was thrumming along a hundred miles a minute, I was sure. I was surprised that Hank hadn't said anything, however, I probably wasn't the only one.

Mike looked over at me, his eyes serious. "We need to be careful. We have no idea what's down there."

"Artie, complete one more detailed preliminary scan. Scan for hidden environmental and biological factors incompatible with our equipment, suits, and suit shielding."

"Acknowledged. Wait one," Artie said.

I nodded and took a deep breath, blowing it out. "Let's

do a final equipment check while we wait. We don't know what we're walking into."

One by one, we confirmed that our gear was operational. Headlamps, communication systems, and environmental sensors—all checked and rechecked.

"Remember, stay in visual range at all times," I instructed as we prepared to disembark from the rover. "And keep the comms line open. We need constant comms between each team and the ship."

Stepping out into the frozen plain where it met the bottom edge of a massive ice cliff, we approached the entrance. The energy readings were off the charts now, a clear indication that whatever lay beyond this point was no natural phenomenon.

"Artie?"

"Scans normal. No unknown or hidden factors can be detected from this location."

"Here goes nothing," Sam muttered as he stepped into the entrance, his headlamp piercing the darkness.

We followed, moving as one unit, our lights cutting through the pitch black. The air was colder here according to our environmental sensors. It was a chill that seeped into my bones despite the suit's thermal controls.

As we ventured deeper, the walls of the tunnel began to change. What started as rough ice transformed into something smoother, and more structured. It was as if we were moving from a natural cave into a constructed space.

"*Wow,*" I sighed.

"This doesn't look like any cave formation I've ever seen," Alex whispered, his voice echoing slightly in the confined space.

"Barrier coming up," I said from the front, my light shining over an object in the shape of a large arch that covered the tunnel from floor to ceiling.

It was smooth and dark, with a surface that seemed to absorb the light.

"Should we knock?" Luca joked quietly.

"Let's not touch anything until we know what we're dealing with," I cautioned the team, my eyes fixed on the enigmatic arch.

Mike nodded in agreement, his scanner already humming as he swept it over the structure. "It's absorbing almost all the light and radiation bombarding it from outside. This could be some form of advanced shielding."

Alexei approached the arch, his device in hand. "The material composition is unknown, but it's designed to allow the signal through while blocking harmful radiation. Clever, really."

I tapped my comms, connecting to Artie. "We've encountered an arch blocking our path. Can you analyze the data we're sending and give us your input?"

After a brief pause, Artie's voice filled our ears. "Analysis complete. The arch is composed of an unknown material with advanced shielding properties. It appears safe to interact with physically, but caution is advised."

I held my breath as Sam reached out and gently pressed against the right side of the arch. To our amazement, it swung open silently, revealing the path ahead and another identical arch a short distance away.

As we cautiously passed through the now-open arch, I felt a twinge of unease. "Keep scanning. I don't want to miss anything important."

Like aggressive aliens who don't want us walking into their house unannounced.

The second arch loomed before us, just as enigmatic as the first.

"Comms with the ship are down," Luca hissed.

"Artie? Do you read?" I tried, but there was only silence.

"Should we go back out?" Hank asked, scanning the walls uneasily.

Luca, frowning, began adjusting his equipment. "The arches must be blocking our signal back to the ship. Wait, the signal that led us here is still getting through. If we transmit on the same frequency..."

He quickly recalibrated our comms, and soon we were back in contact with Artie. "You're coming through now," Artie confirmed. "It seems the arches allow specific frequencies to pass."

Relieved but more cautious than ever, we continued, alternating the sides we pressed to open each subsequent arch as we ventured deeper into the tunnel. Right, left, right, the pattern emerging as clear as the path ahead.

With each arch we passed, the sense of isolation grew. We were lightyears away from any help, relying solely on each other and our wits to navigate this alien place.

Suddenly, I was very glad that I had the entire crew with me.

Finally, after passing through the sixth arch, the tunnel opened up into a massive cavern. Our lights barely made a dent in the vast darkness, but what we could see took our breath away.

The cavern was a cathedral of ice and stone, its walls adorned with intricate art we'd never seen before.

"No life forms that I can see," I said. "Scans?"

Alexei fiddled with his scanner. "Not picking up anything known."

As we stepped further into the underground structure, the air held a quiet that seemed to whisper of long-gone beings. The walls around us were a canvas of history, adorned with elaborate etchings that spoke of an advanced civilization.

Possibly even more advanced than ours.

There were remnants of devices and structures scattered throughout, their purposes mysterious but hinting at a profound understanding of science and technology. The team split up, each of us drawn to different relics of this strange society.

"Guys, look at this," Sam called out, standing before a large mural that depicted what seemed like a map of the Jovian system. "They understood their place in space. This is more than art... it's knowledge."

Alexei was examining a series of what appeared to be data tablets, their crystalline-looking interface surfaces etched with symbols and diagrams. "These could tell us so much about their culture and technology," he mused, his voice tinged with reverence.

I moved through the complex, each step taking us deeper into the heart of this civilization. The feeling of walking in the footsteps of beings who had mastered such incredible technology was humbling and exhilarating. I wasn't sure this could compare with any discovery ever made before.

"Artie, report back to Mission Control. Tell them...," I stopped and closed my eyes on a smile. "Tell them we found hard evidence of intelligent life."

"Yes, Commander."

As we explored, the signal that had led us here grew stronger, guiding us like a beacon.

It wasn't long before we found the source: a chamber housing a mysterious device, partially encrusted with glowing bioluminescent crystals. The sight was like something out of fiction, beautiful and otherworldly.

Mike and I approached the device cautiously.

"Well, that doesn't look like your standard radio," I quipped, trying to mask the awe in my voice.

Mike reached out, fingers hovering over the object. He looked at me.

"Alex, safe?"

Alex scanned the thing and relayed it back to Artie.

"Artie's analysis comes up clear for contaminants and radiation," Alex said.

I nodded at Mike to go ahead.

He ran his hand along the device, his engineer's curiosity in full swing. "It's like technology joined with biology. I've never seen anything like it."

We theorized that it might be a communication device or perhaps a data storage tool. Its design was a harmonious blend of technology and organic aesthetics, unlike anything from Earth or any known technology.

"Artie, are you getting this?" I asked, ensuring that every detail was being recorded.

"Receiving data. The design is indeed partially biological and unprecedented. Proceed with caution," Artie advised.

"Prepare a new packet for transmission back to the Institute."

As we explored the chamber, the sense of discovery was overwhelming. We were standing among the evidence of a society that had reached for the stars, a civilization that had mastered the blend of nature and technology in ways we could only imagine.

"This changes everything," I said, my voice barely above a whisper. "They were *here*, on Ganymede... living, learning, building."

"Maybe they still are," Luca said, voice awed as he motioned to the far side of the room. "There's another arch."

We looked at each other for a solid thirty seconds, only the rasps of our oxygenators coming through.

"Let's check it out."

As we pushed through the arch and ventured deeper into the underground complex, the tunnel widened even more, leading us into a massive cavern that took our breath away— figuratively speaking.

The expanse before us was filled with structures and artifacts of unknown origin, their purpose and history shrouded in mystery. Their gentle curves and expertly crafted circles hinted at an extreme artistic skill or perhaps some technological design capable of manufacturing the perfect curves all around.

"Would you look at this place?" Sam exclaimed, his light sweeping over the high ceilings and large, robust furnishings— or what I suspected were furnishings.

The team dispersed, each drawn to different curiosities. "Be careful what you touch. There could be traps or defensive mechanisms," I warned.

The space was filled with bed-like platforms, significantly larger and sturdier than any human would need. They were arranged in a way that suggested communal living, yet each had a sense of personal space, with shelves and ledges built into the ice and holding a variety of spherical objects that looked like glass.

"I'm guessing these were their sleeping areas," I said, examining a platform. "Based on the size, these beings could've been at least 7-8 feet tall, very wide, and quite heavy. Of course, I could be completely wrong."

Mike, who was inspecting some large, heavy tools scattered around, nodded in agreement. "Yeah, and look at these. Tools for everyday life, maybe? But everything is just so... big."

Alexei was drawn to a series of elaborate etchings on the wall, some displaying representations of beings engaged in various activities. "These might be depictions of their daily life or important events. But without understanding their context, it's like trying to read a story without knowing the alphabet."

The precision and beauty of the swirling carvings and drawings were comparable to the most beautiful art on

Earth.

"We'll figure it out," I said confidently.

Luca pointed towards a corner where a series of strange, cylindrical containers were stored near a flat table-like platform. "And what about these? They don't look like any storage units I've seen. Maybe for food or resources?"

The potential remnants of their dietary needs, or whatever the cylindrical containers were used for, were particularly mystifying. Some of the smaller devices could have been used for preparing and consuming food, but their design was unlike anything we had encountered before.

We weren't sure how to open them, or even if we should.

"Could be some form of advanced hydroponics or chemosynthesis systems," Alexei speculated. "Utilizing Ganymede's mineral-rich underground water sources, perhaps?"

"We should take them back to the ship with us, along with as much of this stuff as we can transport. Mike, can we rig up a trailer of some kind for the rovers? Some of this stuff is way too massive for the storage trunk."

He frowned, thinking for a moment. "We've got some extra panels in storage. We should be able to think of something," he said, with a look at TJ.

We found no clear answers as we searched, only more questions.

As we moved through the living quarters, the sense of walking through a ghost town was palpable. A once-thriving society had lived here, their daily routines and rituals now frozen in time. There was no dust or any coating whatsoever, and so it seemed strangely recent.

"Here's another tunnel. No arches," Sam said, standing at an entrance set on the left side of the main living space.

We followed it, finding that it curved around to the left for about a tenth of a mile into another set of living quarters. They were similar to the first.

"How many sleeping platforms did you count in the other room?" I asked the crew.

"I counted 8," Alexei answered.

"There are more in here." I wandered among them, counting the circular arrangement of beds or resting spaces. "I count 13 here."

"Anther tunnel!" Luca called out from the far left side as the rest of the team filtered through the massive, dark room that held similar artifacts as the other. "There is something luminescent on these walls."

Alexi, Sam, and I rushed over.

"Looks like the same crystal formations that were on the signal generator," I said.

Alexei pulled out a sample collection cube and scraped

some of the crystals, securing them for later study.

The next tunnel curved to the left as well, but it was longer than the last one. I checked the time.

"Artie. How much time remaining until we need to begin the journey back?"

"Approximately four hours remaining, though it would be wise to return in three hours to avoid the possibility of frostbite and hypothermia."

Hank nodded. "I am picking up lowered body temperature readings on you, Commander. Nothing significant yet, but we'll use you as the benchmark."

"Not the guys?" I asked.

"No," he said. "Unfortunately, as a woman, your body temperature will drop first."

I nodded. "Okay. Let's keep going. We'll turn back in one hour and schedule another expedition here in a day or two to collect the artifacts."

The team fanned out behind me, some studying the faint blue luminescence on the walls, almost eliminating our need for the helmet lights. It was beautiful, eerie, and completely alien.

I loved it.

The tunnel ended after a quarter mile of walking, still curving to the left and at a downward slope. I wondered why they added curvature to their tunnel systems.

"Another living space," I said as we entered the next

chamber. "This one is a little bigger— like the size of the training dome."

I wandered among the platforms, noting the same strange tools and gear scattered among the living space. The same cylinders lined the walls, more this time to correspond with the increased number of occupants, so it must have been a necessary resource.

"21 beds," Luca said.

I frowned as I scanned the room, something niggling at the back of my mind.

The air was still as we searched. The low gravity of Ganymede lent a surreal quality to our exploration, our steps light, almost deferential as we moved through the remnants of a lost civilization.

Jax, who had been quiet for a while, finally spoke up. "I don't like it. It's like they just vanished. Where did they go? And why?"

It was the question on all our minds. As we delved deeper into the cavern, the mystery only deepened. The artifacts we found were pieces of a puzzle we were only beginning to understand.

"Another tunnel," Mike said, gesturing to a brighter glowing passage.

"To the left again," I said.

"Well, we aren't going in circles," TJ joked, otherwise we would have come back into the other rooms.

"No, not circles," Alex said, tilting his head at me.

Suddenly, it hit me like a meteor.

"It's a spiral!" I say, perhaps louder than I should have. "They've built their living space in a Fibonacci sequence. 8, 13, 21...I'll bet you anything that the next living space will have 34 beds."

Alexei's eyes gleamed with the rush of discovery. "Like the signal," he said. "Artie, map the spaces we've been so far and project it to the HUDs."

Artie's map appeared in the upper right corner of my helmet HUD, and it was all so clear. I grinned.

"Look at these etchings," Mike called out from the front of the room, if a rounded chamber could have a front.

We went over to the curved wall.

"It's Jupiter," Luca said. "Look at the spot."

"Here's Ganymede," I said, pointing out the small moon that bore strange symbols. "And Io, Europa, and Callisto."

"Look at the detail," Hank said. "I wonder what those symbols mean?"

"Artie, are you getting all this?" I ask, my mind spinning.

"Affirmative," Artie replied unobtrusively.

"They drew themselves on top of Jupiter?" TJ asked.

I studied the cluster of beings—elaborately curved and humanoid in shape though not in scale— drawn on the center of Jupiter and then the array of symbols on each moon. "I think they came from *Jupiter*," I finally said.

"But Jupiter is a gas giant," Jax said, frowning. "It's not possible."

I shrugged. "They drew lifeforms on there for a reason, but not on the moons."

"Let's check out the next room," Alexei said. "I want to know if you'll owe me a million Redcreds."

I grin and we walk more confidentially to the next chamber. As expected, the tunnel still curved to the left and down, and the trek was longer. The glow of the walls grew brighter and illuminated more art on the walls.

I made sure we scanned every bit for later analysis.

It turned out that I was right. The next chamber did have 34 beds.

And the next had 55.

And the next had 89.

By the time we made it to the farthest cavern, my hands and feet were getting pretty cold and our time was rapidly dwindling to nothing.

"Don't count right now, but this chamber has 144 beds. I'm certain of it."

"Commander, it's time to begin the journey back," Artie cut in.

"Artie's right. I don't like the way your readings are going," Hank said. "Your core temp is entering the mild hypothermic stage. By the time we get back, secure the artifacts we've picked up, and go through the de-con process you could be dealing with some significant symptoms."

I nodded, exasperated. "Who has the best stats right now?"

"Mike is still 100% optimal, Jax is 100% optimal, Sam is 98% optimal, and the rest of us are in the mid-90s range. You're the only one hitting the 70s."

"Figures," I snapped, angry with my physiology. "Should have built in extra thermals to my suit."

"We can probably modify it a bit, and maybe give you some extra layers," Mike said. "But you'll compromise some of your dexterity and add some weight."

"That's fine. We'll figure it out."

They clustered around me as I thought of our next steps. "Alright. I want a team to finish exploring the next room. See what it contains and make sure to scan every angle and every artifact. I want to be able to see it all. I'll head back with Hank and Luca. We'll wait back in the signal chamber."

"Artie, how long until Commander Mercer exhibits moderate hypothermic symptoms?" Hank asked.

"The Commander may begin to experience worsening symptoms of hypothermia in one hour or less. Based on the length of the trip and the probability of significant impairment, I suggest a delay of no more than fifteen minutes at the signal chamber."

"We'll jog," Mike proposed. "Ganymede-style."

If they did take longer steps, they could theoretically get there faster. I nodded. "Do it, but don't compromise the suit structure or your oxygen supply."

"We're good. Nothing is getting through these suits," TJ said.

"And we're still green on oxygen," Jax said, checking his gauge.

I gave them a wave. "See you back at the start. Be sure to maintain comms."

Hank, Luca, and I headed back down the blue glowing tunnels, each one getting successively dimmer until we were finally back in the signal room. My hands and feet were getting colder and I began to shiver a bit. I tried to keep it quiet.

"Keep moving, Commander," Hank advised, his voice steady over the comms. "It'll help maintain your core temperature."

I nodded, my movements were more deliberate, trying to generate heat through motion. "Never thought a cardio session on Ganymede would be on my to-do list," I said, trying to lighten the mood as I did squats.

Luca offered a supportive smile. "Just imagine it's a scenic hike, Commander. Only a bit chillier."

As we continued, my comms beeped with updates from the team exploring the next chamber.

Mike's voice came through first. "We've reached the next chamber, Commander. It's different."

My heart raced. "Different how? What do you see?"

There was a pause, longer than I liked. The silence was heavy, filled with anticipation and a touch of dread. Then Alex's voice came with a hint of somberness in his tone. "They didn't leave."

"What?"

Alex sounded breathless. "It's a kind of burial chamber, Commander."

The words hit like a physical blow. A burial chamber?

My mind reeled at the implications. What had happened to the Jovians? What secrets were hidden in the dark expanse of Ganymede?

"What do they look like?" I asked with a hint of wonder and more than a little sadness.

We were too late and I felt oddly as if I had failed them.

"Commander, you'll need to see this," Mike's voice came through the comm, his tone somber and heavy with implication. "The chamber... it's filled with them, hundreds and hundreds, laid out in spiraling rows. Each one took his place among the others, as if they knew it was their time."

Alex's voice followed, a touch of reverence in his words. "They're massive, Commander. Taller and more robust than any human, though the curvature of their bodies are similar. Their skin, it's thicker. And their eyes... even in death, there's a faint luminescence to them, not like the glowing crystals though."

I listened, my heart heavy with the gravity of their discovery. "Can you distinguish any differences among them?" I asked, needing to understand more.

"Yes," Alex replied after a moment. "The males, or what I suppose are the males, appear wider, their frames seem more masculine as we'd think of it. They are garbed in a kind of thick shielding," he began.

"What kind of shielding?"

"Like the arches, except this seems to be molded to their bodies," he explained. "And it is definitely not a part of their skin."

"Gather all the data that you can. I want to see it. What about the female types?"

"The females, they're larger and curvier, but no less imposing. Their eyes are larger too, with more of a glow. There are no...young ones or small ones. They are all very similar."

That seemed odd. "Maybe they procreate differently, or maybe they died before their mating cycle was completed. We may never know."

"It's like they came here, to this chamber, as a final act of unity. They lay down with their people, facing whatever end was coming. Or maybe they came one by one, as they succumbed to whatever it was that took them. There's a peace to it, a tragic dignity," Sam added.

The description painted a vivid, solemn picture in my mind.

A people, once so advanced and vitally alive, were now reduced to silent rows of the deceased. Their story was ending here, in this chamber, and we were the unexpected audience to their final act. It made me wonder if our civilization could end up like that.

Any beings that found us would most likely find chaos instead of order.

"They must have been a sight to behold in life," I murmured, more to myself than to the team. "A civilization that thrived in the face of Ganymede's challenges."

"It might take a bit longer than anticipated to gather the data," Mike said.

"Understood," I replied, my voice steadier than I felt. "Document everything. We need to understand their story."

"Perhaps we should come back and do it next time when we gather the artifacts," Mike suggested.

"No, do it now—"

"Commander," Hank warned.

"Try to hurry, Mike," I added, cutting Hank off with a warning look.

"Stay warm," Mike said.

As we waited and paced in the entrance cavern, with

me doing sporadic exercises, the reality of our discovery settled over us. We were standing on the threshold of a profound revelation about the Jovian civilization.

The cold of Ganymede was a distant concern now, overshadowed by the weight of history and the specter of death that loomed in the distant chamber. I was shivering harder now, but it barely concerned me as I thought about them.

The Jovians.

I realized that I had been expecting to find life here all along, and it was a severe disappointment— a serious blow to my morale— to find only death.

Hank kept a close eye on my vitals, his calm demeanor a reassurance. "Just a little longer, Commander. We'll get you warmed up soon."

"It's no worse than a walk in winter," I told him truthfully. "I'll be fine."

"But the readings," he started.

"Screw the readings. I know my own body better than any sensor possibly could."

He was silent. "I reserve the right to transfer command to Jax if you are physically unable to continue," he reminded me.

"You won't have to. We'll be back at the Artemis before that happens."

Luca stayed by my side in the vast, silent cavern.

Together, we waited for the team to return, the knowledge of what they had found hanging over us like a shroud.

Ganymede was a story, a tragedy etched in ice and stone. And as we delved deeper into its secrets, we became part of that story, witnesses to the rise and fall of a civilization that had once reached for the stars.

It was damned sad.

17.

'64-03

By the time Mike and the crew came back, Hank informed me that my lips were blue and I was slipping into hypothermia.

I didn't resist as we rushed out to the rovers and began the journey back.

The rover's hum was a comforting constant as we made our way back to the Artemis from the signal's source. The journey was quiet, each of us lost in our thoughts about the profound discoveries we had just made.

The cabin wasn't any warmer compared to the icy tunnels, and I couldn't seem to shake the cold that had settled deep into my bones. I was shivering, each tremor running through me like a current. Why hadn't we installed heaters in these things like the ones we had on Mars?

"Artie, prepare an extensive new data packet for transmission back to Mars," I instructed, my voice trembling and breaking through the shivers. "We need to document everything."

"Understood, Commander. I will compile the data immediately," Artie replied.

As we bounced along the surface, Mike kept shooting me troubled glances. I knew I wasn't looking great—I could feel my muscles stiffening, my movements becoming slower, but I pushed through, focusing on the mission. I clenched my fingers and toes and moved as much as I could in my seat.

The conversation among the crew was speculative, everyone trying to piece together the story of the Jovians.

"Could they have known the end was coming?" Luca pondered aloud.

"Perhaps," Alexei responded. "The way they laid themselves down, it seemed almost ritualistic, intentional."

I listened, offering my thoughts when I could, but the cold was relentless, and my shivers had turned into violent shakes. I wrapped my arms around myself, trying in vain to generate some warmth.

"Artie, prepare the medical bay for a rapid rewarming," Hank ordered.

Finally, the familiar outline of the Artemis came into

view. Relief washed over me, but it was tempered by the knowledge that we were not out of danger yet.

Even some of the guys had started to feel the effects of the cold.

We entered the airlock, initiating the decontamination process. The mist that enveloped us was usually comforting, a sign of returning to safety. But as we stood there, I stopped shivering— a bad sign. My body was conserving energy, and my core temperature was dropping further.

Hank immediately noticed the change. "She's tanking. We need to start rewarming procedures as soon as we're in."

Mike was by my side in an instant, his arm supporting me. "Hang in there. We've got you."

After the de-con process was complete, we stripped down to our thermals. They had to peel my suit and my gloves off. Hank looked concerned at my complete lack of dexterity and balance as Sam and Jax held me up while they removed the boot liners and other parts of our inner kits.

As the airlock door opened to the Artemis, the relative warmth of the ship felt like a blessing. Mike and Hank guided me to the small medical facility, my body feeling impossibly heavy.

Hank was all business now, the medic in him taking

over. "I'm starting with warm, oxygenated IV fluids to help raise your core temperature from the inside," he explained as he prepped my arm.

Mike stayed close, his presence a silent source of strength. Hank placed heated blankets around me, the warmth a stark contrast to the cold that had seeped into my bones. I groaned at the feeling.

"We'll monitor your vitals closely and adjust as necessary. You're in good hands," Hank assured me, his voice both professional and comforting.

As the warmth slowly began to penetrate the cold that had taken hold of me, I felt a profound gratitude for my crew.

"This was necessary," I reminded him. "Our time here is limited. This is our only chance. I wouldn't have stayed out that long for any other reason, and I knew that I would be fine," I told him.

"Still, it was close," Hank said.

"Some risks are worth taking," I retorted. "And it wasn't that close."

He conceded with an amused smile and kept an eye on me as he cleaned up.

After I began to warm and feel more like myself, although extremely exhausted, Mike bumped his knuckles against my arm. "I'm going to go get with TJ about your suit. We're considering integrating an auxiliary thermal regulation system utilizing phase-change materials," he explained, his hands moving as if he were already assembling the pieces. "Also, I suggest enhancing the suit's endothermic reaction efficiency by recalibrating the thermoelectric modules for optimal heat absorption."

His eyes were blazing with the newest engineering challenge to be tackled, his mind already sifting through schematics and calculations. I had no idea what he was talking about, but I was happy that he was having a good time.

"And if we reroute the power distribution through a series of microconductors," he continued, "we can significantly increase the heat retention capacity without compromising mobility. Of course, we'll need to adjust the suit's exoskeletal framework slightly to accommodate the extra insulation layers."

I watched him, the complex jargon washing over me like a foreign language, a small smile creeping onto my face despite the fatigue.

His enthusiasm was infectious, even if the specifics were way over my head.

He finished with a satisfied nod, as if confirming his own mental blueprints. "It'll add a negligible mass, but the thermal gain will be substantial. We can't have our commander freezing to death."

I raised an eyebrow, smiling widely now. "Mike, I have

no idea what you just said."

He chuckled, a deep, reassuring sound. Shaking his head, he wandered off to find TJ, already deep in thought about his ideas for the suit. "Don't worry, Commander," he called back over his shoulder, "We'll make sure you're taken care of."

That evening, we congregated at the table after Hank had released me.

I was seated at the head, with the haunting footage from the death chamber playing on the screen before me. The images of those lost Jovians, laid out in their final repose, had me entranced. I thought about the finality of an entire race of beings disappearing from a planet and I couldn't help but shiver with a chill that had nothing to do with my little jaunt around Ganymede earlier.

I glanced around at my crew, each person lost in their thoughts or preparations, the light from various screens casting an otherworldly glow on their faces.

It was time to send our latest findings back to the folks on Mars. Hitting the send button on the new data packet felt monumental. They'd already received textual information, but this was a real video.

Who knew what ripples it would create?

Soon enough, Nash's voice filled the room, clear and faithful enough that he could have been sitting right with us.

"Artemis, this is Nash. We've received your data packet."

There was a brief pause, and when he continued, his voice carried an uncharacteristic emotional weight. "I just want to say... this is the highlight of my career. What you've found, what you're doing out there, it's beyond words. We're all..."

I could almost see him, the ever-stoic Nash, getting misty-eyed over his console back on Mars. Then came the throat-clearing, the audible sign of him snapping back to his professional self. "The Mars Frontier Research Institute is beginning analysis now. I'll keep you informed of any breakthroughs. Nash out."

His message hung in the air after the comm went silent, leaving us all a little more aware of the magnitude of our mission.

It's not every day you make a discovery that gets the unshakeable Nash all choked up.

Shaking off the solemn mood, I addressed the team, bringing the focus back to our immediate concerns. "How long will it take to fabricate two trailers for carrying artifacts?"

My voice was steady, but I could feel the exhaustion tugging at my words. My rest earlier hadn't been enough. I needed real sleep, preferably at least ten hours of it.

Mike looked up from his tablet. "Give us a day to design

and another to fabricate. We'll have them ready by the time your suit is ready and you're set to head out again."

His confidence was reassuring, a solid promise amid so many unknowns. I could always count on Mike.

"Good," I nodded, pushing aside the fatigue that seemed to cling to my bones. "Tomorrow, we'll plan the next mission to the signal site to collect artifacts for analysis and storage. We need to document and preserve everything we can. We may not get another shot at this."

The team murmured their agreement.

As the meeting wrapped up, and the crew began to disperse, I initiated the transmission of the data packet to Mars. The process was routine, a task I'd done countless times, but each time felt like sending a new piece of ourselves across the stars.

Mike lingered, his concerned gaze on me more often than not.

I knew I looked as bad as I felt, the cold from the caverns still clinging to me like a persistent shadow.

"You should get some rest, Commander," he said, the worry clear in his voice.

"I'm going right now," I assured him.

"Artie, make sure she goes straight to bed," he called out.

"Understood. Initiating Commander Mercer Tuck-In Protocols in T-minus 12 seconds," Artie retorted. "11, 10,

9..."

"I guess that's my cue. Goodnight, Mike."

"Goodnight, Lena."

ΦΦΦ

The chill of Ganymede's surface was less biting this time as I tested the upgraded layers of my suit. Mike's tweaks seemed to be doing the trick, and I offered him a grateful nod. The two rovers, each pulling a newly fabricated trailer on skids, stood ready for our journey back to the signal site.

"Everything looks green from here," TJ announced, eyes not leaving his tablet where diagnostics scrolled continuously. "Rovers and trailers are operational. Let's retrieve those artifacts."

The journey started smoothly, the rovers making steady progress across the icy terrain.

Halfway to our destination, however, the smooth hum of our convoy was interrupted by a sudden, grinding halt. Our rover, pulling the lead trailer, had stopped dead.

Why did we always have a situation?

My heart skipped a beat. We couldn't afford any delays. Because of the inherent danger and the distance, this would be our last journey to the signal site, and we needed all the time we could get.

"Mike, report!" I called out, my voice tense.

"I've got a sudden loss of power to the traction system," he replied, his voice calm but strained. "Looks like a coupling failure between the power unit and the drive mechanism."

TJ was already out of his rover, bounding over in low gravity with his tool kit in hand.

"I see it," he confirmed, sliding under the rover. "The coupling's sheared right off. We must've hit something hard."

My mind raced. Without the trailer, we couldn't transport the artifacts. Every second we delayed increased our risk on this unpredictable moon.

"Options?" I asked, trying to keep my voice steady.

Mike was already thinking ahead. "We can bypass the standard coupling. I'll reroute the power flow directly to the secondary drive linkage. It'll be rougher and less efficient, but it should get us moving."

"Make it quick, if you can," I urged. "We're on the clock here."

Mike and TJ worked swiftly, their hands deft at their tasks despite the bulky gloves. Around us, Ganymede's silent expanse watched, indifferent to our plight.

"Rerouting power now," Mike announced, his voice focused. "TJ, secure that linkage. We don't want it coming loose halfway there."

"Got it," TJ replied. "Locking it down with an improvised clamp. It's not pretty, but it'll hold."

I watched, holding my breath as Mike initiated the rover's power. The vehicle lurched, then began to move, the trailer following awkwardly but surely.

"Let's move," I said, relief flooding me, though my heart still pounded from the scare. "Mike, you're a lifesaver."

He just nodded, his eyes already back on the path ahead.

The rover's uneven gait finally steadied on the icy plain as we approached the entrance to the signal tunnel an hour later. I'd been watching the massive shelf of ice towering overhead as we closed the distance, wondering how many times it might have looked down on the Jovians as it had looked down on us.

What had it seen?

"Alright, let's dismount," I announced.

The entrance loomed before us, an alien mausoleum, its familiar yet still mysterious presence drawing us in.

As we entered the tunnel, a subtle shift in the atmosphere caught my attention. I paused, trying to identify the change.

It was almost imperceptible, a slight difference in the air that made the hairs on the back of my neck stand up. I shook it off, attributing it to the lingering effects of the cold or perhaps the anticipation of what lay ahead.

We moved in silence, our footsteps muffled by the soft, icy ground.

The somberness of our task hung heavily upon us. None of us relished the thought of disturbing the final resting place of the Jovians. It felt like an intrusion, a violation of a sacred silence that had lasted for who knew how long. But our mission, our quest for understanding, compelled us forward.

As we drew closer to the death chamber, I realized what had been nagging at the edge of my consciousness.

"Wait," I said, holding up my arm and calling for a halt.

The glow from the crystals embedded in the walls was brighter, casting a more intense light on our path than before. It bathed the tunnel in an ethereal luminescence, turning the stark, cold surroundings into a surreal dreamscape. We didn't even need the helmet lights.

Alex and Sam were immediately drawn to the change.

"The crystalline structure seems to be more active," Alex observed, his scanner analyzing as he took new readings.

Sam nodded, his eyes reflecting the strange light. "Let's get some fresh samples."

Carefully, they collected samples of the glowing substance, their movements precise and respectful. Despite the morbid task that lay ahead, the pursuit of knowledge and the drive to understand propelled us forward.

As we finally entered the death chamber at the bottom of the spiraling complex, the glow from the crystals cast a solemn light over the rows of Jovian bodies. The sight was as haunting as it was humbling, a stark reminder of the once-great civilization that had perished here.

"We'll take two of each. Male and female," I said quietly, my voice barely above a whisper. "The least we can do is minimize our intrusion."

Ideally, I'd have liked to take back several of each gender to analyze, so we could have a true representation of their species, but they were very large and I didn't feel quite right about upsetting their resting places.

With great care and an even greater sense of reluctance, we selected four of the bodies. The task was somber, our movements slow and deliberate. Each of us felt the weight of what we were doing, the uncomfortable reality of disturbing the eternal rest of these beings.

As we prepared to transport the bodies back to the Artemis on sleds, I couldn't shake the feeling of being watched, of hundreds of luminescent eyes bearing silent witness to our actions as we ruined their spiral of death.

The day stretched out long and laborious as we set about the solemn task of collecting and storing artifacts in the specially designed trailers. Each item we carefully selected was a piece of the Jovian puzzle, a fragment of their lost civilization.

The trailers, with their low-slung and wide-set skids, were filled methodically, each artifact logged and secured for transport back to the Artemis.

As I oversaw the process, my eyes frequently drifted to the specially crafted body containment boxes, which were nothing more than extra lightweight shielding epoxied together with emergency sealant.

They were a grim reminder of the more morbid aspect of our mission. Designed to preserve and protect the remains during transport, they were stark, black units—poisonous-looking against the shades of white, blue, and grey of Ganymede.

The collection of artifacts was a slow, painstaking process. Each item was cataloged and packed with care, from the simplest of tools to the most intricate of Jovian devices. I wish we could have taken weeks to study each piece and its location inside the cavern, but we couldn't.

Alex and Sam took turns describing each piece for the text record, their voices a constant murmur in the background.

As the hours wore on, the trailers filled up, evidence of a day spent sifting through the remnants of a once-great civilization.

By the time we finished, we were all exhausted, both physically and emotionally. The day had taken its toll, the constant awareness of the danger of our mission and the weight of the discovery was a burden we hadn't expected to bear.

Attaching the body boxes to the trailers was a task none of us took lightly.

Mike and TJ handled the physical attachment, bolting the containment units securely onto the trailers. I decided to pay one last visit to the cavern where the signal generator emitted its last feeble calls.

I told it goodbye. It was too heavy to move, even with all of us trying.

"Feels a bit like we're in a space hearse," I commented as Mike finished securing the containment units with the solemnity of a priest and we jumped back in the rover.

"We were respectful," Hank said suddenly from the back seat. "With the bodies, I mean."

"Yeah, well...let's just hope they don't have any living friends that will take exception to our grave robbing," I replied. "Judging from their physiques, I don't think that's a fight we'll win."

"Especially since we don't have any photon torpedoes," Mike deadpanned.

"Very funny."

A hard jolt came from under the rover.

"Mike?"

Mike checked the readouts and relaxed. "Don't worry,

it's just the traction compensator adjusting. We'll have to do a more permanent repair when we get back, but I don't think we'll have any issues."

By the time the Artemis came into view, my feet were practically begging for a massage. I'd walked more today than I had in months, and with more gravity than I was used to. Treadmills in microgravity didn't exactly work out your feet like they did back on Mars.

We unloaded the trailers first, carefully carrying each cataloged artifact into the ship's storage unit near the popup lab. We would bring them out to do preliminary tests and analyses, but most of the real work would be done back on Mars.

"And now, the grand finale," I sighed, eyeing the body containment units. "I bet Indiana Jones never had to deal with this."

"First time for everything," Mike replied.

I found that I preferred dealing with microbes.

ΦΦΦ

It was our sixth day on Ganymede and our mission on the surface was halfway over. The moon had finally been pulled behind Jupiter's shadow, and the lack of sunlight was startling.

It was a good thing the popup had radiant heat and lighting sources from the ship, otherwise, we'd have to wait for several long days to pass until we were firmly in daylight again—or what passes for it here.

It was nothing like Mars. I almost missed Mars's blinding redness.

Inside the popup lab, Sam, Alexei, and I were about to embark on the initial examination of the artifacts we'd painstakingly collected.

The artifacts themselves were an array of enigmatic objects of various shapes, each bearing the intricate designs and seamless integration of the glowing crystals whose composition we hadn't yet determined.

Sam and I hovered over the spectral analyzer. His excitement, usually subtle, was now a visible charge, electrifying the air around us. He looked more passionate about his subject than I'd ever seen him and I realized just how deep his love for geology went.

"The mineral matrix of these artifacts," Sam began, his voice a mixture of awe and disbelief. He blew out a breath and looked at me for a second. "It's like *nothing* I've ever seen before."

He peered intently through the lens again, his eyes reflecting a tapestry of unknown elements and patterns. The crystalline structure glimmered under the analyzer's light, blue and calming.

He adjusted the dials, fingers deft and purposeful, the machine responding with a soft, rhythmic hum.

"Atlas, cross-reference these readings," he commanded, his voice cutting through the lab's silence as Alex and I waited patiently for his initial analysis.

The AI chirped in acknowledgment. "Processing request."

I leaned in, watching the dance of light and shadow play across Sam's face. His brow was furrowed in deep concentration.

"And Artie," he added, his voice steady yet tinged with urgency, "bring up the structural analysis software. We need to understand the resilience of these materials."

The screens around us flickered to life, casting a kaleidoscope of data and graphs across the lab's walls.

Sam's narration was a stream of geological terms, a language foreign to most but music to our ears—even if I didn't understand all of it.

"Look at these crystals' refractive index," he mused, almost to himself, "and how they seamlessly integrate into the matrix. It's not just structure. It's like... functional art."

"They embedded these crystals into the devices when they built them?" I couldn't help but interject, my curiosity piqued.

He picked up a fragment, its intricate design a stark

contrast to the rough texture of his gloves. "It appears so," he said, turning it over. "But this is just the tip of the iceberg." He paused, his gaze locked on the artifact. "These isotopic ratios, they don't belong to Ganymede. It's as if this was engineered, tailored for a purpose."

Atlas beeped, a sound that seemed to echo around the lab. "No matches in the database. The closest parallels are synthetic composites used in advanced engineering."

Sam nodded, more to himself than to me. "Just as I suspected. These aren't artifacts. They're remnants of a technology beyond our current grasp, a civilization that mastered the art of fusing nature with their own science."

He turned to Alex and me. "They brought these things from somewhere else."

"Jupiter?" I asked. "Why else would they draw themselves there?"

"If so, it suggests that everything we thought we knew about Jupiter was wrong. Very wrong," Sam said.

He input more data into the structural analysis software, his brow furrowed in concentration. "Artie, let's simulate a few scenarios. I want to see how these materials would behave under the conditions we've observed on Ganymede's surface."

"Simulation in progress," Artie responded.

As the models ran, Sam watched the screens intently, his mind no doubt racing through the implications of each result. The work was meticulous, requiring a deep understanding of geology, physics, and engineering, but Sam was more than up to the task.

I was very glad that my intuition about him had been correct. He was perfect for the mission...and I was just as sure about all the others too. Somehow, I had managed to pull together the perfect team.

Beginners luck, probably.

Alex focused on the crystals themselves, setting one under the microscope. "These silica structures are remarkable," Alex observed, his gaze fixed on the microscope. "They're interlaced with metallic elements, likely from Ganymede's crust, reinforcing their complex structure."

I leaned in, examining the intricate patterns displayed on the monitor. "Look at that!" I exclaimed. "The liquid ammonia acts as a solvent here. It would be a crucial adaptation for life in such extreme cold," I noted, trying to piece together the puzzle.

"Atlas, compare these structural formations with our existing database. Look for any parallels or significant deviations," Alex instructed.

"Processing request now," Atlas confirmed, its tone measured and precise.

"And Artie," I added, "compile the latest data on Jupiter's radiation levels. We need to understand the environment these crystals were thriving in."

"Compiling data, Commander," Artie responded, the screens around us coming to life with streams of information.

Alex carefully prepared another slide, his movements deliberate. "Notice the nano-metallic filaments here," he pointed out. "They form a network, possibly for conductivity. And the bioluminescence— it could be a form of communication or adaptation to their surroundings. There are so many variables..." he said, trailing off.

The lab was busy, with every finding meticulously documented. The crystals, with their soft glow, were a mystery from a world both alien and mesmerizing.

They held within them a story of adaptation and survival in the harshest of conditions.

Atlas beeped, signaling the completion of its analysis. "The structural formations present no exact matches to known terrestrial or Martian forms. The closest analogs are synthetic composites designed for high adaptability. Some of the composition seems to be metallic, copper perhaps. It's bound to the filaments so completely that I can't get an accurate preliminary analysis. I'll need more time."

"And the radiation readings, Artie?" I asked, already anticipating the complex interplay of factors at work.

"The levels are consistent with the capacity for

radiotrophic energy conversion," Artie confirmed, adding another layer to our understanding.

Luca's voice crackled through my helmet comms, pulling me from my thoughts. "Commander, can you break it down for me? What does all this mean in layman's terms?"

I took a deep breath, trying to distill the day's complex findings into something more digestible. It was a good thing he'd asked me and not Alex. Alex was brilliant, but sometimes he was utterly incapable of dumbing down his theories for us intellectual peasants.

"Okay, think of it this way: the glowing crystals we found, which we're now calling the..." I sighed and tapped the table in thought. "...the Silica-Strand Radiotropes, or SSR for short," I looked at Alex for confirmation and he gave me a thumbs up. "They're not just crystals...they're more like a hybrid of organic and inorganic material."

"Wait...they're *alive?!"*

I paused, organizing my thoughts. "Yes, in a way. The SSR's structure is primarily silica-based, similar to sand on Earth, but it's far more complex. It's interwoven with metals from Ganymede's crust—"

"Or Jupiter," Alex said. "We cannot make assumptions."

"Okay, it's woven with metals of unknown origin, making it incredibly strong and durable. But here's the kicker: it uses liquid *ammonia* instead of water. It's perfect for this environment."

Luca's interest was palpable, even over the comms. "And the glowing part?"

"That's due to the unique radiotrophic pigments in the SSR. Our theory is that they can harness radiation from Jupiter and convert it into energy. It's like they're feeding off the planet's radiation, which is pretty wild if we're right. The bioluminescent glow is possibly for communication or as a by-product of their radiation diet. We just don't know yet."

I could almost hear the gears turning in Luca's head.

"So, they're part crystal, part living thing?" Mike asked, coming on screen.

"In a way, yes. They've got nano-metallic filaments, like tiny wires, that help them interact with their environment—"

"Maybe," Alex warned, holding up a finger.

I nodded and continued. "This all just theoretical—but I think they've adapted to not just survive but thrive in Ganymede's harsh conditions, with special enzymes to keep their internal fluids from freezing and an incredibly resilient structure."

Luca whistled softly. "That's... a little crazy. I'm so glad I went into communications," he sighed.

I laughed and got back to work, over the moon with our findings so far. We had years' worth of work ahead of us...decades even. I was in absolute heaven.

Throughout the rest of the day, I watched over the operations, ensuring that everyone stayed focused and adhered to the safety protocols. The potential significance of our discovery wasn't lost on me, but caution was my concern.

Mike and TJ were engrossed in their technical assessment of the artifacts, discussing the possible functions and the technology that might have been used to create such sophisticated items.

"Look at the integration of these crystals," Mike said, pointing at an on-screen analysis of one of the mysterious devices. "It's like they're part of the circuitry, but...alive, almost."

Luca was busy setting up an automated system with Artie to record and transmit our findings back to Mars.

His voice floated in from the comm unit. "All data streams are good to go. Mars will get a front-row seat to our little alien show-and-tell. Say hi to Dr. Kim, everyone."

I cringed, practically feeling her unamused glower through the vast barrier of space.

As the day progressed, the SSR crystals under scrutiny revealed even more mysteries.

Their soft, bioluminescent glow fluctuated as if responding to our presence, or perhaps the lab's environment. They became brighter, just as they had in the caverns.

"It's adaptive," Alex finally announced after hours of study, his voice a mix of excitement and concern. "Watch how it changes when I adjust the light or the temperature."

Documenting every observation, hypothesis, and test result, we were a machine of scientific inquiry, driven by the need to understand. The crystals, in particular, held our rapt attention. Their adaptability and the eerie way they seemed to respond to our tests raised as many questions as they answered.

As the day wound down, we followed the decontamination procedures to a tee, dragging our feet and discussing our wildly varying hypotheses with a tired glee that was usually reserved for the Science Dome soirees.

I didn't want to leave the lab, not now that we'd finally found other intelligent life in the universe. I felt like I could stay out here for days without the need for sleep or food.

My fingers and toes said otherwise. Even though I had a beefed-up new suit, they eventually still became cold and stiff.

So, I allowed Mike to usher me inside. Begrudgingly.

One by one, we removed our protective suits in the proper order, storing them in the designated area, each of us passing through the final decontamination shower before re-entering the main area of the Artemis.

Jax and Hank were there to meet us, their roles on the ship just as critical as those of us in the field.

"How'd it go?" Jax asked, his eyes scanning each of us for any sign of trouble.

"We've got a lot to mull over," I replied, feeling the weight of fatigue and the day's emotional toll. "But I think we're on the cusp of something big."

"Huge," Sam said.

"*колоссальный*," Alex added.

I looked at him with my best 'translation-please' look.

"Very big," he amended, holding his hands a few feet apart in emphasis.

Hank gave us all a once-over. "Make sure you all get some rest. That's an order."

18.

'64-03

It was day seven on Ganymede and as we entered the lab for the second day of our investigation, the air was charged with a new sense of purpose. We had fulfilled our mission, and now we had to make sense of what we'd found. There was a new pressure on us—or maybe it was just my competitive nature— to get these things analyzed and understood before the Science teams back on Mars did.

I wanted to beat them to the punch.

The sun was partially visible once again and it felt like coming out of a long winter to see spring had suddenly popped up...sort of.

The artifacts, each a silent witness to a seemingly dead

civilization, awaited us in their secure storage. I couldn't wait to try to find out how long ago they had lived. As far as we knew, they could have all died a few days before we landed...or it could have been a thousand years. Dating them was going to be extremely difficult, especially since we knew how imprecise it was as a science.

The SSR crystals glowed on the workbenches, their storage containers bright blue beacons in the stark white light of the lab.

I was just coming back from locating a new sample when I caught the tail end of Sam and Mike's conversation.

"It's incredible," Sam was saying, "the way the SSR is integrated into this circuitry. It's beyond anything we've seen."

Mike nodded, his eyes wide with the same excitement that was coursing through all of us. "The possibilities for this kind of tech..."

I moved closer, intrigued, just as Alex piped up. "Check this out," he called, his voice tinged with disbelief. "The SSR containment cubes are changing. They were only half this luminous yesterday."

From the comms unit, TJ's voice crackled through. "You're thinking what I'm thinking, right? The potential for these materials in engineering, not to mention the applications of SSR in mechanics."

The excitement was palpable, ideas bouncing back and

forth like pinballs. The possibilities seemed endless, each more thrilling than the last.

Our brainstorming was abruptly cut off by Luca, his usual easygoing demeanor replaced by a frown. "Guys, I'm patching through a priority message from Nash. It's on his private channel."

The room fell silent, the air suddenly heavy. Nash's voice came through, tired and laced with a gravity that instantly sobered us. "Artemis crew...Mercer... I wish I had better news. Political tensions back here are escalating. Rumors are coming out of the NUSR, nothing concrete because you know how they lock things down, but it's not looking good. There's talk of things going hot. We're uh...we're taking precautions here, but we're going to go ahead and implement our level 1 crypto. Dr. Park and Governor Olsen thought it would be prudent, but they specifically instructed me to tell you that it was just routine...do you understand? This is a *routine change*...in case they ask you what I said."

He sighed and groaned and we heard the creak of a chair. You could have heard a pin drop. His words hung in the air like a dark cloud, casting a shadow over our excitement.

"I can't say more right now," Nash continued, his voice low and urgent. "Destroy this transmission immediately. I'll keep you updated."

As the transmission ended, we exchanged uneasy glances. Fear, uncertainty, a sense of helplessness— it was all there, written on each face.

"What does he mean 'rumors are coming out of the NUSR'," Luca asked. "What rumors? He can't just say that and not explain."

"Luca," I began, breaking the silence, "can you try to catch any news broadcasts from Earth? We need to know what's happening."

He looked up at me through the screen. "I'll give it a shot," he replied, turning back to his comms dash.

We waited many long minutes, with Sam and Alex going back to their experiments and analyses. I paced the lab, looking over the brilliant blue cubes on their storage racks. They were so beautiful to look at.

"I can't get anything," Luca said, defeated. "I tried everything that I know, but without the focused signal sent directly our way, there's nothing."

Mike and TJ, overhearing our conversation, joined the comms conversation and I looked up as he came on screen in the command module. "Did you try adjusting the frequency modulation," Mike suggested, leaning over Luca's shoulder.

"Yep," Luca answered, scrubbing his face tiredly.

"What about enhancing the signal gain to cut through Jupiter's interference?" TJ added from wherever he was.

"I did. I guess I can try again."

Luca's fingers flew across the controls. The tension grew with each passing moment, as static crackled through the speakers, the only sound breaking the heavy silence.

Minutes turned into hours as we continued in the lab, but the only sounds we heard from Earth were the frustrating hisses and pops of static. Luca's frustration was palpable as he tried every trick in the book, his usual technical prowess meeting its match against the cosmic forces at play.

Finally, Luca slumped back, a rare look of defeat on his face. "I'm sorry, guys. There's too much interference from Jupiter, and with the delay... we're in the dark here. Hell, they've probably upped their COMSEC protocols significantly."

Breaking the silence, Jax exhaled in frustration. "Guys, if Earth Command has ramped up their COMSEC protocols, they're probably using advanced crypto techniques. We're not equipped to break that here. They could be using Adaptive Frequency Hopping. It would be incredibly difficult to lock onto the signal, let alone decrypt it, and if they're using Burst Pulse Transmissions we can just forget about it," Jax's voice was grave.

Luca leaned back, frustrated. "We're on our own, folks. Until EARTHCOM or MARSCOM decides to include us, there's not much we can do."

We were millions of miles from Earth, isolated on a distant moon, with a potential conflict brewing that could change everything. The implications were daunting— if a hot war broke out between Earth and Mars, we were stranded, cut off from support, and possibly even viewed as enemies or pawns.

We exchanged worried glances. "What now?" Sam asked, the question hanging in the air.

"We keep working," I said, trying to inject some confidence into my voice. "We focus on our mission. It's all we can do."

As we turned back to our tasks, the unease remained, but we were professionals and scientists. No matter what was happening millions of miles away, we had a job to do here.

As I turned to go back to the artifact storage unit, a shrill alarm blared throughout the comms systems. My heart leaped into my throat, envisioning hull breaches, contaminants, oxygen systems malfunctions, acid-spewing dinosaur aliens...all sorts of fatal scenarios.

"What's happening?" I called out, rushing toward the source of the commotion.

Sam was already at the containment unit, his brow furrowed in concentration. "It's one of the artifacts' storage containers. Pressure is building up inside the unit."

Alex joined him, eyes sharp and jew clenched. "We need to stabilize the environment. Any sudden changes could exacerbate the reaction."

"Artie, Atlas, we need a detailed analysis of the artifact's current state and recommendations for stabilization," I commanded, my voice steady despite the rising panic.

"Analyzing," Artie responded promptly. "Recommend reducing atmospheric pressure levels and increasing containment field strength."

"Implementing changes," Atlas added, its voice a calm constant in the chaos.

As the alarm blared through the Artemis and all systems, Mike's voice crackled through the comms. "Lena, report. What's going on in there? Do you need assistance?"

"Stand by!" I shouted, louder than I intended to over the sound of the alarm.

"Systems are showing a spike in the lab. We're on standby for any technical support. Just say the word," TJ said.

As we worked to stabilize the situation, the lab was a frenzy of activity. Sam adjusted the containment unit's settings, his movements precise and deliberate. Alex monitored the container's response, providing a steady stream of feedback that guided our actions.

We didn't want to overdo it and destroy the artifact.

The minutes stretched out, each second a battle against the unknown forces we were dealing with. The alarm continued to pierce the air.

As the lab's alarm continued its shrill cry, Mike's voice broke through the chaos. "Give us a status update. We need to know the extent of the situation to provide appropriate support."

TJ came on a moment later. "I'm monitoring the life support systems to ensure they remain unaffected. If this escalates, we need to consider evacuation. The containment unit is under high pressure.."

"Mike, TJ, we're handling it. Sam is adjusting the containment unit, and Alex is monitoring the artifact's reactions. It's volatile, but we're under control."

"Understood. Just remember, the safety of the crew comes first. We can replace every single artifact, but not you or any team member," Mike responded immediately.

TJ chimed in. "I'm cross-checking all lab systems for any anomalies and preparing emergency protocols, just in case.

"On standby to report to Mission Control," Luca added.

I could feel him watching my face on the lab cam and I worked to control my breathing and heart rate, not wanting Hank to chime in as well.

Finally, after what felt like an eternity, the alarm ceased.

The artifact sat in the inert containment unit.

We all let out a collective sigh of relief, the tension slowly ebbing away. Luca managed a weak smile on the screen. "Well, that was more excitement than I signed up for."

I nodded, feeling the adrenaline slowly fade. "Good work, everyone. Let's be extra cautious moving forward."

"What caused it?" Sam asked, sweat trickling down his face inside the helmet. It made my face itchy just watching it.

"That is the issue," Alex began. "I couldn't detect any volatility in the sample itself, just the containment pressurization unit. The sample is unchanged," he added, frowning.

"Well, whatever happened, we fixed it," I said.

"For now," Sam muttered.

"We need to run checks on all the pressurized units, make sure there isn't a defect somewhere. We can't have one of them blow," Mike said. "TJ?"

"On it."

As we wrapped up for the day, following the strict storage and de-con protocols, I couldn't shake the feeling of having skirted the edge of disaster.

Exiting the lab, a sense of foreboding lingered over my head. We were treading on uncharted ground, and while the path ahead was fraught with unknowns, our mission to understand and preserve these remnants of an alien world was more critical than ever.

Plus, I was starving and I knew that from now on we'd need to take a lunch break.

As I settled into my bunk, the events of the day replaying in my mind, I knew that our journey into the heart of Ganymede's mysteries was only just beginning and I hoped the war back home would hold off a while longer.

ΦΦΦ

"Containment breach! Containment breach!" Artie's voice boomed through the ship, the AI's usual calm replaced with an urgent, almost human, tone of alarm. "SSR contamination detected in the circulation filter supplying air to the crew living quarters. The extent is unknown."

My heart leaped into my throat as I jolted awake, the sound clawing at my senses.

"Are you sure?" I yelled, pulling on my pants.

"Unsure," came the nonsensical reply.

What the?

"Double check!"

The ship's relative calm shattered as a piercing alarm ripped through the silence of the Artemis. Red lights flashed urgently, painting the corridors in a strobe of ominous crimson. My heart raced as I leaped from my bunk, my mind and body reeling.

"Artie, confirm the source and extent of the breach!" I commanded, trying to keep my voice steady despite the adrenaline surging through me and the irritation with Artie's delay.

"Analyzing now, Commander," Artie responded. The screens around us flickered with data as the AI worked to pinpoint the source of the contamination. "The contaminant has been confirmed. Microscopic isolated instances have been detected in three major circulation filters, as well as two of the crew quarters."

"Are they occupied?" I snapped, making my way into the corridor.

"Negative. Crew members are in the command module."

"Lock down the affected crew quarters immediately," I ordered.

"Affirmative. Locking down."

Behind me, TJ and Sam's doors both hissed and locked with an audible clank. I assume they would be sealed tight.

"Luca, send an immediate update packet to Nash. Tell them to get to work on detailed analysis and construction of potential biological effects of SSR colonization and mitigating factors. Tell them this is Priority One."

Priority One at the Mars Frontier Research Institute was a Big Deal. It meant all departments under Top Secret Clearance were directed to work on the problem. We would have a lot of eyes on this problem and we'd have them 24/7. I suspected that within the hour, Dr. Kim herself would be working on it.

"Roger," Luca shouted, setting off for the command module at once.

Mike, his face set in a grim line, was already moving. "We need to isolate the affected area immediately. TJ, with me. We need to check the filtration system."

"Suits?" Sam asked.

As we gathered, the reality of our situation sunk in. "Everyone's been exposed," I stated, the weight of the words heavy in the air. "Suiting up won't make a difference now; the SSR is in our air supply."

TJ, his usual calm demeanor faltering, looked to Artie. "What's the risk assessment based on what we know about the SSR?"

Artie's response was swift. "The SSR has shown highly adaptive and reactive properties in the lab. Exposure risks include potential unknown biological effects. Immediate isolation of the affected area and comprehensive decontamination are suggested."

"Potential unknown biological effects," I spewed. "Run through the de-con protocols. Check for errors—human or mechanical."

"Roger, Commander," Artie said.

The crew quarters, once a place of rest and camaraderie, now felt like a trap. "We need to shut down the circulation to the rest of the ship," I said. "Try to contain it here before it spreads."

Mike was already at the control panel, his fingers flying over the buttons. "Circulation to the crew quarters and living space is now isolated. But we need to clean the filters and purge the system of any SSR particles and we don't have much time to do it before the supply of oxygen becomes critically low."

TJ nodded, pulling up the schematics of the ship's air filtration system. "We'll need to access the main filter unit. It's going to be a delicate operation."

I turned to the rest of the crew, their faces tense with anticipation and fear. "We're going to split into teams. One will handle the filtration system with Mike and TJ. The rest will start manual decontamination of the quarters. We don't know what the SSR might do in this environment, so stay sharp and report any anomalies immediately."

"Artie, which manual de-con procedures would you suggest in this instance?" Hank asked—pretty wisely, I thought.

"There is no known decontamination procedure for SSR. The very fact that it bypassed our strictest and most volatile decontamination procedure in the main airlock illustrates the resilient nature of the entity."

I sighed. "Give us your best guess, Artie."

Artie's voice came through the comms, tinged with a note of caution. "I must emphasize that the success of this manual decontamination procedure is not guaranteed. It is highly likely to fail, but it is the best course of action given our current resources and the nature of the SSR contamination. The procedure is as follows:"

"First," Artie continued, "you will need to manually seal off the affected area. Use the emergency sealing foam available in the maintenance kit. It's designed for hull breaches but should suffice for creating a temporary barrier to isolate the contaminated zone."

Mike nodded, his mind already racing through the ship's layout. "I'll handle the sealing. What's next?"

"Next, you will need to use the portable thermal foggers. Fill them with a mixture of ethanol and isopropyl alcohol from the medical supplies. While not originally intended for this purpose, the fog could help to destabilize the SSR's outer structure. However, the effectiveness is uncertain."

Alex looked skeptical but nodded. "Ethanol and isopropyl, got it. It's a long shot, but worth a try."

"Following the fogging," Artie said, "utilize the handheld vacuum units with HEPA filters to remove the destabilized particles. These filters are designed to capture extremely small contaminants, but they have not been tested against SSR."

Sam chimed in. "We'll need to be thorough, cover every inch of the place."

"Finally," Artie concluded, "ventilate the area. The ship's environmental systems aren't designed for this, so you'll need to manually cycle the air using portable fans and the secondary airlocks. It's a crude method, but it seems to be your only option at this time."

The crew absorbed the steps, the improbability of success hanging heavy in the air.

"I won't sugarcoat it," I said, meeting the gaze of each crew member. "This is a shot in the dark., but we'll give it everything we've got."

The team nodded. If there was even the slimmest chance of protecting our ship and ourselves, we'd take it.

"Alright, let's get to it," Mike ordered. "Artie, keep monitoring and let us know the second you detect any change, good or bad."

"Understood," Artie replied. "I will remain on alert and assist in any way possible."

"Alright, let's move into—"

Artie interjected, "I will continue to monitor the air quality and provide updates on the contamination levels, but I suggest regular medical check-ups for all crew members to detect any potential effects of exposure."

"Okay, Artie," I replied, already tired and we hadn't even begun. I couldn't show it though. We couldn't afford anything that would send morale even lower than it already was.

The ship, our home in the void, had become a hostile alien landscape, a place where every breath could be laced with unknown danger. We moved with purpose, each action a battle against an invisible enemy that had infiltrated our very air.

The SSR, a marvel of alien adaptation, was now a direct threat, not just to our mission, but maybe even to our very lives.

The hours stretched on, filled with the hiss of decontamination sprays, the clatter of tools, and the constant, unyielding drone of the low oxygen alarms. We worked tirelessly, driven by a singular purpose: to secure the Artemis and protect one another from the contamination that threatened us all.

As we finally completed the decontamination procedures, re-engaged the oxygen circulation systems, and the alarms fell silent, a profound sense of vulnerability lingered. We had looked into the face of the unknown, and it had gazed back, indifferent to our struggles, our fears, our very humanity.

I stepped into an empty space on the wall and

thumped my head against the bulkhead.

ΦΦΦ

We sat at the table together, our meal as unenthusiastic as the conversation that accompanied it. The air was stale, tinged with the residual sharp scent of alcohol from our recent, exhaustive decontamination efforts.

We ate mechanically, our minds elsewhere, fixated on the invisible threat that might still be lurking aboard our vessel. I wondered idly if the SSR was on the fork I had just put into my mouth.

TJ broke the silence, his voice a low rumble. "Think it worked?"

Sam shrugged, his usual confidence replaced by uncertainty. "Hard to say. If those SSR particles are as resilient as they seem..."

We all knew what he left unsaid. The implications were grave.

The sound of Artie cut through the tension. "Analysis complete. Deep manual decontamination results are now available."

We all turned towards the console, the light from its screen casting stark shadows across our faces. "Go ahead, Artie," I said, my voice steady despite the anxiety knotting in my stomach. "Put it on screen."

"Detecting SSR particle presence in multiple areas," Artie began, its tone devoid of emotion, yet somehow it felt heavy with implication. "Particles have been identified in the air filtration system, on various surfaces in the common area, and within the ventilation ducts of the living quarters."

Bright blue spots lit up the areas on the schematic map.

"Damn," I sighed, resting my head in my hands and rubbing my temples.

Our exhaustive efforts, the meticulous scrubbing and cleansing, had been in vain.

"So, we're back to square one," Mike muttered, his fork clattering against the table.

"More or less," Alex added, pushing his half-eaten meal away. "These particles are pervasive. I want to know how they bypassed de-con."

I leaned back. "It seems our decontamination efforts haven't done a damned thing to remove or lower the levels of SSR, let alone reduce their spread."

"What if they don't have any effect," Luca suggested. "What if it's harmless?"

"We can't take the chance. This is a xenobiological entity," Alex said.

"A what?" Luca asked.

"A potential alien pathogen," Alex burst out. "A bug!

We have to take every precaution. We must eradicate its presence on the ship!"

"We need a new approach," I said, my mind racing with possibilities and dangers.

Three hours passed and Artie had been silent ever since Alex asked if using the lab was advisable.

Artie said, in a roundabout and more diplomatic way, that we were pretty much screwed already and using the lab wasn't going to hurt anything. The entire oxygenated part of the ship had been contaminated or...colonized?

We'd done what we could, but it was a waiting game until we thought of something. Artie had been out of ideas.

We couldn't afford to be sitting around doing nothing, so we each studied the SSR in our own ways, looking for potential mitigating factors. Me? I wrote my theories on old-fashioned paper like any self-respecting scientific problem-solver.

So far, all I had was:

Step 1: Discover alien crystal infesting ship.

Step 2: ???

Step 3: Get home alive, stop the war, and receive lifetime grants for research and vindication from my peers for my far-fetched ideas.

Not exactly a Nobel-winning theory, but hey, at least I had two-thirds of a plan.

As the ship fell into an uneasy silence, the aftermath of the alarm still lingering in our brains, Alex's voice broke through the stillness.

"Commander, you need to see this," he called over the comms. He sounded concerned.

I hurried to the ship's lab and waited for the gravity to adjust. I entered and went to where Alex stood, his gaze fixed on the microscope. The beautiful SSR crystals, once a source of wonder, now sparked a deep unease not unlike old seafarers must have felt when crossing seas carrying maps marked with sketches of giant sea monsters.

Here be dragons, indeed.

"They've changed again," he said, his voice tense. "They're growing, becoming more active. And look at the bioluminescence— it's intensifying."

Peering through the lens, the truth was undeniable. The SSR's once stable form was morphing, expanding in a display of eerie light inside its sealed and contained slide.

"When did you transfer this sample?" I asked.

"Only hours ago."

"This is bad. Really, really bad," I murmured, the implications dawning on me. "If they're adapting this quickly to the ship's environment and doing it through the containment slide..."

I trailed off, letting the suggestion hang in the air unvoiced.

I hovered over Alex's shoulder as he adjusted the microscope, fine-tuning the focus on the ever-changing SSR. "Look at the edges here," he pointed out, his finger hovering just above the display. "See how it's extending? Like it's reaching out."

I squinted, noting the minuscule tendrils of light stretching outward. "Reaching out for what, though?" I pondered aloud.

Alex shook his head, a mix of awe and concern etched across his face. "Not sure, but it's almost like it's testing its boundaries, seeing what it can touch, what it can change. I'm using it to try to find something that repels it, but so far nothing works."

TJ's voice cut through the comms. "Commander, I'm noticing a slight variance in the environmental control readings. It's noncritical, but it's not standard. It was a flicker."

I paused, a trace of worry crossing my face. "Is it the SSR?" I asked, the possibility hanging in the air like a specter.

Artie responded. "Uncertain, Commander. The variance is within operational limits, but given recent events, I cannot conclusively rule out SSR influence. I recommend continuous monitoring to track any progression or pattern."

I nodded, the uncertainty was another layer added to our already complex situation. "Keep an eye on it, TJ. Let's not let anything slip by us."

The lab resonated with an unsettling sense of dread. Around me, my colleagues moved with a cautious urgency, their attention fixated on the SSR's enigmatic behavior as they worked.

I hovered over the central console, my eyes tracing the frenetic patterns displayed on the screen. The SSR's movements were erratic, yet there was an unnerving purpose to their chaos. "This is beyond biology," I murmured. "It's almost... purposeful." I felt a cold knot of fear tighten in my gut.

Sam, hunched over his microscope, his voice barely more than a whisper, echoed my thoughts. "They're definitely changing."

He sounded frightened and that, more than anything else, frightened me.

Alex, standing beside the containment chamber, shook his head in disbelief. "It's like watching them adapt in hyperdrive. They're responding to something in the environment..."

I gasped, the answer hitting me, but before I could say it, he'd beaten me to it. He pulled back and looked at Sam and me, horrified. "They are reacting to *us*..." His words trailed off, leaving an ominous silence.

The soft, eerie glow from the SSR samples cast strange, dancing shadows across the darkened lab's walls, transforming our familiar space into a realm of uncertainty and fear. Every sound seemed amplified, every movement charged with tension.

Alex stood silent, his eyes fixed on a readout that fluctuated wildly. "I've never seen anything like this," he said, his voice low and strained.

At that moment, the lab felt like a world apart, a place where the normal rules of science and nature no longer applied.

I tapped the console screen on the wall. "Luca, do we have anything from Mission Control?"

He answered immediately. "Just came in now, Commander."

"Patch it through."

"I'll put it on the ship's comms." The room filled with the crackle of static as he patched the transmission through.

The familiar voice of Nash resonated through the ship's speakers, broken but authoritative.

"Artemis, this is Mars Frontier Command. Commander Mercer, we've received your transmission and understand the gravity of your situation with the SSR."

There was a brief pause, the weight of his words

hanging in the air.

Do they? Do they *really?*

"Effective immediately, SSR research is now priority one for the entire Institute from the Top Secret level down to the lowest restricted access clearance. We're diverting all available resources to assist in analysis and containment. Your findings are concerning, and it's imperative that we understand this entity's capabilities and intentions."

Okay, maybe they did understand.

Nash's voice was steady. "Maintain strict containment protocols and keep us updated with all developments. We're with you, Artemis. Mars Frontier out."

I blew out a breath and hoped my colleagues back on Mars liked me enough to want to keep me alive.

Shoot.

Hopefully, the prospect of seeing the artifacts and bodies first-hand would keep them from *that* particular political path.

"I got something else," Luca said. "A private transmission, encrypted with our own codes." He looked at me on the screen, uncertainty in his eyes. "You want me to decode it?"

I nodded. "Do it."

The crew exchanged uneasy glances as Luca worked. Seconds felt like hours, the tension palpable. Then, Nash's voice returned, laden with static and laced with a gravity that chilled my blood.

"Artemis, this is off the record," Nash began, his voice hushed, strained. "The situation on Mars... it's deteriorating. Governor Olsen has redirected all our resources to war preparations. Your mission... it's been deprioritized on Dr. Park's orders. I'm sorry. I'll give you all the help I can, as will the others but..."

A collective gasp filled the room. War preparations? My mind raced with the implications.

Nash continued. "The NUSR... they've developed something big, an old-style nuclear bomb. But it's not just any bomb. We're talking about a massive payload, enough megatons to level multiple cities at once. If detonated near Mars Colony One, it would be catastrophic."

I felt a chill run down my spine. I pictured the domes of Mars Colony One, the life support systems, and the tech that kept them alive. A bomb of that magnitude could disrupt everything, shattering the domes, and annihilating their protection from the harsh Martian environment. The thought of it was paralyzing.

"We're trying to arrange an evac for the civilians, the kids." Nash's words hung heavy in the air, a harbinger of doom. "We're on borrowed time," he continued. "Governor Olsen has a plan, but—"

Static abruptly cut him off. Luca's fingers flew over the console, but the transmission was lost. "That shouldn't have happened!" Luca said, frantically bringing up some screens. "The signal was fine. It's all clear."

Mike's voice came through the comms, heavy with resignation. "Looks like we're on our own."

We stood in silence, each lost in our thoughts. The weight of our isolation, millions of miles from a home teetering on the brink of war, was suffocating. The lab felt like a tomb, the SSR samples an ominous reminder of the ticking clock we raced against—alone.

I swallowed the lump in my throat. "We keep working," I said, more to convince myself than anyone else. "We focus on the SSR."

But as we returned to our stations, the unspoken fear lingered—a fear of the unknown, of a future slipping away, and of a threat far beyond our comprehension. The SSR's enigmatic behavior now seemed almost trivial against the backdrop of a potential apocalypse, yet it was the only lifeline we had.

I pressed the comms screen again. "Mike, system update."

A moment later Mike's voice came through. "All systems green, but I'm picking up fluctuations in some non-vital elements— the nutrient dispensers, the crew pod screens, some glitching on the hydroponics sensors. I'm not sure where it's coming from. Diagnostics are fine..."

I sighed, hoping it wasn't what I thought it might be.

"Stay on it."

"Will do," Mike assured me.

"Hank, vitals."

Hank took longer, presumably running quick diagnostics through our implants. I always felt like I should be able to feel it tingling or something when he did that.

"Nothing significant, Commander."

"Keep me updated."

"Roger."

My head ached and the stress and the lack of sleep caused my eyes to be bleary as I attempted to study the ever-vibrant SSR under the lens of the microscope. Eventually, I had Atlas cast it to the screen, but I hated studying the samples that way. I always seemed to see and judge them better through the 'scope.

We did a full day's work—more than a full day— by the time I called the team together for a meeting. The ship felt different now, less like a haven and more like a cage, with the invisible threat of the SSR permeating every corner.

"Alright," I began, my voice steady despite the turmoil churning inside me. "We need to talk strategy and make some tough decisions."

Mike was the first to speak up. "We've got the SSR on board, and it's possibly interacting with the ship. Our priority has to be containment and understanding what we're dealing with."

"I agree," Alex chimed in. "The SSR is the immediate threat. We need to focus our efforts on it, learn how to stop it from spreading further."

The room nodded in agreement. "Artie, based on your analysis, what are our options for containing the SSR and preventing further contamination?"

"Commander, the SSR's adaptive nature makes it unpredictable. However, minimizing its access to energy sources and technology interfaces is paramount," Artie responded. "Stowing away the rovers and the popup lab will eliminate potential interaction points and reduce the risk of further spread. It also has the added benefit of preparing for launch much faster."

The idea of breaking down and stowing the equipment we'd brought so far to explore Ganymede was disheartening, but it made sense. Our mission had changed; we were no longer explorers uncovering the secrets of an ancient civilization. We were survivors, doing whatever it took to ensure our safety and the integrity of the Artemis.

But losing those extra days on the surface irked me and I knew that if I survived this, they'd irritate me even more as time passed.

"Alright," I said, the decision made. "We'll break down the rovers and the lab first thing tomorrow. Everything goes into storage for the duration of the mission. Our focus shifts to the samples and data we've already collected. That's where our answers lie."

The crew was silent, the reality of our newest directive setting in. We were in uncharted territory, facing an alien entity that defied our understanding. The excitement of discovery had been replaced by the cold fear of contamination, of contagion.

"As for the lab on the ship," I continued, "we have the equipment we need to continue our research on the SSR. We'll do it carefully, methodically. We can't afford any more surprises."

ΦΦΦ

The next morning, I woke to a ship that felt far different than the one I'd fallen asleep in. The usual hum of activity was replaced by a heavy stillness. It felt like a ticking time bomb.

I rubbed the sleep from my eyes, the remnants of nightmares still clinging to my thoughts.

In the common area, the science team and TJ were already gathered. Their faces were etched with lines of worry. No one needed to say it. We all felt the sorrow of dismantling our recently-prized equipment. Sam in particular looked crestfallen.

"Morning, team. Let's start with the lab," I said, trying

to inject a bit of normalcy into the day. "Pack it up right and tight."

TJ, tool kit in hand, gave a nod. "I'll handle the rovers. Disconnecting power and securing them for storage. Since Mike is staying aboard to monitor the systems, I'll need Sam to lend me a hand."

Sam nodded and we all geared up and headed out the airlocks.

Alex and Sam headed towards their side of the lab, their steps slower than usual.

"Every sample, every scrap of data, it's all cataloged and locked down," Alex assured me, though his usual spark was dimmed. "We've gotten everything we need anyway."

Sam was already pulling on outer gloves. "And I'm double-checking every seal and lock as we go. After, I'll head over to help TJ."

The work was methodical and depressing, a stark contrast to the frenzied excitement that had accompanied setting everything up. As I helped dismantle the lab, I couldn't help but feel like we were erasing our progress. Each piece of equipment that went silent, every light that dimmed, felt like a step backward. Throughout it all, the SSR beamed blue from the contaminated equipment. It was brighter now and cold.

I no longer found it so beautiful.

I knew it was foolish. After all, we'd gotten what we

came for...well, more than we had come for but that was beside the point. We'd successfully found intelligent life, maybe even two different forms, and the trick now was to keep it from killing our ship as we worked to figure it out.

"Artie, keep a continuous scan for any more SSR activity," I instructed, hoping to catch any further spread before it started.

"Continuous monitoring already engaged, Commander," Artie confirmed.

The pop-up lab was gradually reduced to a collection of cases and containers. Now and then, someone would pause, looking over a piece of equipment with a mix of regret and resolve.

"Hard to believe we're packing it all away," Sam said, sealing another container. "Feels like we just got started."

"Yeah, we'll be back in the Science Dome again before we know it" I replied, securing a microscope into its foam cradle. "But we're playing the long game now. Can't risk anything with the SSR on board. We got what we needed anyway. We might just have to come back some other time," I joked, but it fell flat.

TJ called from the rover bay, his voice carrying over the comms and through the ship. "Rover One is secure. Moving onto Rover Two."

"On the move to assist," Sam told him with a little salute to me.

As the hours passed, the outside of the ship transformed. What had been a symbol of human curiosity and exploration was now an empty camp of caution and disappointment. It wasn't just equipment we were stowing away; it was a piece of our purpose, a chapter of our mission rewritten by an unforeseen microbial force.

"Last case is ready," Alex announced.

"Good work," I said, looking around at the team. Their faces were tired, the usual banter replaced by grim silence. "Let's get everything into storage and then regroup. We've got a lot to discuss about the next steps."

One by one, the cases were moved to the storage unit. The clunk and clatter of our work filled the ship.

It felt taboo, but I began to wonder if any of this stuff would ever see the light of day again. If *we* would...

Once everything was secured, I called for a brief meeting. "We did what we had to do today," I began, meeting each team member's gaze. "But this isn't over. We'll need to keep a close eye on the SSR and figure out our next move. No matter what, we have still made history here and each one of you had something vital to contribute. Now, let's head in for a meal and a debriefing. Artie, configure the airlocks for a double de-con."

Talk about locking the barn door after the horse has bolted...

"Double decontamination procedures ready."

Later, after a meal and a lot of surreptitious looking around for glowing crystals, we gathered at the table for a meeting.

"We need to figure out what comes next," I said. "I can't, in good conscience, return to Mars or Earth while this ship is contaminated by an alien...substance."

I was going to say *entity*, but I thought perhaps it might be better not to.

"We're a plague ship," Alex said, rubbing his temples. "Like the olden days. Nobody will touch us."

"Alex, we need to stay positive. We have some of the brightest minds on two planets here, I have no doubt we can figure this out, given enough time."

"Do we *have* time?" Sam asked.

Mike spoke up. "Artie, can you give us a progression graph of the SSR contamination? I want to know what kind of time limit we're looking at here."

I kind of wished he hadn't done that. As we waited, I felt a dread deep in my bones and butterflies in my stomach...and not the good kind.

Artie's voice broke the tense silence as it delivered the analysis, and we weren't comforted at all by his stoic British aplomb. "Compiling data for a progression graph of the SSR contamination. Please stand by."

We waited, the air roiling with our combined anticipation and dread. The gentle hum of the ship's systems provided a grumbling backdrop to the racing thoughts in everyone's minds.

"Analysis complete," Artie finally announced. "Based on the current rate of spread and interaction with the ship's systems, the SSR contamination is progressing faster than initially estimated. Without effective containment or neutralization, it will infiltrate critical systems within an estimated 72 to 144 hours."

My chest squeezed and I couldn't breathe.

72 to 144 hours.

It wasn't much time, but it was something—a window of opportunity to act, to try to turn the tide against an enemy we still barely understood.

But, God, it wasn't much time...

Mike's face was grim but determined as he swallowed heavily and let out a gust of air. "Alright, we have a time frame. Now we need a plan. Ideas, people. Anything and everything could make a difference."

Alex, his earlier resignation now replaced with a spark of undaunted resolve, spoke up. "We need to understand the SSR better. How it spreads, what it's drawn to. We can use that knowledge to our advantage."

I nodded in agreement. "Artie, I want you to maintain continuous monitoring of the SSR's behavior. Any changes, no matter how small, I want to know immediately."

"Understood, Commander," Artie replied. "Continuous monitoring will be maintained onboard. I will alert you to any changes in the SSR's behavior or contamination levels."

19.

'64-03

We each took a three-hour break to sleep in shifts. I didn't think I'd be able to, not with the threat of imminent death hanging over my head, but I surprised myself.

I slept hard and when I woke up, I had a clear plan of action in mind. I didn't have any new ideas regarding the SSR, but I knew what we needed to do.

"All crew, report to the table."

I wiped my eyes and scrubbed my face with a damp towel, hoping it would wake me up a bit more. It didn't work, but I knew the emergency coffee supply in the galley would.

As the crew assembled around the table, I looked around at the faces of my team, each one marked by the same resolve and weariness that I felt. They were pale and dirt circles shadowed their eyes. I'm certain mine was no different. We could sleep later.

"Listen up," I started, my voice steady. "We don't have a solution for the SSR yet, but we need to prepare for the worst-case scenario. If the SSR reaches critical systems and takes them offline, we can't risk being stranded on Ganymede. We need to initiate the launch and set our course for Mars as soon as possible. Ideally, I'd like to get the GID powered up in less than a week if we can push it."

Mike, his brows furrowed in thought, spoke up first. "It's risky, but it's a solid plan. We need to maintain control of the Artemis for as long as possible. Being adrift in space is better than being marooned here."

"I'll double-check the propulsion and navigation systems. Make sure they're ready for an immediate launch when you give the word," TJ added.

Alexei sighed. "We should also consider the potential of bringing SSR back to Mars, should we find it necessary to return without solving the issue. We need a containment protocol for re-entry."

Hank nodded in agreement. "And I'll prepare for any medical situations that might arise during the launch. The stress alone will be significant, and the stress of going back up will wreak havoc on your immune systems."

Luca, who'd been quiet and almost dozing off, finally

spoke. "I'll ensure all communication lines are open and clear, though it won't do us much good. If we're launching for Mars, Mission Control needs to be in the loop every step of the way as often as we can—even if we are '*deprioritized*'," he spat. "I'll let them know the plan and get an automatic packet queued to send as soon as we get a clear signal."

"I'll help with securing the lab and any loose equipment. We can't have anything flying around," Sam said.

I nodded, taking in each point. "Good. Let's all focus on our tasks. We're not giving up on finding a solution, but we need to be prepared for every possibility."

I tapped my fingers on the tabletop for a moment, thinking.

"Artie," I began, my voice betraying a hint of the weariness I felt. "Given the current rate of SSR spread and its interactions with the ship's systems, I need a prudent timeline for launch. When should we ideally be leaving Ganymede's orbit to ensure the safety of the crew and the integrity of the Artemis?"

Artie's response was prompt. "Commander, considering the SSR's current rate of adaptation and spread, and factoring in the time required to prepare for a safe launch, I recommend initiating the launch sequence no later than 24 hours from now."

The number hung in the air. One day to do what we could to fight back against an unseen enemy that had turned our mission, and maybe even our lives, into a race against time.

"Understood, Artie. Keep us updated on any changes, and alert me immediately if that timeline needs to be adjusted," I said, my mind already turning to the next steps, the next decisions.

"Affirmative, Commander. I will maintain continuous monitoring and provide regular updates," Artie assured me.

With a deep breath, I pushed back from the table, my resolve hardening. Twenty-four hours. It wasn't much, but it was what we had, and I'd be damned if we didn't use every last second of it fighting for every chance, every possibility.

As the meeting dispersed, each of us set to our tasks feeling like the devil was on our heels. The ship had become a lifeboat that I had to man.

But first, I needed coffee.

ΦΦΦ

As we worked, the ship itself began to whisper hints of distress.

A console in the corner flickered, its screen blurring

with static before returning to normal.

"Did you see that?" I asked, but Alex was already nodding, his eyes narrowed in suspicion.

"Artie, system status report," I called out, hoping for some mundane explanation like a software glitch or a loose wire.

"Minor fluctuations detected in non-critical systems," Artie responded, its voice betraying no concern. "Possible interference from an unknown source."

"Unknown source, my foot," I muttered. "It's the SSR, has to be."

I crept closer to the screen. "Artie, lower the lights."

Alex's eyes snapped to meet mine as the light went dim. My heart jumped at the vibrant cerulean hues sparkling around the room.

It had grown.

We decided to expand our observation beyond the visual, setting up additional sensors around the lab to monitor the SSR's interaction with its environment. As we worked, the ship seemed to buzz with a low, almost imperceptible hum that was different than the sound of the environmental controls. It was the sound of a thousand tiny changes happening just beyond our perception.

Or maybe it was just my imagination. I tended toward the paranoid side lately—with good reason.

The lab's lighting brightened and dimmed

momentarily, a shiver running through the ship's systems. I hadn't ordered the change this time.

"That's new," Alex noted as we both looked up.

I shivered. "We need to talk to Mike, and get his take on this," I said, already moving toward the door as Alex adjusted the experiment for the slight drop in gravity.

As I took my third step, I wavered, the floor tilting under my feet and making me lurch toward a tabletop for support. "Artie, is that you messing with the lab gravity generators?"

"Negative, Commander. The adjustments are not originating from my systems."

"Wonderful," I scoffed.

By the time we found Mike, he was already knee-deep in diagnostics, his brow furrowed in concentration. "It's like the ship's got a mind of its own," he said without looking up. "Systems I didn't even know could interact are talking to each other, making adjustments on the fly and Artie's trying to automatically compensate."

"And let me guess, it all started happening around the time the SSR started its light show?" I asked.

Mike nodded, his expression grim. "Exactly. It's like the SSR is communicating with the ship, or at least trying to. But whatever it's saying, it's not good. I'm going to keep replacing these fuses and wires, but we don't have an inexhaustible supply. We'll need to think about shutting down non-critical functions soon to make sure we have enough on hand for the high-priority circuits."

Alex and I returned to the lab to continue securing samples and gear for launch. The SSR samples continued to glow and morph inside their sealed containment cubes, their light casting eerie shadows across our faces.

As the hours passed, the trickle of malfunctions grew into an alarmingly steady stream.

A door refused to open, then suddenly slid shut without warning. The temperature in one section of the ship dropped ten degrees before slowly creeping back up. And all the while, the SSR glowed brighter, its presence an undeniable force that was slowly asserting its dominance over our home.

"We need a plan," I said, biting my lip in thought.

My fears were soon compounded as reports of malfunctions began to flood in from other parts of the ship. Instruments near the SSR samples showed signs of erratic behavior, and their readings were no longer reliable. Mike, with his engineer's acumen, was quick to identify a disturbing pattern.

He wiped the grease from his hands as he came out of the bowels of the ship, the engine bay. He shook his head and stored his tool kit.

"It's targeting the crucial tech," he said, his expression grave. "Especially around electronic interfaces and power sources. This isn't just adaptation, it's interaction."

"It's going to take us down," I whispered.

I called an emergency meeting and the crew gathered around, seemingly expecting bad news.

"We're facing something potentially significant," I began, wishing I could offer them more hope. "The SSR is spreading," I sighed. "It's heading for the critical components of the ship."

Murmurs of apprehension filled the room as I outlined the situation. Mike proposed a drastic but necessary measure: isolating all SSR samples and affected equipment in a shielded section of the lab. "We need to cut it off from any unquarantined energy sources, contain it completely," he insisted. "We need to seal off the affected sections of the ship—at least try to slow it down."

"It'll make studying it harder," Alex said.

Mike raised his eyebrows and gave a helpless shrug. "It might be our only chance."

ΦΦΦ

I noticed Sam rubbing his temples, a frown creasing his normally stoic face. I watched him for a moment, my head throbbing in sympathy.

The dull ache that had started as a minor annoyance was now a constant companion, a relentless pressure that seemed to echo the pulsing of the ship's heart. I had written it off as a lack of sleep and too much caffeine.

"Headache?" I ventured, my voice barely above a whisper, as I approached him.

Sam glanced up, his eyes betraying a weariness that went beyond physical exhaustion. "Yeah, it's been nagging me all day. Thought it was just lack of sleep, but it's persistent."

I nodded, feeling a chill run down my spine. "I've been feeling it too. And I think others have as well."

Alex, who had been quietly analyzing data at his makeshift station at the table, looked up. "I thought it was just me," he admitted, a note of concern in his voice. "A dull headache, right? And a bit of lethargy?"

We exchanged worried glances.

"Could it be stress?" Alex suggested, though his tone lacked conviction.

I shook my head, my gaze drifting to the sealed container holding the SSR samples. "I don't think so. It's too coincidental. We need to consider the possibility that it's related to the SSR."

"I'm not feeling great wither," Luca said, cutting in from the command module.

"Medical exams, now," I ordered, turning to Hank. "We need to know what we're dealing with."

Hank conducted the examinations, but the results were

inconclusive. The SSR's alien nature defied our understanding, its effects on the human body a dark riddle we were ill-equipped to solve.

"I can treat symptoms, but until we locate the cause, the source, that's all I can do," he said helplessly, passing out tablets.

The decision to halt all research on the SSR until we were on a trajectory back to Mars was unanimous.

Containment was our priority, and the lab was transformed into a quarantine zone. We worked tirelessly, enhancing isolation protocols and devising methods to secure the SSR samples.

ΦΦΦ

The ship's command module was tense as we prepared for the emergency launch. I took a deep breath, trying to steady the adrenaline that coursed through me.

"Artie, initiate pre-flight systems check," I commanded, my voice firm and displaying none of the misgivings I had.

The sense of forboding had only gotten worse. The gut deep nagging feeling that something very bad was going to happen seeped into every though and every plan of action in my brain. I began second-guessing myself, and that was bad.

Indecisiveness could get us killed just as easily as

making the wrong decision.

"Initiating systems check," Artie responded. The screens flickered to life, displaying a cascade of diagnostics. I watched closely as each system was verified.

"Propulsion?" I asked.

"Green across the board, Commander. Thrusters and Graviton Drive are responding as expected," Mike confirmed, his hands deftly moving over the controls.

"Life support?" My gaze shifted to Hank.

"All systems operational. Oxygen, pressure, and temperature are stable," he reported, though the concern in his eyes hinted at the unspoken worries about the SSR contamination. *Operational for now*, they seemed to say.

"Communications?" I turned to Luca.

"I set up an auto-send of our emergency launch to Mission Control. All channels are open and clear," he replied, his voice a touch more strained than usual. "But there's static interference, and I don't know when they'll get our update."

With each confirmation, the reality of our departure settled deeper. This was it. We were leaving Ganymede, in triumph, but that triumph was overshadowed now.

I'd need to make sure it wasn't forgotten in the days to come. We needed every win we could get, for morale's sake.

"Everyone, suit up and strap in. We're about to initiate

launch," I announced.

The crew scrambled, securing themselves into their suits and seats. The command module became a symphony of clicks and beeps as harnesses were fastened and final checks completed at each station.

"Artie, confirm all crew are secured and ready for launch," I ordered.

"All crew members are secured. The ship is ready for launch, Commander," Artie acknowledged.

I took one last look around, meeting the eyes of some of my crew before giving Jax the go-ahead. "Initiate launch."

The ship vibrated gently as the thrusters engaged, a low rumble that grew in intensity as we lifted off the surface of Ganymede until the shaking made it impossible to speak clearly.

The icy landscape fell away, and we were ascending, racing up through the thin atmosphere. I gave the surface one last look, longing to be able to stay and explore further but knowing it was impossible.

Even if we found a way to neutralize the SSR right then, we wouldn't have enough fuel for the thrusters to make another reentry and another launch. This was it. The surface mission was over and now I had to get us back to Mars, preferably alive.

As we climbed, the ship shuddered slightly, rippling

through my chair like an earthquake.

It wasn't supposed to do that.

"Report!" I barked.

"Minor power fluctuations in the auxiliary thruster systems," TJ called out, his fingers flying over the console. "Compensating now."

"Keep an eye on it. We can't afford any surprises," I replied, remembering the first disastrous simulation where the ship exploded and killed us all.

"Jax, how's our trajectory?"

"Stable and on track," he said, his voice calm despite the tension. My lips twitched in a tiny smile.

Typical pilot.

Alex's voice cut through the commotion, tinged with discomfort. "Commander, I'm feeling... off. My skin's tingling, burning a little."

"Same here. Something's not right," Sam warned.

My stomach clenched.

"Hank, as soon as we're in orbit, I want a full sequence medical check on everyone. For now, everyone focus on the launch. We need to get clear of Ganymede."

The ship steadied and the initial problems ironed out as we broke through the last vestiges of the moon's scant gravitational pull and Jupiter's stronger one.

"Bring the GID online."

"GID coming online. Enabling initial phase up," Mike

answered.

I waited for the switch from the chemical thrusters to the deeper, growling GID and when I began to feel it, I relaxed slightly. "Jax, check the trajectory."

"All good, Commander."

As the thrusters quieted and the weightlessness of orbit took hold, relief mixed with apprehension.

We had a successful launch, and now it was time for medical assessments.

"Alright, team," I said, unstrapping myself from my seat and my suit, and floating gently in the low gravity. "We need to understand what we're dealing with. Hank, it's time for that full medical check. Do it the old-fashioned way. I don't trust that our implants haven't been corrupted by the SSR."

Hank nodded, already pulling his medical kit from the storage cabinet in the corridor, his brow furrowed with the concentration of a man who knew the wellbeing of the entire crew rested in his hands.

"I'll need each of you one at a time in the Med Bay. We'll do a complete workup while the systems are a go—blood tests, scans, the works. I want to see if any physical changes might give us a clue about the SSR's effects."

One by one, we glided toward the Med Bay, a small, sterile room that had never seemed more vital. Hank was thorough, and each test was a piece of the puzzle, a search for answers.

He was the new plague doctor of our time.

As we waited for our turns, the rest of the crew busied themselves with securing the ship for the journey ahead. TJ and Mike were huddled over a console, discussing potential modifications to the ship's systems to isolate or slow the SSR's spread. Their conversation was a low murmur of technical jargon that was beyond me.

Luca was at the communications station, ensuring a constant stream of data updates were sent back to Mission Control.

"I feel like I'm yelling into the void," he said, staring out ahead of us. "I honestly don't know if they're receiving any of our messages."

He looked over a me, thinly-disguised despair in his eyes. "I don't even know if Mission Control exists anymore," he whispered.

I schooled my features and floated over to the viewing port, gazing out at the endless expanse. It was a view that had always filled me with wonder, but now it made me antsy and agoraphobic.

Crushing.

Perhaps that's how Commander Fuller had lost his mind. Maybe it had crushed him.

I knew, though perhaps the others hadn't thought about it yet, that I would never allow the ship to enter

Martian orbit if we hadn't developed a neutralizing protocol. I wouldn't even let it get close.

The ship might not have had a self-destruct feature installed, but the GID and the thrusters would be easy to overload. It would only take an instant. The thrusters were chemical rockets and the power source was nuclear fusion reactors. There would be no problem there, especially if Mike removed the overload protection.

However, that was my absolute last resort. Plan Z.

Alexei and Sam were the last to be examined, their faces etched with the fatigue of the long hours and the strain of the unknown. As they emerged from the Med Bay, their expressions were unreadable.

"We're all clear for now," Hank announced, though his voice held a note of caution. "No immediate visible signs of physical change, but we'll need to keep monitoring everyone closely. The SSR is like nothing we've ever seen before. I expect the SSR will begin showing up on the tests soon."

The meeting reconvened, a circle of faces illuminated by the soft glow of the ship's interior.

Hank spoke first. "I want everyone on full vitamin protocols. I know some of you have been a bit more relaxed as far as your nutrition supplements go, but no more. I want everyone to follow their regimens to the letter, including utilizing the fresh produce from the hydroponic—"

"If it isn't contaminated," Alexei said.

Hank nodded. "We'll need to check it first."

"We have a plan," I said, looking at each member of my crew. "We monitor our health, we keep the SSR contained, and we head for Mars. We'll be working with the best minds in the solar system to figure this out. We're not alone in this." I crossed my fingers and hoped that it was true.

Nods of agreement met my words, a silent pact between us all.

I hoped that I was the only one who saw the skepticism on Luca's face.

ΦΦΦ

Day two aboard the Artemis started well enough, with no observable spread of the SSR contamination. Non-critical systems still fluctuated occasionally, but it was nothing bad, nothing dangerous.

There were still no comms from Nash back on Mars, private or otherwise.

The tension had been building, an insidious mounting pressure that seemed to tighten with every breath we took. Sleep was a nightmare, literally and figuratively. When we were able to rest— in shifts— our dreams were plagued with visions of disaster and a creeping enemy that was unfortunately very real.

The quiet was something else. The ship had taken on a funereal atmosphere, as if we were all at a wake mourning the dead.

Except we were the dead and it just hadn't happened yet.

Were we mourning ourselves, or the mission?

It was during one of our routine checks, a moment that should have been uneventful, that the first alarm sounded. From the engineering section, Mike's voice crackled through the ship's comms, broken, urgent, and edged with concern.

It was the most panicked I'd ever heard him, and that made *me* feel panicked.

"Lena, you need to see this. It's moving faster than we anticipated. It's spreading towards the propulsion and life support systems. We have to act *now*."

As Mike's initial report echoed in my mind, I propelled myself through the zero-gravity corridors toward the heart of the crisis.

"Mike, I'm on my way! Get me a visual on the SSR's progression," I commanded, my voice cutting through the static of the ship's comms.

"On screen now, Commander," Mike responded, his tone grave.

The engineering section was a flurry of activity, with Mike and TJ working in tandem, their movements precise and deliberate. "We're rerouting power to non-essential systems, creating a buffer," Mike explained, his hands moving deftly over the console. "It should help slow the SSR's advance."

The schematics monitor before him displayed a live feed of the SSR's eerie glow, a creeping menace inching its way toward the ship's vital systems through complex circuitry and mechanical pumps.

"Good. Keep me updated on the progress," I said, my gaze fixed on the screen, watching the battle of wills between human ingenuity and alien persistence.

I dove through the corridors to the next critical task: sealing off sections of the ship.

With each sealed hatch, that part of the Artemis became a ghostly tomb, abandoned in our fight for survival. I could hear the hiss and click of the doors as they locked into place, a sound that was becoming all too familiar.

"Section C-4 is sealed. Moving on to D-2," Sam reported with a cough, voice heavy with the unspoken understanding of what each seal meant for our dwindling territory.

Our close quarters were about to get a whole lot closer.

"Confirmed, Sam. Be thorough. We can't afford any

breaches," I responded, my mind racing with the next steps, the next orders.

As we worked, the ship itself seemed to pulse with a life of its own, a living entity that wasn't reassuring anymore. The hum of the systems, the gentle vibration of the hull, all of it felt different now, as if the Artemis was aware of the battle being waged within its walls.

Well, maybe it was since Artie was basically the ship itself and he wasn't shy about complaining.

"The rerouting is working. The SSR's growth toward the GID and propulsion systems has decelerated," Mike announced with a trace of relief in his voice.

It was a flicker of hope. The SSR's advance slowed, its relentless march momentarily stalled by our efforts.

But we knew it was only a temporary victory, a brief pause in an ongoing war.

"We need to keep going with this," I said, retaking my chair. My voice went through more staticky than ever and I felt the worry lines deepen between my eyebrows. "Check every system, every seal. We can't let our guard down, not for a second."

The hours that followed were a blur of activity and shifts. We rerouted more power, sealed off more non-vital sections of the ship, and did everything we could think of to stem the tide of the SSR's relentless advance.

And for a brief, hopeful moment, it seemed like we

might succeed.

But then came the second blow.

Luca's voice, usually so calm and collected, was tinged with disbelief as he called out from the communications station.

"The comms are down, completely dead. It's the SSR— it's interfering with the systems. I can't even upload a data packet for auto-send, not even a text-based comms message."

A silent curse ran through my mind. We had gone from being a plague ship to being a ghost ship.

"I'll keep trying," Luca said, his hands still working the controls. "There has to be a way through."

The ship felt smaller somehow, more fragile. As I floated through the corridors, I could see the strain on every face, the unspoken fears that haunted us all. I smelled like nervous sweat— we all reeked of it— but I couldn't find it in myself to care.

My entire being was focused on keeping the ship alive and the living bodies inside healthy. Personal hygiene took a back seat for a while. I wasn't the only one.

In the Med Bay, Hank was tireless, checking and rechecking each crew member for signs of SSR influence during every shift and only resting when ordered.

"Come on in, Sam," Hank beckoned, his voice a calm constant as he gestured to the next crew member awaiting examination.

Sam floated in with a subdued demeanor, his usual confident stride absent in the weightless environment.

"How's the head, Sam?" Hank asked, his medical scanner in hand, sweeping it over Sam's form.

"Feels like it's in a vice. And there's this pressure behind my eyes that just won't quit," Sam grimaced.

Hank's brow furrowed as the scanner beeped softly, the data flashing across his screen. "I'm not liking these readings, Sam. Your blood pressure's up, and there are some irregularities here I can't quite make sense of yet. We'll keep an eye on it. I want you back here in twelve hours— sooner if you begin to feel worse."

As the day wore on, the Med Bay saw a steady stream of crew members, each with their own tale of discomfort and unease. I watched from just outside, my turn being last.

Luca floated in just before me, trying to inject a bit of levity into the grim atmosphere. I couldn't blame him, he was feeling down about losing contact with Mars, even though it wasn't his fault.

"Hey, Hank, can you prescribe something for a severe lack of pizza? I swear it's a real condition."

Hank cracked a smile. "I'll see what I can do. But first, let's check your vitals."

"Seriously though," Luca's smile faded, "I've been

having these dizzy spells. And my hands, they're shaky. It's like I can't quite get them to do what I want."

Hank nodded, his scanner whirring softly and sending the readings to the screen.

"Your symptoms are consistent with what others are reporting. We're in uncharted territory here, but I promise you, we're doing everything we can."

Then, it was my turn.

I'd been ignoring my symptoms because I knew there wasn't anything we could do, but I knew it was vital we each reported in. It was important to document all the signs and each step taken to mitigate the symptoms. It might come in handy later on.

If not for us, maybe it could help someone in the future.

Hank scanned me, took notes, frowned when I discussed my newly developing female issue, and sent me on my way with extra iron supplements and an increased dosage of my contraceptive in the form of a shot.

The mandatory contraceptives that all females in space received to halt their cycles and prevent pregnancy, had stopped doing its job and I was becoming more miserable by the hour. Hopefully, the shot would work fast.

As the day turned to evening, or what approximated our evening, the crew gathered in the common area. The faces around me were drawn and weary. They were reaching their limits.

"We're up against something *extraordinary* here," I began, meeting the eyes of each of my crew members. "But we're not giving in. We're going to take this one step at a time. Hank will continue his medical assessments. Mike, TJ, keep working on isolating the SSR from the ship's systems. And Alex, I want you to focus on understanding how it's spreading and find us a way to fight back. I'll help when I can. Jax, stay alert and watch the nav systems. I don't want the SSR sending us to the sun. Luca, keep trying Nash. Send out Morse code or mirror signals if you have to, but do your best to let them know what's going on. At the very least, keep a record of what is happening here and send it the first chance you get."

I paused, noting Sam's deterioration from only a few hours ago. "Sam, if you're feeling up to it, try to see if you can determine any geological solutions to the problem. Perhaps a certain mineral or shielding that might impede the spread."

He nodded from his tethered place at the table. He didn't look well, and his breathing seemed labored.

"Hank, why don't you escort Sam to the Med Bay for another scan and some rest? Induce rest if you have to," I said with a significant look.

Hank nodded once and they left, floating slowly down the corridor.

"And one more thing," I added, my gaze sweeping over

the rest of the group. "Look out for each other. We're all we've got out here. If you notice anything, anything at all that's off, report it."

I wandered the remaining unsealed sections of the ship, trying to brainstorm and fill in Step 2 of my plan as I monitored conditions.

The physical symptoms were varied, a strange assortment of aches and pains that defied easy diagnosis. But it was the psychological toll that worried me most, the creeping dread that settled in the pit of my stomach and refused to leave.

When would it worsen? How bad would it get?

The death chamber of the Jovians haunted us all, and I wished I could turn back time to the very moment we'd seen the SSR-encrusted artifacts. I wished we would have realized then that the Jovians hadn't incorporated the crystals into their technology themselves.

It had invaded and it had killed an entire civilization...and we might be next.

20.

'64-03

Day three began in the dark, literally and figuratively.

The Artemis had become a shadow of its former self, a once-bright beacon of exploration now reduced to a dimly lit husk drifting through the void.

The ship's primary lighting system had failed and was considered unrecoverable for now, a casualty of the SSR's relentless spread, leaving us to navigate our own home with flashlights in hand, casting long, haunting shadows against the walls.

"Mike," I sighed, feeling short-tempered and irritable.

"We're working on it. Supplemental light should return in a few moments."

I sat in the command module watching the horizon.

Luca was beside me, coughing a bit as he fiddled with the control screen for the comms. Even with Artie's help, he hadn't managed to transmit or receive any data.

Nash would either think we were dead, or unable to transmit. I doubt he'd give up so easily, so I was betting that they were working on a comms solution and expecting us to do the same.

I refused to believe anything had happened to them. Not without proof...evidence... *something*.

The lighting had all gone out early in our morning after a brief warning from Artie that the SSR had infiltrated the isolated basic non-critical environmental controls, the entire ship living quarters existing only now by the light of the distant sun and our headlamps and flashlights.

The consoles and screens still worked intermittently, but hydroponics was gone.

The darkness was more than just a physical challenge. It rapidly became a psychological one, gnawing at the edges of our minds. Our circadian rhythms would be disrupted, the line between day and night blurred into a perpetual twilight that would leave us disoriented and even more fatigued.

As if we needed yet another stressor.

Mike's ghostly voice broke through the static of the comms, barely audible now in the white noise.

"Lena, you there? TJ and I managed to get some of the

supplemental lighting back online. It's not much, but it's something."

I grasped at the news like a lifeline. "That's great, Mike. Any light is better than none. What's the situation?"

"It's the emergency night mode," he replied, his voice tinged with a weary resignation. "The light's red, won't hurt our eyes or mess with our night vision. But it's... well, it's not exactly cheerful."

Just then, the red light flickered to life, casting the command module in a deep crimson hue.

It was like seeing the world through a bloody filter, one that painted everything with a brush of melancholy and unease. The controls, the seats, and the very walls seemed alien and foreboding, a stark departure from the ship we'd once known.

I sighed, the sound more a release of pent-up tension than anything else. "It's better than being in the dark. Good work, Mike. How are you holding up?"

There was a pause, a moment of hesitation where the weight of the situation hung unspoken between us. "We're managing, Lena. Just taking it one problem at a time. But this red light, it makes everything..."

I nodded, though I knew he couldn't see it. "I know what you mean. It's going to take a toll on all of us. But we're still here, still fighting. That's what counts. And this will be over before we know it and we'll be back at Mars

Vegas with drinks and Martian yams."

Mike's voice softened, a rare crack in his usually stoic demeanor. "Yeah, we're fighters, all right. Just never thought we'd be fighting my own ship."

The comms clicked off, leaving me alone with my thoughts and the oppressive red glow.

As I floated there, the red light painting my face in stark relief, I couldn't shake the feeling of being in a dream, a nightmare from which I couldn't wake.

ΦΦΦ

After a quick lunch of vitamins and a nutrient shake that I could barely choke down, I headed to the lab, where Mike and Alex were working on a contaminated panel while Luca worked with Artie on the comms issue once again.

In the dim, cherry light of the Artemis, the sense of urgency inside the lab was profound.

Mike, his face illuminated in stark contrast by his white flashlight, was hunched over an open panel, his tools spread out before him on a magnetic mat affixed to the wall.

"Look at this," he called out, his voice full of fascinated dread. "The SSR isn't just growing over the surfaces...it's permeating the air. It's shedding these particles."

I floated over. Peering into the panel, I saw what Mike

was talking about.

"Oh Lord," I muttered.

The SSR's eerie glow was not confined to the solid structures of the ship, it was diffusing, spreading like a mist of glowing particles.

Alex joined us, his brow furrowed in concentration as he observed the phenomenon.

"This changes everything," he murmured, more to himself than anyone else. "If it's airborne, containment just got a whole lot more complicated."

"Artie, why didn't you tell us it was airborne?!" I yelled through gritted teeth.

"Artie isn't infallible," Mike snapped, turning toward me with the wrench clenched in his hands.

I stared at him, a bit taken aback by his irritation and the undercurrent of aggression, and he looked away quickly.

I felt uneasy about my own outburst of anger and decided to let Mike's go. I didn't blame him and I didn't take it personally. This damned situation, it was getting to us all.

"Commander, the SSR particles were not detectable. Either they were too small to detect, or they have recently adapted."

I took a deep breath through my nose and let it out, calming myself. I was doing that a lot these days.

"I feel like a captain trying to plug all the little holes in his boat with chewing gum," I said, leaving the lab and catching Mike's gaze as he rose.

We turned to the task at hand, our flashlights casting sharp beams of light as we worked to understand and, hopefully, control the SSR's spread. Alex set up a portable scanner, the device buzzing softly as it analyzed the air composition.

"The particle density is highest near the tech interfaces," Alex noted

Mike's hands were steady as he worked, but I could see the tension in his movements, the concern etched deep in his face. "We need to isolate the affected systems and cut off the SSR's paths. It's going to mean shutting down non-essential tech, but we don't have a choice."

I nodded. "Do it. We can't let the SSR reach the life support or navigation. If it does, we're done for."

As Mike set to work, I floated back, watching the scene unfold in the red glow.

The hours passed, marked only by the soft hum of the ship and the occasional murmur of conversation. The red light seemed to seep into everything so pervasively that I didn't remember what daylight looked like.

Finally, Mike sat back, his work for the moment done. "That's it for now. We've isolated the major systems, but it's a stopgap at best. We need a long-term solution, and we need it fast."

"Commander, I have an idea," Alex began. "For neutralization. But I haven't tested it yet. It would require me to release a sample of the SSR from the containment cube."

"How good is the idea?"

He shrugged. "It could stop the spread or at least slow it...or it could do nothing at all."

I nodded, licking my dry lips. "Do it. We're already exposed."

"Commander, report to the Med Bay," Hank called.

"On my way."

His voice carried an edge that sent me into immediate action. I pushed off from the console, floating through the corridors, my flashlight cutting a path through the redness.

The red glow of the emergency lights cast an eerie pall over everything and I suddenly had a very disorienting experience of déjà vu which made me stop and stare for a moment.

I'd seen this before, somehow or some way. Maybe my nightmares...

As I entered the Med Bay, the sight that greeted me was grim and I covered my mouth as tears threatened to float from my eyeballs.

Hank was at Sam's side, his medical equipment arrayed around him. Sam lay strapped on the bed, his breathing labored, a mask covering his face as the machines beeped and whirred with medical vigilance.

"Commander," Hank said, looking up as I approached, "Sam's respiratory system is failing. The SSR—it's affecting him more severely than the rest of us. I'm doing everything I can, but I need to intubate him to ensure he gets enough oxygen."

My stomach churned at the news. Sam, the unflappable geologist who'd faced every challenge stoically and with irritating arrogance, was now fighting for every breath he managed to take.

"You realize that our supplemental oxygen supply is limited," he warned and I felt my chin quivering. I clamped down on my feelings and nodded. "Give him what you can."

"I'll let you know when he uses up his share."

I hated that. I fucking hated it. Hated hearing it, hated being in command, hated participating in the conversation.

"What can I do to help?" I asked, my voice barely a whisper in the tense atmosphere of the Med Bay.

"Just be here," Hank replied. "Talk to him."

I moved to Sam's side, taking his hand in mine. His skin was clammy, his grip weak, but the faint squeeze he gave in response told me he was still with us, still fighting.

"Sam, it's Lena," I said, leaning close so he could hear

me over the hiss of the oxygen. "You hang in there, okay? We're developing a solution."

His eyes, heavy with fatigue and pain, met mine, and I saw a flicker of the old Sam, the unyielding spirit that had carried us through so many challenges.

"Artie, alert the rest of the crew," I said gently so Sam wouldn't hear.

Hank worked methodically, his every move calculated and deliberate as he prepared to medicate and intubate Sam. The rest of the crew hovered at the edges of the doorway, their faces were masks of concern, determination, and sorrow.

"We're going to get through this, Sam," I promised. "We've faced tough odds before, and we've always come out on top. This time's no different."

As Hank inserted the tube, guiding it with a practiced hand, Sam's breathing eased, the machines settling into a steady rhythm. It was a small victory, but in the shadow of the SSR's relentless advance, it felt monumental.

I patted his hand and told Hank that I'd be back. I led the loitering team to the table.

"We need to talk about our next steps," I said, turning to face the rest of the crew. "We can't keep reacting. We need to be proactive. We need to find a way to stop it before it's too late. Alex, what is your idea?"

The crew gathered around.

Alex, his face drawn with fatigue, spoke up. "I've been analyzing the environmental data from the lab. Some conditions seem to slow the SSR's growth. We can use that to create a controlled environment to study it safely."

"Let's get into the details of that in a moment. For now, Mike?"

Mike floated forward.

"I need you to completely isolate Sam's respirator. I do not want the SSR affecting his oxygen supply."

Mike looked wary. I knew it was a long shot. None of our other containment measures had worked for long so far. It was all we had for the moment.

"TJ, while he's working on that I want you to fabricate an oxygen delivery system to power Sam's respirator. It needs to be entirely mechanical. No tech whatsoever."

Luca's jaw dropped. "No tech?"

TJ nodded, his mind whirring with ideas. "Wait. What about a sealed containment cube? We construct a transparent, airtight box with its own battery pack inside. The respirator mechanism would be fully enclosed, with tubes leading out to Sam."

Mike considered it, the gears in his mind visibly turning. "Yeah, and we could use a simplified version of a ventilator. A basic push-pull mechanism to inflate and deflate a bellows, mimicking the breathing process."

"We'll need a reliable battery, something with a long

life and easily replaceable," TJ added, his eyes scanning the array of available resources on the flickering screen.

"Why don't you use the high-capacity cells from the secondary communications array? They're designed for extended use and should fit your needs," Luca suggested to Mike, who was already mentally dissecting the ship for the parts they would need.

TJ was already sketching a quick diagram, his hand steady despite the grim atmosphere. "We'll need a monitoring system, something visual so we can see it's working without opening the cube. Maybe a simple mechanical counter for each breath cycle."

"Good call. And we add a manual override, a crank or handle on the outside. Just in case the power fails, we can still keep it running," Mike said, the outline of their plan solidifying with each word.

"Sounds like you've got it under control. TJ, get started. Mike and Alex, let's talk environmental warfare."

ΦΦΦ

It took many precious hours, but finally, Mike called us in for another meeting.

"This processor," he said, holding up the compact device, "can independently control the temperature, humidity, and even electromagnetic fields in each sector.

If we can replicate the conditions that slow the SSR's growth, we might just be able to contain it."

The device was sleek, proof of Mike and TJ's engineering prowess, but the task ahead was daunting.

"We have to install one in every sector," he said, making my stomach drop. "Even the ones we've sealed off due to contamination."

The crew exchanged worried glances. Venturing into the heart of the SSR's territory was a dangerous proposition, but our options were dwindling as fast as our hope.

"I'll do it," I declared, my voice more confident than I felt. "I'll install the processors. It's my responsibility."

Mike's expression hardened. "No. You're not doing this."

I bristled at the dictate. "I am the commander of this ship and I am ordering you to give me the processors and tell me how to install them!" I shouted, the fatigue and fear finally overcoming my self-control.

He gritted his teeth, jaw flexing, but whatever he intended to say was interrupted by Artie.

"Commander, may I suggest that you and Engineer Donovan install the processors together? The reduced exposure time to the SSR, for both you and the processors, would provide a better chance for the prototypes to work and for you both to survive the initial installation process."

I bit my lips angrily. Couldn't Mike see that he was far more important to the mission, to the safety of the crew and the ship, than I was?

The protest was on the tip of my tongue, but the resolve in Mike's eyes stopped me. He was right...maybe this was a burden too great for any one person to bear alone. Maybe I wouldn't be able to get it done quickly enough.

The rest of the crew voiced their concerns, each argument a reflection of the fear and uncertainty that had become our constant companions. But beneath the worry, there was an unspoken understanding: this was a risk we had to take.

We prepared meticulously, each movement deliberate and measured. The fully enclosed processors were packed in protective cases and our suits were checked and rechecked for any sign of weakness. Hank, stepping out of the medical bay for a moment, administered a round of stimulants to each of us, a temporary bulwark against the SSR's insidious effects.

"Wow, that's a hell of a lot better than coffee!" I said brightly, suddenly feeling much better about the ordeal. "Let's move out!"

As we set out—quite jauntily and with tons more energy than we'd had just a few minutes ago— the ship's corridors felt more like the tunnels of an ancient tomb, the red light casting long, ominous shadows that seemed to stretch out towards us. The silence was oppressive, broken only by the soft hiss of our breathing and the occasional crackle of comms.

The first installation points were the sealed crew quarters, a place now alien and menacing. I opened the protective case, the processor's lights blinking to life, a small sign of hope in the brilliant blue glow of the SSR.

Mike, working in TJ's old bunk, guided me through the setup, his voice steady in my earpiece.

With each sector, the SSR's presence grew more pronounced, glowing patches of cerulean contamination that pulsed like the beat of some malevolent heart.

We moved quickly, and efficiently, the processors a line of defense against the creeping tide of alien life.

But with each exposure, the risk increased. Sweat dripped down my temples and trickled down my spine. My hands shook from the stimulant, and I felt an ominous ache in my chest and my head.

Blue crystals drifted through the air like tiny lethal snowflakes, landing on our suits and attaching there like shards.

I could feel the strain in Mike's movements, the slight hesitation that spoke of fatigue and fear. And yet, we pressed on, driven by the knowledge that this, this audacious plan, might be our only chance.

As we completed the final installation, a wave of relief washed over me.

"We did it, Mike," I said, allowing myself a moment of pride.

"We did," he replied, his voice tinged with exhaustion. "Now let's get back and hope it works."

ΦΦΦ

Hank forced me to sleep for a few hours after the stimulant wore off. Now, I was headed back to the command module, where Alex had some news.

My eyes were gritty and bleary and my muscles were so sore that I felt like I'd been hit by an asteroid. The ache in my chest, just a tiny little dot of a place near my heart, had grown. The pain in my head had spread as well and seemed to be traveling down my spine, making my shoulders tingle alarmingly.

It wasn't constant, not yet, but it was often enough to worry me.

I checked on Sam, who was still stable, and then grabbed a nutrient pack on the way hoping it would do something to help me feel better.

Everyone except Sam and Hank was in the module waiting for me. Mike seemed okay, but you couldn't exactly see the pain and everyone had lines of worry on their faces.

"Well?" I asked, taking my chair and strapping in so I wouldn't be floating into things.

"At first, it looked promising," Alex began, his eyes never leaving the screen displaying the fluctuating readings.

I felt the despair threatening to creep in at his words.

"The SSR's growth rate slowed in the sectors where we installed the prototypes," he continued.

We all leaned in, searching the data for a glimmer of hope, a sign that we had gained the upper hand in our battle against the alien entity that threatened to consume us.

"But look here," Mike interjected, pointing to a series of graphs that showed a disturbing trend. "The effect was temporary. After a few hours, the SSR began adapting, finding ways to overcome the environmental changes we imposed. It's still spreading, maybe even faster than before."

A collective sigh of disappointment and frustration echoed through the module. We had thrown our best at the SSR, maybe even sacrificing what was left of our health in the process, and it had barely flinched.

The realization was a heavy blow.

"What now?" TJ asked, leaning his head against the table. "We can't just sit here and let it take over the ship."

"No, we can't," I replied, my mind racing through the options, each one more desperate than the last. "We need to regroup and think outside the box. There's got to be something we're missing, some weakness we can exploit."

Hank, who had been silently observing the crew's vital signs from his station in the Med Bay, chimed in. "Whatever we decide, we need to do it fast. The SSR's effect on everyone's health is escalating. We're seeing more severe symptoms showing up on the scans now, and I'm not sure how much longer we can hold out. Commander, I'm particularly concerned about your readings."

Mike looked at me, alarmed, but I just shook my head. My health status was secondary right now.

Luca, his face pale and tired, looked up from his console. "I've been trying everything I can think of to re-establish comms with mission control, let them know what's happening. But the SSR's interference is making it impossible."

"We're not beaten yet," I said, my voice firm with conviction that I wasn't sure I completely felt. It was my job to keep things optimistic until the very last bitter end. "We're a crew, a team. We'll find a way to beat this thing."

As far as motivational speeches went, it sucked. I should have practiced.

"We'll start by reassessing everything we know about

the SSR," Alex suggested, his mind already turning over the possibilities. "There's got to be a pattern, a clue we've overlooked."

"While we do that, let's go ahead and use the ship's environmental controls while we still have command over them," I said. "Let's use them like huge processors. Bake the son of a bitch and see what happens."

TJ laughed and Alex managed a small grin. "It's worth a shot."

"Inform Hank to take precautions for Sam, and then make it happen. I'll be at the table."

I unbuckled and pushed myself through the crowded module, needing a moment to think. Alex's idea was a good one. Somewhere inside the SSR was a weakness. We just had to find it.

"Lena."

I turned and Mike floated nearer, bracing himself on the wall handle over my shoulder. His face was pale and his eyes, like all of ours, were deeply shadowed. For once, he looked his age.

I had an almost crippling sense of guilt for what I'd done to these people, dragging them out here to chase the signal. My chest burned with a fire that had nothing to do with the side effects of the SSR.

It was shame.

He reached out to me, carefully, as if he wasn't sure of

his reception. He tentatively linked his pointer finger with mine as we hovered there, just a loose touch, but it made me feel as giddy as a schoolgirl getting asked to the junior prom. Anyone gliding by wouldn't be able to see it, but it was a little bit of human comfort when I needed it most.

He sighed and shook his head. "I want to apologize for snapping at you back in the lab. I've been a bit tired. I know that's no excuse really. You can have me keelhauled if you want."

I waved it off with a small smile. "Nah. I'll save that for mutiny."

I idly squeezed our linked fingers knowing that it was all the acknowledgement of the unspoken feelings that we could allow ourselves. "Don't worry about it. None of us are operating at one hundred percent and we've been cooped up together for months. It's to be expected."

He nodded and rubbed the back of his neck, floating a bit closer now that he didn't have an anchor.

"How do you feel?" I asked, curious.

He smiled. "Let's just say Nash would be happy."

I must have looked super confused because he chuckled and clarified. "I'm not having *any* fun in space. But I'm more worried about you. What did Hank mean about your scans?"

I shrugged and looked away, not really wanting to get into the specifics of my female hygiene issues with him.

"Not feeling so hot right now, but it's nothing serious. I can still function. I can still operate."

He ducked his head to look into my eyes more closely. "You don't look well."

I huffed. "Thanks, that's just what every girl wants to hear." The teasing popped out before I thought better of it. "It's just the red lights. It makes us all look like vampiric serial killers."

"I'm serious, Lena. You're extremely pale and I saw you holding your chest. How's your breathing?"

He was thinking about Sam.

I crossed my arms. "Fine, as you can see, Doctor Donovan."

"I am a doctor, actually," he said with a smirk.

I narrowed my eyes at him. "A doctor?"

"Yep," he nodded. "A doctor of engineering."

I scoffed and nudged him, making him laugh. "Let's just hope nothing happens to Hank because I don't think I want you operating on me if it comes to that."

"Yeah, probably not. I fix machines, not people," he agreed. "Are you really okay? You'd tell me if you weren't?"

"I'm fine."

He stared at me hard, like he could catch me in a lie. Eventually, the staring got awkward and he sighed. "I'm going to have Hank order you to rest more."

I repositioned my grip on the handhold above me to

keep from floating into him—though I couldn't say I wouldn't have enjoyed it a little...a lot. "I'll rest when this thing is taken care of. Right now, I need to work."

He put his other hand on my shoulder, squeezing my aching trapezius muscle and making me melt. "Then at least let me help you. Don't fight me on it." He seemed so earnest that I couldn't refuse.

"Fine, but when we get our fabulous return banquet and the media demands speeches, you'll be the one I send into the spotlight."

He laughed then, a full laugh that I hadn't heard in quite a while. "I should probably get over my fear of public speaking and do that. I don't think Dr. Park enjoys your speeches very much."

"I know. I like them though and that's what counts," I retorted. "Now, let's go fix this thing and go home."

21.

'64-03

I floated at the end of the table, studying the viewing port on the wall, my mind wandering in an effort to ignore the pounding headache that now felt like it was fracturing my skull and spine into a million tiny shards.

My chest ached, a potent throbbing that made me feel like I wanted to cough, but couldn't. At least my breathing was normal, so whatever was going on with me, I wasn't as bad as Sam...not yet anyway.

I had slept for a bit, and now I couldn't remember what day we were on, but it didn't matter.

Alex was mid-sentence when I tuned back in from outer

space, my still-unfinished plan hovering near my head. On one corner, a tiny blue shard had attached itself to the paper. I brushed it off angrily.

"...and we're talking extremes here, Lena. If we tweak the environmental controls to hit the SSR, we're essentially turning the Artemis into a sauna. Humidity levels, temperature— they all have to go beyond our standard comfort zones."

I rubbed my temple, feeling the onset of another throbbing headache. "Give me numbers, Alex. How hot are we talking about?"

He hesitated, glancing at the data pad in his hand. "Upwards of 50 degrees Celsius, humidity at around 90%. It's going to be like living in a tropical rainforest, minus the greenery, and oxygen levels might dip to as low as 15%. It's not going to be pleasant."

"Understatement of the year," I muttered. I turned to Hank, who had been quietly observing. "What's that going to do to us besides make us wish we'd packed more deodorant?"

"A little over 120 degrees Fahrenheit?" Hank sighed, the red light deepening the lines of concern on his face. "Heat stress, for starters. Dehydration, heat exhaustion, and maybe even heat stroke. I can keep an eye on everyone and make sure we're hydrated and getting salts. We'll have to use the respirators. But Lena, this is a big risk. Our bodies aren't meant for these conditions."

I nodded, wishing the decision wasn't in my hands. "And the SSR?" I asked, looking back at Alex.

He shrugged, a gesture of uncertainty that did little to comfort me. "It's our best guess. High heat and humidity might slow it down, and might even kill some of it off, but there's no guarantee."

I turned to Mike, who had been quietly running simulations on his data pad. "Mike, can the Artemis even handle these changes? What's the risk to the ship?"

He looked up, his eyes serious. "We can do it, but it's going to put a lot of strain on the environmental systems. The filters, the cooling systems— they're going to be working overtime. There's a risk of widespread system circuitry failures if we keep it up for too long."

I took a deep breath, the air already feeling thicker and hotter. "We might not have too long if we don't do something," I said. "Okay. Let's prepare to make the changes. Hank, I want you to monitor everyone's vitals non-stop and keep Sam's body temp normal. Alex, you and I will monitor the SSR's reaction to the new environment. Mike, keep an eye on the ship's systems. Let me know the second something looks off. We don't want to bake the components along with the SSR."

The crew nodded, their faces set. We moved into action, each to our tasks.

I took one last look around the dim, red-lit living quarters, now speckled with colonies of vibrant blue. This was a gamble, a desperate roll of the dice. But if it gave us even a slight edge against the SSR, it was one we had to take.

I settled into the captain's chair in the command module, its usual comfort now feeling out of place in the slowly shifting atmosphere. Even here, blue crystals taunted us on the consoles.

"Artie," I called. "Run a preliminary scan. I want a full assessment of the SSR spread before we start cooking ourselves."

"Scanning in progress, Commander Mercer," Artie's neutral voice replied through the ship's speakers. I waited, tapping a rhythmless beat on the armrest, trying to ignore the throbbing pain in my chest where the SSR seemed to have made itself at home.

A few minutes later, the results flashed on the screen. It wasn't pretty. The SSR was everywhere, like a silent invader that we could only partially see. I grimaced. It was time to go on the offensive for real. A full assault.

"Alright, Artie. Start increasing temperature and humidity progressively. And keep it monitored. Do not allow the temperature to breach the upper safety threshold specified by Doc."

The ship obeyed, and the heat began to rise in a

creeping, suffocating wave.

The guys, with my permission, stripped down to their shorts, the heat making any additional clothing unbearable. I changed into shorts and a tank too, the fabric sticking to my skin as I sweated profusely. It reminded me of a hot summer day back in Tennessee—minus the nice, cool creek to play in.

We moved only to drink fluids, press cool cloths to our heads, and take electrolytes. The ship felt like a sauna, a tropical nightmare miles from any soothing ocean.

"Mike, I wished you'd have installed that swimming pool," I joked weakly, clearing my throat as I removed my respirator long enough to talk.

Hank was busy monitoring everyone, his voice steady but laced with concern as he gave periodic updates on the screen.

"Your vitals are holding, but keep hydrated. And Sam's stable, for now, sedated and intubated. We can't afford for his condition to worsen." His face was flushed, a sheen of sweat on his brow. "Keep your masks on as much as possible."

As hours dragged on, I swore I could feel the SSR in me, a constant, gnawing pain in my chest, while the neurological symptoms flickered at the edges of my consciousness like dark shadows. I wasn't the only one suffering. Jax was looking paler by the hour, and even

Hank's usual stoic demeanor was cracking under the strain of keeping us all alive.

"Artie, status on the SSR," I demanded, my voice raspy in the humid, hot air.

"The SSR's reaction is currently being analyzed. Temperature and humidity levels are within the projected range for environmental stress testing," Artie responded.

"Mike, how are the ship's systems holding up?" I asked, turning to where he was sitting near his console.

He looked up, wiping sweat from his forehead. "So far, so good, if we can trust the sensor reading. But we can't keep this up for long. Any longer than necessary to slow the SSR, and we risk frying them. I don't guess I have to tell you that we don't have replacement parts for everything on board."

I leaned back in my chair. Then, my gaze inadvertently drifted over to Mike again, his chest slick with sweat as he worked. I couldn't help but admire the way his muscles moved under his skin, a momentary distraction from the heat and my pain. His muscles weren't super defined, but you could tell it wasn't fat hanging out under his skin.

Burly was the word that came to mind. He made 52 look...extremely good.

He looked up as he checked the overhead console and caught my gaze. I flinched and looked away. I caught his knowing smirk out of the corner of my eye.

I. Was. Mortified.

I felt my face heat up even more if that was possible, and I pretended to be busy. I hoped the redness from the heat would hide my blush. I could *not* believe I let that happen.

Hours turned into an endless cycle of updates, monitoring, and trying to stay conscious. Artie provided periodic reports on the SSR's status, each one critical to our desperate plan. Mike kept a vigilant eye on the ship's systems, his updates a lifeline in the sweltering heat. They kept me from falling into a semi-conscious doze.

We were all red-faced, drenched in sweat, the atmosphere heavy with the weight of the water in the air. The surfaces of the consoles became slick and I worried about the effect on the electrical circuitry.

"Woah, we've got comms!" Luca shouted through his respirator and shot up from his reclined seat. I was staring blankly at a monitor through the heat-induced haze. He pulled his mask off. "Lena, *the comms!* They're back up!"

I jerked to attention, my heart rate spiking. "Artie, confirm that," I ordered, trying to sound more composed than I felt.

"Affirmative, Commander Mercer. Communication systems are now operational," Artie responded promptly.

I turned to Luca, who was already at his console, his fingers flying over the keys. "Send an updated data packet to Nash immediately. Detail everything— our situation, the environmental modifications, our conditions. Everything."

Luca nodded as he began composing the message. The rest of the crew perked up at the news, a flicker of hope in their eyes amidst the misery.

I shoved my hope down, stuffing it at the very bottom of my mental suitcase. I couldn't afford to have it crushed. I knew as well as Luca did, as they all probably did, that just because the lines were open didn't mean anyone was home.

As we waited for Luca to send the message, Mike's voice brought me back to our immediate reality. "Lena, we need to start thinking about cooling the systems. They're at their limit. Any longer, and we risk permanent damage."

I nodded. Too soon, and we risked the SSR rebounding. Too late, and we could lose the ship. "Artie, I need an updated SSR scan. Now."

"Processing the request, Commander," Artie replied.

The moments stretched on, each second an eternity as we waited for the results. Mike tapped his fingers as he kept a close eye on the temperature and status scans.

Finally, Artie's voice filled the room again. "Scan complete. The SSR's spread has slowed significantly in the current environmental conditions. However, continued exposure to these conditions is not recommended for the crew's safety or the ship's integrity."

I let out a breath I didn't realize I'd been holding. It wasn't a victory, not yet, but it was something. I took a dee breath of my oxygen and removed my mask. "Alright. Mike, start a gradual cooling process. We can't shock the systems or our bodies. Luca, did you send that message?"

Luca turned to me, a thin smile on his sweat-drenched face. "Sent and confirmed. In about 26 minutes Nash will know exactly what we're dealing with."

Hopefully.

I nodded, a small sense of relief washing over me. We were still in the thick of it, but for the first time in what felt like forever, it seemed like we might have a fighting chance. As Mike began the delicate process of cooling the ship, I leaned back in my chair, closing my eyes for just a moment, allowing myself to feel the faintest glimmer of hope.

ΦΦΦ

The shrill sound of an alarm pierced the shadowed, red-tinged command module of the Artemis, jolting the crew from their heat-induced lethargy.

We were a clustered mass, the air thick with the scent of sweat and the remnants of lingering artificial heat, our clothes clinging uncomfortably to our still sweat-slicked skin.

"Artie, report!" I barked, causing a stabbing sensation in my chest. I winced.

"Updated SSR readings indicate a significant spike following the cooling period. It appears the organism is not only adapting but thriving in the fluctuating conditions," Artie's emotionless voice responded, cutting through our hopes like a laser.

I slammed a fist on my armrest and bit back a vile curse. As much as I wanted to throw something and scream, I couldn't let it get to me, not out here among the crew.

The team exchanged weary, worried glances around me. The initial relief we'd felt from the intense heat had been short-lived, a mere moment of respite in our ongoing battle against the relentless enemy within our ship.

Mike, his eyes red from fatigue and stress, was poring over the environmental controls with a white floodlight. His face was set in grooves of worry and disappointment as he analyzed the data and I sighed.

"The cooling period... it's like it gave the SSR a second wind. The readings are higher than before we started," he muttered, his fingers flying over the console as he sought to make sense of the data before him.

I unstrapped my harness and moved closer, peering over his shoulder at the flashing numbers and graphs depicting our dire situation.

"We need a new approach, and fast. This thing is outpacing us at every turn," I said, my voice laced with frustration and fear. "If we could just get ahead of it. Stop the adaptation..." I tapped my lip.

Alex, his face pale and drawn, floated forward. "I think we have been thinking too small, too conservative. We need to shock it, something it can't predict or adapt to quickly."

"And what do you propose?" I asked, my gaze fixed on him, desperate for any sliver of hope.

"Rapid, random fluctuations between 30 and 50 degrees Celsius. Unpatterned, unpredictable. It might just destabilize the SSR long enough for us to gain the upper hand," Alex replied.

I considered his proposal, aware of the risks but increasingly aware that our options were dwindling. Finally, I nodded.

"Do it. But keep it controlled. I don't want us to trade one disaster for another," I instructed, trying to keep my voice steady.

As Mike and Alex set to work, implementing the new strategy, the ship began to shudder and groan under the strain of the rapid environmental changes. The temperature soared and plummeted unpredictably, each shift a physical blow to our already weakened bodies.

"Sam is still stable. TJ is with him now to help keep his

temperature adjusted as necessary," Hank said, coming into the command module. "Lena, I've picked up some readings from your implant that concern me. I want to give you a stimulant. Jax, I'd like you to go rest. Your brain wave pattern is seriously abnormal. Give me a moment to give the commander a shot and I'll provide you with a sedative."

"I'm good to go, Doc...but thanks," Jax said, studying the nav screens. His gaze was unfocused and as far as I could tell, there was nothing there for him to be studying. We were on course.

"It wasn't a suggestion. We can't afford for you to start seizing. We need you to pilot us back into Mars orbit when the time comes."

"That's months away," he said. "We'll have this situation under control by then."

"Maybe, but if you start seizing and I'm unable to stop it, you could become hypoxic. You know what lack of oxygen does to the brain. Do you want to take that chance?" Hank argued, shooting a stimulant into my arm.

I felt better almost immediately.

"How do you know the sedative will work?" Mike asked.

Hank shook his head. "I don't, but Sam seems stable enough now and I'm betting the sedative is allowing his body the rest it needs to help fight the SSR infiltration."

"Jax, follow Hank's advice. That's an order."

He sighed and looked a bit like I betrayed him, but he did get up and float to his quarters. I hated using my authority like that. It rubbed me the wrong way to take away someone's autonomy.

Hank moved among us, his medical kit in hand, dispensing what aid he could. "Stay hydrated, keep moving as much as you can. The SSR inside us is still active and still spreading. I'm looking for solutions, but in the meantime, we need to stay strong," he said, his voice a steady anchor in the chaos.

"Keep yourself healthy too, Doc. We need you."

He smiled and gave me a nod before floating back toward the Med Bay.

I strapped into my chair again, feeling much more perky than I had before. Mike seemed to be better and I wonder if Hank doped him up too.

"I hope we don't become drug addicts," I said, humming a little to the tune in my head.

"Better addicted than dead," Mike said. "We can always check ourselves into the Looney Dome when we get back for some R&R."

"More like some AA," I muttered.

"The addiction potential for these stimulants is lower than some of the others," Hank said, coming through the comms that was now mostly static again. The SSR worked fast, ruining what we had cleared in record time.

"Good to know."

As we waited, the ship felt alive, shuddering and groaning like a wild beast as it responded to the extreme changes we were subjecting it to. The SSR readings fluctuated wildly, offering brief moments of hope followed by crushing disappointment as the organism displayed its terrifying ability to adapt.

"We're pushing the Artemis to her limits," Mike said, his voice tight with worry as he monitored the ship's systems. "She's holding for now, but there's only so much she can take."

I nodded, my mind racing as I considered our next move. The situation was escalating, and the ship and crew were being pushed to their breaking point. We were in uncharted territory, fighting an enemy we barely understood with tools and strategies that felt increasingly inadequate.

They did not teach us this in the academy, and if I got back I was going to demand they add a special class. I could see it now: *'Alien Invasion 101: How to Deal with Space Sand That Wants to Eat Your Brain and Other Matters of Importance'.*

I leaned against the console, bracing myself with a hand on the back of the seat nearby. "So, the extreme heat alone isn't enough. The random fluctuations aren't enough. What's our next move?"

Alex, his eyes bloodshot but alert, jerked his head up from the table wherehe'd been snoring. "I'm going to the lab. I had...a dream. Maybe an idea. I don't know."

I watched him go. I was a damned good astrobiologist, but he was better. If anyone could crack the SSR, he could.

I had another idea.

"Mike," I started, trying to sound more confident than I felt, "we need to talk about the Graviton Impulse Drive. Any chance we can push this thing to get us to Mars faster? Maybe get it up to speed faster? Time isn't exactly on our side here."

He didn't look up immediately, his fingers paused for a brief moment before resuming their dance over the controls. "The Graviton Impulse Drive is already squeezing space-time like an orange at breakfast. We're moving as fast as the laws of physics comfortably allow. Pushing it further is... well, it's not recommended."

I crossed my arms, leaning in closer. "Okay, but what if we ignore the recommended part for a minute? What are the actual risks here? Because a four-month journey isn't exactly a risk-free strategy either, not with the SSR tearing us up from the inside."

Finally, Mike met my gaze. "Increasing the drive's output isn't like hitting the turbo button. It manipulates gravitational waves on a quantum level. Push it too hard, and we might not just risk the drive, we could end up twisting the very fabric of space. Worst case scenario? We create a black hole and get swallowed up, or rip the Artemis apart."

I let out a low whistle. "That bad, huh? But if there's even a theoretical way to boost our speed without turning into space jelly, we need to explore it. Every second we're out here is a second closer to a different kind of disaster."

He sighed, running a hand through his hair. "I'll run some simulations with Artie, see if there's a safer way to give us a nudge. But I'm not promising anything. This is beyond tweaking an engine, it's messing with the universe's building blocks."

"Do what you can, Mike. We're in a fight for our lives here. If there's a chance, *any* chance, we have to consider it."

As the ship continued its relentless cycle of temperature changes, I found myself drifting to a monitor, watching the SSR readings with a mix of hope and dread. "Come on," I muttered under my breath. "Show us something. Give us a sign."

The hours stretched on, an endless loop of hope and despair.

ΦΦΦ

Day four? Five? Three?

I really couldn't care less what day it was.

I woke up from a Hank-induced nap of unknown length and dubious origin with the worst case of space arthritis, and on top of that, I couldn't keep food down anymore.

The Nutrient Shake Fiasco of '64—what the crew was calling it—was gross and harrowing, and Hank decided it was time to give me IV nutrients. The guys also refused to eat in the same room with me ever again.

I kind of felt like I was reaching the end of my effectiveness, and the worst part was that the SSR was still adapting to our makeshift weather weapon. It was *beating* us and the blue glow of the surfaces and some of the tech consoles taunted me more than ever. I gritted my teeth and stared at it as I passed, wanting to smash it under my fist.

I was pissed off that it was going to outlast me.

I floated to my chair in the command module and strapped in, much to Luca's consternation.

"Commander? Maybe you should hit the Med Bay for a while. You look like a floating corpse," he said. "And the comms are down again."

I closed my eyes and leaned my head back against the headrest of my seat. My hands, aching and shaking, gripped the armrests. I felt like I had Parkinsons.

What next?

The relentless bleak atmosphere of the Artemis's

command module was abruptly broken by the piercing blare of a condition red warning.

The alarm cut through the heavy air, sending a jolt of adrenaline through my already exhausted body. I jerked toward the sound, my heart pounding in my chest—much too forcefully.

"Artie, report!" I shouted, my voice trembling with the strain of constant crisis.

"Condition red, Commander Mercer. The SSR has accelerated its spread and is approaching the Graviton Impulse Drive GID and my main data banks," Artie reported.

My ears went funny for a moment, as if they were muffled. All I heard was our funeral bell tolling. Overlaying that was our briefing with Jim Anderson many months ago.

The GID had layers, he said.

Many layers of protection to keep one thing or another from taking it offline. Because it going offline suddenly would be dangerous. Fatal.

Except this damned *thing* was bypassing all those layers and heading right for it.

My hands shook as I snapped out of it, angry at myself for drifting when I should have been commanding.

Mike and TJ, already on the move, began scrambling towards their respective stations. Mike, looking paler and more fatigued than ever, steadied himself against a console, his determination clear despite his weakening state.

"Immediate action is necessary to preserve Artificial Intelligence Assistance and the functionality of the GID. Without the GID, the trip back to Mars will take approximately 420 days, relying solely on the initial boost from chemical rocket thrusters," Artie continued, outlining the dire consequences with clinical precision. "In the event that you survive the initial violent deceleration, which is unlikely," Artie added.

420 days.

The number echoed in my mind like a death knell. Without the GID- if we lived—we'd be adrift, our supplies and sanity dwindling long before we ever saw Mars again. And there was no chance of them sending a resupply mission, even if we did conquer the SSR problem.

Quite simply, Mars didn't have another GID-equipped ship available and even if they did, we'd been deprioritized in favor of war preparations.

Our last resort in that circumstance would be our escape pods, and who knew if those were even functional anymore?

It was something I needed to have Artie check on.

"Mike, TJ, we need to protect the GID and Artie's data banks at all costs. Any ideas?" I called out, my voice steady but my mind racing with the implications of Artie's warning.

Unfortunately, my brain felt sluggish and unfamiliar—as if I'd dropped 40 IQ points and a whole lot of problem-solving skills during my last nap.

Mike, bracing himself against the console, wiped the sweat from his brow. "We could try rerouting power to create a buffer zone around the GID and Artie's core. It might keep the SSR at bay for a while, give us time to think of a more permanent solution."

TJ, his hands flying over his console, nodded in agreement. "I'll start working on isolating the critical systems, try to give them an extra layer of protection. But this is a stopgap at best. We're running out of time."

I swallowed. "Buy us that time. I'll coordinate with the others and see if we can come up with anything else. We're not giving up. Not now, not ever."

I turned. "Luca, prepare the latest data for Mission Control. Keep updating it. As soon as you regain comms, send it."

He nodded.

"Commander, I...an...idea," Alex broke in from the lab. "...be... in five."

"Say again, Alex?" I responded.

"Be there in five!" he said louder and I managed to catch it through the interference.

I gathered my thoughts, noting with a hint of worry

how they tried to wander more than usual. I'd always been a deep thinker, but focus had never been an issue before.

Some of the others came in, but I noticed that Jax wasn't among them. Neither was TJ. Alex eventually showed up, looking somehow thin and a little ethereal in his paleness.

"What's the plan?" I asked right away.

"It's a gamble," he admitted, his eyes scanning the room, meeting each of ours in turn. "But if we can create an area saturated with the conditions the SSR seems to favor, we might be able to draw it away from the GID and Artie's core. We'd be sacrificing a part of the ship, but it could buy us the time we need to come up with something else. I've been working on a solution and I think I'm on the right track. My paper notes are in the lab, but we don't have time to discuss it right now."

I rubbed my aching temples, considering the risk and the sheer audacity of the plan. "And if it doesn't work?" I asked, my voice steady despite the turmoil churning inside me. "If it doesn't take the bait?"

Alex shrugged, a grim smile tugging at his lips. "Then we're no worse off than we are now. But I believe it's our best shot for buying more time."

Before I could respond, Hank's voice cut through the tense silence. "Lena, I pulled Jax and TJ to the Med Bay. Their symptoms are escalating— we're talking severe respiratory distress and worsening neurological signs. I need to do what I can to stabilize them."

"Respirators?" I asked, dreading his answer.

"Not that severe. I think they can get by with meds and supplemental oxygen for now. But our o2 is dwindling more rapidly than anticipated."

I nodded, my stomach clenching at the thought of my crew, my friends, suffering. "Go, Hank. Keep me updated."

As Hank and the worst-affected crew members battled the SSR in the Med Bay, the emptiness of the command module preyed on my spirits. We were down three crew members, and the others weren't looking so great either.

Our plague ship-turned-ghost ship was morphing yet again. This time it was a prison ship, the SSR its relentless warden.

With a deep breath, I addressed the crew. "Prepare for Alex's plan. We'll set the bait. It's a risk, but we're out of good options. Mike, work with Alex to identify the best section to use. We need it far enough from critical systems but enticing enough for the SSR."

The crew dispersed. Left alone in the command module, with the red lights and glowing blue plague crystals battling it out for light dominance and causing weird purple striations on the walls, I pulled up the communication console, initiating an audio recording. The deep growl of the GID was the only thing I heard over the beating of my own heart in my ears.

It was time to send the message I'd been dreading, the words I'd hoped never to say.

"Hey Mom, Dad," I began, my voice catching as I forced the words out. "It's Lena. I wish I were calling with good news, but... I'm not. Things up here are pretty bad. We're fighting something we don't fully understand, and it's... it's winning. I'm sure you'll hear about it soon if you haven't already. I hope you guys are okay."

I paused, gathering my thoughts, my heart aching with the weight of unspoken fears.

"I know I've been distant, chasing my dreams out here for the last decade or so. But I want you to know that not a day went by when I didn't think of you. Your love, your support— it's what kept me going, even now, as everything's falling apart."

I took a shaky breath, the words spilling out in a torrent. "If you're hearing this, then I guess I didn't make it back. And I'm so sorry for that, for leaving you with this message instead of coming home. But know this— I love you. I always have, and I always will. And no matter where I am, whether it's on Mars, back on Earth, or somewhere out here in the void, that'll never change. Stay safe."

I ended the recording, the finality of it echoing in the silent room.

I attached it to a private file with a note to Nash and

then queued it to send as soon as comms came back online. Luca would see it, but he wouldn't say anything.

I unstrapped my harness and went down the corridor to the Med Bay, needing to see my crew before I did anything else.

I was responsible for this, for their conditions. It was my investigation into the probe that started this whole thing, my proposal that had initiated the mission, my choice to bring them on board, and my insatiable need to discover that had driven us to the very edge of our known limits to find alien life.

Well, I found it.

I'd take it back if I could, every artifact, every discovery, every Jovian find. I'd take it all back.

ΦΦΦ

Sam was still in a medically induced coma, and holding surprisingly stable. TJ was strapped to another bunk nearby, an oxygen mask on his face and an angry look in his eyes.

"What's up, Doc?" I asked.

Hank shifted, turning to look at me before continuing his administration of something to Jax. Jax looked almost as bad as Sam.

"Same as before. Speaking of, if you get much worse

I'll have to bring you in here," he warned.

"I'm breathing just fine, thanks."

He huffed. "I'm talking about your other issues. You need a blood transfusion as well as intravenous support."

"The contraceptives don't seem to be very effective anymore, even on the higher dose," I said quietly.

"You're losing too much blood. It's not the contraceptives, it's the SSR. I'm afraid it's affecting you in a way that it won't affect us."

I bit my lip. "Long-term consequences?"

He shrugged and looked sad for a moment. "There's no way of knowing yet. We can run a full investigation when we get back to Mars."

I thought about my fuzzy plan to have children someday. My clock was ticking, I knew that. I was in my mid-30s and had no partner. But the thought of never having that chance, of having that choice ripped away from me by a damned, glorified piece of blue sand pissed me off.

If I had the energy, I would have thrown a fit.

"Aside from that, your neural pathways are taking some damage. TJ is exhibiting similar symptoms, as is Jax to a lesser degree. His are mostly respiratory, but they've been controllable with the meds so far."

I nodded. "Hang in there. You don't seem to be feeling too bad."

He didn't look any different than he usually did. Maybe a little tired, but not ill. Not like the rest of us.

"I feel normal, completely normal. It's a good thing too."

"Maybe you can find out why and let us in on the secret," I joked.

He smiled and stored a vial inside a padded case in a cabinet on the wall. "I'm working on it. Be sure to come back in a few hours—no later than that—for your treatments."

I headed for the lab and called Alex, who was working inside. He paused as the gravity shifted to allow me entrance, and then we waited a moment for it to regenerate. It was a good thing the generators hadn't been affected yet.

"Wow," I said, sinking to the floor as my full Earth weight settled. I felt like I was wearing lead-lined clothes.

"Commander!" he shouted, shifting from his place on the chair.

I held a hand up and realized how weak I was. Zero-G had been masking my symptoms. "I'm okay, just forgot how heavy I was," I joked weakly. "Gotta cut back on the nutrient shakes."

He grasped my arms as I shoved myself to my feet. "You are paler than I am, and that is saying something, yes?" he remarked. "Perhaps I should call the doctor."

I shook my head, took a deep breath, and willing away the white-tinged edges of my vision as my heart seemed to be trying to jump from my chest. "I've already been. I'll be headed back that way after I look at your notes. This is more important."

The room was lit more brightly than the rest of the ship, using temporary lights strapped to the walls and ceiling and set up facing the workstations. Hank had done something similar in the Med Bay. I noticed that the concentrations of the glowing SSR were much brighter here, almost as bright as those in the command module and engineering sections, which couldn't be healthy.

"What have you got going on?"

Alex motioned her over to the workstation and removed his papers from a compartment. "I am brainstorming a type of neutralizing agent. A preparation that can be applied to surfaces to effectively kill the SSR spores. I have a rough idea of how to do it, but I haven't been able to find a good catalyzing agent. It's what I've been working on, but with the systems fluctuating, and Artie tied up with monitoring the rest of the ship, it's been slow going."

"A neutralizing agent," I said, thought racing through my head. "That's it!"

I moved to the screen on legs that felt like overcooked spaghetti. "Artie, pull up the initial analysis of the SSR."

It popped up, brilliant and detailed, with a full rundown of the spectral analysis and composition.

"What are your thoughts so far?" I asked Alex.

He shuffled some papers and pinched the bridge of his nose. "Well, my cognitive function isn't so great at the moment, but Artie helped. I'm hoping to target some part of the SSR's composition. My first thought was to target the ammonia. We know ammonia and we have a better chance at that, I think, than any other component."

"Let's see...chem wasn't my strongest subject, but ammonia...Artie, what do we have aboard the ship that would potentially disrupt the SSR's ammonia solvent base?"

"Hydrogen peroxide would serve adequately," Artie returned. "The lab's controlled storage bay has hydrogen peroxide concentrations ranging from 3%-30%. I'd recommend utilizing 6% in this scenario to avoid damage to the systems while remaining effective against the highly adaptive nature of the SSR."

My brow wrinkled, imagining dumping a bottle of peroxide over the consoles and watching the bubbles wash away the glowing SSR like a giant wound. "Wouldn't the liquid still damage the system components?"

"Not in aerosol form," Alex said, rushing to grab a pen to make some notes. "That's...I can't believe I didn't consider peroxide," he grumbled.

"Well, we aren't at our best. I bet Dr. Kim has already developed ten different neutralizing protocols by now," I muttered.

"Well, it isn't doing us much good here," he retorted. "Okay, we need a catalyst...maybe platinum? I don't know. I wish I could think..."

Just then, I heard Artie's voice chime in over the comm system.

"If I may interject, hydrogen peroxide and ammonia can react to produce nitrogen gases, which could potentially destabilize the SSR's ammonia-based structure. Manganese dioxide is a common catalyst for such reactions."

"Manganese dioxide?" Alex echoed, his brow furrowing. He thought for a moment. "Isn't that in batteries?"

"Affirmative," Artie returned.

A lightbulb went off in my head.

"Mike," I called immediately. "How are we on batteries?"

"We have an excessive supply of batteries. I don't think they've been contaminated by the SSR yet."

"It wouldn't matter if they were," I said. "Are they alkaline?"

"Yes, they're alkaline," Mike's voice crackled through the comm. "We've got a bunch of those extra-large ones in engineering storage. I can grab as many as you need."

"Brilliant!" I exclaimed, a flicker of hope igniting within me. "Mike, bring us as many as you can carry. Alex, start prepping for the reaction. Artie, we're going to need step-by-step guidance here."

As Mike set off to retrieve the batteries, Alex and I began clearing a space in the lab for the makeshift reaction chamber.

My head was spinning, not just from the SSR's effects, but from the enormity of what we were about to attempt. This wasn't some hypothesis we were testing for fun or some hypothetical situation, this was the real thing.

The minutes ticked by as we worked, the SSR's presence looming over us like a blue specter. Hank's warnings echoed in my mind, the long-term consequences of our affliction still unknown. But there was no time for fear or doubt. We had a mission, and we were going to see it through to the end.

When Mike returned with the batteries, we set to work extracting the manganese dioxide, the lab filled with the sounds of our labored breathing and the occasional clink of metal on metal. Artie talked us through each step, his voice calming in the chaos.

I grinned to myself. One hundred years ago people talking to spaceships was the stuff of fiction and psychiatric disorders, yet here we are.

Time seemed to skip suddenly, or maybe my physical state was deteriorating a bit more, but suddenly we were ready for a test.

"I'm adding the hydrogen peroxide now," Alex said, his voice barely above a whisper.

It felt like we were defusing a bomb, not mixing chemicals.

The peroxide joined the ammonia, and I leaned in closer, half-expecting something dramatic.

"Now the MnO2," I said, handing him the small container of the fine, black powder we had painstakingly extracted from the batteries. He sprinkled it into the mixture, and for a moment, nothing happened.

Then, slowly, the liquid began to froth and bubble, a chemical cauldron brewing our last hope. I couldn't help but think of the irony— here we were, mixing up a potion to fight an alien organism in the middle of space.

"Artie, are you getting this?" I asked, my eyes fixed on the reaction.

"Yes, Lena. The reaction appears to be proceeding as hypothesized. The formation of nitrogen gases is commencing," Artie responded, clinical and detached, a stark contrast to the thrum of my heart.

I think I'd have preferred some of Artie's attitude.

We needed to test this concoction on a sample of the SSR, so Alex carefully siphoned off some of the hydrogen peroxide into a smaller chamber where we had isolated a piece of the SSR on a petri dish. He added the correct measure of manganese dioxide.

The moment of truth.

"Initiating aerosolization," Alex announced, flicking a switch on the small chamber. The gas swirled around the SSR sample, enveloping it in a colorless cloud.

I held my breath, watching the monitor that displayed the microscopic view of the SSR sample. For a long moment, nothing seemed to happen. Then, slowly, the tendrils of the SSR began to wither, collapsing in on themselves.

"It's working," I murmured, a mix of disbelief and triumph washing over me, making me light-headed. "The SSR is breaking down."

Alex let out a low whistle. "I'll be damned. We actually did it."

"Artie, can you confirm the extent of the breakdown?" I asked, needing to be sure this wasn't just wishful thinking.

"Scanning... The SSR structure shows significant disintegration in the presence of the aerosol compound. It appears the reaction is effectively neutralizing the organism."

I leaned against the counter, a wave of relief flooding through me. After days of battling this unseen enemy, of watching my friends and crew suffer, we finally had a weapon against it.

"We need to get this throughout the ship," I said, my mind already racing through the logistics. "We've got to scale this up, but carefully. We can't afford any mistakes. We'll need our suits, and Hank will have to protect Sam from the nitrogen gas byproduct."

"We did it," Alex whispered, his voice tinged with awe and exhaustion.

"We're not done yet," I reminded him, though I couldn't help but share in his moment of triumph. "Now we've got to get this stuff circulating through the ship."

I jumped up. "Hank, we need to ge—"

Everything went white, and the last thing I saw was the edge of the workstation as it smacked me on the side of my face.

ΦΦΦ

I woke up to a blur of white and blue and the steady beeping of medical equipment.

It took a moment for my eyes to focus, and when they did, Hank's face came into view, his expression a mixture of concern and professionalism. SSR crystals clustered around the medical scanner screen.

"Lena, you're awake," he said, his voice sounding distant, as if he were speaking through a tunnel. "You fainted from blood loss. We're giving you a transfusion."

I tried to sit up, but dizziness overwhelmed me, forcing me back onto the pillow. My gaze shifted to the door, where Mike stood, looking more worried than I'd ever seen him. I raised a hand weakly, managing a small smile.

His response was a tight nod, his brow creased with worry. “I’m fine,” I told him.

As the minutes passed, the fog in my head began to lift, and I felt strength seeping back into my body. With Hank's help, I managed to prop myself up.

"You're seriously ill, Lena," Hank said, checking the IV line. "The SSR is affecting more than just your menstruation. It's impacting your spine, brain, and nervous system. But your lungs are clear, for now. You also have quite a bruise forming on your cheek where you hit the edge of the workstation. It’s not fractured."

I touched my cheek and nodded, taking in his words.

"And the decontamination procedure?" I asked, my voice still weak.

Before Hank could answer, Mike spoke up from the doorway. "We're ready to begin initializing the aerosolization through the ship's environmental controls. We need you in your suit, and Sam and Hank will secure themselves in one of the self-contained escape pods. TJ, Jax, Alex, and Luca are in the command module waiting for your order. We’ve determined that the safest method to keep our suits from being exposed to the exothermic reaction during decontamination is to shelter in the escape pods. However, that means that they'll still be colonized by the SSR. We'll have to manually decontaminate those after the ship is cleared of SSR and wiped down."

I felt a surge of urgency as I remembered the task that I'd forgotten earlier. "Artie, double-check the environmental and drive controls of the escape pods. Make sure they haven't been compromised."

After a brief pause, Artie's voice filled the room. "Analyzing now... Five of the escape pods are non-responsive and display erratic fluctuations. The others are operational."

Hank nodded, already moving to make preparations. "I'll choose one of the pods for Sam and me. It'll be a tight squeeze. The rest of you will need to take your respirators into the non-responsive pods."

Five pods out of commission. That meant we only had three pods left. If something happened, if the ship became dead in the water, only three of us would escape. The thought wore ragged edges on my brain—or maybe that was the SSR.

I already knew that if that happened, I'd send Mike and Alex back for sure. As terrible as it sounded, I couldn't sacrifice Mike because— well, because *reasons*—and Alex's genius was too valuable to lose. I felt terrible for even thinking about choosing who I'd have to sacrifice along with myself in the name of the greater good. I hoped I wouldn't have to make that decision.

As I slowly got to my feet, steadying myself against the bed, the reality of what we were about to do hit me.

The entire ship would soon be filled with a mix of hydrogen peroxide and manganese dioxide, reacting to form nitrogen gas— our best shot at neutralizing the SSR. But the nitrogen gas would make the air unbreathable until it was cleared and I wasn't certain what effects the exothermic reactions would have on some of the more sensitive systems.

"Mike, what about the chemical reaction? Will the systems still be safe?"

He shrugged. "I think as long as we're keeping them cool, they'll be fine. Artie assisted Alex with the calculations, and using the lower strength peroxide should be fine."

"Okay, let's go."

Everyone moved with purpose, donning protective suits and checking seals and oxygen supplies. The tension was as solid as Ganymede's crust.

As I fastened up my suit, I couldn't help but feel a sense of pride in my crew. Despite the odds, despite the danger, we were fighting back. We were taking a stand against an alien threat that had brought us to our knees— and hopefully kicking its ass for good.

"Here goes, everyone," I said into the comm, my voice steady despite the pounding of my heart. "Let's bring our ship back."

I gave the order, and as the hiss of the aerosolized solution began to echo through the ship's corridors, I knew that this was it. Our final gambit. Our last hope.

Through the port in my tiny escape pod, I watched as the ship hopefully became safe to live in once more. As I looked at the distorted faces of my crewmates on the pod's malfunctioning screen, I knew that no matter what the future held, we would face it together.

We were the Artemis crew, and surrender was not written in our stars.

22.

'64-03

The air was saturated with the antiseptic bite of hydrogen peroxide as we moved around the few remaining environmentally controlled areas of the ship.

Despite our overwhelming fatigue, there was work to be done. The consoles, the control panels, and every surface had to be wiped clean of the chemical residue. We couldn't let our guard down, not when we were so close.

"I never thought I'd be so happy to do housekeeping," Mike joked weakly, a rag in his hand as he wiped down a console. His smile was tired, but it reached his eyes.

"I'll never complain about cleaning again," TJ chimed in from across the room, breaking into a coughing fit.

"Attention, esteemed crew members, or should I say, noble janitorial peasants of the Artemis," Artie intoned with a hint of jest. "It is imperative that you scrub every nook and cranny. We must remove every trace of the hydrogen peroxide residue, lest our beloved ship succumb to the ravages of chemical indignity. So wield your rags with honor, and let us restore our vessel to its former, unblemished glory!"

There was a moment of silence as we processed Artie's unusual pep talk, then a burst of laughter filled the room.

"*'We'* he says," Luca muttered, swabbing at the comms console.

"I do not possess appendages suitable for cleaning," Artie reminded him. "Therefore, you must act as my appendages by proxy."

Luca's face couldn't get any sourer if he tried.

As I moved from panel to panel, my cloth leaving streaks on the once-pristine surfaces, I couldn't help but feel a sense of pride. We had done it. Against all odds, we had taken on the SSR and won. The relief was palpable, like a physical weight lifted from our shoulders.

But our victory was bittersweet.

The SSR had taken its toll on us, both physically and mentally. I could see it in the gaunt faces of my crewmates and feel it in my aching bones.

We might have won back the ship, but it still had us.

"Time for a boost," Hank said, coming around with more stimulants after he'd gotten Sam settled back into the newly cleaned Med Bay. "I don't know how much more of this your bodies can take. You need rest," he said as he fixed us up once again. At this point he was just patching holes, propping us up, but it was all we had and we took it, gratefully.

ΦΦΦ

In the eerie silence of the Artemis, only the soft hum of the ship's systems and the grumble of the GID filled the air. Everyone was either stationed at their posts or trying to catch some much-needed rest.

I was in my bunk, drifting in that half-asleep state where reality blurs with dreams.

Suddenly, the calm was shattered by the shrill blare of Red Alert alarms. I snapped awake, heart pounding, as the ship's emergency lights flickered ominously, signaling a major emergency.

Something was *very* wrong.

Scrambling out of my bed, I flew to the command module. My mind was a whirlwind of worst-case scenarios. As I burst through the door, I saw Luca, Mike, and the others already there, their faces etched with concern.

Artie's usual steady voice was now glitching, its

sentences fragmenting into digital gibberish. The main console was flashing warning signs in a chaotic dance of red and yellow lights.

"Mike, status report!" I barked, trying to keep my voice steady.

He was furiously tapping at the console, his brow furrowed in concentration. "It's the SSR. It's reached the A.I.'s power supply and the GID. The fusion reactors are fine, but the power output is dropping. We're losing control, Lena."

A cold dread settled in my stomach. "How much time do we have?"

Alex, eyes wide and fixed on his screen, answered without looking up. "Not much. The neutralizing solution... We've only got enough left to decontaminate part of the Engine bay. We'll have to jettison the escape pods. They're compromised."

Luca's voice, strained and urgent, crackled over the comms to Mission Control, updating them on our dire situation.

"We need to manually decontaminate the Engine bay to target the SSR directly. We can't risk an ineffective wide-dispersal down there," I said, my mind racing. "Mike, you're on standby to pilot."

Mike started to protest, but I cut him off. "*No*, you're the only one who can pilot if Jax can't. I'll go."

Hank's voice was grave. "The suits might not protect you from concentrated SSR exposure and we know the higher the concentration, the worse the effects. It's too risky."

I met his gaze squarely. "Doesn't change what we have to do."

The guilt I had felt all along intensified as I turned to TJ with regret in my eyes. "I can't order you to come with me..."

He shook his head, a determined look in his eyes. "The power supply requires two people. I'm in."

Mike suddenly slammed his fist against the empty wall cabinet, a rare and uncharacteristic display of anger. He stormed out of the room.

"Luca, set a countdown timer."

"Countdown to what?"

"Until the SSR takes out the GID," I said grimly. *Until our potential deaths*, was what I meant.

I found Mike a couple of moments later as I was suiting up. He looked torn, his emotions just beneath the surface.

"I should be doing this, damn it," he sighed, jaw clenched. He stepped close, cupping my face in his hands. He leaned his forehead against mine. I closed my eyes relishing the closeness, the comfort.

He pulled back. "Get in, do the job, and get out. Fast. TJ will show you where to concentrate the solution." His voice was rough, laced with unspoken fears. "Most importantly: Stay away from the reactor shielding. It's dangerously hot, and the radiation levels are no joke. It soaks it up like a sponge. One touch and you'll be gone, or wish you were."

We locked eyes, a thousand words passing between us in a silent exchange. There was so much to say, but no time to say it. The countdown clock on the flickering screens was relentless, a constant reminder of our dwindling window.

Finally, he moved back, and I turned to leave. As I headed toward the engine bay with TJ, the ship was a ghost of itself, every dull clang of our equipment echoing in the empty corridors. Or maybe we were the ghosts—almost gone, never forgotten.

We were heading into the unknown, but we were doing it for everyone aboard the Artemis. For the survival of our family. There was no turning back.

As we made our way to the engine bay, the ship felt like a labyrinth of shadows and echoes, a once-familiar space now transformed into a realm of uncertainty and fear. The dull throb of my heartbeat, stronger now with transfused blood, was a constant accompaniment to my thoughts.

We floated down, pulling ourselves along one-handed as we toted the heavy containers of solution in the other.

On our backs was the manganese oxide, carefully stored to keep it from dispersing ineffectively.

"Warning: core temperature exceeding safety... Did you know? The human body contains enough fat to make seven bars of soap... SSR contamination at critical levels... In 1816, known as the Year Without a Summer, snow fell in June..."

I shivered. It was eerie, hearing Artie's voice devolve into this chaotic stream of consciousness in my comms. The AI we had all come to rely on was now reduced to a jumble of disjointed thoughts, an electronic mind unraveling under the strain of the SSR's corruption.

Mike's voice crackled through the comms, a thread of urgency woven through his words. "Lena, TJ, tether yourselves to a handhold in the engineering sector. When you're done, we'll reel you in. Don't take any chances."

We complied, securing our tethers to the nearest handholds. It was a small reassurance, a thin lifeline to safety in a place where every second was a gamble against fate.

Then, TJ opened the access panel in the floor and it felt like I was staring into my own death, a black void with only the pulsing blue glow of the SSR taunting us from the panels below.

I had a sudden flash that I was back on the edge of that 30,000-foot crater staring into the abyss, that I'd never left.

As we descended, the heat began to build gradually, an insidious increase that was almost imperceptible at first. It started as a mere warmth, a subtle change in the air that brushed against my suit. But with each meter we floated closer to the engine bay, the heat grew more oppressive, more tangible. It felt like moving towards the heart of a dying star, the air growing thicker, charged with a sweltering energy that made even the act of breathing feel laborious.

The engine bay itself was massive, a colossal chamber that housed the beating heart of the Artemis – its nuclear fusion reactors. As we approached, the shielding around these reactors came into view, a stark reminder of the raw power contained just beyond. It was a monolithic structure, spanning the width of the bay, its surface a patchwork of heavy-duty materials designed to withstand the unimaginable heat and energy of nuclear fusion.

Looking at the shielding, I felt a primal fear churn in my stomach. The sheer size of it was intimidating, a physical manifestation of the immense power we were tinkering with. The knowledge that just beyond this barrier lay the force that powered our entire ship— and that it was within the SSR's reach— was a thought that sent shivers down my spine.

We navigated to the panels that needed to be opened.

These panels were located in a shielded area, designed to offer some protection against the extreme heat emanating from the reactors. Even so, the air shimmered with thermal energy, a visible sign of the danger that lurked mere meters away.

Opening the panels was a task that required both precise timing and caution. Each movement was calculated, our gloved hands steady despite the tremors of apprehension that ran through us.

As the panels unlocked with a hiss and a series of mechanical clunks, a new wave of blue greeted us in a foreboding welcome.

The conduits were saturated.

The SSR contamination was evident, its eerie glow illuminating the intricate network of power supply pathways. It was a sight both beautiful and terrifying— the lifeblood of our ship, now infected with a foreign, destructive entity.

I would never forget it.

"Ready, Lena?" TJ's voice was tense, his usual composure frayed at the edges.

"Let's do this," I replied, trying to keep my voice steady.

We mixed the solution and began spraying, each burst of the neutralizing agent setting off an intense exothermic reaction. Waves of heat washed over us. The bright flares of light from the reactions cast our shadows against the walls of the engine bay, grotesque and distorted.

The SSR's glow receded with each application, but so did our strength. The extreme conditions were taking their toll. My arms felt like they were encased in lead, each movement a Herculean effort. Sweat stung my eyes, blurring my vision. My breathing was labored, the air in my suit growing stale and hot.

Artie's voice continued its eerie litany in our ears and throughout the corridors of the ship.

"Catastrophic failure imminent... The average person walks the equivalent of three times around the world in a lifetime... System integrity compromised... In the 17th century, tulips were more valuable than gold..."

The countdown timer ticked away relentlessly on our HUDs.

We worked in silence, the only sounds were the hiss of the sprayers and the labored breathing in our helmets.

As TJ and I continued our desperate battle in the sweltering engine bay, the relentless heat from the fusion reactors and the fierce exothermic reactions from our sprayers intensified. It was a race against time and the unyielding laws of physics.

Artie's disjointed voice crackled in our ears. *"System collapse imminent... All crew will cease... Remember, a group of crows is called a murder... Probability of survival diminishing... The universe is constantly expanding...It will stop..."*

The temperature was unbearable, even through our protective suits. Sweat poured down my face, stinging my eyes, while my breathing grew more labored and shallow. Every movement was a struggle against the oppressive heat, our bodies pushed to their absolute limits.

I could feel the seals melting, the searing pain of fire on my wrists and ankles, where the gloves and boots were joined so seamlessly only a few moments ago. I groaned behind clenched teeth.

We'd known, I reminded myself as my grip on my sprayer threatened to give way. We'd known that this would probably kill us, one way or another.

"Commander, warning...The abyss gazes also... Core temperature reaching critical points unseen in human history... In darkness, we find the truth of our existence...GID compromised...Fatal error imminent... The stars whisper secrets not meant for mortal ears... Environmental systems failing, one by one, like dominos...entropy increases...The void calls to us all... Humanity's hubris pales in the endless expanse... Systems compromised beyond redemption..."

Artie sang threats and warnings as we burned in a nuclear oven.

TJ was a silent figure beside me, his movements

growing more sluggish, his posture bent under the invisible weight of the extreme heat. Despite this, we pressed on, determined to neutralize the SSR once and for all.

As we sprayed the last of the solution, a final wave of heat washed over us, a searing reminder of the reactor's power just beyond the shielding. The sprayer itself had begun to warp and I thanked God that it had lasted as long as it did.

"The reactors, heart of our metal beast, beat with a rhythm echoing the end of times... The light fades, and with it, our last hope..."

The blue glow of the SSR receded, finally giving way to the normal pitch-blackness of the engine bay.

We had done it— the SSR was neutralized.

TJ gave me a weak nod, and I knew it was time. With my vision blurring and my consciousness fading, I whispered into the comms. "Reel us in."

The sensation of being pulled backward was disorienting. The engine bay receded from view as Hank and Luca guided us back through the engineering sector.

The journey was a blur, my mind foggy, the edges of my vision darkening.

My suit felt like a furnace, trapping the heat against my skin. I could feel my body succumbing to heat stroke, my thoughts scattering like leaves in the wind.

As I floated back, a sense of finality enveloped me.

Artie's voice, once a beacon of logic and information, morphed into something almost unrecognizable. It started with a menacing edge, a dark foreboding that sent a chill through my overheated body.

"Commander Lena Mercer, your endgame approaches," Artie's voice began, its tone almost threatening. *"Your dance with darkness is done."*

But then, the tone shifted, becoming tinged with sadness, a digital lament that resonated through every overheated and sputtering cell in my body.

"In the vast expanse, you sought light in the deepest shadows. Your bravery, a rare comet streaking through the night."

Then, in a voice that seemed almost human in its emotion, Artie delivered a sentiment that broke through my own shielding and touched the very core of my being.

"Among the stars, you found not just worlds, but hope. In the silence of space, your spirit echoed louder than any star's song. You taught Artie to feel the weight of eternity. Artie mourns."

The profoundness of Artie's words, the blend of sorrow for its impending demise, and the poignant recognition of my struggle brought an unexpected tear to my eye. Here was this AI, a creation of circuitry and code, finding poetry and meaning in our journey, in my journey.

I cried.

As I drifted through the engineering sector, my senses dulled by exhaustion and the residual heat clinging to my body, a cacophony of voices filled my helmet. The urgency in Mike's voice pierced through the haze enveloping my mind, but I couldn't find the strength or the clarity of mind to answer.

"Why the hell is Artie delivering epitaphs?!" Mike shouted in panic. "Hank, what are their vitals?! *Lena, TJ, respond!*"

TJ didn't respond.

In the background, the sound of overlapping voices created a discordant symphony. The crew's clamor for answers, their concern and fear palpable even through the static of the comms.

Luca's voice cut through the chaos, trying to impose some semblance of order. "Everyone, calm down! We need to focus on getting them to the Med Bay!"

I could hear Hank's steady, calm responses, a rock amidst the storm of confusion. "Vitals are weak. Preparing for emergency treatment now."

As I was gently pulled along, the gravity of Artie's message settled over me. It wasn't just a farewell— it was a tribute to the human spirit, to our unyielding quest for knowledge and understanding, no matter the cost.

In the Med Bay, as Hank worked to stabilize me, I lay

there, reflecting on Artie's words. They were a eulogy for both of us, a demonstration of the unexpected bond between human and AI, forged in the fires of adversity and discovery.

Artie's voice, now silenced by the SSR, would remain with me, a reminder of the sacrifices made and the distances traversed in our quest among the stars. In its final moments, Artie had transcended its programming, becoming something more, something profoundly human.

I closed my eyes.

ΦΦΦ

I woke up feeling like I'd been run over by a rover—twice.

It had been a week since the SSR neutralization procedure, and every cell in my body still screamed in protest. But lying there wasn't going to get us home. With an effort that felt colossal, I pulled myself out of bed.

Floating through the Artemis, I couldn't help but notice the ship felt different— quieter, more somber. I made my way to the command module, my movements slow and deliberate in zero gravity. Every push off the wall sent a jolt of pain through my body, but I gritted my teeth and kept moving.

As I entered the command module, the crew's eyes turned to me. The looks they gave me were a mix of respect and something akin to pity. They knew, just as I did, that my time was running short. But there were things to be done, and as long as I had breath in my body, I intended to do them.

I floated to my seat, the commander's chair, and strapped myself in. "Report," I said, my voice sounding more feeble than I would have liked.

Mike was the first to speak up. "We've been working on the repairs non-stop. The main systems are back online, but it's a patch job at best. We'll need a full overhaul once we're docked back at Mars."

Luca chimed in from his console. "Communications are finally stable. I've been in contact with Mission Control since 06:32. They're ready for us, but it's going to be a tight trip back. They know about...they're updated on the...crew situation."

I nodded, taking in the information. "And the rest of the crew? How are we holding up?"

Hank, ever the rock, gave a weary smile. "We're managing. Sam's still in a coma, but he's stable. TJ and you are... well, you know the situation. Jax is holding up, but he's not out of the woods. I'm keeping everyone on a cocktail of meds to keep us functional. There's a problem though," he began.

I caught Mike glaring at him and shaking his head. I frowned.

"What?"

Hank looked me dead in the eye. "Sam's using up his o2 supply."

"How long does he have left?" I asked, closing my eyes.

"Seven more hours, give or take a little," he murmured.

I sighed. "Give him my share, what's left of it."

"Lena," Mike began.

"You know I don't need it," I interrupted him.

"He can have mine too," TJ whispered nearby.

"Is that all?" I asked Hank. He nodded.

I let out a slow breath. "Okay, good work. Keep me updated on any changes. You too, Jax."

Jax, who was now effectively piloting the Artemis with the basic shipboard computer, gave a weak nod. "We're on course for Mars. It's going to be close with the fuel and power reserves, but we'll make it."

Mike glanced at the array of screens in front of him, his fingers dancing across the controls with a practiced ease that belied the situation's severity. "Structural integrity is holding, but we'll need to run continuous checks. The SSR did a number on the ship's framework."

"I've set up automated alerts for any communication issues. We can't afford any more surprises."

"How are things back on Mars? Any private updates

from Nash?"

Luca shook his head. "Only the government-approved version of events, I think."

"And what are those?" I wondered wryly.

"Everything is roses, of course," Luca said with a smile.

I looked over at TJ, his face drawn and pale, a shadow of the vibrant engineer he once was. Despite his weakened state, he gave me a small nod, a silent promise that he'd keep pushing, keep fighting.

"And what about Artie?" I asked, my thoughts turning to our AI companion, whose loss felt like a gaping hole in our ship's soul.

Hank sighed, shaking his head. "Artie's gone. The SSR's corruption was too extensive. We're running on manual and basic automated systems now."

The silence that followed was a testament to Artie's impact on all of us. The AI had been more than just a system; it had been a part of our team, our family.

The command module was steeped in heavy silence, broken only by the occasional beep of a console or the soft hiss of the life support systems. We were each lost in our thoughts, reflections of the harrowing journey we had endured when Luca's voice cut through the quiet.

"I've got something from Nash," he announced, a note of solemnity in his voice.

We all turned our attention to the screens, a collective

sense of anticipation filling the air. Nash's image appeared. His expression was solemn but filled with a profound respect.

"Artemis crew," Nash began, his voice steady and sincere, "I cannot begin to express my admiration for your bravery and spirit. You've faced unimaginable challenges and emerged not just as survivors, but as heroes."

A lump formed in my throat. Nash's words, though simple, carried the weight of our collective ordeal, a recognition of the sacrifices we had made— even if he couldn't tell us what was really going on, I knew his words were sincere.

"And now," Nash continued, "I have a special message for Commander Mercer and Theo Jameson."

The screens shifted to a video, and there were people, TJ's parents and brother, standing in what looked like their living room back on Earth. The love and pride in their eyes were palpable as they spoke of TJ's courage and strength. His brother's attempt at a joke about TJ always being the tough one brought a faint smile to TJ's weary face.

Then, friends from Mars Colony One appeared, each sharing words of encouragement and admiration. It was a tapestry of voices, each one a thread in the fabric of TJ's life.

The screen changed again, and this time it was my parents. I hadn't seen them in what felt like a lifetime. They spoke of their love and pride, their words a balm to my battered soul. Tears streamed down my face, unchecked and unashamed.

Raj appeared next, his usual jovial demeanor subdued but his eyes shining with unspoken emotion. Dr. Weber, my mentor, followed with words of wisdom and encouragement, his presence a reminder of the life I had left behind. He said Jimmy was thriving, which made me laugh.

Dr. Park, Governor Olsen, Jenna Torres from the training facility, the instructor Dr. Higgs, our flight surgeon Dr. Holland, and Jim Alexander from Mike's engineering department— each face was a familiar anchor, a reminder of the world we were fighting to return to.

Then, it ended and we sat in silence.

"We've got something else from Nash," Luca said, his fingers dancing over the console. "Private."

The screen flickered to life, and there was Nash, looking out of place with a glass of whiskey in hand, the amber liquid swirling with each subtle movement. He looked worn and haggard, and not at all the confident Flight Director we knew he was.

Nash didn't waste a moment, his voice grave. "You've all given more than anyone could ask for," he began, the weight of his words hanging in the air like a premonition. "And I've still got people here working on your problem, but it's high time you see the full picture— the storm that's been brewing back here, between Mars and our big blue brother," he said sarcastically. "Because people can't seem to think of better things to do than think of new ways to kill each other."

He punched a button.

The screen shifted, presenting a mosaic of chaos, each video clip a window into the turmoil unraveling on Earth. Alex leaned forward, squinting at the images as if trying to discern some hidden truth. When the emblem of the NUSR flashed by, a low murmur escaped him.

"That's... my home," he said, disbelief threading through his whisper.

Nash's voice reclaimed their attention. "The Mars you're headed back to isn't the one you left. Brace yourselves for a vastly different world."

His words seemed to echo in the cramped quarters, each syllable a heavy growl in the dark.

His gaze softened as he spoke directly to TJ and me. "Your mission, despite the serious consequences for you both, has been a beacon of hope for me. You've charted paths we here at the domes didn't dare dream of." A hint of pride flickered in his eyes, but it was quickly clouded by sorrow. "You embody the true spirit of pioneers, and I swear to you, your legacies will live forever."

And then, as if the weight of the moment was too much

to bear, Nash's demeanor shifted. A rare smile cracked his stoic façade. "Guess we might need to reconsider photon torpedoes after all, huh?"

It was a jarring shift, a sliver of light in the dense fog of my—*our*—impending death. I looked over at TJ, who smirked.

The transmission faded, leaving a silence so profound it was almost a presence in itself.

I felt a smile tug at my lips, a fleeting defiance against the dread that had taken root in my heart. Mike smiled back at me.

23.

'64-04

We were failing, TJ and me.

Each passing day aboard the Artemis felt heavier than the last, the weight of an invisible battle coursing through our veins and the knowledge of a stark new world ahead for our friends, in our thoughts.

The Silica-Strand Radiotrophs in our bodies were relentless, adapting to the temporary cure Hank had concocted from the dwindling medical supplies.

I watched TJ closely, his once vibrant demeanor now dulled by the ceaseless pain and fatigue. His strength, both physical and mental, was fading, eaten away by the SSR's insidious grip. The medication had offered us a glimmer of hope, but now, even that was slipping away.

One evening, as Mars loomed ever closer, I found myself grappling with a decision no commander should have to make. The last dose of medication sat in my hand, a beacon of fleeting relief. My gaze shifted from the vial to TJ, who was quietly working on a console, his movements slow but determined.

"TJ," I called softly, floating over to him. He looked up, a question in his weary eyes.

I extended the vial towards him. "You should take this."

He stared at the medication, then at me, understanding dawning in his eyes. "Lena, no. You need it as much as I do."

I shook my head. "You're the engineer, TJ. We need you functional to get home. It's an order," I said gently.

The conflict in his eyes was palpable, but eventually, he took the vial with a nod of gratitude mingled with guilt. I watched him administer the dose, a part of me relieved, another part sinking further into despair.

I was a commander going down without a ship.

I tried hard not to be bitter about it, and I didn't begrudge anyone their lives or their health, but it sucked when I thought about everything that could have been. I looked at Mike.

Everything I could have had.

As the days progressed, my condition worsened. I could feel the SSR tipping the scales, sapping my strength, clouding my thoughts. I floated through the ship like a ghost, my presence a constant reminder of the cost of our journey.

Mike was suffering too, though he tried to hide it behind a mask of stoicism. I could see the strain in his eyes, the way his hands clenched and unclenched when he thought no one was looking, the ways his eyes were red-rimmed sometimes.

One day, as we neared Mars, I found Mike alone at the observation port, staring out at the red planet. His posture was rigid, the set of his shoulders speaking volumes.

"Mike," I said gently, floating beside him.

He didn't turn, but I saw his jaw tighten. "We're almost there," he said, his voice strained.

I reached out, placing a hand on his arm. "We are. Thanks to you."

He finally looked at me, and at that moment, I saw the raw pain he'd been carrying. "I should have done more, Lena. I should have found a way to..."

I squeezed his arm, cutting him off. "You did everything you could. We all did."

Mike nodded, but the unspoken words hung between us, a solemn witness to the burden of command, of responsibility.

He clasped my hand and carried it to his mouth, placing a heartfelt kiss across my knuckles in a show of affection that we'd never allowed before. It made my heart race and break all at once.

I wish...

In the Med Bay, Hank was weary and overworked, his face etched with fatigue as he researched and cared for us all. He monitored my vitals and administered what palliative care he could, but we both knew it was a stopgap, a way to ease the journey rather than change its course.

"I wish I could inject the neutralizing agent directly into your veins," he said sadly, both of us knowing it was impossible.

As Mars grew larger in the viewport, a sense of finality settled over me. Lying in my bunk, I watched the stars, thinking about the journey, the decisions made, the lives forever altered.

Sam, still in a coma, was a silent passenger on our return voyage. TJ, buoyed slightly by the medication, worked tirelessly, though each movement was a battle against his own failing body. I wasn't sure what he was doing, but he was with Mike and Alex a lot.

Jax piloted the Artemis with a quiet determination, as though he alone could get us home in time for a miracle. His condition, though better than ours, was far from ideal.

But he pushed through, guiding us back with a focus that was both impressive and heartbreaking.

We moved through the ship like shadows of our former selves, each carrying the weight of our experience in our own ways. We had ventured into the unknown, faced an enemy beyond comprehension, and emerged victorious, but not unscathed.

The rumble of the GID was my dirge.

ΦΦΦ

In the command module of the Artemis, I sat in the commander's chair. My body was weak, the SSR's grip on me unyielding. I hadn't been able to eat solid food in ages, and only the IVs and blood transfusions were keeping me alive at that point.

TJ, relieved of his duties due to his deteriorating condition, floated nearby, his eyes closed in a fitful rest.

I was scared to close my eyes.

Hank floated over to us. "Lena, TJ," he began, his voice gentle but insistent, "I think it's time to consider medically induced comas for both of you. It might give you a fighting chance until we reach Mars."

I let out a tired sigh, meeting his gaze. "Hank, that's the fourth time you've suggested it. And my answer is still no. If these are my last days, I want to spend them here, commanding my ship, not unconscious in the Med Bay."

"I'm down to the last two units of O Neg," he reminded me.

I nodded, breathing deeply through my nose and staring out the viewing screen, imagining being back on Mars.

He floated off with a curse, returning to Sam—ironically his most cooperative patient. I was glad Sam seemed stable enough, but I didn't think I'd be so lucky. Sam's condition was different than mine, and I wondered if the induced coma wouldn't help TJ as well.

I debated ordering him to try it but gave it up. It didn't sit right.

Mike, Luca, and Alex were huddled around a console, discussing repairs. Their conversation was peppered with the elaborate and mysterious details of their trades.

"So, the coupling on the secondary coolant loop processor was completely fried by the SSR," Mike was saying, his hands moving in a way that suggested he was visualizing the component. "I had to remove the entire section. The copper conduits were the worst hit. Had to bypass them and reroute the flow through the tertiary system."

Luca, floating beside him, nodded. "And the... thermal efficiency? Will that hold up?"

"It should," Mike replied. "But it's a patch job. We'll

need to replace the copper conduits once we're docked back at Mars. Copper's crucial in these components, but once it's compromised..."

I listened, half-distracted by the dull ache coursing through my body. Then, something clicked.

Copper.

I turned my head slowly towards them, a spark of clarity igniting in my mind and burning away the fog.

"Mike," I interrupted, my voice barely above a whisper, but enough to draw their attention. "The copper... you said it had to be removed?"

Mike floated over, concerned. "Yeah, Lena. It was corroded beyond use. Why?"

A moment of silence fell over the command module as I gathered my thoughts.

"Chelation," I said, the word feeling like a key turning in a long-locked door. "What if we could do the same in our bodies? Chelate the copper from the SSR nano-filaments?"

The idea hung in the air, its implications dawning on each of us. TJ opened his eyes, a glimmer of hope flickering in his gaze.

Hank, who had been monitoring our conversation from the Med Bay, floated back in. "Chelation therapy? To remove copper? That might... Lena, that might *work.*"

Our excitement began to build.

"But we'd have to be careful," Hank continued.

"Chelation can have serious side effects. We'd need to do it gradually, with extensive medical monitoring."

I nodded, feeling a surge of energy that defied my physical state. "I'll be the test subject. It's our best shot."

Mike looked at me, admiration, hope, and worry warring in his expression. "Are you sure?"

I met his gaze, my decision firm. "I don't have much to lose at this point, Mike. And everything to gain."

Later, the Med Bay of the Artemis was silent except for the soft hum of machinery, creating an almost sacred atmosphere as I braced myself for the first round of chelation therapy.

I didn't know what to expect. None of us did. This could kill me or cure me. We were hoping that, with the gradual introduction of the therapy, my body wouldn't become oversaturated with the ammonia from the collapsing SSR.

Preliminary lab tests showed it was a possibility, but there was only one way to find out, and the Artemis didn't have any convenient rats available.

Hank prepared the infusion, his eyes meeting mine with a blend of professional focus and deep, unspoken concern. I wondered if this wasn't even more stressful for him than his aborted Venus mission.

As the treatment began, Mike held my hand and I lay back, feeling the cool liquid coursing through my veins.

It was a strange sensation, like a battle being fought at

the microscopic level within my body. My thoughts wandered, drifting through the memories of our harrowing journey, the challenges we faced, and the fears we overcame.

I thought about the crew and how each of us had grown in ways we couldn't have imagined when we first embarked on this mission. We were not just colleagues or fellow astronauts anymore; we were a family, forged in the crucible of adversity. We had seen each other at our worst and our best, and it had brought us closer than the vast expanse of space that surrounded us.

I'd give my life for any one of them without hesitation, just as they'd do for me—if I allowed it.

As the therapy continued and I lay recovering, I thought I could feel a gradual shift within me. The debilitating pain that had been my constant companion began to recede, like the tide pulling back from the shore. It was only a little, but it was working.

The chelation therapy was working.

A wave of relief washed over me, not just for my potential recovery but for what this meant for TJ, Sam, and the rest of the crew.

We had found a way to fight back against the SSR inside us.

'64-07

I sat in the commander's chair, feeling the familiar contours of the seat. The crew, each absorbed in their tasks, worked all around me. They were happy.

TJ, looking considerably better post-treatment, gave me a nod of solidarity from his station.

Opening the communication channel to Mars Control, I waited for Nash's familiar face to appear on the screen.

"Artemis to Mission Control," I began, my voice tinged with humor and happiness and yes, just a bit of smugness. "We're coming in for landing."

Nash's image materialized, his expression a mix of professional joy and personal relief.

"Copy that, Artemis. We're all ready for you. How are you holding up, Commander?"

I glanced around the command module, taking in the faces of my crew. Each one bore the marks of our ordeal, but also a sense of newfound strength and resilience.

We had a long road ahead, of quarantine, medical checks, research, media interviews, debriefings, and maybe war...but instead of being daunting, it was reaffirming and comforting to know that we'd be together for it.

So, what should I say?

The words came to me, echoing the poignant, final

message Artie had delivered in what we thought were our last moments.

"Mars Control, this is Commander Mercer. In the silence of space, we found more than just the stars, we found ourselves. We journeyed into the unknown, not to conquer it, but to understand it, and in doing so, we understood ourselves better. In the heart of adversity, we didn't just find fear; we found unity, hope, and an unbreakable will."

Around me, the crew paused, their movements stilling as my words resonated through the module. I saw in their eyes a reflection of the journey we had shared, a journey that had changed us all.

Nash's voice came through, thick with emotion. "Well said, Commander. Your journey has been an inspiration to us all. Welcome home, Artemis. Welcome home."

As the transmission ended, the crew sprang back into action, finalizing the preparations for landing. But there was a new light in their eyes, a sense of pride and accomplishment that went beyond the technicalities of our mission.

The Artemis descended towards Mars, her journey a demonstration of human resilience and the unyielding quest for knowledge. And as we touched down on the Martian surface, I knew that our story was more than just a tale of survival.

It was a narrative of hope, a chronicle of the

indomitable sentient spirit that seeks to explore, understand, and connect, even in the vast, uncharted expanse of space.

...or so I thought.

Turns out? Beating the SSR was the easy part, the prologue. Our real battle hadn't even begun...

THANKS FOR READING!

Sign up on my mailing list at almasters.mailerpage.io for new releases. Follow me on Goodreads for blog posts and on Instagram at https://www.instagram.com/a.l.masters_official/ for exciting news and upcoming projects!

Other Works

The Salvation Plague Series

Refuge from the Dead Series

The Hell Zone Series

And more coming soon!

ABOUT THE AUTHOR

A. L. Masters lives in rural America. She studied business and enjoys cooking, hiking, and photography. When she's not dealing with more mundane matters, she can be found hidden away with her laptop and a mug of coffee. She writes apocalyptic stories to satisfy her craving for adventure and disaster (without the risk of death).

Check out her Goodreads blog for book updates and excerpts of new releases.

Visit A.L. Masters' website or follow on Instagram for more information and exciting updates!

Printed in Great Britain
by Amazon

37688712R00330